"Oh, how I love this series! Officer Megan Luz has an LOL dry humor and wit rivaling that of Kinsey Milhone. Her K-9 partner, Officer Brigit, is smarter and more protective than any three men on the force put together. Add some of the more bizarre cases in the whole Fort Worth Police Department, and handsome firefighter Seth and his bomb-sniffing dog, Blast, and the reader is treated with a deliciously intense novel."

—*Open Book Society* on *Enforcing the Paw*

"Four Paws Up! This is a fabulous series that is sure to win the hearts of mystery fans and dog lovers alike!"

—*Books and Trouble*

ST. MARTIN'S PAPERBACKS TITLES BY DIANE KELLY

THE PAW ENFORCEMENT NOVELS

Paw Enforcement
Paw and Order
Upholding the Paw
(an e-original novella)
Laying Down the Paw
Against the Paw
Above the Paw
Enforcing the Paw
The Long Paw of the Law
Paw of the Jungle

THE HOUSE-FLIPPER NOVELS

Dead as a Door Knocker

THE TARA HOLLOWAY NOVELS

Death, Taxes, and a French Manicure
Death, Taxes, and a Skinny No-Whip Latte
Death, Taxes, and Extra-Hold Hairspray
Death, Taxes, and a Sequined Clutch
(an e-original novella)
Death, Taxes, and Peach Sangria
Death, Taxes, and Hot-Pink Leg Warmers
Death, Taxes, and Green Tea Ice Cream
Death, Taxes, and Mistletoe Mayhem
(an e-original novella)
Death, Taxes, and Silver Spurs
Death, Taxes, and Cheap Sunglasses
Death, Taxes, and a Chocolate Cannoli
Death, Taxes, and a Satin Garter
Death, Taxes, and Sweet Potato Fries
Death, Taxes, and Pecan Pie
(an e-original novella)
Death, Taxes, and a Shotgun Wedding

PRAISE FOR DIANE KELLY'S PAW ENFORCEMENT SERIES

"Kelly's writing is smart and laugh-out-loud funny."
—Kristan Higgins, *New York Times* bestselling author

"Humor, romance, and surprising LOL moments. What more can you ask for?" —*Romance and Beyond*

"Brimming with intelligence, a devious plot and plenty of imagination."
—*Romance Junkies* on *Laying Down the Paw*

"Outstanding!"
—*Night Owl Reviews* on *Laying Down the Paw*

"Fabulously fun and funny!" —*Book Babe*

"An engaging read that I could not put down. I look forward to the next adventure of Megan and Brigit!"
—*SOS Aloha* on *Paw Enforcement*

"Sparkling with surprises. Just like a tequila sunrise. You never know which way is up or out!"
—*Romance Junkies* on *Paw and Order*

"A completely satisfying and delightful read. By being neither too 'cute' with its police dog lead, nor too dark with its serious topic, the author delivers a mystery that is a masterful blend of police detective and cozy fiction."
—*Kings River Life* on *Enforcing the Paw*

PAW OF THE JUNGLE

Diane Kelly

St. Martin's Paperbacks

First published in the United States by St. Martin's Paperbacks, an imprint of St. Martin's Publishing Group.

PAW OF THE JUNGLE

For information, address St. Martin's Publishing Group, 120 Broadway, New York, NY 10271.

www.stmartins.com

ISBN: 978-1-250-19737-5

Our books may be purchased in bulk for promotional, educational, or business use. Please contact your local bookseller or the Macmillan Corporate and Premium Sales Department at 1-800-221-7945, ext. 5442, or by email at MacmillanSpecialMarkets@macmillan.com.

Printed in the United States of America

St. Martin's Paperbacks edition / December 2019

10 9 8 7 6 5 4 3 2 1

To all the brave and dedicated folks fighting the illegal animal trade.

ACKNOWLEDGMENTS

Thanks again to Colonel (Retired) Patricia A. Mance for suggesting the title for this book. I'm lucky to have such dedicated and creative readers.

Thanks to Cecilia Conneely and Police Officer B. Conneely for answering my questions about police gear and recommending police shows and videos for information and inspiration.

As always, much appreciation goes out to the team at St. Martin's Press who shepherd the books along from idea to published product. Thanks to my editors, Hannah Braaten and Nettie Finn, for all you do in refining my work. Thanks also to Allison Ziegler, Kayla Janas, Talia Sherer, and the rest of the team at St. Martin's for getting my books into stores and libraries, and into the hands of readers, reviewers, and librarians.

Thanks to Danielle Fiorella and illustrator Allen Douglas for creating such fun book covers for this series.

Thanks to my agent, Helen Breitwieser, for all you do to advance my writing career.

Thanks to Liz Bemis and April Reed of Spark Creative for your work on my Web site and newsletters.

Thanks to fellow authors D. D. Ayres, Laura Castoro, Angela Cavener, Christie Craig, Cheryl Hathaway, and Angela Hicks for your feedback and friendship. It's been fun taking this ride with you all.

And thanks to you readers who chose this book! I couldn't do this without you. Have fun with Megan, Brigit, and the gang!

ONE
SECOND CHANCES

The Poacher

Please say yes.

He knew it was dumb to cross his fingers, that the childish gesture wouldn't change anything, but he needed any help he could get.

The man leaned back in his chair and crossed his arms over his chest, sending a pointed look over his desk. "We've taken chances on ex-cons before. It hardly ever works out."

The guy's words weren't exactly encouraging, but he wouldn't have offered an interview to a felon if they weren't desperate to fill their openings. Besides, he'd said hardly ever, not never. *How can I convince this guy to give me the job?*

"I got early release for good behavior," the Poacher said. "I'll do what I'm told. I just want to earn an honest living. I'm not the same man who—"

"Stole from his employers?" The man's brows lifted, his forehead ridged like corrugated metal.

The Poacher's gut tightened. He'd planned to say he wasn't the same man who'd made those stupid mistakes years ago, but there was no point in arguing with the guy—especially when he was right. Even so, the Poacher had only been trying to provide for his family, to give them the things they needed and deserved. He hadn't done it for himself. He wasn't a bad guy. But trying to explain himself or excuse his behavior wouldn't get him anywhere.

"I learned my lesson," he said, quickly adding "sir" even though the guy interviewing him was his own age or younger. "Look. I really need this job. I've got a wife and three kids to take care of." Well, he had the three kids, anyway. Despite a dozen heartfelt proposals, Vicki had never agreed to make their relationship official. *Maybe she'll change her mind if I land this job.* "I promise if you hire me, I'll work hard and won't give you any trouble."

The man grunted, still not fully convinced. "The job requires working outside in all kinds of weather."

"No problem." After eighteen months in a concrete cage, it would be a treat to be outside, even in rain or sleet or wind.

The interviewer narrowed his eyes and cocked his head. "You willing to work weekends?"

The Poacher leaned forward earnestly. "Whatever you need. I'm your man."

The guy sat back in his chair and released a slow, long, and loud breath. "All right," he said finally. "You can start tomorrow. But one screwup and you'll be out on your ass. Understand me?"

"Yes, sir." For the first time in a year, his mouth spread in a sincere smile. *Things are finally turning around.* He stood and offered his hand across the table. "Thank you. You won't be sorry."

The man took his hand, but gave him a skeptical look in return. "We'll see."

Vicki's narrow face wore that same skeptical expression when she opened the door of the tiny wood-frame house.

Seemed he'd been looking at skeptical faces all his life. *Ugh.* In addition to the cynical scowl, she wore skintight jeans, high-heeled ankle boots, and a V-neck sweater that revealed another V formed by her cleavage. Some had called her trashy, but the Poacher had always called her beautiful. His groin tightened at the sight of her lean curves, her baby-blue eyes, and those wild copper curls. It had been far too long since they'd been together. The state of Texas didn't allow conjugal visits. *Talk about your cruel punishments.* He hadn't realized when he'd been sentenced to a year and a half in the slammer that he'd also been sentenced to a case of blue balls. He wondered if another man had since been meeting Vicki's needs. The thought made him want to punch the siding. But he knew he wouldn't win her back if he got angry.

"Hey, babe." His breath fogged in the winter air as he offered her a grin. Hell, it was the only thing he had to offer her. He'd been given a mere fifty dollars on his release from prison, and he'd spent most of that on the cab ride to get here. He leaned against the door frame, hooking his thumbs in his belt loops and crooking his arms to emphasize the biceps he'd developed in the prison gym. "I'm home."

A spotted cat twined around her ankles as she eyed his new muscles. She put her cigarette to her lips and took a deep drag before shooting smoke out the side of her mouth. "How can you be *home*? You've never lived here."

True. When he'd left for prison, they'd been sharing a tiny two-bedroom apartment a couple miles away.

"Besides," she added, "that's my decision. Not yours."

She had a point. This house belonged to her. She'd somehow managed to save enough of her tip money to put a down payment on the place and convince a bank to give her a mortgage. He'd never been able to save a penny, and there was no way he'd qualify for a loan. His credit score approximated his IQ. They'd even had to put his pickup truck in her name. The car dealer wouldn't have sold it to him otherwise. The truck was parked in her driveway now. *She hung on to my truck. That says something, don't it?*

"I missed you," he said softly, locking his gaze on hers. "You were the first thing I thought about when I woke up every morning and the last thing I thought about when I fell asleep every night." In between, he was mostly thinking of ways he could avoid getting the shit beat out of him . . . or worse. "I counted each second until I could see you again. It was the only thing that kept me going." He ran his gaze down her sweater and jeans to her boots, and back up again. "Is it my imagination, or did you get even sexier while I was locked up?"

She softened ever so slightly at his sweet talk, the change perceptible only to one who knew her so well. Taking a chance, he took a step toward her. She turned her head away. He recognized the gesture. It meant she was giving in, but felt ashamed of herself for it. He reached out to touch her hair but she moved like a ninja, raising her arm to block his hand. Ashes fell from her cigarette to the porch. She dropped her cigarette after them, grinding out the butt with her heel.

"Come on, Vicki," he pleaded. "Let me come in. It's cold out here."

She crossed her arms over her chest, making no move to let him past. "You've brought me nothing but trouble. Give me one good reason why I should let you in."

"Because I love you," he said. "I bet you still love me, too."

She rolled her eyes. "Been there, done that. All it got me was heartache. You're gonna have to come up with a better reason for me to let you back into our lives."

Our lives? A hot spark flared in him. Their children were as much his as they were hers. Despite that fact, she hadn't once brought them to see him in prison during the year and a half he'd spent inside. But now that he was out, he could enforce visitation if he had to. Still, no sense getting her all riled up. "I've got a job." He'd been taught some job skills in prison, ones that would help him stay on the straight and narrow. "They're starting me tomorrow. I'll be able to pay you that back child support I owe you." *Eventually.*

She issued a derisive huff. "I've heard this story before. It always ends in you getting fired."

"Not this time!" He closed his eyes and took a breath to calm himself. When he opened his eyes, he said, "I'm going to work hard, make something of myself. Take care of you and the kids."

"I'll believe it when I see it."

A sweet little voice came from behind him. "Daddy?"

He turned to see the yellow school bus rolling off down the side street and his seven-year-old daughter standing on the cracked sidewalk. She wore a puffy white jacket with black sleeves. Black ears stood up from the hood, which featured the face of a panda bear. Pandas had always been her favorite animals. Her hands gripped the front straps of the backpack slung over her shoulders. His heart soared. He knew a father wasn't supposed to play favorites, but he couldn't help it. He loved his two little boys, but Harper, his firstborn, had always been his pride and joy, a daddy's girl through and through.

When she realized the man on her porch was, in fact, her father, her lips curled up in a smile that revealed a big gap between her teeth. When he'd last seen her, she'd still had all her baby teeth, and both she and her hair were several inches shorter. He'd missed out on a big part of her life, another gap for the two of them. *I'll die before I let that happen again.*

"Hey, squirt!" He bent down and stretched out his arms.

She ran full speed right at him, her backpack slapping against her small shoulders. She nearly knocked him over as she hurled herself into his arms, but he wouldn't have minded if she'd broken every bone in his body. His heart filled with so much emotion it was a wonder it didn't explode. The overwhelming emotion was joy, but regret was in the mix, too.

"I missed you so much," he said into her hair, his voice breaking. He'd really messed things up last time. But when he'd been released, he'd vowed to be the kind of father his children needed, the kind they deserved. Seeing his precious daughter only made him more determined to get things right this time.

She tried to push him back and get a look at his face. "Are you crying, Daddy?"

"'Course not." He was, but he didn't want Vicki to know. She'd already made him feel like half a man. He discreetly turned his head, wiping his tears on the hood of his daughter's black-and-white coat. "How was school?"

"Good!" She eased out of her backpack and unzipped it, reaching in to retrieve a piece of wide-lined notebook paper and thrusting it in his face. "Look! I got a hundred on my spelling test."

He took the paper. The list included some difficult words for a seven-year-old. "Because." "Caught." "Bright." That last word certainly described his daughter. Although he'd like to think otherwise, he was smart enough to know she didn't get her brains from him. He'd never done well in school, even when he tried. His father had always said he'd been born stupid and had only grown stupider since. *As if that man were some kind of Einstein.*

Harper blinked her hazel eyes. *At least she got something from me.* "You done good," he told her. "Made me and your mama proud."

She beamed. "I made this, too."

She pulled another paper from her backpack, this one green construction paper cut in the shape of a Christmas tree. Gold glitter drifted down to the porch like fairy dust. Harper must've used a whole jar of the stuff on her picture. The tree featured a bunch of plastic beads, too, strung on yarn to resemble lights. She'd written her name on the back, adding a curl to the tail on the letter *p* as she'd done since she first learned to write in kindergarten. She said the curl made the letter prettier, and that it wasn't fair for the lower-case *g*, *j*, and *q* to get a curl but not the *p*. Luckily for Harper, the teachers didn't seem to mind.

"Come on, Daddy." Harper grabbed his hand and pulled him inside. "Let's hang them on the fridge."

Vicki frowned as they squeezed past her, but made no attempt to stop them.

He glanced around as his baby girl led him into the living room. The place was a cluttered but comfortable home. The scent of cigarettes and the morning's cinnamon toast hung in the air. A space heater whirred in the corner, warming the small den. Cheap secondhand furniture filled the room, mismatched but functional. He recognized most of it from their old apartment. A playpen sat in the corner, blankets and teethers strewn about inside. Toys in all shapes and sizes littered the scratched hardwood floors. He knew instantly which ones were Harper's—the stuffed animals, the plastic barn complete with a set of farm animals, the collectible horses.

Harper hung her backpack on a hook by the front door. As she pushed back the hood of her jacket, static electricity caused some of the shiny strands of her red hair to stick up in gravity-defying wisps. She unzipped her jacket, slid it off, and hung that on the hook, too. She'd always followed the rules, seen the world in black-and-white, just like the colors of the panda on her coat. She turned to him. "Are you going to live here, Daddy?"

He cut a glance at Vicki. Her expression said she still hadn't made up her mind, but if anyone could convince her to let him stay it was their daughter.

"That's up to your mother," he said.

Vicki's expression turned sour and she cut him an icy glare. "Thanks a lot. Now I'll be the bad guy if I say no."

He flashed his most charming smile. "Then don't say no."

"Pleeeeease, Mommy!" begged their daughter, tugging on Vicki's sweatshirt. "Please let Daddy stay with us!" She turned to him. "You're gonna be good this time. Right, Daddy?"

A lump of emotion clogged his throat. He gave his girl a single but definitive nod. *Yes. I'll be good this time if it kills me.*

Vicki looked from him down to the little girl at her waist. "All right," she said finally. She returned her gaze to him. "But you can only stay if you pay half the mortgage and bills, and you've got to pick up your truck payments. You owe me for the ones I paid while you were gone, too. And you're sleeping on the floor in the boys' room."

"Fair enough." He kept a straight face, but on the inside he knew he had her. *I'll be back in her bed in no time.*

TWO
BLUES AND GRAYS

Fort Worth Police Officer Megan Luz

It was a crisp Wednesday morning in mid-December when a shrill sound stabbed into my brain. *Bleep-bleep-bleep.*

I reached over to the bedside table and slapped blindly at my phone until my fingers found the button to turn off the alarm. *Getting up before the sun is unnatural.* My eyes were still closed, but my mind slowly cleared from the fog of sleep, discerning a warm body stretched along my left leg, a furry head draped over my thigh. Brigit was taking full advantage of my body heat. When the two of us were at work, the enormous shepherd was my partner and a highly skilled tool for sniffing out illegal drugs, trailing suspects, and taking down criminals. But when we were at home, she was my playmate, my cuddle buddy, my Briggie Boo-Boo. I reached down and ruffled the dog's ears. "Good morning, girl."

Seeming to know the alarm meant I should be getting up, the calico cat who belonged to my roommate leaped up onto the bed and landed on my bladder like a furry kettle bell. *Oof!* Nothing like a sucker punch to the gut to open your eyes. As I scowled down at Zoe, she proceeded to stroll up my ribs and stopped to stand on my right breast.

Ow. She locked her laserlike feline gaze on mine. Realizing she had my full, if irritated, attention, she placed her breakfast order. *Meow.*

"Fish breath."

Ignoring my insult, she hopped down from the bed and waltzed to the bedroom door, glancing back to make sure I was moving. *Bossy cat.* As I sat up in bed, Brigit stretched her legs out straight, working out the kinks in her muscles. She slid off the bed and onto the floor where she shook herself fully awake, her tags jingling like Christmas bells.

I climbed out of bed, tiptoed into the hall, and took a peek into Frankie's room. Sure enough, she was fast asleep, the covers pulled up high around her face, the spiky points of her blue hair sticking out above them. Frankie had come off a twenty-four-hour shift at the fire station at four o'clock yesterday afternoon and followed it up with an evening of roller derby practice. Two physically and mentally exhausting activities. Can't say that I blamed her for sleeping in.

I set about feeding the animals and myself, showered, and slipped into my Fort Worth police uniform. I wound my long, dark hair up into a tight bun on the back of my head, slapped on a quick coat of mascara and lip gloss, and performed a quick mental rundown to make sure I had all of my gear. *Gun? Check. Baton? Check. Radio? Check. Partner?* I looked around. *Where is that dog?*

I found Brigit on her back on the living room rug, wriggling around playfully as Zoe swatted at her tail.

"C'mon, girl," I called to Brigit. "Duty calls."

She deftly leveraged herself to her feet and trotted over so I could attach her lead. *Partner? Check.*

Of all my tools, Brigit was by far the most useful. While I had to rely on my eyes and ears when searching for a suspect who'd fled or hid, she had a top-notch nose at her disposal. That skilled snout made her instrumental in finding contraband narcotics, too. No more time-sucking car searches for me. Brigit could sniff out drugs in mere seconds. She could also run faster and farther than me, and take down large suspects that, admittedly, the thought of wrangling with scared me to death. Since partnering with her, my arrest statistics had gone through the roof. Though she deserved the lion's share of the credit, I received the bulk of the pay, including a small additional stipend for her care. She didn't seem to mind that she never got a raise. She wasn't in the law enforcement game for the glory. She was in it for the liver treats.

I slid into my jacket and gloves, and out the door we went. Another day, another dollar. Also another day closer to making detective, which was my ultimate goal.

As we headed down the porch, my boyfriend Seth pulled up to the curb in his seventies era blue Nova complete with flames painted down the sides and a license plate that read KABOOM. Seth worked as a firefighter. In fact, he was the one who had initially interested my roommate in joining the department. He also served on the city's bomb squad along with his K-9 partner, Blast, who was trained to detect explosives. Blast stood on the backseat, looking out the window. When he spotted Brigit, his tail began to whip back and forth. The yellow Lab had an incurable crush on my partner. But who could blame him? She was smart and fun, with beautiful big brown eyes and lots of shiny fur. She could even be sweet when she wanted to be.

Seth parked and climbed out of his car. "Glad I caught you!" he called, his breath visible in the frigid air. Seth stood five feet ten and sported broad, muscular shoulders formed from countless laps swimming the butterfly stroke at the local YMCA. A former explosives ordnance specialist in the army, he continued to serve in the reserves and kept his blond hair shorn short in regulation. He had gorgeous green eyes and a manly army eagle tattoo that spanned his back and those aforementioned strong shoulders.

He turned back to reach for something inside his car and, as I approached, held a large cardboard coffee cup out to me. Steam wafted through the tiny hole in the lid.

I gave him a smile as I took the cup. *What a thoughtful gesture.* "This is a nice surprise."

"Thought you could use a hot drink this morning." He quirked his brows. "'Course I'd rather keep you warm another way."

"I bet you would." *I bet I'd enjoy every minute of it, too.* Though we didn't officially live together, Seth kept clothes, a toothbrush, and a razor at my place. He also stayed here on most of the nights when my roommate was gone, and he and I were both off work. Otherwise, he lived in a patchwork house in east Fort Worth with his mother and grandfather, a surly Vietnam veteran named Ollie. Still, Ollie had been noticeably less surly since I'd introduced him to Beverly, a burglary victim I'd met on an earlier case. *Nothing can change a man like the love of a good woman.*

I took a sip of the luscious latte and moaned in bliss.

Seth groaned in return. "You trying to torture me?"

I gave him a coy smile. "How was your shift?" While working as a police officer and firefighter had distinct differences, all first-responder jobs shared some similarities. Long periods of downtime broken by bursts of frenetic action. Dealing with people in highly emotional situations. A tight bond with coworkers who had your back and, like yourself, put their lives on the line each day.

"A day-care van caught fire on Rosedale this morning," he said. "Luckily all the kids got out and there were only minor injuries. Alex had put a box of colored bandages in the ambulance. It was a great idea. Even the kids who weren't hurt wanted one."

"Alex?" Because Seth's station sat within my beat, we covered the same general area and I'd met all of the firefighters and paramedics assigned to his station at one time or another. I didn't remember an Alex.

"New paramedic," he replied. "Started a few days ago."

I made a mental note to stop by the station and introduce myself. "Gotta go or we'll be late." I leaned in and gave Seth a kiss that was nearly as warm as the latte. *Let the neighbors gawk and talk.*

When I stepped back, he said, "I'm off the next two days. Why don't I come by tonight? We could watch some TV, maybe order a pizza."

"Sounds good."

Brigit let out a bark to let us know pizza sounded good to her, too. *Woof!*

A half hour later, I downed the last of the latte as Brigit and I cruised our beat in our specially equipped K-9 cruiser. The vehicle had the standard equipment in front—laptop stand, radio, dashboard-mounted camera. But, rather than the usual backseat, a carpeted platform spanned the space, enclosed by metal safety mesh. I'd added a comfy cushion for Brigit to lie on, as well as an assortment of chew toys to keep her occupied during the dull downtime. Now that the weather had grown colder, I'd added a fleece blanket to keep her cozy. With the blanket and toys strewn about, her enclosure resembled a child's playpen.

As we meandered about our beat, waiting for a call to come across the radio, my mind pondered the irony of law enforcement driving black-and-white vehicles when the situations we dealt with every day were rarely clear-cut black-and-white, but varying shades of gray. Depending on a suspect's mental state or abilities, the accused could be guilty of a crime or found innocent. Sometimes people did illegal things for good reasons, such as speeding to the emergency clinic with a passenger suffering a serious asthma attack. Or they violated the law, but prosecuting them would do no good for anyone, such as when two otherwise friendly neighbors get in a minor shoving match at a backyard barbecue after a few too many beers. *Shake it off and shake hands, guys.* People loitered about on occasion for no other reason than that they had no other place to go, or simply needed to stop and think. Though we liked to think of police work as a game of the good guys versus the bad guys, the concept of good and bad could be quite fluid.

Whoa. All that caffeine had me feeling philosophical, huh?

Of course Brigit's world was more black-and-white than mine, though not entirely so.

All dogs relied more on their noses than they did their eyes, especially dogs like Brigit who were trained to scent for drugs or lawbreakers who'd fled or were hiding. Still, it was a myth that dogs were color-blind. As I'd learned in my K-9 handler training, their color spectrum was more limited, given that their eyes had only two types of cones while human eyes had three. Their range included yellows and blues, but, thanks to evolution, filtered out common background colors like greens and browns to make other objects, such as their prey or predators, stand out more readily. And, despite their limited color range, canine eyes had much better night vision and could detect movement much better than the human eye.

My radio came to life. "Report of a fender-bender at Pennsylvania and Hemphill. Who can respond?"

I grabbed my mic from the dash and pressed the button. "Officer Luz and Brigit responding."

The wreck was resolved in twenty minutes, both vehicles dented but functioning, no tow trucks required. I issued a citation to the driver with the crumpled hood, who, according to witnesses, was looking down at her cell phone and failed to stop in time. The remainder of the morning was spent sending truant teens back to class at Paschal High School, issuing a speeding ticket to a college student near the TCU campus, and unsuccessfully scouring the area around the Shoppes at Chisholm Trail for a shoplifter who'd run off in a brand-new pair of sneakers when security had spotted her slipping her own worn shoes into the box to leave behind.

Around one o'clock, the outdoor temperature had risen to nearly sixty degrees and my butt had grown numb from sitting in my seat. *Time to get out of the cruiser and get moving.* I cast a glance at Brigit in my rearview mirror. "Want to walk the zoo?"

On hearing two of her favorite words, Brigit's ears perked up and she issued an excited *arf-arf!*

Minutes later, we were making our way inside. One of the perks of patrolling this beat was free admission to the zoo while we were on duty. I raised a hand in greeting to the ticket seller, a sixtyish black woman named Janelle whom I'd introduced myself and Brigit to a few months back. Janelle wore a broad smile and a yellow knit hat to keep her head warm.

"Back again?" she called through the open circle cut out of the glass in her booth.

"Brigit insisted. It's her favorite place to patrol." Still, the worst offense I'd witnessed on the premises was when one bonobo stole a piece of fruit from another while the latter turned his head.

"You two have fun!" Janelle called after us.

"Thanks!" I called back. "We will!"

I let Brigit take the lead, determining where we'd go and what we'd see today. While we walked, I spun my nightstick. I'd been a twirler in my high school band, and old habits never die, right? Besides, I found the motion and sound soothing. *Swish-swish-swish.*

My partner strolled past the giraffes and gorillas, stopping when we reached the red wolf exhibit. As I'd learned from a zookeeper on an earlier visit, the wolves were critically endangered after being mistakenly blamed for killing livestock and slaughtered indiscriminately. Brigit stared into the exhibit, making eye contact with a wolf lying under a tree. She issued a soft whimper, as if sympathizing with their plight.

As we meandered about, it dawned on me that, like my police cruiser, many of the animals here were black-and-white. The zebras, of course. The white tiger. The aptly named eastern black-and-white colobus monkey. The rockhopper penguin and Andean condor. The zoo even had a fish called the "convict tang" that was white with four black vertical stripes.

We soon found ourselves at the black rhino exhibit. According to an informational sign, black rhinos were critically endangered, like the red wolves, but for a different reason. Some cultures wrongfully believed rhino horn had medicinal qualities or served as a powerful aphrodisiac, fueling demand for horns. *If it takes ground-up animal parts to make someone horny, maybe they should look for a partner they're more attracted to or just read a darn book instead.* The placard noted the black rhino population, once widespread and numerous in southern Africa, had decreased to a mere 3 percent of its 1970 level by 1992, nearing extinction. Due to the scarcity of the animals, their horns were more valuable than gold. Though attempts had been made to protect the animals, brutal poachers routinely killed the animals for their horns, sometimes murdering park rangers, as well. The sign noted that the loss of habitat to agriculture played a role, too, and conservationists realized too late that more of their focus should have been on preserving the habitats. When an ecosystem was disrupted and the only specimens of a species were in captivity, there was little chance the creatures could be returned to their native lands.

A thirtyish white man in a long-sleeved green T-shirt, khaki pants, and a safari-style vest worked inside the enclosure, while a zookeeper kept an eye on the rhinos lounging on the other side of their pen. This buddy system was a wise arrangement. A few years back, the zoo had been cited by the Occupational Safety and Health Administration for safety violations after a zoo worker was injured by an elephant tusk. The practice of "free contact," in which there were no barriers between zookeepers and animals, could be controversial. No problems today, fortunately. Though rhinos could be extremely dangerous in the wild, these enormous beasts paid the man and the overseer little mind, accustomed to humans in their environment.

While one of my duties as Brigit's handler was to clean up after her, the droppings she produced were tiny compared to the cantaloupe-sized rhino poops. It was no wonder the man's well-developed biceps strained the fabric of his sleeves as he used a flat, wide shovel to scoop the piles of excrement into a rolling bin lined with a plastic garbage bag.

Brigit looked up at me and issued a soft *woof.* Looked like she needed a potty break of her own. I led her over to a landscaped area where she crouched and did her business. I tugged a biodegradable bag from the dispenser on my belt and used it to retrieve the mess. As I was tying the bag closed, a gate opened and the man in the green shirt emerged, pushing the rolling bin. The name tag attached to his vest identified him as Danny L.

I smiled at the man and raised my bag. "Looks like your job description and mine have some overlap."

He chuckled. "I've learned more about animal dung on this job than I ever wanted to know. At least the rhinos poop in one spot. Makes it easier to clean up."

As I'd learned from the informational display at the exhibit, the rhinos' communal dung piles were called "middens." The display also noted that the dung contained chemicals that rhinos could read, telling them the age, health, sex, and reproductive status of other rhinos in the area. Rhinos sniffed the dung piles for the same reasons dogs sniffed each other's rears, fire hydrants, and light poles used as common urination spots. Though I sometimes envied Brigit's heightened senses, I was glad that, as a human, I could refrain from such sniffing. If I wanted to know someone's age and status, I could read their Facebook profile.

"Need someplace to ditch that bag?" When the custodian raised a palm to indicate his bin, my eyes spotted a small tattoo below his thumb—five dots configured like the five sides on dice, with four dots in a square and one in the middle. The tattoo was a common prison tattoo. The shape was symbolic, the center dot representing an inmate trapped inside four walls. Most likely, the tattoo had been applied using a sewing needle or paper clip. The ink had probably been drained from a ballpoint pen. Not exactly hygienic.

I wondered what he'd been in for. It couldn't have been a violent crime or he would never have been hired here, where he'd have contact with the public. *Drugs, maybe? Some kind of theft?* Those were the most common nonviolent crimes. But whatever he'd done in the past, I was glad the guy had found work now, been given a second chance. If he was smart, he'd make the most of it, stay out of trouble. Recidivism rates for convicts with steady jobs were significantly lower than for the unemployed. Unfortunately, unskilled, convicted felons had an uphill battle finding legitimate work. Many employers assumed they'd be unreliable and untrustworthy. Studies showed this assumption was incorrect. Offenders, especially those under supervision, tended to be more productive than the average worker, especially when maintaining employment was a condition of their early release. Employers who hired ex-cons also reported lower turnover rates, which helped their bottom lines. Many who'd done time did whatever it took not to return to the clink. I'd visited prisons myself. They were far from pleasant places.

To reduce recidivism, prisons offered work-training programs ranging from custodial work to information technology. They also taught barbering, cooking, plumbing, HVAC installation and repair, welding, and other construction trades. Heck, there were even programs for animal training, with convicts taught how to train horses and dogs. Given the bias against former inmates, civil rights advocates were pushing "Ban the Box" or "Fair Chance" legislation to preclude employers from asking on job applications whether an applicant had a criminal record. Eleven states had adopted such laws. Texas, which prided itself on being tough on crime, was not among them. Ironically, the tough-on-crime pride didn't extend to sexual violence. The state had a huge backlog of untested rape kits. Rather than pony up the money to test this critical evidence and take violent offenders off the streets, the legislature voted to allow residents to make a donation for this purpose when renewing their driver's licenses, essentially a GoFundMe program with no guarantee of raising a single dime. Frankly, I thought the legislature should go "fund" itself for showing so little regard for victims.

My curiosity got the best of me. Besides, part of community policing was getting to know the people on my beat. The more I knew, the better I could do my job. "What were you in for?" I asked the man.

His cheeks reddened with what I assumed was shame. "Felony theft. I used to be an orderly at the children's hospital. One of the nurses caught me taking diapers and baby formula from a supply room. My kid needed the stuff and I couldn't afford it on my pay."

Per the Texas Penal Code, felony theft involved property valued between $1,500 and $20,000, and carried a penalty range of 180 days to two years in prison and a fine up to $10,000. Not the worst crime a person could commit.

His eyes narrowed. "How'd you know I did time?"

I gestured to his hand. "The tattoo is a dead giveaway."

He looked down at the tattoo and frowned. "I should get that thing removed."

"First offense?" I asked.

"First and last. I got no interest in going back to jail."

"Don't blame you." I cocked my head. "I'm surprised your sentence wasn't probated." Many first-time offenders were placed under supervision rather than incarcerated. Under the circumstances, it seemed a judge might go easy on him.

He shrugged. "I'd confessed to the cops. The prosecutor made a big deal about me stealing from a kids' hospital. Said it was heartless. I had a lousy defense attorney, too."

Most court-appointed attorneys did a competent job, but they were paid poorly. Some took on excessive caseloads to make ends meet and didn't have time to fully prepare each case for court. My heart squirmed in my chest. Sure, the guy had broken the law, but his reasons for doing so weren't selfish or hateful. He'd done it out of desperation. This situation was another instance of the gray areas we in law enforcement confronted constantly.

My mind went to Jean Valjean of *Les Misérables*, a man forced to work on a chain gang after stealing bread to feed his starving nephew. After living as a pariah due to his status as an ex-con, Valjean assumed a fictitious identity and spent the rest of his life attempting to live honorably—not easy when he was constantly pursued by police Inspector Javert, intent on sending Valjean back to prison. I hoped Danny L. would attempt to live honorably, too, though he might find it harder given he couldn't hide behind a fake persona like the hero of the Broadway musical.

I fished a business card out of the breast pocket of my uniform and held it out to him. "We've got a shared interest in your success. If there's ever anything I can do, let me know."

His expression was equal parts surprised and dubious as he took the card, read it over, and slid it into the back pocket of his pants.

Brigit lifted her head to scent the garbage can as I tossed her small bag of poop into the bin. "Thanks." I raised my hand in good-bye to the custodian. "Enjoy the rest of your day."

Brigit and I walked around for another fifteen minutes. We passed the Nubian ibex, a type of large mountain goat with a long beard and huge, curved horns. We also passed the more delicate-looking springboks, antelopes with distinguishing white faces and bellies, and two small horns that curved toward each other, like a lyre. The springboks came by their names honestly, able to leap several feet into the air in a move called "pronking" intended to distract predators.

When we left the springboks, Brigit stopped to watch errant squirrels scurry about in the bushes, making a last-minute attempt to gather acorns for winter. You'd think the dog would have had enough of squirrels with the dozen or so that constantly skittered around our backyard.

After a minute or two, I urged her to move on. "Let's go, girl. Squirrels are boring."

Brigit gave me a look that said she wholeheartedly disagreed with my assessment of the entertainment value of squirrels. Nonetheless, she left them to their nut gathering.

As we approached the exit, my shoulder-mounted radio crackled to life, dispatch looking for an officer to handle a theft of jewelry from a residence in the adjacent Berkeley Place neighborhood. I pressed the button. "Officer Luz and Brigit responding."

Brigit looked up at me, her eyes bright with anticipation. She seemed to know that my response meant we might see some action. Brigit loved her job, lived to trail and chase suspects. I, on the other hand, was working as a beat cop only until I had four years under my belt and could apply for a detective position. Depending on the particular shift, working patrol could be either incredibly slow and boring or extremely fast and frightening. To paraphrase Forrest Gump, police work was like a box of chocolates. You were sure to encounter some nuts, and things could get sticky and messy. You had to learn to stomach quite a bit to avoid getting sick.

We hurried out to the lot and I opened the back door of our cruiser. "In you go, girl."

Brigit hopped up onto her platform. I closed her door, slid into my seat, and off we went.

Guided by my GPS, I drove to the victim's house, pulling to the curb in front of it. While many of the houses in the exclusive Berkeley Place neighborhood were well kept but decades old, this house was more recently constructed, its predecessor having been razed. The home was a single-story ivory stucco, featuring a heavy wooden front door and rustic shutters in a dark finish. The diminutive bushes that lined the front bed had not yet had time to spread and fill the space, giving the house a spare look.

Brigit and I made our way to the door. I knocked and the door was promptly answered by an attractive Asian woman in her early thirties, only a few years older than me. The woman's dark hair was worn in a low side ponytail that draped forward over her thin shoulder. She wore sneakers along with a long-sleeved black T-shirt and a pair of teal exercise pants bearing the Lululemon logo. *Cute pants.* Too bad I'd never be able to afford designer athletic clothes on a cop's salary.

In her arms was a male Shiba Inu, a smaller breed of curly-tailed spitz that had recently grown in popularity. The dog took one look down at Brigit, drew his lips back, and snarled. Brigit took one look up at the dog and seemed to realize he posed no threat whatsoever. In fact, I would swear I saw Brigit roll her eyes at the dog's attempts to scare her.

"Come in." The woman shifted the dog to her left arm to hold the door for us. She had long, slender fingers and a festive manicure, sparkly white snowflakes on a blue background. I seemed to have a natural affinity for detail, noting such things. Not to brag, but not much gets by me.

Brigit and I stepped into the tile foyer. I extended my hand. "Hi. I'm Officer Megan Luz."

"Nanami Ishii," she replied. "Call me Nan."

The woman took my hand in hers. *Wow. How does she get her skin so soft?* As much as I would have liked to ask what type of lotion she used, it would be unprofessional.

Our introductions complete, I pulled out my notepad and pen. "I understand some jewelry has gone missing?"

"Yes. My engagement ring and wedding band. I was feeding my dog a few minutes ago when I noticed I didn't have my rings on. I only take them off to shower. The diamond gets tangled up in my hair when I wash it."

I nodded. I'd had the same issue with some of my rings. Of course, I'd never had a diamond ring. But if my relationship with Seth continued on its current course, I might have one in another year or two. Who knew?

She pointed behind her, down a hallway. "I always leave my rings in the dish on my vanity so they won't accidentally get knocked into the sink and go down the drain. But when I went to get them, they weren't there. A plumber was in the bathroom earlier today, installing new shower heads. He had to be the one who took them. He's the only one who's been in the house today other than me. My husband is on a ski trip in Colorado with some of his old friends from college."

I jotted a quick note. *Plumber installed shower heads. Hubby in CO/skiing with buddies.* "Can you show me where they were?"

"Sure."

Brigit and I followed Nan down the hall and into the master bedroom. The space was decorated in turquoise and chocolate brown. On the wall over the king-sized bed was a nearly life-sized wedding portrait of Nan and a man who wasn't quite old enough to be her father, but maybe a youngish uncle. I'd put fifteen years between them. The photograph had been reprinted on canvas and showed them from the waist up. Nan's hands were wrapped around the base of her white rose bouquet, her ring set clearly visible.

I stopped and pointed to the picture. "The rings that were stolen. They were the ones in this picture?"

"Yes."

I walked to the head of the bed and leaned over to take a closer look at the rings in the photo. The wedding ring was a simple, wide gold band. The engagement ring was similarly understated, though the marquise-cut diamond was quite large. "Mind if I snap a photograph? It could help us identify the rings if we come across them."

"Of course," Nan agreed.

After I snapped a few pictures of her rings, she led me into the spacious master bath and pointed to the vanity. A variety of tubes and bottles containing expensive beauty products sat on the marble countertop, along with a box of tissue and a porcelain ring holder, essentially a small bowl with a raised center spike on which to place rings. Three other rings encircled the spike. One was silver with a heart-shaped charm dangling from it. Another was silver with a large oval of turquoise. The third was gold with an intricate filigree.

She pointed to the bowl. "That's where my rings were. In the bowl with the others."

My gaze moved about the cluttered countertop. "You're certain?"

Irritation flickered across her face. "Absolutely. I go through the same routine every morning. I take off my rings, put them in the bowl, then undress and shower. After I get dressed and fix my makeup and hair, I put my rings back on."

I hated to point out the obvious, but . . . "You don't appear to be wearing makeup." The splayed ends of her ponytail told me she hadn't curled or straightened her hair before pulling it into the elastic holder, either. I had my own routines, ones I went through on autopilot, my body doing things out of habit while my mind paid little, if any, attention. But those routines could be thrown off if unusual circumstances intervened. Given that she'd forgotten to put the rings back on after her shower, it was also possible she'd never put them in the bowl to begin with. Maybe she'd lost them elsewhere earlier.

"Since the plumber was coming," she said, "I took the day off from work. There was no reason to put on my usual makeup or fix my hair. I was just going to catch up on some cleaning. I didn't plan to leave the house."

"So you haven't been out of your house today? Not for a run or an exercise class? Or maybe to check the mail?"

"No. I've been inside all day. I let my dog into the backyard, but that was it. I didn't go out with him."

So much for that theory.

I turned my attention to the shower. It was a wide, walk-in style, with multiple shower heads at various heights. The heads had variable settings, everything from a soft drizzle to full-on, hurricane-force blast. *Must be like showering in a car wash.* "Did the plumber show you his work when he was done?"

"Yes. He demonstrated the different settings and showed me that everything was working properly so I'd sign off on the paperwork."

"Did you ask him about the rings then?"

"No. I didn't notice they were missing until after he was gone."

"Have you called him?"

"Yes," she said. "He claimed he hadn't seen my rings, but there's no other explanation. He has to be lying."

Or does he? People were often too quick to blame missing items on housekeepers or other service providers who'd been in their homes, when often they'd misplaced the items themselves.

I said my next thought out loud. "Any idea why he would have taken only your wedding and engagement rings and not the others?"

She glanced over at the ring holder and shrugged. "Those three aren't as valuable. Maybe he could tell. Or maybe he thought if he left some of them it would be less obvious."

I eyed the bowl. "How much are the missing rings worth?"

"I don't know exactly," she said. "My husband picked them out and surprised me with them."

"Any chance he's got a receipt for the rings? It would be helpful to have a copy to include with my report." I explained that the DA would also want proof of the value of the items in order to determine if the theft constituted a felony and of what degree. "You'll need a receipt to file an insurance claim, too."

"My husband handles our finances," Nan said. "He scans the important documents. It might be on his computer."

She led Brigit and me down the hall to a home office with French doors. She stepped over to a desk that faced the wall. An open laptop sat on it, the screen in easy view. Still holding the dog, she dropped into the rolling chair, situating the little beast on her lap. After booting up the computer and typing in the password, she ran a search for a file that included the word "ring." Two file names popped up. One was RECEIPT—JORDAN WEDDING RING. The other was RECEIPT—WEDDING & ENGAGEMENT RING SET.

She pointed at the latter. "That must be it." She clicked on the file, quickly skimmed the screen when the document popped up, and dipped her head in confirmation. She ran her finger over the built-in mouse pad, clicked a couple of times to print out the receipt, and handed it to me, hot off the desktop printer.

Hmm. For someone who claimed to have little knowledge of their finances, she sure found the receipt quickly. Then again, her husband seemed to be well organized.

I ran my eyes over the page. The receipt was dated seven years prior and included a charge for an inscription that had been engraved inside the wedding band. *Sierra and Jordan forever.* Confused, I returned my attention to Nan. "Is Sierra your first name?"

"No." Her voice was as tight as her yoga pants. "Sierra was Jordan's girlfriend before me."

Nan's husband had proposed to her with an engagement ring purchased for another woman? *Ouch.* Still, it was hard to blame him. He'd paid over twenty grand for the engagement and wedding ring set. Not exactly chump change.

"Did the ring still have the inscription?" If so, it could help us identify the ring if it were recovered.

"No. Jordan must have had it removed before he gave it to me." Nan's eyes narrowed briefly in what was likely distrust, hurt, or anger—maybe all three.

"Was there a new inscription?"

Again, her answer was no. Again, her eyes narrowed. And, again, I couldn't blame her husband. *Why pay for another inscription when the first had been a waste of money?*

I wondered if Nan had known about the inscription before now, whether she'd been aware the rings were originally intended for another woman, whether that fact bothered her. "I can dust the bowl for prints, see if we get a match. Unless the plumber is already in the system or agrees to supply a print, it might not get us anywhere, but it's worth a shot. Just to warn you, though, the dust makes a bit of a mess."

"That's okay," she said. "I can clean it up."

I returned to my cruiser, retrieved my fingerprint kit, and the four of us headed back to the master bathroom together. While a crime scene team normally handled this type of evidence collection on bigger cases, beat cops were trained to lift prints in more routine cases like this.

After brushing the black powder about the small bowl, a number of fingerprints were revealed. Some were very well defined, probably left by Nan soon after she'd applied lotion or oil. Others were less distinguishable. I applied the tape and lifted the prints, affixing the tape to the fingerprint card for the lab to look at. Careful to keep out of snapping range of her dog, I also took prints from Nan so the lab could identify any that were hers.

"Cute manicure," I said as I rolled her index finger back and forth on the card, which I'd placed on the countertop.

"Thanks. I usually paint them myself, but my office holiday party is this weekend so I decided to go all out."

We returned to the foyer, where I snapped a photo of the invoice the plumber had left with Nan. The invoice contained his name and phone number.

"I'll get in touch with him," I told Nan. "It's likely he'll tell me the same thing he told you, but we'll see."

She thanked me and, after one last snarl from the dog in her arms, Brigit and I headed out to the car. Once I was seated in the cruiser, I phoned the plumber. After identifying myself, I asked if I could come speak to him in person.

He paused a moment, processing my words. "I'm finishing up a job," he said, keeping his voice low. "If people see my van and cops coming around, they'll jump to conclusions."

"I understand." Whether he was guilty or innocent, I couldn't blame him for not wanting me to show up on a worksite. It wouldn't be good for his business. "Let's meet at a public place nearby, then." I asked for his current location, plugged it into my phone's mapping app, and suggested we meet at a convenience store a half mile away. He agreed.

Twenty minutes later, the plumber, Brigit, and I stood face-to-face to furry face in the side parking lot of a 7-Eleven on north University Drive. The location was slightly outside the bounds of my designated beat, yet close enough that I could still respond to emergency calls if needed.

There was no point in beating around the bush. My time was important, and so was his. Heck, at the rates plumbers charged, his time was more valuable than mine. "Mrs. Ishii noticed that some of her jewelry was missing after you left her residence."

"And she told you I took it?"

I lifted a noncommittal shoulder. "She said you're the only one who's been in her house recently."

He issued an indignant huff. "The nerve of that woman. Accusing me of stealing from her even after I gave her a new-customer discount. No good deed goes unpunished, huh?" He rolled his eyes before returning his focus to me. "I didn't take anything. I installed the showerheads and that was it." He raised his callused palms. "Don't know what else to tell you."

"Did you touch anything in the house other than the shower?"

He looked up in thought. "Not that I remember. She opened the front door for me on my way in and out. The bathroom door was already open so I didn't have to touch the handle."

"Would you be willing to provide fingerprints?"

"Hell, yeah!" he replied without hesitation. "If it'll clear my name you can have fingerprints, a blood sample, whatever."

He certainly was being cooperative. Might as well make the most of it. "Would you let me take a look in your van?"

He swept his hand toward his vehicle. "Be my guest."

I peeked into the glove compartment, ashtrays, and console of his truck. No rings. Ditto for his toolbox and cargo bay. I did spot a well-used pair of heavy-duty work gloves, though, as well as a box of disposable latex gloves. The discovery wasn't surprising. Given the nature of his work, gloves would be needed for some jobs. While the thick work gloves would've made it harder for him to snag the rings, he could've donned a pair of the latex gloves and snatched them without leaving a print. *Hmm.*

I backed out of the van and returned to my cruiser for a fingerprint kit. After obtaining his prints and handing him a wet wipe to clean the ink from his fingers, I thanked him for his cooperation.

"I hope you find her jewelry." He gave me a pointed look. "For her sake and mine."

"Me, too."

Brigit and I returned to our cruiser. I made a quick call to Nan to inquire whether the plumber had worn disposable gloves while at her home. She said she hadn't noticed him wearing gloves, but she'd been in the living room and kitchen while he'd been working. She made a quick round of the house and confirmed he hadn't disposed of any gloves in the bathroom trash can or elsewhere.

By then, my shift was up. I drove Nan's and the plumber's prints back to the station, and Brigit and I headed back home for an evening of sitcoms, Seth, and snuggling.

THREE
FUR SHAME

Brigit

That furry little sissy had been acting like a darn fool with all that snarling. Brigit should've told him to pick on someone his own size—like a flea! *Heh-heh.*

Despite having the occasional run-in with these types of amateur wannabe watchdogs, Brigit loved working as a police K-9. She was taken on way more walks than the average house pet, and had fun exploring the city, including great smelly places like the parks and the zoo. Sometimes, she even got to chase humans and tackle them to the ground. Other dogs were punished for that kind of behavior, but Brigit was rewarded for it. *Best job ever!*

She had the best pack, too. Megan always carried liver treats in her pocket, and gave Brigit lots of nice scratches and ear rubs. Megan did weird things sometimes, like when she picked up Brigit's droppings and carried them around in a bag like a party favor, but Brigit had noticed that humans did all sorts of strange things. They bathed every day, willingly! And they ignored squirrels for some reason. Didn't they realize the rodents were launching an uprising to take over the world? But even though Brigit would never fully understand Megan, she loved her partner from the tips of her ears to the tips of her toes, and she knew Megan felt the same way about her.

FOUR

TOO GOOD TO BE TRUE

The Poacher

For once in his life, everything was going good.

He liked his job okay. He had to work outside and it could be cold sometimes, especially in the mornings, but overall the weather hadn't been too bad. His coworkers were all right, too. None had given him any problems. He'd turned over most of his first paycheck to Vicki, hanging on to just enough of the cash to buy gas to get to work.

Vicki had been happy to see the money. She still hadn't let him back into her bed, but when he'd snuck up behind her yesterday at the stove and slid his hand up under her top, she hadn't pushed it away. Too bad Harper had chosen that exact second to barge in and ask when dinner was going to be ready. *Kids and their crappy timing* . . .

The boys didn't remember when he'd been a part of their lives before, but they were slowly warming up to him again. It helped that he'd used some sheets and blankets to turn their bunk bed into a cool fort. Maybe prison would've been more fun if he and his cellmate had made a fort out of their bunk bed, too.

Even his truck seemed to be running smoothly. He'd made this month's payment on it. Covered the insurance on it, too. Once the loan was satisfied, and he got Vicki paid back for the payments she'd made while he'd been in prison, he'd see about having it put into his name instead of hers. It only seemed right that a man's truck should be in his own name.

Never in his life had everything seemed to be going his way. *Damn.* He might've just jinxed himself. *Better knock on wood.* He reached out a clenched hand and rapped twice on the scuffed coffee table. *Particle board counts as wood, don't it?*

FIVE
BYE-BYE BIRDIES

Megan

The following Monday afternoon, I turned again into the parking lot of the zoo. Brigit and I were working a swing shift. Well, *I* was working. My partner snoozed away on her cushion behind me, snoring softly. The warmth and white noise of the heater in the patrol car threatened to lull me to sleep, too. *Better get my blood flowing before I drift off behind the wheel.*

The afternoon was cold and windy, but a blustery blast of wintry weather was just what I needed to wake me up. I slid on a pair of gloves, a knit hat, and my heavy police jacket before opening the cruiser's back door. Brigit looked at me with sleep-droopy eyes and issued a yawn. Her nose twitched, her keen sense of smell working to identify our whereabouts better than her eyes could. When her nose told her we were at the zoo, she rose to all fours and hopped down to let me attach her leash. The brisk breeze parted Brigit's fur as we made our way to the front gate.

In her ticket booth, Janelle was bundled up in a heavy hooded coat. A scarf encircled her neck, covering the bottom half of her face. She pulled it down as we approached, her breath fogging the cold glass in front of her. "You'll have the place to yourselves today. Not many people willing to brave this weather."

A light crowd was fine with me. Fewer people to maneuver around, better visibility into the exhibits, less chance of a child accidentally stepping on Brigit's paw.

Many of the animals on exhibit were warm-climate species, better suited for the hot Texas summers than these occasional cold snaps. The zebras huddled in a herd to fight the frigid wind. Of course the chilly weather had the opposite effect on animals from colder climates. The black bears felt frisky, a pair loping about in play, a third backed up to a tree, rubbing his rump across the bark, treating himself to a nice butt scratch. The speakers mounted on poles and buildings throughout the zoo played holiday tunes. When the soundtrack launched into "I Want a Hippopotamus for Christmas," I found myself singing along. *Dang!* No doubt the song would become an earworm, playing through my brain the rest of the shift.

As we made our way, I noticed zoo employees scurrying down walkways and looking up into trees. *What's that about?* Soon after, we rounded the bend leading to the Parrot Paradise exhibit. The large, walk-through aviary was dome-shaped, with a heavy-duty, tightly woven mesh roof to keep even the tiniest birds from flying the coop. Bamboo and other varieties of trees provided perches for the birds, while a waterfall and pond provided ambiance and drinking water. Dozens of brightly colored parakeets, cockatiels, and parrots made homes in the space, chirping, squawking, and twittering as they went about their day.

As we approached the entrance to Parrot Paradise, I spotted the custodian I'd chatted with last week about our mutual doody duty. The man I knew only as "Danny L" sported a hoodie with the zoo logo today. A gray-haired woman also in khaki pants and a jacket faced him, her back to me. Danny held a push broom in one hand and plunked the handle down on the ground before him, holding the broom in a pose reminiscent of the stoic farmer and his pitchfork in the famous *American Gothic* painting. His other hand clenched the handle of his rolling litter bin so tight it was a wonder it didn't snap under the pressure. The tense expression on Danny's face and the woman's stiff posture told me the subject of their exchange was serious and unpleasant. The woman said something I couldn't hear, and Danny's eyes flashed with alarm. Brigit and I soon drew near enough for me to hear their conversation.

"You failed to follow protocols," the woman said. "That's grounds for dismissal."

"Please don't fire me!" the custodian cried in a desperate plea. "I've got mouths to feed. Give me another chance. I'll do everything by the book. I promise!"

Uh-oh. Though employment matters were none of my business, emotional situations sometimes got out of hand. The custodian's broom could make an improvised weapon. Better let them know Brigit and I were ready to step in if needed. I walked up. "Everything okay?"

The woman turned to me. "Not at all. Our pair of hyacinth macaws is missing. Fabiana and Fernando. They must have escaped when Mr. Landis was cleaning the entrance area."

Landis. Now I knew what the *L* on the custodian's name tag stood for. "And you are . . . ?" I asked, sticking out my hand.

"Sharon Easley." She took my hand. "The zoo's director."

After introducing myself and my partner, I nodded to the custodian and likewise stuck out my hand. "Mr. Landis."

He pulled off his work glove, again revealing the prison tattoo by his thumb. He gave my hand a single, firm shake before slipping the glove back on. Niceties complete, I glanced over at the bird exhibit. The entrance was designed with self-closing gates at either end of an enclosed walkway to prevent the birds from making an easy escape. Dog parks had similar gates, the outer gate designed to trap animals in the entry area if they managed to sneak out the interior gate. The sally port at the police station served the same purpose, giving officers a contained environment in which to safely unload suspects from a cruiser before taking them into the building for booking. Of course the design could fail if both ends were open at the same time. Hence the posted warnings, advising visitors not to hold gates open and to ensure the gate closed behind them.

His boss having already determined him guilty, Mr. Landis attempted to defend himself to me. "Some kid dropped a full bottle of apple juice from a stroller. It made a big, sticky mess all over the concrete. I made sure no birds were by the inside gate before I propped it open, and I only had both gates open long enough to hose down the pavement." He released his bin and threw up his hand. "I'm sure I would've seen those birds if they'd flown out!"

He had a point. The hyacinth macaws not only bore bright blue feathers, but they were also large, measuring around three feet long, including the tail feathers. A parakeet might not be spotted making an escape, but the macaws would've had a hard time sneaking out unnoticed.

Easley wasn't having it, though. "The birds were in the exhibit earlier and now they aren't. There's no other explanation."

Maybe. Maybe not. The aspiring detective in me knew every angle should be examined before reaching conclusions. Plus, I'd hate to see an ex-con lose gainful employment. Getting fired could increase the odds Landis would reoffend. At the risk of overstepping my bounds, I asked, "Could the enclosure have been breached in some other way?" Maybe a limb had come off a tree and damaged the wire roof, bent it to allow escape.

"Several employees inspected the exhibit," the director replied. "Everything looks fine."

I'd been inside the Parrot Paradise exhibit before and had noted a private door built into a fake stone façade at the back. The door had a tinted window on the top half and a security keypad mounted on the wall beside it. Presumably, the door was used by zoo personnel and led to a room used for storage or for veterinary examinations. More than likely, there was another door that led from that space to the outside. "What about the door at the back of the exhibit? Could the macaws have gone out that way?"

"I checked with security," she said. "That door was last used early this morning, before the zoo opened, when staff put out feed for the birds. The macaws were seen afterward."

"By whom?" I asked.

"One of our ornithologists. He was checking the winter birdhouses that were installed a few days ago. He went in and out through the visitor entrance, not the staff entrance."

In other words, it was likely Landis or a guest was responsible for the birds' disappearance. But weren't other precautions taken to keep the birds from flying off? "Were the birds pinioned?"

"No," Easley said, "but their flight feathers are clipped every few weeks. The macaws were due."

With their feathers grown out, it was the perfect time for the birds to mount an escape.

A beefy black man in a jacket embossed with the word SECURITY stepped up to our impromptu powwow. Apparently, he'd been summoned to assist. He gave me and Easley a nod.

Landis was clearly having mixed emotions, his expression vacillating between fear and anger. "Please don't fire me!" he begged Easley. "I been doing good. Ask my supervisor. He'll tell you. I don't know what happened to the birds, but I was very careful!"

A horrible thought crossed my mind. "Could the birds have been intentionally taken?"

"Intentionally taken?" Easley repeated. "You mean stolen?"

The custodian's voice reached a pitch so high he seemed to be channeling the itty-bitty blond Broadway star Kristin Chenoweth. "Are you accusing me of stealing those birds?"

I raised my palms. "Just trying to consider all possibilities. If they were stolen, I'm not saying you were necessarily responsible." But I wasn't saying Landis *wasn't* responsible, either.

Landis seemed to realize my theory could work in his favor. His face brightened and he stood straighter. "If somebody stole the birds, that means it's not my fault they're gone."

"Zoo thefts are rare," Easley said, her gaze shifting between me and Landis, "but they're not unheard of. I suppose it's possible the birds were stolen. They're worth thousands of dollars."

I eyed Landis, wishing I could read his mind. Did the saying "once a thief, always a thief" apply here? He'd stolen from an employer before, and a moment earlier he'd mentioned having mouths to feed. A person under pressure could do something stupid or wrong. But before I threw accusations around, I'd better get my ducks in a row. "Are there cameras on the aviary?"

"No," Easley said. "We didn't see the need for cameras inside the zoo. Staff keep an eye on things while the zoo's open, and we've never had problems after hours. We've got some cameras on the perimeter. Not sure they'll help. Most are aimed at the parking lot."

The decision was understandable. Why spend funds on cameras when it could be better spent improving the habitats? Still, staff couldn't keep a constant eye on every corner of the zoo.

"Can't hurt to take a look at the footage," I suggested.

The custodian's cart rattled as Easley and the security guard escorted me, Brigit, and Landis to the main administrative building. Landis left his bin outside by the door. We walked down the hall and into the security office, where Easley introduced us to the chief security officer, or CSO, a burly man with close-cropped curls the same dark brown as the zoo's bears.

After names and handshakes were exchanged, the CSO turned to Landis. "Wait outside."

The custodian's nostrils flared. "I got a right to see the video, too!"

The CSO stepped toward Landis, forcing him to back out the door. "You can take a look after we've gone through it." The chief cut his eyes to the guard who'd escorted us here, silently directing him to watch over the janitor. The man stepped out into the hallway with Landis.

The CSO retook his seat at his desk and turned his attention to the oversized monitor in front of him. "I'll start the footage at eleven fifteen. That's when the birds were last seen."

As Easley and I gathered behind him, he maneuvered his mouse and started the video stream, running it at several times the real-time rate for efficiency's sake. The feeds from half a dozen cameras ran simultaneously on his screen, showing views of the zoo's entrances and exits, as well as the parking lot. Adults and children filtered in and out of the camera range, their movements robotic and awkward at high speed. Many wore bulky winter coats or pushed large strollers draped with blankets, but none was obviously smuggling two large birds out of the zoo.

As we watched, Landis rolled his big garbage bin out of the zoo's front gate. The CSO clicked on the pane to enlarge the feed to full screen and slowed it so we could take a closer look. We leaned in and watched intently. Several garbage bags were inside the huge bin. They shook as the bin rattled down the sidewalk, but none moved enough to evidence animals inside, struggling to escape. Of course I wasn't an expert on bird behavior. *Don't birds become quiet and still in the dark? Isn't that why people cover their cages?* I raised the issue.

Easley shrugged. "Animals may behave atypically when they're frightened."

The security guard made another point. "He could have hidden a cage under the bags."

If the birds were in a cage, it would explain the lack of movement among the bags. *Hmm.*

Landis continued to a trash can on the sidewalk that led to the parking lot, removed the plastic lid, and tied the bag inside closed. He lifted the bag from the receptacle, placed it in his rolling bin, and lined the can with a new bag before returning the lid. He repeated this process with a second trash can farther down. He then rolled the bin out of camera range.

I wondered aloud. "Could he be taking the birds to his car? Or handing them off to someone?"

"Could be," the CSO mused. "But there's a dumpster at the far end of the lot. He might have only been taking his bin there to empty it."

We continued to watch. Minutes later, Landis rolled back into sight, his bin empty. Had the birds been in the bin? Who knew. I had nothing definitive, certainly not enough evidence to get a search warrant. Even so, the guy seemed eager to clear himself. Maybe he'd voluntarily allow us to search his vehicle. We watched until the time the birds were discovered missing, then invited Landis in to view the footage himself.

"The video's inconclusive," I pointed out. "Will you allow us to search your car?"

"Be my guest," he said. "You won't find anything."

The CSO, my partner, and I followed Landis out to the parking lot. Easley opted to remain in the administrative building where it was warm. Couldn't say I blamed her. Landis stopped at a cheap white sedan produced a decade earlier. The steering wheel and seats sported fuzzy purple covers that looked to be made of Muppet pelts.

The CSO slid Landis some side-eye. "*This* is your vehicle?"

"No." Landis pointed the fob at the car to unlock it. "I drove this one today because mine's in the shop getting brake work done."

The CSO and I opened the doors and looked around, searching for feathers or other evidence the birds had been in the vehicle. We removed the seat covers and checked the trunk. *Nothing.* We returned to the security office. The CSO informed Easley we'd come up empty.

"So?" Landis asked, his hopeful gaze moving among us. "We good?"

Easley exhaled a sharp breath and shook her head. "If anything, I'm more convinced than ever that the birds escaped while you were cleaning. I've got to let you go. Sorry."

Clearly, that wasn't what the guy wanted to hear. "This is bullshit!"

The CSO gestured to the staff ID card hanging from a lanyard around the custodian's neck and held out his hand. "I'll need your badge, Mr. Landis."

Landis snorted a frustrated breath and yanked the lanyard over his head, cursing as he cast it to the ground. Knowing things that fell to the floor were often delicious, Brigit lowered her head and sniffed the card. When she realized it wasn't a tasty tidbit, she backed away and sat down by my side, issuing a disappointed doggie sigh.

While I could understand the shock and anger at being fired, acting like an ass wasn't going to do anyone any good, least of all the custodian. I picked up the card and handed it to the security guard. "I'd be happy to help escort Mr. Landis out, if you'd like."

Landis turned to me. "Why? You think I'm gonna go off and do something stupid, like coldcock him?" He gave an angry shake of his head. "Not my style."

He was quiet from then on, his jaw clenched as tight as a bear trap as the security guard and I walked with him to the employee locker room. Once he'd gathered his coat and returned his uniform vest and jacket, we proceeded en masse to the exit. Janelle looked up from inside her booth, her eyes wide and wary. The security guard took up a post just outside the entrance, probably to make sure Landis didn't attempt to return. Brigit and I followed Landis into the lot.

He cast an irritated glance my way. "You don't gotta follow me. I'm gonna leave."

"That's not why I'm here," I said.

He stopped walking. "What do you want, then?"

"Are you on parole?" Inmates who fulfilled their full sentence were released with no strings, but they received no ongoing support. Those released early for good behavior were required to check in regularly with a parole officer. The POs helped parolees stay on track and find work. "If you are, maybe your PO could help you find another job."

The man tossed me a sour look. "The best job he could find me before was shoveling shit, and you see how that turned out. I wanted to take some of the other classes in prison, but there weren't enough open spots. The warden steered me to the janitorial program."

I would hate to see this guy give up and become a statistic, another recidivist. I reminded Landis of his options. "There are other job-training programs you can attend now. Or you could go to school. There are churches and nonprofits that help with reintegration, too."

"Or you can give me two grand to get through the month," he snapped.

"If I had any extra cash, I wouldn't be wearing these shoes." I raised my foot to show him the duct tape holding the sole onto my tactical shoe. In a recent moment of weakness, Brigit had resorted to her old, shoe-chewing ways. But given that she'd just barely survived being shot, I'd let her indiscretion slide.

He took one look at my shoe and snorted. "Maybe you should look for a new job, too."

"Point taken." As we parted ways, I pushed the button on my shoulder-mounted radio and notified dispatch about the missing macaws, asking officers to be on the lookout. "The birds are bright blue with yellow rings around their eyes," I explained. "About three feet long."

With any luck, the birds would be found in a nearby tree and returned to the zoo soon. I started the car and turned on the heater, my frozen bones happy for the warmth. It was half past four and the sky was rapidly darkening. I turned on the headlights and prepared to shift the car into reverse when a voice came across the radio, the haughty intonation of my former partner, Derek Mackey. While he claimed he'd been given his nickname because he sported an unusually large male member, it was more likely he'd been dubbed the "Big Dick" because he often acted like one. It was such behavior that had led to me Tasering him in the nards and being reassigned to work with Brigit.

"Hey, Megan," Derek said. "I've spotted those birds you're looking for."

"You did?" My heart soared with hope. "Where?"

He rattled off an address on Eighth Avenue, a mile and a half by road and even closer as the crow flies.

"Thanks! I'll be right there." I backed up and zipped out of the lot, driving as fast as I dared. In less than a minute, I turned into the parking lot of a Fiesta Mart grocery store. Derek's patrol car sat at the front curb, his beefy body filling the front seat, his reddish hair reflecting the lights of the sign above him. I glanced up through my windshield, but saw no birds in what few trees surrounded the lot. No birds were perched on the light posts, either. I pulled up next to him and unrolled my window. "Where are the birds?"

With a smirk, he pointed through the front window of the store at a display of parrot piñatas hanging inside. "Right there." He guffawed, punched the gas, and roared off.

Jackass. Fuming, I aimed for the fire station. After all, people called the fire department about cats stuck in trees. Maybe they'd call if they spotted the big blue birds in a tree, too. It couldn't hurt to let Seth and the others on duty know about the escaped macaws. Still, a part of me wondered if they had truly escaped. Though we'd found no clear evidence they'd been stolen, we'd found no decisive proof they hadn't been, either.

Due to the frigid temperature, the bay doors were closed when we pulled into the station. Both Frankie's red Juke and Seth's blue Nova sat in the lot, along with other cars belonging to the first responders on duty. I retrieved Brigit from her enclosure and we headed inside through the regular door. My partner slowed and raised her nose to sniff the air, but it didn't take a canine's superior senses to detect the scents of sugar, vanilla, and chocolate. *Someone's baking.* Hearing voices coming from the kitchen and unable to resist the enticing aroma, Brigit and I made our way down the hall and stopped in the doorway.

Seth, Frankie, and three of their fellow firefighters sat at a table playing penny-ante poker, their focus on the cards in their hands. Blast lay under the table at Seth's feet, his eyes closed as he dozed. A woman I'd never seen stood at the stove. She looked to be in her early twenties. Her fresh face was fully made up, a thick swipe of liquid liner accenting her big green eyes, pink-hued gloss giving her lips a natural glow. She'd pulled her caramel-blond hair up in a sleek, shiny twist atop her head, as if she had a prom to attend. She wore a paramedic uniform and darn if it didn't look good on her. She must've had it altered to fit her curves. She plucked small balls of baked brownie dough from a cookie sheet, stopping once to blow on her singed fingertips. She rolled the balls in a mix of powdered sugar and cocoa, and arranged them on a plate. She carried the plate over to the table and set it down next to the pile of coins. "Eat up."

Seth picked up a ball and juggled it between his hands. "Ow. Hot."

"They're best warm." She grabbed the ball from the air, gently blew on it to cool it off, and turned to Seth. "Open wide." When he opened his mouth, she put her fingers to his lips and popped the treat inside.

What the—? It took everything in me not to whip out my nightstick and give her a pop of my own. Brigit seemed none too happy with this situation, either. She raised her snout and issued a sharp *arf!* All heads snapped to look in our direction.

"Hey, Megan." Seth smiled as he stood. "Didn't hear you come in."

Frankie waggled her fingers. "Hey, roomie."

Blast lifted his head and, spotting Brigit, rolled to his feet to greet his best girl.

As I stepped into the room, the young woman walked up to stand next to Seth. Seth introduced us, holding out a hand to indicate Alex. "Megan, this is Alex, our new paramedic."

When he'd told me a few days back that the station had hired a new paramedic named Alex, he hadn't mentioned that Alex was female. *Hmm.* That was funny. It was also *not* funny.

"Alex"—he moved his hand to indicate me—"this is Megan. She's a cop with the Fort Worth PD."

Alex giggled. "I'd already guessed that, Seth. The uniform clued me in."

Despite the slight nausea their chumminess brought to my gut, I forced a smile and held out my hand. "Nice to meet you, Alex."

She took my hand. Her skin was nearly as soft as Nan Ishii's had been. *I might have to start paying more for my lotion.*

From her seat, Frankie held up the plate. "Try one of these, Megan. They're sooo good!"

I took one of the baked cocoa-covered balls from the plate and bit into it. *Mmm.* Frankie was right. They were yummy. I shoved the rest into my mouth and licked the powder from my fingers. "Delicious." I turned back to Alex. "What are they? Rum balls?"

Alex lifted her slim shoulders and giggled again. "I call them 'Reindeer Droppings.'"

Of course you do.

Brigit looked up at me and issued an insistent bark that said *I want to try one, too!*

I ruffled her head. "Sorry, Brigit. Chocolate's not good for dogs."

Seth patted his leg. "Come with me, girl. I'll get you a hot dog instead."

Brigit and Blast followed Seth to the fridge and wagged their tails as he finagled a package of hot dogs out of a drawer. He nuked two of them in the microwave and cut them into pieces before returning to the table and pulling out a chair for me. As we fed our furry partners, he asked how my shift was going. I told him and the others what happened at the zoo.

"Would y'all mind keeping an eye out for Fabiana and Fernando?" I asked. "They've lived at the zoo for years. They probably don't know how to forage for food. They might not be able to survive in the wild." Maybe they'd luck out and find a house with a full bird feeder.

They all agreed to watch for the macaws. Seth said he'd ask the captain to send a notice department-wide in case the birds flew farther out.

My cell phone buzzed in my jacket pocket. The read-out indicated it was an incoming call from the station. I accepted the call, stood, and stepped away from the table so they could resume their poker game. "Officer Megan Luz."

It was the crime scene lab calling. "Got your fingerprint results," the tech said. "All of the prints you lifted match Mrs. Ishii's."

So either the plumber hadn't stolen the rings, or he'd managed to snatch them from the bowl without leaving a print. Either way, barring a confession, the plumber could be ruled out as a suspect. I thanked the tech, tucked my phone back into my pocket, and turned back to Seth and Frankie. "I better get back out on patrol." I raised a hand in good-bye to the group and directed a nod at Alex. "It was nice to meet you."

"You, too!" she said. As I reattached Brigit's lead, Alex scurried over to snatch a small plastic bag from a box on the counter, filled the bag with a dozen balls, and handed it to me. "Here. Take some Reindeer Droppings to go."

I hadn't liked how comfortable she'd seemed with Seth, but she was making it really hard for me to be annoyed with her. "Thanks." I tucked the bag into my pocket alongside my phone.

Seth stood. "Blast and I will walk you out."

Alex's brows angled slightly as her gaze went from me to Seth. She appeared confused, as if she hadn't realized Seth and I had a personal relationship.

Seth hadn't bothered to put on a jacket, and as we walked out into the parking lot he shivered involuntarily. "Brr."

Alex probably wouldn't mind keeping Seth warm. "Wimp," I teased.

He hugged himself. "Guilty as charged." We both knew he was anything but. Wimps don't go looking for explosives, detonate bombs, or run into burning buildings to save people.

I watched him closely as I opened the back door of the patrol car and signaled for Brigit to hop inside. "Alex seems nice."

"She likes to cook," he said. "That's a big plus around here."

I closed the door. "Is she a good paramedic?"

"This is her first job, but she's getting there. We've got to get her up to speed as quick as possible. The holidays are coming. You know what that means."

Did I ever. To civilians, the holidays meant gifts, feasts, and fun times with family and friends. To first responders, the holidays meant burglaries, domestic violence, drunk drivers, and dry Christmas trees going up in flames. While everyone else slowed down to relax, law enforcement, firefighters, and medical professionals worked overtime.

Seth leaned in and gave me a kiss that warmed me down to my toes. He rested his forehead against mine, his cocoa-scented breath soft against my cheek. "Be careful out there."

"I will. You be careful out there, too." *And in there, where Alex is.*

Seth and Blast stepped back, but remained outside, waving as Brigit and I drove off.

As we made our way to Nan Ishii's house, I found myself feeling a little uneasy. *My relationship with Seth is solid, isn't it?* Sure it was. We cared deeply about each other, relied on each other, our lives having become slowly yet hopelessly entangled over the time we'd dated. We enjoyed each other's company, as did our dogs. While we weren't the most demonstratively romantic people, we found ways to show each other how much we felt. Alex wasn't a threat, was she? Of course not. I was being ridiculous, feeling insecure for no reason. Still, I couldn't shake the image of her sliding her baked goods into Seth's mouth any more than I could shake that hippopotamus for Christmas song from my brain. I sent a quick text to Frankie. *Seth didn't mention Alex was female. Should I be concerned?*

Her reply came right back. *Not a bit. He knew you'd find out sooner or later.*

True. Police and fire stations often coordinated in emergencies. Still, I found myself wondering whether Alex had set her sights on Seth and, if so, whether he was aware of it. But before I could think too much about it, I arrived at the Ishii residence. Because my conversation with Nan would be brief, I left Brigit in the cruiser as I went to the door and rang the bell. Given that it was now full dark outside and the porch was lit only by a small coach light, I kept my head up so Nan could easily identify me through the peephole.

A moment later she pulled the door open, her little dog cradled again in her arms. Her left hand was buried in his fur, her ring finger obscured. "Hi, Officer Luz. Any news?"

"That's why I'm here. The lab results are in. All the prints on the ring bowl were yours."

She frowned. "Fingerprints or not, the plumber must have taken my rings."

"Sorry. Without prints or a confession, we have no grounds to make an arrest."

"I understand." She shifted the dog in her arms, her left hand now out in the open. The porch light glinted off her new ring set like it was reflecting off a disco ball. *Whoa.* The round stone in her engagement ring was one of the largest I'd ever seen, probably close to two carats. The glitzy wedding band featured a row of channel-set diamonds in a platinum setting. The set was gorgeous, if gaudy. She'd wasted no time replacing her earlier set, as if she knew she'd never see them again. These new rings were also an entirely different style. *Hmm* and *hmm.*

I gestured to her hand. "Your husband already replaced your rings?"

"No. He's still in Colorado. He extended his ski trip. He told me to pick out whatever I wanted, so I did." She held out her hand and smiled at her new rings, shrugging as she did so.

Wow. Must be nice not to have to wait for the insurance

check to be able to afford expensive new jewelry. "I've circulated the information to local pawnshops," I said. "If anything turns up, I'll let you know. In the meantime, you might want to take a look online, see if the rings show up for sale on eBay. If they do, let me know."

She thanked me, and I headed back to my cruiser, knowing the chances of her rings being found were slim. Stolen property was rarely recovered. I could only hope Alex wouldn't try to steal Seth's heart.

SIX
SCROOGE

Brigit

The hot dog Seth had fed her wasn't bad, but Brigit would've liked to try one of those round brown things the humans had been eating. Megan had a bunch of them in her jacket pocket. Brigit could smell them. She didn't know why Megan was being so stingy, refusing to share. *But two can play this game . . .*

She stood and whimpered through the mesh that separated her from Megan. As expected, Megan pulled the cruiser into the parking lot of a school, let Brigit out of the back, and attached her leash. Brigit followed Megan over to a grassy area, but instead of squatting to pee, she took her time, sniffing around. *La di da . . . La di di . . .*

"Come on, girl!" Megan begged after a few seconds. "It's cold out here! Hurry up!"

With her thick fur, Brigit could last much longer outside than her partner. *Humans and their inadequate coating of hair. Heh.*

She sniffed around some more. *La di di . . .*

"Brigit!" Megan scolded. "Go potty! Now!"

But Brigit refused to go. Instead, she lifted her snout

and nudged the jacket pocket that held the chocolate treats. *Gimme, gimme.*

"Sorry, girl." Megan walked over to a metal trash can, pulled the baggie from her pocket, and tossed it into the can. The chocolate treats landed on the bottom with a *klunk*. "How about a liver treat instead?"

Brigit wagged her tail. While she would've liked to try a brownie ball, she wasn't about to pass up one of her favorite liver treats.

Megan tossed her one treat and, when Brigit issued an *arf* to insist on another, tossed a second into the air. Brigit expertly snatched it on its way down. Megan bent down and put her shivering hands on either side of Brigit's face. "You know I love you and I only want what's best for you, right? I don't want you to get sick."

Brigit wasn't sure exactly what Megan's words meant, but she decided that all was forgiven. After all, she trusted Megan. Whatever reason her partner had for denying her must've been a good one. She popped a quick squat and the two trotted back to the warm cruiser.

SEVEN
MONEY BAG

The Poacher

At first, the birds had kept quiet and calm in the dark, but now these stupid parrots wouldn't stop squawking and talking and fluttering their wings.

"Shut up!" he yelled at the garbage bag moving about the floorboard.

One of the birds squawk-mocked him from inside the bag. "Shut up!"

"No, you shut up!" he hollered.

"No, you shut up!" the bird hollered back.

Ugh. The damn birds were getting on his last nerve but, even so, he felt sorry for them. They had no idea what was going on. At least they'd be going to a good home. He assumed so, anyway. Someone who was willing to pay thousands of dollars for a bird would surely treat it good, wouldn't they?

He'd taken the birds on impulse after overhearing someone say how much the birds sold for. It had been almost too easy, with the birds and a garbage bag in easy reach. They'd barely fit inside his big winter coat. He knew he'd been lucky. He could have been caught and sent back to prison. *What's the sentence for bird-napping?*

He turned into the parking lot of a Dollar General store, taking a spot as far away from the doors and other cars as he could. Didn't want someone hearing the birds and getting suspicious.

He scurried inside and headed straight for the prepaid phones. The last thing he needed after being fired from his job today was to spend money, but what choice did he have? He had to make a call, and he couldn't make it from the cell phone he already owned. He had to make sure this call couldn't be traced to him.

EIGHT
SHOPPING MALL FREE-FOR-ALL

Megan

By Wednesday evening, the fickle Texas weather warmed up quite a bit and I decided to take Brigit on a stroll through the Shoppes at Chisholm Trail. The mall was one of those newer open-air structures, with a food court, carousel, and administrative offices situated inside an enclosed central atrium.

Though I loved to window-shop at the mall, I couldn't come here without being reminded of the day not long ago that a bomb had gone off, people narrowly escaping with their lives. They owed those lives to my partner. Heck, I did, too. Brigit wasn't trained to scent for explosives but, for reasons known only to her, she'd alerted on the bomb. In just the nick of time, too. I'd cleared the area only seconds before the device went off. Sometimes I wished I could get into that furry head of hers. She'd be able to tell me if she smelled the macaws on Danny Landis and his rolling bin, whether he'd stolen them from their enclosure. The spilled apple juice could have been a ruse, an explanation for their disappearance. After all, the birds were probably worth more than he'd earn in months on the job. *Will I ever know for certain?*

With the Christmas holiday rapidly approaching, the mall was alight with colored bulbs and abuzz with shoppers looking for the perfect gift for that special someone, or at least a good bargain. People milled about, some with smiles on their faces, others showing signs of stress. The hectic season could be overwhelming. Best to pace oneself.

As for me, I'd started my shopping online on Cyber Monday. I'd ordered Seth a high-tech swimsuit like the competitors wore in the Olympics. He refused to wear a Speedo—*thank goodness*—but this form-fitting, knee-length suit would enable him to glide through the water like a dolphin without making a spectacle of his naughty bits. I'd ordered him a new pair of goggles, too, Swedish-style ones, which were supposed to be favored among serious swimmers according to various Web sites I'd perused. I'd also ordered my mother a new backpack. She'd dropped out of college when she became pregnant with me, and recently decided to go back and finish. She'd been carrying my old backpack to class, but it was looking tired. I still hadn't decided on something for my father, my brothers, or my sister Gabby. Maybe I'd find ideas for the others on my list as Brigit and I walked the mall this evening.

The decorations along the mall's southwest walkway portrayed a Twelve Days of Christmas theme, all the way from a dozen drummers drumming to the five golden rings to the partridge in a pear tree. *Cute.*

Of course the five golden rings reminded me of the rings missing from Nan Ishii's home. They hadn't turned up anywhere. I wasn't sure what to make of that. It still seemed possible she'd somehow lost them herself without realizing it. But the possibility that the plumber had pocketed them couldn't definitively be ruled out, either. Nor could I dismiss the chance that Nan might have intentionally ditched the rings herself to have an excuse to replace them. She might have summoned the police to give her story credibility.

As we walked along, it struck me how many birds there were in the classic Christmas song. Seven swans a-swimming. Six geese a-laying. Four calling birds. Three French hens. Two turtledoves. And, of course, the iconic partridge in the pear tree. The flock of various birds along the pathway took my mind back to the zoo's Parrot Paradise exhibit and the missing hyacinth macaws. Despite repeated pleas to the public on the local news to report any sightings, Fabiana and Fernando had not been spotted. It was as if the pair had taken wing and headed down to South America, where the species originated. But the vast majority of parrot species didn't migrate. Rather, they remained within a certain range for all of their lives. And even if they had been a migratory breed, it wouldn't explain how the birds had exited the enclosure.

No other birds had gone missing since, so the exhibit must be intact, as Easley had claimed. If they hadn't been purposely swiped, the macaws must have gone out through the visitor gates, then. It would be the only way out. Still, I found it hard to believe they'd snuck past Danny Landis while he was cleaning the walkway. Then again, he'd have been looking down as he'd tackled the apple juice spill. The birds could have flown over him. But wouldn't he have heard their wings flapping? Maybe they'd pulled themselves along the wire mesh, essentially sidestepping out the gate. It seemed highly unlikely, though. Could errant zoo visitors have left both gates open earlier in the day, after the ornithologist checked the winter houses but before Landis arrived to clean up the juice?

Out of curiosity, I'd run a search online and learned zoo escapes had occurred before. Several big cats escaped from a German zoo after flash floods damaged their cages. Two lions had previously escaped in Germany and, sadly, one was shot dead. A snow leopard escaped from a U.K. zoo after a keeper left its pen open. The leopard, too, was killed. In 2004, a gorilla named Jabari escaped his enclosure at the Dallas Zoo. He injured several people, including children, before being shot to death. I couldn't imagine having to end the life of an innocent animal, apex predator or not.

As Hurricane Katrina approached, staff at Marine Life Oceanarium in Gulfport, Mississippi, left dolphins, sea lions, and a seal to fend for themselves at the park, which was already under scrutiny by animal welfare activists. The animals were swept away in the storm. Some were never found. Debris killed or injured others. Miraculously, all of the dolphins were recovered. While the other dolphins beached themselves on mats to be transported back to captivity, one named Jill, who had lived in the wild before, had to be lassoed and dragged back in.

Of course not all animals missing from zoos had escaped. Others were, in fact, stolen. My research led me to a report of eleven animals taken from a zoo in Florida, including a squirrel monkey, nine turtles, and a Solomon Island skink, whatever that was. A lemur stolen from a California zoo was subsequently abandoned at a hotel. Thieves used a net to steal a horn shark from the San Antonio Aquarium, and wheeled the shark out in a baby stroller. Luckily, the thieves were nabbed and the shark was recovered.

Though I had not personally encountered illegal wildlife traffickers, I'd heard stories through the law enforcement grapevine. Not long ago, smugglers abandoned an unconscious Bengal tiger cub in a duffel bag near the Mexican border. Fortunately, the cub was found by border patrol and survived. Due to the popularity of parrots as pets, as well as their high price tag, illegal trade in wild-caught parrots was rampant in the Caribbean and Latin America. A man from Guyana was intercepted at JFK Airport with a carry-on full of live finches immobilized inside plastic hair rollers. Jason Shaw, an exotic-pet dealer in the nearby city of Arlington, had been charged in the country's biggest animal cruelty case after numerous dead or starving animals were found in his possession. Shaw fled the country. Outrage ensued when the heartless creep returned home and got off in a sweetheart deal in which he pleaded guilty to a single misdemeanor charge and paid a paltry fine of $15,000. Never mind that the city and animal welfare groups had spent hundreds of thousands of dollars caring for the animals. I wouldn't want to shoot an escaped zoo animal, but I'd happily put a bullet in that heartless bastard.

This unpleasant reverie led me to wonder, once again, whether someone had taken the hyacinth macaws with the intent to sell them. Were the missing macaws hidden in a stroller, like the shark? Or had Danny Landis rolled them out of the zoo in his refuse bin? He'd stolen from an employer before. Then again, there's a big difference between taking necessities like baby formula and diapers, and stealing a valuable, living creature. Would he even know how to go about selling such a bird? I supposed it could be arranged online easily enough. After all, the Internet made it easy for drug dealers, human traffickers, and pimps to sell their wares. Or maybe Landis had been approached at the zoo by some creep who'd offered him money if he could snatch the birds. Or maybe my job had made me overly cynical and suspicious. This was the time of year when we were supposed to come together, see the good in each other, spread joy and goodwill and maybe some influenza from kissing under the mistletoe.

As Brigit and I strolled along, keeping an eye out for

shoplifters and suspicious activity, we passed the mall's nail salon. A poster on the back wall read GET YOUR HOLIDAY HANDS HERE! The poster featured a pair of female hands, each fingernail painted in a different holiday theme. Candy-cane stripes. Christmas trees. Wrapped gifts. You could even have your nails decorated in men—gingerbread men, snowmen, or the big man himself, Santa.

Under the sign, three tables sat side by side, displays of colorful polish atop them, technicians seated behind them. All three of the techs were blond, though they ranged in color from platinum to dishwater to strawberry. A client sat at each table, two more waiting in plastic chairs for their turn. The techs hunched over the hands on which they worked, carefully applying polish, glitter, and gems, giving their clients the perfect look for the holidays.

As much as I'd like to get my nails done, too, there wasn't much point. I kept my nails short so they wouldn't interfere with my work. Couldn't risk a lengthy nail getting in the way of using my weapons. Besides, bad guys might not take me seriously if I had candy-cane stripes on my fingers, and if someone thought I was wasting taxpayer dollars by handling personal matters on the clock, they might call the chief to complain.

My partner and I continued on to the glass doors that led into the expansive atrium. Santa sat atop an elevated throne inside, a couple of elves tending to the children waiting in line to tell the jolly old elf what they wanted for Christmas. Though the carousel horses made their rounds, gleeful children riding upon their backs, the music was muted so as not to compete with the high school choir performing upon a set of portable risers a few yards away. Parents and siblings stood watching and listening, snapping video and pics on their cell phones to memorialize the performance. Sometimes I found myself longing for the good old days of my early childhood, before cell phone cameras, when people simply enjoyed the moment without the need to document every second of life. Then again, I was guilty of the same offense. My phone contained at least three hundred snapshots of Brigit doing something cute or funny.

Brigit lifted her snout, scenting the garlic, pizza dough, and grilled meat aromas in the air as we meandered past the food counters. Was that dog ever *not* hungry?

Serhan Singh, a Turkish man who ran the kebob booth, raised a hand and offered a smile in greeting. He and I had met during the earlier bombing investigation. He looked down at my partner. "Would you like a snack, Brigit?"

She put her front paws on the counter in front of him, wagged her tail, and woofed softly. *Yes, please!*

Singh layered strips of beef and chicken in a disposable paper tray and held it out to me. "Here you go."

I took the food from him. "Thanks."

He looked down at my partner. "Enjoy your meal, Brigit. Be sure to eat it all so you will be strong enough to chase the bad guys."

He needn't worry. Finishing a meal had never been a problem for her.

I led Brigit over to one of the few empty tables in the food court, and pushed aside the trash that another customer had carelessly and inconsiderately left on the tabletop. Left to her own devices, Brigit would wolf down the meat without taking time to chew it. She wasn't one for table manners. Lest she give herself a tummy ache, I used a plastic knife to cut the meat strips into small pieces and fed them one by one to Brigit. When she was done eating, she issued a satisfied burp, much to the amusement of the young boy sitting with his parents at the adjacent table. He followed up with a burp of his own.

After disposing of our trash, Brigit and I headed toward

the doors on the opposite side of the space. The choir was gone now, the risers empty, a strolling barbershop quartet having taken their place. The four men were singing the quick-paced classic "Sleigh Ride." The men ranged in age from thirtyish to fiftyish, and were dressed identically in black top hats, white shirts with ruffled sleeves, green and red plaid vests, black capes, and black pants. One of the men was tall, six feet two or so. Two of the others were average height. The thirtyish one on the end stood only around five feet six, not exactly a Tiny Tim, but undeniably on the short side. Even with the top hat on his head it was clear he was balding, and his vest fit snug around his belly. While he might not be a perfect physical specimen, he was nonetheless charming, taking a female shopper's hand and going down on one knee while the quartet finished with the "giddy yaps" and sang about how grand it was to just hold your hand. He'd certainly committed to his character. Soon, all four were singing and bouncing up and down in an imaginary sleigh. The choreography was entertaining and playful. Whoever had come up with it deserved kudos.

Brigit and I continued out the doors to a different wing. Along this walk, we spotted one of the mall's security guards rolling toward us on a three-wheeled scooter.

He slowed as he approached. "Hey, Officer Luz. Brigit." He rolled to a stop and reached down to pet my partner.

"How's everything going?" I asked.

"Busy," he said. "We've nabbed six shoplifters today alone."

I wasn't surprised. People thought the crowds would hide them from view as they snuck items into their pockets or purses. They took chances, and merchandise, that they shouldn't.

The security guard's radio came to life. "We've got a runner at Macy's."

The guard hooked a U-turn. "Here we go again!"

Brigit and I ran after his scooter. Shoppers turned as we rushed past, Brigit's tags ringing like jingle bells. As we neared the store, a teen girl bolted out the door. She sported a bright pink coat and pom-pom beanie. *Sheesh. If you're going to shoplift, have the sense to wear something inconspicuous!* A purse tucked under her arm, the girl weaved around shoppers with the agility of former Dallas Cowboy Emmitt Smith. The store's doors burst open again as a security guard ran out in hot pursuit. The four of us joined forces, chasing the girl toward the parking lot. The guard I'd followed hopped off his scooter and left it at the curb. Without looking, the girl sprinted into the driving lanes. *SCREECH! HOOONK!* She whirled like a frenzied ballerina before continuing her mad dash. I didn't dare deploy Brigit to chase the girl given the number of cars cruising up and down the rows. My partner's life was worth more than any purse.

Bleep-bleep! The girl might be quick, but she wasn't quick-witted. She used a key fob to open the locks on an SUV a row ahead. The lights flashed, telling us which car was hers. Given the near gridlock in the lot, she'd be easy to apprehend in her car. If she escaped on foot, we could identify her from the car's registration. Either way, this twit was toast.

As she reached the car, she turned and saw us gaining on her. Realizing she'd never be able to drive off, she flung the purse in our direction. Brigit caught the bag in her teeth as the girl took off again. The men and I collided as we tried to squeeze between cars. In the split second it took for us to wriggle free from each other, the girl disappeared.

"We'll track her." I wrestled the purse from Brigit. It was a Radley London brand, a "Hobo Bag" according to the tag. *As if a homeless person could afford a two-hundred-dollar purse.* I handed the bag to the men and issued Brigit the order to trail. My partner put her nose to the ground and I stayed by her side as she scampered on a zigzagging trajectory to the edge of the lot, where we found the pink coat and hat abandoned behind the bushes.

Nose still down, Brigit circled back to the mall and led me into the Forever 21 store, the men trailing us. They waited outside while Brigit padded into the dressing rooms and scented her way to a room at the end. I caught a glimpse of dark hair hanging down as the girl took a quick peek under the door. From inside the dressing room came a hissed "Shit!"

I put my hand to the door and knocked. *Rap-rap-rap.* "Jig's up. Come on out."

The sounds of locks releasing and hinges creaking filled the air as every door down the row opened except the one I stood in front of. Curious heads peeked out.

The girl feigned innocence. "What do you want with me?"

So that's how she's going to play this, huh? "I'm helping Santa. He's checked twice. You're on his naughty list." Okay, so I was being a smart-ass. But if she was going to dish out BS like it was figgy pudding, I was going to serve her some right back.

The girl emerged wearing a scowl, skinny jeans, and a polka-dot sweater. She'd be the cutest criminal ever booked at the station. *That sweater would look cute on my sister Gabby, too.*

I pulled my cuffs from my belt and circled my finger. "Turn around." I snapped the cuffs on her, took her by the arm, and led her out into the store where the security guards waited.

"I didn't steal anything!" she cried, turning her plea on them. They ignored her. She might not be green or come from Mount Crumpet, but she was the Girl Who Stole Christmas.

Leaving her temporarily in their custody, Brigit and I returned to the dressing room. Various clothing was strewn about the floor. Stashed under a wadded fleece pull-over was a variety of security-tag removers. The girl had likely ordered them online. Just as the security business was booming, so was the business in security-defeating devices. We went back out and I showed the gadgets to the men before turning to the girl. "Didn't steal anything, huh?"

I grabbed a bag from the cashier for the evidence and retook possession of the suspect. She kept her head down to avoid the condemning looks of other shoppers as I led her to the door.

A clerk folding sweaters at the front glanced down at the polka-dot sweater she had just added to the display and eyed the girl. "Did she pay for that top?"

The sweaters on the stack were the same as the one the girl was wearing.

"Are you kidding me?" I snapped. *Trying to steal more items right under my nose? The nerve!* I turned to the salesclerk. "Got one of those sweaters in a small?" Nobody could fault me for shopping while I was stuck waiting for an officer to take this little lawbreaker off my hands.

Minutes later, my backup arrived in the form of my former partner, the rusty-haired, foulmouthed Derek Mackey. Without a word, he took custody of the girl, now dressed in her own clothes. I'd swing by the station to fill out her booking paperwork once I paid for Gabby's sweater. All in all, it was a productive night.

NINE
FEATHERY FAKERS

Brigit

The treat she'd been fed at the mall had been delicious. But Brigit couldn't understand why there were so many artificial birds along the sidewalk. When she'd first spotted the big swans, she thought she'd be in for a fun and noisy chase, like when she ran after the ducks and geese at the pond in the park. But then she realized these birds weren't moving. She confirmed with a sniff that the birds were nothing more than Styrofoam, glue, and old feathers long since plucked from other fowl. *Boring!*

At least she'd had some fun trailing that girl. Her quarry had made it extra tough by zigging and zagging through the parking lot like a rabid squirrel, then turning back the way she'd come, leaving a second scent trail on top of her first. Of course even with the tricky tactics, the teen had been no match for Brigit and her nifty nose.

Dogs 1, humans 0.

TEN
BAD DAY

The Poacher

"You're gonna be good this time. Right, Daddy?"

His daughter's words echoed through his head as he lay on the hard floor in his sons' bedroom, a sleeping bag that smelled suspiciously like cat piss for his bed. The morning sun peeked around the crooked miniblind in the dusty window as guilt puckered his belly. He'd tried to be good. He really had. As usual, it just hadn't worked out.

He still hadn't told Vicki he'd been fired. He couldn't take that look of disappointment on her face, the "I told you so" she was sure to dish out. He'd wanted to prove her wrong, to prove to himself that he could hold down a good job without screwing it up. He couldn't even tell her that it wasn't his fault he'd been fired, that he'd been wrongfully accused. She'd never believe him.

His parole officer had suggested he apply for jobs farther out of the city where there would be less competition, maybe make some cold calls. In the meantime, he'd found the Poacher another job, this one at a Christmas-tree lot. The work was part-time, temporary, and paid only minimum wage plus tips. Not many people tipped him, even when he got scratched and covered in sap tying the trees to the top of their cars. *Cheapskates*. He'd hoped to give Vicki and the kids a good Christmas with lots of presents, but there was no way he could even pay half the mortgage and bills on what he earned now, let alone his truck payment. He didn't want to think what he'd have to do if he didn't find a better-paying job soon . . .

Oomph!

His older son had jumped down from the top bunk and landed on his stomach like an anvil. The gut that had been puckering in guilt now exploded in pain. If the Poacher could draw any breath, he would've screamed in agony.

"Sorry, Daddy!" the boy said as he climbed off the Poacher. "I forgot you were down here." With that, the kid traipsed out of the room, leaving his father to writhe in pain, wondering if something inside him had ruptured.

A moment later, Vicki came to the door to rouse their other son from the bottom bunk. Grimacing against the raw tenderness of his bruised belly, he forced himself to sit up on the floor. He gave her his best smile. "Good mornin', gorgeous."

"I quit my job last night," she said, getting right to the point and making no attempt to work up to the big news.

"You *what*?" He felt as if he'd taken another sucker punch to the gut. But surely he hadn't heard her right. Vicki had worked the dinner shift at the restaurant the night before, covered for a coworker. With dinner tickets being higher than lunch tickets, it had been a chance to put a little more money in her pocket. He'd already been asleep when she got home.

"I quit," she repeated, crossing her arms and leaning against the doorjamb. "A customer tried to play grab-ass with me at closing time. The manager wouldn't do nothin' about it, so I walked out."

As much as the thought of another man touching his

woman would normally enrage him, the emotion that overtook him in that moment was pure panic. "Can you take it up with the owners? See if they'll do something about it?"

"What's the point?" Vicki snapped. "I'm sick of waitressing anyway. People are rude and demanding, and they treat servers like dirt."

It felt as if hands had wrapped around his throat and were squeezing the life out of him. He could barely get words out, and when he did they sounded shrill. "What're you gonna do?"

She shrugged. "You're making good money. I figured I'll take off through Christmas and New Year's, look for a new job after the holidays. It'll give me some time to spend with the kids and catch up on things around the house."

He knew he should be honest with her then, tell her what had happened, that he'd lost his job and couldn't support them on his measly earnings from the seasonal gig at the tree lot. But he couldn't bring himself to do it.

He knew what he had to do. He had to take care of his family. *He had to be bad again.*

ELEVEN
CHRISTMAS BALLS

Megan

It was half past one o'clock in the afternoon on the last Saturday before Christmas. My gift shopping was done, but the macaws still hadn't been located. The story had quickly become old news, buried under a barrage of holiday parades, sales, and performances. But I still hadn't forgotten the birds. Maybe it was silly to be so concerned about Fabiana and Fernando. After all, there were plenty of humans in bad situations, too. But having another species for a partner had taught me that, whether our outsides were covered in skin or fur, we weren't that different. At heart, we all simply wanted food, shelter, and comfort. Surely the same applied to creatures with scales and feathers, too. If the birds hadn't been stolen and sold, they were probably hungry and scared, looking for somewhere safe to nest.

I hadn't planned to take Brigit to the zoo today, but when we stopped at the adjacent Forest Park so she could stretch her legs and relieve herself, she tugged on the leash and pulled me toward the entrance.

"Okay, girl," I told her. "We'll go visit your animal friends."

Janelle and I exchanged waves as Brigit and I made our way past the ticket booth. The weather was brisk but sunny, and the zoo was bustling with parents and children excited about their upcoming vacation from work and school. I wouldn't be getting a vacation. Brigit and I were scheduled to work Christmas Day. But at least I'd be able to spend Christmas morning with my family.

As Brigit and I made our way past the giraffes, a father bent down next to his adorable gap-toothed daughter, who looked to be seven or eight years old. She wore a black-and-white coat with a panda face and ears on the hood. She gaped up at the creatures while her younger brothers sat one in front of the other in a double stroller, their focus entirely on the soft pretzel they were sharing.

When a giraffe opened its mouth to snatch a leaf from a tree, the girl looked up at the man and tugged on his sweatshirt. "Hey, Daddy. How come their tongues are purple?"

"I don't know, squirt." Her father shrugged. "Maybe they ate grape popsicles for breakfast."

She giggled. "That's not right! Let me look it up on your phone."

The father reached into his pocket as we continued past them.

A smile curved my mouth. I'd been an observant and curious young girl like her once, trying to understand the world around me. Of course my childhood stutter had kept me from asking too many questions, but it didn't keep me from getting the answers. I spent quite a bit of time in the library or online, looking up information. I was still a curious person, a good trait for an aspiring detective. But, fortunately, barring a rare occasion, my stutter had abated.

A squeal came from the older boy in the stroller. "Ew! It's pooping!"

I glanced back to see that the giraffe who'd been feasting on leaves was now dropping a load of small pellets similar to the scat left by rabbits. Of course these droppings had much farther to fall than the ones produced by bunnies. Like Danny Landis, I now knew more about animal excrement than I truly cared to.

As Brigit and I walked on, dispatch came over the radio, looking for a unit to respond to a call from Colonial Country Club, which sat directly across University Drive from the zoo. Apparently there was some type of disagreement taking place at the tennis courts. I pressed the button on my mic to let dispatch know my partner and I would take the call.

"Let's go, girl!" I called down to Brigit.

With a call of "See you next time!" to Janelle, the two of us jogged out to the parking lot and climbed into our cruiser for the short drive across the street. I started the engine and waited, my eye on my side mirror, as a couple with a stroller passed behind my car. *Hold on. Is that Danny Landis?*

I unrolled my window and called out to the man's back. "Mr. Landis?"

The man turned around. *Yep. It's him.* He handed something to the woman. "I'll meet you at the gate," he told her before walking to my window.

I gestured to the zoo. "What are you doing here?"

"Same as everyone else," he said. "Taking my family to the zoo. They gave me a bunch of free passes when I was hired here. Might as well use 'em up. Can't afford to take them anywhere else. You know what a movie costs these days?"

"An arm and a leg." If you added butter to your popcorn, it could also cost you an artery. "At least you won't have to scoop poop today," I offered, trying to help him look on the bright side.

He issued a mirthless chuckle. "I suppose there's that."

I raised a hand in good-bye. "Have a good time."

"I'll do my best," he replied as he backed away from the cruiser.

As I watched him walk away, the same old thought haunted me. Had Danny Landis stolen the valuable birds? I wished I could figure it out, put my suspicions to rest.

The lot behind me now clear, I backed up and headed to the exit, gunning my engine to make it across all four lanes of University Drive. As we curved down Colonial Parkway, my gaze moved up to the bare trees. A plastic grocery bag was stuck in one of them. Two squirrels chased each other up another. An old nest sat vacant in the crook of a third, waiting to see if its former occupants might return in the spring to raise another brood. But there were no hyacinth macaws sitting on the limbs, waiting to be rescued.

While Colonial Country Club was most widely known for hosting an annual PGA tour, the club also offered thirteen tennis courts, ten outdoors and three indoors. The outdoor courts would be lighted come dusk for evening play. To celebrate the season, the perimeter fence around the courts sported a festive garland with red bows placed every six feet or so, affixed to the chain-link exterior.

As Brigit and I approached the courts, the telltale sounds of tennis being played met our ears. The *thwock* of a ball being served or returned, the *thomp* as it bounced off the court, the grunts of exertion and cries of delight and despair as players either returned a difficult ball or missed it. My partner's ears perked up and her tail wagged. Like these tennis players, Brigit loved to chase the fuzzy yellow balls.

"Sorry, girl," I told her. "This isn't playtime."

From outside the first court, a woman wearing tennis

shoes and a black Nike warm-up suit raised her arm and snapped her fingers to flag me down, the way an impatient customer might signal an overworked server. "Over here, Officer!"

The woman's short hair was dyed a stylish but unnatural reddish tone, akin to an oaky cabernet. A tennis tote sat at her feet, the handle of a racquet sticking out of the specially designed pocket on the side. Two other women stood nearby. Both were club employees. The tall, thirtyish Latina wore pumps, dress pants, and a blazer embroidered with the club's seal on the breast pocket. The other was a sturdy fiftyish white woman with salt-and-pepper hair. She wore work boots, work pants, and a jacket embossed with the same seal.

As we stepped up, a faint scent of peppermint met my nose. Maybe the wine-haired woman had tennis elbow and used one of those mint-scented pain creams to treat it. I looked from one of the women to the other. "Someone called for assistance?"

The woman in the warm-up suit raised a hand to her shoulder. "That was me." Her fingers were tipped in a festive holiday manicure. The base was white and featured green holly leaves with red berries. "I just finished playing a couple of tennis matches. I always take my rings off when I play and I put them in this pocket." She bent down and opened the tote to show me a small zippered pocket sewn inside. "When I was done, I went to get my rings but they weren't there." She pointed to the woman with the salt-and-pepper hair. "She had been working around the courts and moved my bag. I hate to sound accusatory," she said, doing just that, "but I don't see who else could have taken them. Nobody else was around."

The story was similar to Nan Ishii's. *Déjà vu.* I turned to the accused.

Before I could even ask, she said, "I didn't take anything." Her voice contained a calm control that the firm set of her jaw told me was forced. "I only moved her bag so I could reattach a bow. Some of them had come loose." She cast an annoyed glance at the club member. "I requested that she move the bag herself, but she told me to do it."

The woman gave a derisive but dainty huff. "I was in the middle of a game."

My focus shifted to the woman in the blazer. She raised her palms slightly as if to say *I don't know what happened or what to do about this.*

"You're a manager?" I asked.

"Assistant manager," she replied.

I glanced around, noting security cameras mounted on the tennis clubhouse, which sat near the courts. I gestured to them. "Can we take a look at the video footage?"

"Of course," she said. "Security will have to set it up, but it shouldn't be a problem."

I cast a glance at the older woman who'd been accused. She didn't object, nor did she appear worried in the least. In fact, she appeared to be gloating. *She didn't do it.* While I couldn't claim to be an expert in psychology, I had studied criminal psych at Sam Houston State University as part of my criminal justice degree. If this woman was guilty, she'd be making excuses or at least displaying signs of anxiety. She did neither.

Twenty minutes later, the three women, Brigit, a male member of the club's security team, and I were gathered around a large monitor in the assistant manager's office inside the clubhouse, watching the footage. On the screen, the maintenance employee walked up to a droopy piece of garland and attempted to reattach the loose bow from the outside of the court. Unfortunately, she couldn't get her hands through the mesh far enough to secure the back. She proceeded to open the entrance to the courts and slunk along the fence, doing her best not to interfere with the game being played on the court a few feet away. As she reached one of the loose bows, she looked down at the sport bag leaning against the fence directly below it. Her head turned toward the players as she waited for an opportune time to address them. When one of them missed a ball, she called out to them. The woman with the cabernet hair called something back, and the staff member reached down, took the handle of the bag, and lifted it, moving the bag a few feet farther down. She immediately turned her attention back to the bow, secured it, and circled around the bag to fix another bow near the far end of the court. When she finished, she walked out of the court, still sticking close to the fence, but never again touching the bag. She returned to the tall gate and exited.

The employee looked directly at the tennis player and raised a brow that said, *You going to apologize for wrongfully accusing me, bitch?*

To her credit, the woman did, her face blushing nearly as red as her hair and her eyes bright with bewilderment. "I'm so sorry! I just didn't think there was any other explanation." She looked up, as if trying to force a memory to appear. "I mean, I had them on when I got here, didn't I?"

"We can look and see." The security guard restarted the footage, this time beginning as the woman arrived to play. Though we could see her retrieve her balls and racquet from the bag, at no point did she appear to remove any rings.

"Oh, no." Her hands moved to her cheeks. "Where did they go? What did I do with them?"

I attempted to help her train of thought move along the track. "Where else have you been today?"

She removed her hands from her face. "I did some Christmas shopping and then I got a mani-pedi."

"Did you take your rings off when you got your nails done?" I asked.

"Yes," she replied. "The girl gave me a hand massage with peppermint lotion."

That explained the minty smell.

The woman continued. "I took the rings off before she started. I remember because she had a hand-shaped holder to put them on. It was covered in red velvet. Very kitschy."

I pointed out the obvious. "Maybe you left the rings at the salon."

She shook her head emphatically. "No. I specifically remember the girl reminding me not to forget my rings when she finished. I know I put them back on because they slid on really easy with the lotion on my hands."

Again, I pointed out the obvious. "If they slid on easily, they could slide off easily, too. Maybe they fell off somewhere."

She gasped and covered her mouth, her eyes darting wildly around. "They could be anywhere. The court. The clubhouse. My car. I cut across the grass after I parked. Oh, Lord! I might never find them!"

Despite the member having wrongfully accused her of stealing the rings, the woman with the salt-and-pepper hair offered to help the lady search for the rings. The assistant manager also agreed to help.

At that point, the situation was more of a treasure hunt than a police matter. I handed the tennis player my business card and wished the trio luck. "I hope you find them."

TWELVE
FINDERS KEEPERS

Brigit

Megan led her outside and away from the place where the humans were hitting the balls around. Brigit was disappointed she hadn't had a chance to chase any of the balls. Next to chasing down a suspect, playing ball was her favorite sport. She was way better at it than those humans. They kept missing. Maybe they should try using their teeth instead of those weird stringed sticks.

But at least Brigit had come away with a ball. While the humans had been staring at the screen in the office, she'd lain down next to a bag that the woman who smelled like peppermint had placed on the ground. Despite the overwhelming scent of mint, Brigit's skilled snout was also able to detect the telltale scent of rubber that told her there were tennis balls in the bag. She'd stuck her nose through the top, pushed the zipper further open, and snatched a ball. Nobody had complained. She wasn't even sure they'd noticed. But really, wasn't anything on the floor fair game for a dog? Sure it was. Everyone knew that was the rule. If nothing else, she had *paws*ible deniability.

THIRTEEN
THE WEATHER OUTSIDE IS FRIGHTFUL

The Poacher

It was so damned cold outside he couldn't feel his toes or his nose. He didn't know why the owners of the tree lot even bothered keeping the place open. Christmas was in four days. Anyone who hadn't bought a tree yet wasn't going to buy one at all. Besides, the only trees left were small, sparse, and dry. They'd make lousy Christmas trees. The only thing they'd be good for was firewood. To hide their decrepit condition, the boss had handed him a case of flocking spray and told him to cover the trees with the fake snow.

While the lot's owner watched television, drank whiskey, and kept warm in his RV, the Poacher was out here like an idiot in a Santa hat with a plastic sign that read ALL TREES 50% OFF! He'd tried spinning the thing like his boss told him to, but the sign had gone as haywire as a helicopter hit by enemy fire. It whirled into traffic, nearly causing an accident. After riding half a block on the windshield of a pickup truck, the sign had blown off and promptly been run over by a city bus, another pickup, and some hipster in a Prius with a handlebar mustache, a flannel shirt, and five cat decals on his back window. The Poacher had risked his life retrieving the sign from the road, wiped the tread marks off as best he could, and settled for moving the sign left to right in his hands.

A rattling sound came from the RV and his boss stuck his head out the window. "Don't just stand there!" he hollered. "Trying dancing or something!" He slid the window shut with a *slam*.

Dancing? What did the guy expect? The only dancing the Poacher had ever done was at the high school prom, pressed up against Vicki during a slow song with his hand cupped over her butt cheek. But if that asshole wanting dancing, the Poacher would give him dancing.

He started by doing his best impersonation of Kevin Bacon in *Footloose,* and segued into *Napoleon Dynamite.* When he was done with that, he went full-on John Travolta, starting with the pointed disco finger from *Saturday Night Fever,* moving on to a *Grease* montage, attempting a one-person two-step à la *Urban Cowboy,* and ending with the dance he'd performed with Uma Thurman in *Pulp Fiction,* making a V with his fingers and sliding it past his eyes while shaking his butt. The warden in charge of movie night had been a huge Travolta fan. The Poacher had seen every one of his movies at least three times.

When he tired of the Travolta shtick, he grabbed a couple cans of flocking spray and danced around, shaking them. The metal balls inside gave off a *clankety-clank* as he shook the cans. Cars slowed as drivers tried to get a better look at him. A couple honked, and one issued a wolf whistle out his window. "Shake it, baby!"

The burner phone buzzed in his jacket pocket. He was moving so fast he hardly noticed at first. He stopped and closed his eyes, both grateful and ashamed.

He pulled the phone from his pocket and jabbed the button to take the call. "Yeah?"

Two minutes later, he hurled the sign toward the RV like a Frisbee. As the sign slid under the vehicle, he climbed into his pickup and started the engine.

His boss poked his head out the window again. "Where in the Sam Hill do you think you're going?"

The Poacher ripped the Santa hat from his head and tossed it out the window. "I quit!" Not that it much mattered. The job was scheduled to end in four days anyway. He punched the gas and roared out of the lot.

FOURTEEN

MONKEY SEE, MONKEY DO, MONKEY SOMEHOW LEAVE THE ZOO

Megan

Just three days until Christmas. Fort Worth was in a festive frenzy, people rushing around to find last-minute gifts, exchange cookies, and stock up on groceries for their holiday meals. It was mid-afternoon and Brigit and I were working another swing shift. It was also freezing cold outside, the temperatures dipping into single digits once the wind chill was factored in. Mother Nature seemed intent on torturing north Texas today, sending gusts of wind that whipped your exposed skin and threatened to topple anyone out in the weather.

Good thing I'd worn a pair of thermal underwear under my uniform. I'd also brought along a fleece-lined police-dog vest for Brigit. With any luck, she wouldn't need it. I had no intention of performing any unnecessary foot patrol today. We'd stay in our warm patrol car, thank you very much.

As we waited at a traffic light near the TCU campus, the wind whistling around the cruiser, dispatch came over the radio. "Got a report of a missing monkey at the zoo. Who can respond?"

So much for staying in the car. I finagled the mic from its holder and let dispatch know the crack team of Megan Luz and Sergeant Brigit were on their way. "Officer Luz and Brigit responding."

As we aimed for the zoo, my mind went in a million different directions. *A monkey is missing now? What are the odds the macaws and the monkey escaped on their own? Has the zoo staff been negligent again, or is someone stealing these animals? If so, who and how? Have I been right to be suspicious of Landis?*

I parked the cruiser, attached Brigit's leash, and dressed her in the vest so she wouldn't get cold. Together, we trotted to the front gate, partly to keep warm, partly to hurry things up. There, we found Sharon Easley, the zoo director who'd fired Danny Landis. She wore a tan parka trimmed with faux fur along with her khakis today. Standing off to the side was the same security officer who'd escorted Landis to the gate after his termination. He paid me no mind. His attention was focused on those leaving the zoo. Janelle watched from her ticket booth. We exchanged nods before I turned to Easley.

The director gave me a quick rundown. "The primatologist on duty noticed one of the colobus monkeys was missing when she went to feed them an hour ago. We had a full count of five at closing last night, but there are only four in the enclosure now. She says it's the male who's missing, an eighteen-year-old monkey named Sarki. The security records for the card reader show that the only people who entered the enclosure since last night were one of our veterinarians who was checking on a female with a dental issue and the keeper who reported the monkey missing."

"And you suspect foul play." It wasn't a question, really. She'd summoned law enforcement so she must've thought something criminal had taken place.

"It seems that way. The hyacinth macaws have already disappeared, and we can't see how the monkey could have gotten out of the exhibit on its own."

When I'd first been paired with Brigit, she'd used several of my shoes for chew toys, and subsequently defeated nearly every security measure I'd taken to protect my remaining pairs. She had also surreptitiously stolen a tennis ball from the woman's bag at the country club. She held the thing as far back in her mouth as she could, covering it with her jowls. I hadn't noticed until we'd returned to our cruiser and she dropped it in her enclosure. I decided to let her keep her loot. By that point, it was soaked in dog saliva and the woman probably wouldn't want it back. Besides, it would be embarrassing to admit my trained partner had committed misdemeanor theft right under my nose. Yep, animals could be clever, crafty, and downright devious when they wanted to be. Of course these zoo professionals knew that as well as I did. In fact, exhibits were designed to take every potential escape route into account and eliminate them. And if one monkey had somehow managed to escape, why hadn't others escaped, too? Theft seemed the more likely explanation.

"I'd like to take a look at the exhibit and speak to the veterinarian and primatologist." I also realized it would be a good idea to call the station and speak to one of the detectives. A stolen monkey was unusual, a much bigger matter than the usual petty theft or home burglary. A detective would want to come out and take a look, too.

While Easley used her walkie-talkie to summon the

primatologist and veterinarian to the exhibit, I used my phone to call the station.

Detective Hector Bustamente took my call. "What's up, Officer Luz?"

I gave him a quick synopsis of the situation. A monkey named Sarki had gone AWOL. No means of accidental escape was immediately evident. Given that the pair of macaws had already gone missing, theft was suspected. There definitely seemed to be some monkey business going on.

"I'll be right there," Bustamente said.

Ten minutes later, the detective met me, Brigit, and Easley at the zoo's entrance. Bustamente was a seasoned investigator whose careless appearance was at odds with the careful consideration he applied to his work. He had thick lips, round cheeks, and a winter coat that was snapped closed over his chest but hung open over his midsection. The sides couldn't quite meet across the roll of flesh he'd accumulated over years spent sitting at a desk, pondering clues and evidence.

We strode quickly to the exhibit, stopping at a viewing area. Given the frigid weather, there were no visitors at the overlook, only the zookeeper and veterinarian, who stood side by side, staring into the habitat, their elbows nearly touching. They turned our way as they heard us approach, and Easley made quick introductions all around. The keeper was a petite woman in her mid to late thirties. Her Italian lineage was evidenced by her dark hair, olive skin, and name—Camilla Bellafiore. The veterinarian, Greg Geer, was a tall, fiftyish guy with a lean runner's build, a shiny balding head, and eyeglasses in fashionable blue plastic frames.

Camilla's brown eyes were bright with worry. "We can't find Sarki anywhere. I don't even want to think what might have happened to him."

Greer cringed in a sign of agreement. "I wish I'd realized he was gone when I was here earlier examining Zawadi. We could've started our search sooner."

Their concern for the animal entrusted to their care seemed genuine. I could only imagine the panic I'd feel if Brigit were missing. The mere thought made my skin prickle.

My eyes scanned the exhibit. While it did not have a covering like the aviary to keep animals from escaping out the top, all of the trees inside were contained on an amorphously shaped island of sorts that slanted down on all four sides into a wide, deep gulley. The outer walls of the gulley were high, smooth, and straight, seemingly impossible for this small breed of monkey to climb. At the back of the enclosure stood a mock rock wall, similarly designed with smooth surfaces to be unclimbable. A dark, discolored streak about four feet wide bisected the wall, indicating where a man-made waterfall coursed down the surface in warmer weather. The water had been turned off today, probably due to the risk of the pipes freezing and breaking.

The remaining four colobus monkeys perched on limbs in the center of the stand of trees. They were a beautiful species, mostly black with white tails and white fur encircling their faces. They were also a small species, only slightly longer than human infants at birth. While some of the other animals didn't like the cold, these monkeys didn't seem to mind the winter temperatures. Not surprising, I supposed. The informational display on the viewing deck noted they were native to both coastal and mountainous regions in Africa, including Kilimanjaro.

Although it certainly appeared the monkey had been snatched, we nonetheless needed to explore all possibilities to definitively rule out whether the animal had simply absconded on its own. Tarzan used vines to move around the forest. So did Mowgli from *The Jungle Book.* They'd learned from monkeys, hadn't they? And all sorts of vines and climbing plants grew wild in Texas. Poison oak. Mustang grape. Honeysuckle. They spread easily, helped along by birds who ate their seeds and berries, depositing them elsewhere at the end of the digestive process. While the back wall of the colobus monkey enclosure was smooth, it was built with vertical angles to give it a more natural appearance. Not all of the faces were visible from where we stood.

I turned to the keeper. "Could some kind of vine have grown along the back wall?"

"I looked the enclosure over carefully," Camilla said. "There's no vegetation Sarki could have used for climbing. No growths or damage that would allow him to get a foothold, either."

Looked like he hadn't climbed it like a rock wall, either.

Bustamente turned to Camilla. "How far can these monkeys jump?"

"A long way," she said. "Up to fifty feet from a tree. They bounce off the limbs, use them like trampolines. But this enclosure is designed so all of the trees are more than fifty feet from the outer boundary."

After taking another sweeping glance around the enclosure, the detective asked, "How long has Sarki lived here?"

"More than a decade," Camilla said. "I've worked here ten years and he was already living here when I started."

The detective's head bobbed as he mulled over the information. "Is there any reason why he'd try to make a break now? Has anything changed recently? Has there been some type of threat, or maybe something outside the habitat he'd find particularly enticing?"

"Nothing I can think of." She looked up at Greer. "What about you, Greg?"

I noticed she'd said "Greg," not "Doctor Greer." Though it was common for colleagues to be on a first-name basis and forgo formal titles, I wondered whether the two might have a personal relationship.

When the detective turned his gaze on Greer, the veterinarian affirmed Camilla's assessment. "I'm not aware of anything, either."

Bustamente gestured into the habitat as he posed another question to the keeper. "How do you get in there to feed them?"

"There's a staff door around back," she said. "I'll show you."

Camilla led our assorted parade on a downward-sloping path around the side of the enclosure. She stopped at a six-foot wooden privacy fence with a sign on the gate that read ZOO STAFF ONLY BEYOND THIS POINT. Like Danny Landis, Camilla wore a staff ID card on a lanyard around her neck. She swiped her card through the secured-access device and the lock opened with a *click*. The rest of us followed her through. Camilla stepped back to the gate to ensure it had latched.

We stood in a small concrete courtyard that was enclosed by a wooden fence and contained only a seasonally decommissioned snow-cone stand parked to the side. Camilla headed to a heavy iron gate set in a brick wall at the back.

Rather than risk frightening the monkeys, I ordered Brigit to sit and stay by the snow-cone stand, giving her a head ruffle to show I appreciated her obedience. "I'll be back soon."

Camilla led us through the iron gate into an enclosed

walkway flanked by brick walls. Glass skylights had been installed in the roof to provide natural lighting in the space.

I pointed up. "Has anyone checked the skylights?"

"Yes," Easley said. "None are loose."

It had been a long shot, anyway. The glass panels would be heavy to lift. A small monkey probably couldn't do it on his own. Besides, he would have only made it this far if he'd found his way past the interior gate at the far end of the passage.

As we made our way down to the end of the walk, Camilla gestured to the doors on either side. "The left door leads to the storage area where the monkeys' food is kept. The door on the right leads to an exam room where the vets treat them. There're also small cages where we put the monkeys when they're sick."

She opened each door and gave me and the detective a glimpse inside. The storage room contained a refrigerator stocked with spinach, kale, and other dietary staples for this species of monkey. The space on the right contained an examination table topped with Formica, storage cabinets, and several tall cages.

Bustamente pointed to the cabinets, which had old-fashioned key locks built into them and were large enough to house a small monkey. "What's in there?"

"Medicines and medical supplies," the vet said.

Bustamente cocked his head. "Mind if Officer Luz and I take a peek?"

"No problem." Greer stepped into the space and unlocked each of the cabinets, revealing small bottles of pills and liquids, syringes, and other items similar to what one would find in a doctor's office, but no monkey.

After we'd taken a look at the rooms, Camilla turned to the inner gate. "This leads into the monkeys' enclosure."

Like the outer gate, this gate was secured by a card reader and bordered by brick on the top and sides. In other words, there'd be no way to go over, under, or around the gates without going through the brick or concrete floor. Nowhere on the route had the brick or concrete shown signs of damage or repair. All of the card readers had appeared intact, too. Ditto for the locks.

Camilla stood by the gate until we had all made it through, and closed it behind us, giving it a tug to make sure it had latched just as she'd done with the previous gates. I glanced back to see if there was a security device on the inside of the enclosure. Bustamente did the same, our gazes meeting as we turned our heads. The detective lifted his chin to acknowledge my actions. He'd always said I had good instincts.

Though a manual lock release was in place, there was no electronic security system on the inside of the gates. In other words, while a badge was needed to enter this area, none was needed to exit. The arrangement was typical in commercial structures, designed so people would not be trapped in the event of a fire or other emergency.

Greer stepped up beside Camilla. "Why don't I keep an eye on the monkeys while you show them around?"

"Good idea," Easley said.

The detective and I followed the three zoo professionals farther into the enclosure. I found myself staring out across the space toward the visitor viewing decks, wondering what it would be like to live on display like this, with people watching you go about your life. I looked up into the carefully designed forest and saw four sets of eyes looking back at me, waiting to see what I might do next. *So this is what it feels like.* Of course spectators wouldn't be much interested in watching me eat organic oatmeal in the morning, issue traffic tickets all day, and read books in bed at night.

While the veterinarian stood near the trees and watched the monkeys watch us, Camilla took us on a tour of the enclosure. She explained that the base of the back wall was several feet thick, and showed us the small opening cut into the wall that led to a cave of sorts, offering the monkeys a private location to spend time out of the public eye. As she'd said, the wall appeared devoid of any vines or footholds that Sarki could have used to climb out. We ambled down the concrete slope into the gulley, circumnavigating from one end of the horseshoe-shaped ditch to the other. Again, no vines or footholds were evident along the outer walls. No signs of damage, either. All I saw were dry, brown leaves that had blown into the enclosure and the occasional small mass of dark, slimy poop evidencing the monkeys' high-fiber diet.

Looking up, I mused aloud. "Someone could have come over the back wall on a rope or ladder. Or they could have lowered a rope or ladder into the channel from one of the viewing areas." Once inside, they'd have been able to seize the monkey and go back the way they'd come, or easily exit through the gates.

"Possibly." Bustamente cut me a sideways glance that said he had other theories, as well. He turned his gaze on the keeper. "Who came in with you when you fed them earlier?"

"Nobody," Camilla said. "I take care of the feeding alone."

He pressed on. "Is there any chance someone could have followed you through the gate without your knowledge?"

"No." Her tone was confident. "I always check to make sure the gates have closed behind me."

She'd done exactly that when she'd led us into the enclosure. It seemed to be a natural habit for her.

Easley chimed in on the subject. "Checking the gates is part of zoo protocol."

Bustamente dipped his head. "I see. Good rule." As we circled back around to the gate to exit, the veterinarian fell in line with us. The detective asked him essentially the same questions. "Who came in with you when you examined the female monkey? Did you bring an assistant?"

"No," Greer replied. "It was just me. These monkeys are small and docile, so I can handle a single specimen on my own. Of course it's a different story when I'm dealing with a chimp or gorilla."

"Could someone have followed you into the enclosure without your knowledge?"

"Absolutely not," the vet said. "I always try the gates to make sure they're shut all the way after I use them."

As we stopped in front of the gate, a question popped into my head and out of my mouth. "What would happen if someone forced the gate open from the outside?"

Easley answered my question by pointing at two thin sensors, one mounted at the top of the brick wall, the other mounted on the outer surface of the metal gate. "Those sensors detect when the gate has been opened. An alarm would sound if it was opened from the outside without a key card." She pointed up to a speaker mounted above the gate. "The system would also send an immediate notification to the security team."

Given that neither safety alert had been activated, as well as the fact that none of the locks appeared damaged, it seemed we could rule out that someone had come through the gate without a key card. Even so, they could have exited without one.

The detective glanced around one last time before turning to the director. "I think Officer Luz and I have seen all we need to see here."

We ascended the walkway, Easley and Greer taking the lead, with Camilla closing and checking the gates behind us. Brigit stood and wagged her tail, glad to see me return to the courtyard.

As I rounded up my partner, Bustamente asked a final question of the zoo staff. "Did you take the monkeys anywhere today other than the enclosure or the exam room?"

Each of them answered in the negative. But were they telling the truth? Or was one—or both—of them lying?

FIFTEEN
ROUND AND ROUND

Brigit

When Megan issued the command for Brigit to trail from the metal gate, Brigit wasn't sure which disturbance Megan wanted her to follow. There was more than one here. One of them smelled like the lady who'd just left. The other smelled like the man who'd gone with her. For not the first time in their partnership, Brigit wished Megan could give her more specific instructions. *Too bad Megan doesn't speak dog.*

Brigit did the best she could. She followed the lady's scent first, leading Megan, Detective Bustamente, and the woman in the big coat back to a building near the zoo entrance. When Megan opened the door, Brigit could smell the trail more clearly given that the wind hadn't been able to blow it away. She followed the trail all the way to the door of the room that smelled like the woman in the coat. The trail backtracked there to the monkey exhibit. They ended up back where they started.

Megan gave her a "good girl" and a liver treat before telling the woman in the coat, "She must have been on the keeper's trail."

Brigit's partner instructed her to sniff around some

more, which meant she was to look for additional trails. She picked up the vet's trail and did her best to follow it. It wasn't easy on a windy day like today, when the breeze scattered the scent. More than once she lost the trail and had to raise her nose in the air in an attempt to find it again. She led Megan from the monkeys to the gorilla exhibit.

The woman in the coat spoke this time. "She must be tracking Dr. Greer. He checked in on the gorillas after examining Zawadi's tooth."

Megan took her back to the courtyard a third time, and directed her once again to scent for a trail. *Sheesh. Give a working dog a break, will ya?*

Brigit sniffed her best sniff, flexing her nostrils as far as they would go. She'd smelled the monkey dung behind the snow cone cart earlier, but with this extra effort now she also detected just a hint of a scent on the fence near it. She led Megan over and sat down next to the poop, facing the fence to put Megan on notice.

Her partner bent down next to her and looked at the poop. That was weird. Megan normally issued sounds of disgust when Brigit showed interest in excrement and pulled her away from it. *Humans are so fickle.*

SIXTEEN
MONEY FOR MONKEY

The Poacher

The monkey cowered in the back of the plastic pet carrier, its chest heaving and dark eyes shining with fear. The Poacher had never felt like more of a shit in his life.

His baby girl's voice echoed in his head yet again. *"You're gonna be good this time. Right, Daddy?"*

He wanted to be good. Really, he did. But it wasn't as easy as it sounded. Harper still looked at the world in black-and-white, like that panda jacket she wore all the time. Someday, when she grew up, she'd realize few things were so clear-cut. His family came first. If he had to be bad to take care of them, then he'd do it.

He handed the carrier over, taking the thick white envelope in return. He opened it and did a quick count. Three grand in hundred-dollar bills. *It's all there.*

As he turned to go, the man called after him. "I'll be in touch."

"Don't bother." The job had been risky, and he couldn't take another poor, frightened animal looking at him that way. "I'm not doing this again."

The man had the nerve to laugh. "That's what they all say."

SEVENTEEN
WHO DUNG IT?

Megan

When Brigit sat and issued her passive alert, I spotted another deposit of monkey scat near the bottom of the fence. *Maybe Sarki wasn't lifted out of the exhibit. Maybe he was taken out this way.* Yep, the doo-doo could be a clue-clue. It was smeared, though, as if it had been stepped in. Unfortunately, there was no discernible footprint or sole pattern that could be traced to a particular shoe. Whoever had stepped in the scat must have turned their foot.

"Detective? Brigit found something."

Bustamente came around the snow-cone stand and followed my gaze down. "Aha."

Easley did the same, frowning when the significance of the excrement struck her. "This doesn't look good, does it?"

"Proof that the monkey was taken through a staff-only area with no apparent breach of security?" Bustamente said, staring down at the icky goop. "No, it does not." He raised his head. "Could we go to your office so we can speak privately?"

"Of course," Easley said.

Dusk set in as we followed Easley, retracing our steps to her office in the administrative building near the front entrance. The warmth was more than welcome after the extended time we'd spent outside. A standard desk and high-backed chair sat in the back corner of her office, while a coffee table, a couch, and two end chairs sat at the front, forming a more casual space. Easley took a seat in one of the end chairs, Bustamente in the other. That left me to perch on the sofa. Brigit flopped down at my feet.

Once the three of us were seated, Bustamente leaned forward, his arms resting across his thighs. "Ms. Easley, I hate to tell you this, but in situations where property is missing from a business it's most often an employee who took it. The evidence so far is flimsy at best, but it points to Ms. Bellafiore or Dr. Greer. Maybe both of them."

She let out a slow, loud breath. "I feared you might say that. But why would either of them take Sarki?"

He raised a shoulder. "The only reason I can imagine for someone stealing zoo animals is to keep them as pets or sell them for money." His brows rose in question. "Do either of them seem like viable suspects to you?"

She shrugged this time. "They've both worked here for years and have good performance records. That said, the zoo has hundreds of employees. I don't know these two well, so it would be a stretch to say I could completely vouch for them."

"I understand," Bustamente said. "I'd like to speak to their immediate supervisors and coworkers, any staff who are responsible for the birds or monkeys, see if they might be able to provide any insights. Can you get me a list of these people and their contact information?"

"It'll take me an hour or so to pull that data together," Easley replied, "but it won't be a problem."

"What about the custodian who was fired?" I looked from the detective to the director. "Danny Landis? Could he have come back to the zoo and taken Sarki?" I told them how I'd run into the man in the parking lot with his family after he'd been terminated. "He said he was using the free passes he'd been given when he was hired."

"If he was a custodian," Bustamente said, "that means he'd know his way around the zoo, both the public and restricted areas. He'd be familiar with the routines, too. But unless he was in cahoots with the vet or the primatologist, it wouldn't explain how he'd gotten through the secure gates."

He could have scaled the six-foot fence, though. It wasn't hard. I'd had to do it myself on more than one occasion when chasing a suspect, as well as in the academy training.

I drew a circle in the air with my finger. "And that brings us back to the possibility that he climbed into the exhibit to steal the monkey during the overnight hours. Maybe he climbed into the courtyard with Sarki when he saw a security patrol coming." I looked down at my partner. It was too bad her tracking skills hadn't led us to any definitive answers. But if someone had stolen the monkey overnight, it was understandable that she could no longer find the trail given the amount of time that had elapsed and the blustery wind working against us.

Bustamente began to wrap things up with the director. "To make sure we've covered all the bases, I'll get a crime scene tech out here to dust for prints. Please instruct your staff to stay away from the employee areas of the exhibit until I give you the all clear."

While the detective placed a quick phone call to the crime scene division, Easley used a walkie-talkie to address the zoo staff, letting them know the restricted area at the colobus monkey habitat was off limits until she said otherwise.

Their external communications concluded, Bustamente

said, "I'd like to speak with the head of security. Is that person on-site and available now?"

"I'll check." Easley picked up the receiver on her desk phone and tapped three digits. After a brief conversation with someone on the other end, she said, "He's in. His office is right down the hall. I can take you there."

"Thanks." Bustamente stood and Brigit and I followed suit. "In the meantime," he told the director, "it wouldn't be a bad idea to put the word out over the zoo networks, let everyone know Sarki is missing, ask them to gather as much information as they can and notify us if anyone tries to sell him to another facility. Same for those blue macaws."

"I'll do that," she said. "Unfortunately, though, there's quite a few of those roadside zoos run by unscrupulous folks who put profits ahead of animal welfare. Some shady traveling circuses, too. They'd buy a monkey like Sarki in a heartbeat and not think twice about it. They get little oversight from the state or the USDA, and even when they're found to have violated the Animal Welfare Act, they rarely get more than a slap on the wrist. Regulation in other countries isn't any better, if there's any at all. If Sarki ends up in one of those outfits, God help him. He's not likely to fare any better if he's sold to a private collector. Most people get exotic pets for the novelty and don't have the knowledge or funds to properly care for a monkey. Besides, he won't be happy alone. Primates need to be part of a social system."

My heart writhed in my chest, hurting for Sarki, hurting for the birds, too, wherever they were.

Easley escorted us down the hall, where she passed us off to the chief of security I'd met before. After we exchanged names and handshakes, we took seats and Bustamente launched into a line of questions about the zoo's security systems and procedures.

The first question the detective posed was, "Can you confirm whether Danny Landis's key card was canceled?"

"I can," the CSO said. He typed something into his computer and turned the monitor so the detective and I could see it. On the screen was an alphabetical list of names. "These are the people with currently active key cards. You'll notice Landis isn't on it. Not only did I deactivate his card in the system, but I shredded it immediately after he turned it in."

"Is anyone missing a card?" Bustamente asked.

"Not to my knowledge," the man said. "Whenever I'm notified that a card is lost, I immediately deactivate it and issue the employee a new one. On occasion, a staff member has gotten by for a shift or two by asking others to open secure areas for them, but we've cracked down on these breaches. I send regular reminders to the entire staff that gaining access with someone else's card is grounds for both parties to be dismissed."

Bustamente offered the man a nod in respect. "You run a tight ship."

"I do my best," the man said.

The detective asked about the card access records next. "Is there any way the devices or your computer system could be tampered with to delete a card reading?"

"No computer system is entirely immune from hacking," the man acknowledged, "but we've got several safeguards in place. The data is password protected and encrypted. I've seen no evidence that any of our devices or data have been tampered with, from the outside or the inside."

Bustamente turned the subject to the security cameras.

"Officer Luz mentioned that the only security cameras are around the perimeter. There aren't any on the exhibits?"

"That's correct," the CSO confirmed.

"Could we watch the footage from each camera, starting right after closing time last night?"

"Certainly. I'd planned to take a look myself. We can do it together."

Once again, I found myself gathered around the desk, watching security camera footage on the oversized monitor. We spent the next two and a half hours carefully reviewing each feed.

As for the night footage, most of the cameras showed little more than the trees at the edge of the parking lot swaying wildly in the rough winds and various items of trash blowing by. Another showed a pair of possums parading along the exterior wall before dropping out of sight inside the zoo. Yet another showed a homeless man pushing a loaded shopping cart along the asphalt, his head down and back bent against the wind as he rolled his belongings into Forest Park.

The final feed was from a camera positioned to show the stretch of brick wall that ran along University Drive. The view was limited due to the darkness and the trees growing along the stretch of land between the wall and the roadway. We were watching the feed at six times actual speed when a big, black blob appeared at the base of a tree near the far end of the wall.

I reflexively raised a palm. "Wait. What's that? Did it come over the fence?"

The CSO stopped the feed, went back to when the blob first appeared, and slowed it to half normal speed. It was impossible to tell where the thing had originated given the quality of the feed, the trees blocking the view, and the fact that the winds had been constantly shifting. But as we watched, the black blob rolled away, changing shape as it moved.

"Garbage bag," the CSO concluded. "Looks like the wind blew it away."

"It's moving fast," Bustamente noted. "Whatever's in it must be lightweight."

The colobus monkeys were small, but still weighed enough to anchor a trash bag, even in the relatively high winds that had rocked the metroplex the preceding night. As we continued to watch, the bag rolled toward the neighborhood behind the zoo, eventually rolling out of sight. We went on to watch the footage up to the time Camilla Bellafiore had reported Sarki missing. All we saw were employees and patrons coming and going from the zoo. The footage showed Greg Greer presumably leaving for a lunch break only two minutes before Camilla did the same, and also showed the two returning within three minutes of each other approximately an hour later. It seemed clear the two had met somewhere nearby for lunch. Still, though Camilla had carried a purse with her, neither of them had carried anything out of the zoo that was big enough to hold the missing monkey. Greer's coat had hung open, so he couldn't have had the monkey tucked inside. Camilla's coat, though zipped, was formfitting, leaving no room for her to hide even the smallest of primates.

When we'd finished watching this footage, Bustamente asked to see the footage I'd viewed before, from the day the birds disappeared.

"No problem." The CSO tapped a few keys and slid the mouse around before clicking it.

Once again, I found myself watching the bundled-up zoo guests come and go on the blustery day, Landis rolling his bin out the entrance and emptying the trash cans until he rolled out of sight. He rolled back onto the screen a few minutes later.

After finishing the relevant footage, the detective frowned. "The video tells us little, if anything."

I was afraid he'd say that, though I'd hoped he'd notice something we hadn't. Making sure we'd left no stone unturned, I said, "We've looked all around the monkey area, but could Sarki be hidden somewhere else in the zoo? Maybe someone took him out of his habitat and stowed him somewhere temporarily with the intention of sneaking him out later."

The CSO was a step ahead of me. "I had the same thought. I posted a man at the gate the instant we learned the monkey was missing. Before guests leave, he's checking all wagons, strollers, and large bags." That explained the security officer I'd seen at the visitor exit on my way in earlier. The CSO said he'd also posted team members at the other exit points, which were used for deliveries or garbage collection. "If Sarki is still on the property, he won't be leaving. We'll find him."

Bustamente handed the man his business card. "Let me know if you do."

We'd done as much as we could for the time being and walked out to the parking lot together, the illumination from the lights overhead casting our distorted shadows on the pavement. Bustamente followed me to my cruiser to powwow before he headed back to the station.

Once we were seated with Brigit in the back and the heater warming up, he simply said, "Give me your thoughts."

There were all sorts of ways to approach an investigation like this, but when analyzing a crime I tended to ask myself three basic questions—who, why, and how. Who could have committed the crime? Why would someone commit the particular crime? And how had the perpetrator done it? The questions were interrelated. Sometimes the *who* would tell you *why*, or the *why* or *how* could tell you *who*. At the moment, we hadn't yet figured out how the monkey had been removed from the habitat. That left me to ponder *who* and *why*, questions which we'd danced around already.

"Someone either wants to keep Sarki as a pet or sell him for money. Presumably Danny Landis could use the money. Janitors don't earn a lot and we already know he stole from the hospital he worked at before. We could try to figure out if Camilla Bellafiore or Greg Greer is in some type of financial trouble. The person who took him, or who would buy him, could be either an exotic-animal collector or part of the underground wild-animal trade. It's worth a visit to pet stores and private zoos; people known to collect theses types of animals."

Texas had some of the most permissive laws in the country regarding private ownership of wild animals, so big cats and other exotic species could be found across the state, often in substandard enclosures and conditions. In several instances, the animals had escaped and mauled or killed children and adults. Frankly, I had no idea why anyone would want a big cat for a pet. It was painful enough when Zoe traipsed across my chest while I was asleep in bed, and she only weighed eight pounds. I couldn't imagine how much it would hurt to have a tiger stand on your boobs, even a baby one. Not to mention the cost of tiger chow and the huge litter box you'd need. In addition to people who kept wild animals in their backyards, facilities calling themselves "zoos" were often unaccredited and operated as if Texas were still the Wild West, allowing visitors to interact with wild creatures. It was an incredibly dangerous practice, for both the people and the animals.

"We should look into anyone in the area with an arrest for illegal wildlife trafficking," I added. "It can't hurt to run a search online to see if anyone's posted hyacinth macaws or a colobus monkey for sale, or posted pictures of a bird or monkey they recently acquired."

"Good strategy," the detective said. "Of course I've come to expect that from you, Officer Luz."

My cheeks flushed with pride. "Aw, shucks, Detective. You made me blush."

"Now I'm going to make you *work*." Bustamente gestured for me to start my cruiser. "Let's pay a visit to Danny Landis together. If that doesn't solve the case, you'll check out the pet stores and zoos, and talk to anyone in the area who's been connected with wildlife trafficking. I'll interview Greer's and Bellafiore's supervisors and coworkers. I'll let the captain know I've commandeered you to help me on this case. We'll circle back soon."

Once again, he'd informally deputized me as a junior detective. Not that he'd get any complaints from me. Chasing down clues was much more fun than writing traffic tickets and dealing with domestic disputes. If I could save the birds or monkey in the process, all the better.

By that time it was nearing seven o'clock. Assuming Landis had worked a normal daytime schedule, he should be home by now. While I drove out of the lot, Bustamente pulled up Landis's address on my laptop and plugged it into the GPS. His house was in east Fort Worth, just five miles and less than a fifteen-minute drive from the zoo. We admired the holiday light displays along the way.

Bustamente clucked his tongue at a young boy in a yard who was treating an inflatable Santa as a punching bag. "You'll be arresting that kid someday."

I chose to remain hopeful. "Maybe not. Maybe he'll work out his issues."

The detective cast me a soft smile that was half admiration, half pity. "Not completely jaded yet, are you?"

"I hope I'll never be." If I didn't think the people I arrested could turn their lives around, that my job was more than pushing people through a revolving door, I'd have to quit. That said, I harbored no blind optimism. Thanks to educational and training programs, the recidivism rates in Texas had declined to around twenty percent within the first three years after a convict's release. That meant a lot of ex-cons managed to remain out of prison. Some of them were probably getting away with crimes, but others had gotten their act together, right? Even so, the numbers indicated that one in five former inmates could be expected to reoffend. Problem was, I had no way of knowing which type of ex-con Landis was.

We pulled up to the house and looked it over. It was tiny for a single-family home, around a thousand square feet, I'd say. The exterior paint was a white that had faded to an almost-gray. A small porch stood before the front door, a rusty aluminum carport at the end of the cracked concrete drive. *Could be better. Could be worse.* Who was I to judge? The house I'd grown up in looked like a before picture in a home improvement magazine. With five kids and both limited time and income, my parents had to let some things slide.

I retrieved Brigit from the back and the three of us went to the door. Bustamente knocked and instinctively turned himself at an angle to make himself a smaller target. I did the same. You never knew when someone might be armed.

The woman who answered the door was, in fact, armed—with a potato masher. Evidently we'd interrupted her dinner preparations. She stiffened when she realized it was law enforcement on her porch. We could hear the sounds of a sitcom playing on a television inside, see a small boy playing with a wooden train set on the floor, see the top of a man's head poking up over a recliner facing away from the door.

"Hello," the detective said, his tone calm and polite. "May we speak to Mr. Landis, please?"

The woman heaved a heavy sigh before turning back and calling out to the man in the chair. "Danny! It's for you."

The head turned and Danny Landis's face popped up over the back of the chair. His eyes narrowed when he spotted me. "I'm gonna have to put you down, boy," he said, his head disappearing as he leaned forward. Though I'd thought he'd been talking to a child, I realized I'd been mistaken when a lanky black-and-white tuxedo cat circled around the recliner, swishing his tail, annoyed we'd interrupted his cuddle time. The feline froze when he spotted Brigit in the doorway, then took off like a rocket down the hall. Landis pulled the lever to lower the footrest, climbed out of the recliner, and circled around, too, walking to the door. "What's going on?"

The detective didn't beat around the bush. "There's another animal missing from the zoo." He hadn't specified that the missing animal was a monkey, probably to see if Landis would inadvertently tip his hand by indicating he knew which animal was missing.

"Another bird?" Landis asked.

"No," Bustamente replied.

Landis's forehead furrowed. "Who is it, then?"

His phrasing caught my attention. Most people thought of animals as "whats," not "whos." His words seemed to reveal a connection with the animals, a respect for other species. Of course most people who worked around animals quickly developed an appreciation of their individuality. Apparently this appreciation applied even if one's job was to clean up after them.

"A primate," the detective said, his answer still somewhat vague. After all, the zoo housed a number of primates. Bonobos. Golden-headed lion tamarins. Gorillas. Orangutans. Gibbons.

Landis shook his head and gazed down for a moment before looking back up at us, his eyes narrowed. "You think I had something to do with it, don't you? That's why you're here." He gave his head a quick, angry jerk, as if he could toss the thought away. He stared me down. "I told you before, I'm not trying to go back to prison. I'm trying to keep it together. Whatever happened, I had nothing to do with it."

"Okay," the detective said. "Then tell me where you were today."

"Pounding the pavement!" Landis snapped. "Trying to find a full-time job. Like I told her before"—he cut his eyes to indicate me before returning his focus to the detective—"nobody wants to hire an ex-con."

Bustamente went on to ask him several questions. Did he maintain a relationship with anyone who worked at the zoo? Did anyone ever approach him about stealing an animal? Had he been back to the zoo since he'd been fired?

His answers were "no," "no," and "Yes, you already know that 'cause Officer Luz saw me there a few days ago."

"Look," Landis said, "I'll do whatever it takes to prove I had nothing to do with any animal thefts." He waved us in. "Come search my house. I'll give you my car keys and you can search that, too." He pulled his cell phone out of his pocket. "Look at my call records. I didn't talk to no one from the zoo or anywhere else about stealing animals."

As long as he was being so cooperative, we might as

well take advantage of it, right? Of course it occurred to me that his cooperation might be an attempt to throw us off track. Maybe he'd taken Sarki, but knew there was no evidence of the theft around his home or on his phone. After all, most criminals bought burner phones and tossed them afterward to destroy the evidence.

We searched his house, including the attic and the rusty metal lawn shed out back. Ditto for his last-decade SUV and his wife's sedan. Though we found some black-and-white fur, the length told us it likely belonged to the family cat, not the missing colobus monkey. Still, we rounded some up to take to the lab for analysis. We collected all of the phone numbers in his contacts list and noted in his call logs.

"Do you have another phone?" Bustamente asked him.

Landis pursed his lips sourly. "No. I don't have a burner. Never have had one. No need."

As we left, Bustamente turned back on the porch to thank Landis. "We appreciate you giving us this information and letting us take a look around."

"You're wasting your time," he snapped, "but whatever will get you off my back."

We headed across the yard. As we climbed back into the cruiser, Landis called out, "Can you tell me now who's missing?"

Bustamente and I exchanged glances, and he nodded to me.

"Sarki," I called over the top of my car.

Landis's mouth fell open. "The black-and-white monkey?" He shook his head. "Damn. I liked that little guy."

EIGHTEEN
CAT SCAT

Brigit

Brigit had followed Megan and Detective Bustamente around the house as they'd searched it. The cat who had run off earlier was curious what they were doing. He sneakily followed them, too, peeking around corners, scurrying off every time Brigit turned to look at him.

They came across the cat's litter box in the bathroom. Brigit would never want to be a cat. They were useless creatures as far as she could tell. But she did envy their litter boxes. She had to relieve herself outside, no matter what the weather. It wasn't fun to pop a squat in the pouring rain.

She'd heard the soft patter of the cat's paws as he snuck up behind them again. *One . . . two . . . three!* Brigit whipped her head around. The instant her eyes met the cat's, he'd skittered backward, banged into the wall in the hallway, and ran off. *Heh-heh.*

NINETEEN
SANTA DAD

The Poacher

With cash in his pocket and the perfect presents in his arms, the Poacher felt like the cock of the walk as he snaked through the department store that evening. He slowed when he saw a group of men gathered around a big-screen television, watching basketball, the Dallas Mavericks versus the Houston Rockets.

He stopped at the edge of the group to watch. While half of the men seemed to be rooting for one team and the other half seemed to be rooting for the other, the Poacher didn't really care who won. But he did notice how nice and clear the picture was on the television, much better than the resolution on the cheap TV in their living room now. *Maybe I should buy one of these babies.*

Though he didn't know any of these men, he enjoyed their company. The camaraderie had been the only good part about prison. If you took away the razor wire and armed guards in the towers, it had been a lot like the summer camps of his boyhood. Cinder-block housing. Bunk beds. Group showers. Dirty jokes that he sometimes didn't quite understand.

When the Rockets scored, the guy next to him whooped

and raised both his hands for a double high five. The Poacher set his gifts down on the floor at his feet so he could oblige. *Slap!*

Minutes later, with the score tied and only twelve seconds left on the clock, the game went to commercial. The men around him threw up their hands and hollered and grumbled in frustration.

"Come on!" yelled one of them.

"You gotta be kidding me!" barked another.

Another merely shook his head. "Their timing sucks."

A series of commercials played, all of them for products normally purchased by men. Beer. Boner pills. Pickup trucks. Foot powder. The final commercial was a quick teaser for the evening news, coming up after the game. After the attractive anchorwoman piqued viewers' interest with quick sound bites about politics and the weather, Sarki's photo came up on the screen. His brown eyes seemed to see the Poacher through the screen, to ask *How could you?* As Sarki's photo shrank to fill only the upper right corner of the screen, the anchor looked at him accusingly. "Where could Sarki be now? Stay tuned for an update on this heartbreaking investigation."

The monkey's eyes had been bad enough, but now he heard his little girl's voice echo in his head. *"You're gonna be good this time. Right, Daddy?"*

As he turned to walk away, the game popped back up on the screen.

"Dude!" one of the men called after him. "You're leaving *now*? You're going to miss the end of the game!"

The Poacher didn't care. He felt as if the game were already over for him.

TWENTY
ZOOS, POOS, BUT NO CLUES

Megan

After speaking with Landis, I spent the rest of my shift trying to identify illegal wildlife traffickers living in the area. It wasn't easy. While there were a number of people who'd been convicted of the crime, they weren't required to register a current address with the government like sex offenders were. Animal welfare advocates had suggested a registry should be created for animal abusers, too, to protect pets. *I'd be all for that.*

At any rate, it was up to me to match the names of the convicted to driver's license records, vehicle registrations, or other data that would indicate their current address. What's more, it was possible that people convicted or arrested in other states had since relocated to north Texas and begun to dabble again in their nefarious trade here. Unless I searched every state's criminal database and compared the names of the convicted to the Texas records, I might miss someone. But with the limited time I had, I decided to restrict my research to those convicted of animal trafficking in Texas and the four adjacent states—Louisiana, Oklahoma, Arkansas, and New Mexico.

Unfortunately, the people who'd been brought in for unlawfully trading in animals seemed to have scattered to the winds on their release from prison. A couple had likely returned to their home countries south of the border. Three had landed themselves back in jail for other offenses, and remained incarcerated. By the end of my shift, I was left with only two possibilities, one here in Fort Worth and another a four-hour drive down the road in San Antonio.

The latter guy, Bruno Molina, had been convicted of buying reptiles that had been smuggled into the country from Brazil. He'd resold them in the San Antonio area. One of the iguanas turned out to be sick and succumbed to his illness. The customer demanded a refund, but Bruno stupidly refused. He'd been arrested after the customer reported the incident to the local police. Molina had been released from prison eight months ago. While he certainly could have resumed his despicable business and expanded his stock-in-trade to include macaws and monkeys, it seemed questionable whether he'd be operating in Fort Worth, over 250 miles from home. Moreover, I'd found no reports of animals missing in the San Antonio area. His previous MO didn't involve stealing animals, either.

Still, I hadn't ruled Danny Landis out entirely as a suspect. I pondered the possibility of Landis and Molina being in cahoots. To ensure I didn't dismiss Molina too soon, I consulted the man's criminal record to see where he'd served his sentence. He'd been assigned to the Darrington Unit in Brazoria County, south of Houston. Landis, however, had done his time at the Telford Unit, which sat in Bowie County in northeast Texas. I reviewed their driver's license records back to inception. Landis had obtained his first license at sixteen right here in Fort Worth. His address on every license since had noted a north Texas address. Molina was issued his first driver's license at seventeen. Though he'd moved about the San Antonio area, every address was in the south Texas city or one of its suburbs. In other words, the two men had never lived in proximity to each other and it seemed unlikely they would have crossed paths.

The local guy, Vaughn Waggoner, had been convicted six years ago of smuggling both parrots and pot into the country from Mexico. His illegal activities had been arranged and enabled by a border patrol agent who was on the take and repeatedly let Waggoner pass through the border crossing without a detailed vehicle inspection. Waggoner might still be smuggling his illicit wares had the agent not suffered a sudden heart attack on the job and been transported to a hospital for treatment. When Waggoner arrived at the crossing, he discovered his coconspirator had been replaced by another border patrol officer, who in turn discovered a mother lode of wacky weed and feathered fowl in Waggoner's trunk.

Though Waggoner had been arrested and convicted, his attorney had negotiated a reduced sentence in return for Waggoner's guilty plea and providing testimony against the corrupt agent. On recovering from his heart attack, the border patrol agent was released from the hospital and taken directly to jail to face smuggling and corruption charges.

Both Waggoner's driver's license photo and his mug shot showed a chubby, cherub-faced guy with curly blond hair. But, despite his appearance, he was clearly no angel.

It was the middle of the night when I finally logged out of the computer and roused Brigit, who'd fallen asleep at my feet. We headed toward the front doors of the station. While part of me was exhausted from worry and the long shift, another part of me couldn't wait to confront Waggoner and find out if he was behind Sarki's kidnapping and the disappearance of the hyacinth macaws. Despite the late hour, I decided to swing by Waggoner's place. I couldn't go banging on his door in the middle of the night without concrete evidence of his involvement, but, at worst, I'd waste a little time. And maybe, just maybe, I'd spot something that would help bring Sarki and the macaws home.

Brigit and I climbed back into our cruiser and headed to the apartment complex where Waggoner lived. It was an older complex on Thornhill, comprising two long, rectangular two-story buildings standing parallel at either side of a pothole-ridden parking lot. The building bore a combination stucco-and-stone façade with dark green paint on the railings and doors. A vinyl banner attached to the upstairs railing near the street lured potential tenants with the promise of ALL BILLS PAID!

I cruised slowly down the length of the first building, looking for unit A8. Not an easy feat when the majority of the letters and numbers were missing from the doors. *There it is, on the back corner.* Waggoner occupied a first-floor, end-unit apartment. While many of his neighbors had strung multicolored Christmas lights in their windows or along their door frames, he displayed no holiday decorations. His windows were dimly lit, though, with light coming from inside, behind the curtains. Looked like he was still up. *Good.* I wouldn't have to wait until morning to talk to him.

I pulled into an empty spot at the end of the lot, retrieved my partner, and headed to Waggoner's door. His sporty red Mazda3 sat in the space in front of his apartment. Though his door and windows were closed, I could hear sounds coming from inside. People talking and laughing, loud enough for me to hear them but not so loud a neighbor would complain or call the cops. I rapped softly on the door.

From inside came a man's voice. "That must be X-Ray with our tacos."

"About time!" said another. "I'm starving!"

These guys were about to be sorely disappointed. I wasn't X-Ray and I came bearing no tacos.

The door swung open and I found myself face-to-face with the chubby cherub. He was dressed in jeans and a bright red hoodie. On the couch behind him sat another, equally chubby guy, though the second guy had darker skin. On the coffee table in front of the couch sat several stacks of bills, separated by denomination. Next to the bills sat open boxes of brownies, cookies, and gummy candies, all individually wrapped in plastic. A half-dozen mason jars filled with greenish-brown leafy material sat on the table, too. I had no idea whether Vaughn was still dealing in contraband parrots, but it was clear he'd continued to market marijuana.

A huge orangey-brown fluff ball lay on its side between the coffee table and the door. Judging from the color of his fur and his square face, I'd say the dog was primarily chow chow. Judging from his size, I'd say some mastiff was mixed in with the chow. And, judging from the exposed anatomy, I'd say the dog was an unneutered male. He raised his head and eyed me. *Uh-oh.* I didn't want to have to hurt the dog. He had nothing to do with his owner's criminal activity. Sadly, dogs were sometimes shot by officers who misread their body language and didn't know how to handle them. Fortunately, thanks to the efforts of the Texas Humane Legislation Network and its group of dedicated activists, a bill had been passed in 2015 mandating that law enforcement officers in Texas receive training in canine encounters. As part of my standard police training, I'd been taught how to read a dog's body language and react accordingly, deescalating the situation and minimizing the need for lethal force. The number of dogs shot by law enforcement in the state decreased dramatically after the training was put into effect. Of course I'd learned lots more about dog behavior in my specialized K-9 team training, too.

This dog hadn't raised his hackles, bared his teeth, or even growled, so there were no signs he was about to attack. Even so, it was best not to look him directly in the eye. I averted my gaze, but kept an eye on him in my peripheral vision lest he decide to make a sudden lunge for me or Brigit. Luckily, he didn't seem the least bit concerned about the strangers at his door. Given the business the men seemed to be running from the apartment, there likely were unknown people coming to the door at all times of day and night. Nothing for him to get upset about. In fact, he lumbered upright, ambled over to stand at Vaughn's knee, and wagged his tail in greeting. He certainly wasn't living up to his bully-breed reputation.

Vaughn stared at me for several seconds before his mouth slowly dropped. "Uhhh . . . you're not X-Ray."

Slow reaction time? Bad case of the late-night munchies? This guy's been sampling his wares.

"Nope, not X-Ray," I told him. "Sorry to disappoint you." Not knowing whether there were other people or weapons in the apartment, I wasn't about to enter alone and put myself and Brigit at risk. That said, I wasn't about to let Vaughn shut the door, either. Best to keep him in my sights. I eased the steel toe of my tactical shoe over the threshold where it could serve as a doorstop, if necessary, and used my radio to call for immediate backup. I glanced from one of the men to the other. "Anyone else in the apartment besides you two and the dog?"

"No," Vaughn said. "Just us."

I hoped he was telling the truth. I'd been lied to and unpleasantly surprised before. I motioned with my hand. "Come on out, guys. You're under arrest."

Vaughn cocked his head. "For what?"

Seriously? I lifted my chin to indicate the coffee table. "For your illegal bake sale."

"We're not . . . uh . . . selling that stuff," he stammered. "We . . . uh . . . made them ourselves." He beamed, as if proud of the magnificent cover he'd come up with.

Yep, definitely stoned. "Planning to leave those cookies out for Santa?" The jolly old elf would crash his sleigh if he ate those cannabis cookies. Or maybe he'd park his sleigh somewhere and binge on the baked goods, shirk his gift-delivery duties and leave nice kids wondering why they'd ended up with empty stockings, whether being good all year had been worth it.

Vaughn's friend piled on. "They're Christmas presents. Homemade gifts are where it's at."

That might be true, but I had a hard time visualizing these two poring over Pinterest, looking for crafty gift ideas.

Vaughn added. "It's the thought that counts, you know."

"Oh, yeah? Then you should've put more thought into your lies." *How stupid do these guys think I am?* Or maybe the better question was, *How stoned are these idiots?* "I can see the labels on those cookies and brownies from here. There's marijuana in them."

Vaughn scowled. "You don't know that."

I looked down at my dog. "Is there pot in those brownies, girl?" I gave Brigit the order to scent for drugs, but kept her leash taut. Until my backup arrived, neither one of us was going into the apartment.

My partner lifted her snout and sniffed the air. Her nostrils twitched just once before she sat, staring at the items on the table, issuing her passive alert.

"See that?" I said. "She's alerting on your cookies." I

motioned again for them to step outside. "Come on out, you two. No more games."

"Wait!" Vaughn raised a palm. "Maybe we can work something out. Cops don't get paid much, right? I bet you could use some extra bank for Christmas." He raised hopeful brows.

"What are you suggesting?"

He gestured back to the table. "We could split that with you. Three ways."

"The cash?" I specified.

"Yeah."

"So you're saying if I don't arrest you, you'll give me a third of that money?"

"Yes. Jeez!" Vaughn rolled his eyes. "Do I have to spell it out for you?"

No, but you just spelled it out for my body camera. "Not gonna happen, buddy," I said. How anyone in law enforcement could be on the take was beyond me. *How do they look themselves in the mirror?* "Come outside, guys."

Vaughn took a step forward and the guy on the couch stood. But just when I thought this arrest would go down easy, Vaughn waved his dog out the door. "Get 'em, Sasquatch!"

The obedient dog trotted outside. As soon as the furry mutt crossed the threshold, Vaughn tried to slam the door shut. My steel-toed shoes did their job, both blocking the door and protecting my little piggies. Meanwhile, Brigit and Sasquatch exchanged butt sniffs and did that funny little circling dance dogs do when first meeting each other.

Vaughn's face contorted in confusion as he pulled the door open a few inches and tried to slam it again, meeting with no more success the second time.

I yanked my baton from my belt and flicked my wrist

to extend it. *Snap!* "Cut the crap!" I hollered. "And come out here with your hands up!"

Disregarding my demands, he tried a third time to slam the door. When again it failed to shut, he finally had the sense to look down and spotted my foot. He reared his foot back and mule-kicked my shoe, his heel meeting my toes, my female feet no match for his men's size twelves. Putting his entire body weight against the inside of the door, he slammed it again, getting the door closed before I could insert my foot or baton into the space. I went for the knob but heard the telltale *schwick* of the dead bolt hitting home. *Dang it!*

Headlights turned into the lot to my right. I shielded my eyes. *Is that my backup?* With the glare in my face, I couldn't tell. But as the car rolled toward me and my eyes adjusted, I could tell it wasn't a cruiser. Rather, it was a silver Ford Mustang with a thirtyish guy at the wheel and a Taco Bell bag in his passenger seat. *He must be X-Ray.* My eyes went to his license plate. When the guy saw me he hit the gas, careened around the row of parked cars, and zipped back out of the lot, leaving the sound of tires screeching and the smell of burned rubber in his wake. I pushed the talk button on my radio and told my fellow officers to be on the lookout for the vehicle, giving them the make, model, and plate number.

Lest Sasquatch run off or get upset by the melee that was likely to ensue, I led him over to my squad car and secured him in Brigit's compartment. He stood at the window, looking out, his warm breath fogging the cold glass. I hurried back to the apartment door. From behind it came the whirring grind of a garbage disposal interspersed with the *shushhh-shushhh* of a toilet flushing repeatedly. Vaughn and his houseguest were getting rid of the evidence. *My backup better get here soon!*

I twirled my baton while I waited. *Swish-swish-swish.* My wrist was nice and loose now in case I ended up in a wrestling match.

Headlights turned into the lot once again, this time accompanied by the flashing lights atop the patrol car. The cruiser jerked to a stop behind Vaughn's Mazda and Derek emerged, his expression smug. "You little ladies in over your head?"

I took a deep breath as I'd been taught in the anger-management class I'd been forced to take after Tasering Derek in the testicles, and whispered the calming mantra I'd borrowed from the Catholic Church and modified for my own purposes. "Peace be with me. Peace be with me."

Having quashed my urge to whack my former partner with my baton, I used it to point to the door. "We need to get in that apartment. Now."

Derek didn't ask why. He didn't care. He lived for this kind of thing. He drew his gun, turned sideways, and ran at the door shoulder-first, like he'd learned when playing football in high school. At the last second, he jumped so that his entire body weight, all two hundred-plus pounds of it, slammed against the door. *BAM!*

While the door didn't open, the framing pulled loose and a sliver of the interior light shined through at the edge. Derek backed up and made a second run for the door. This time, the top half of the door fell inward, the upper and middle hinges pulling loose from the frame, the dead bolt bending. Derek raised a leg and used the bottom of his shoe to kick the door the rest of the way in. The man was a pompous ass, but he was also a human battering ram. *Guess I have to take the bad with the good, huh?*

Derek stormed over the door and into the apartment. Brigit and I stepped over it and followed him. Vaughn stood at the kitchen sink, his back to us. The garbage disposal continued to whirr and the faucet, which was running full blast, splashed water all over Vaughn, the countertops, and the floor as he shoved brownies and cookies down the drain. More water ran over the lip of the sink and onto the floor. *Looks like the idiot clogged the pipes.*

Derek stopped at the doorway to the galley kitchen, his gun at the ready, and hollered, "Hands up!"

Vaughn didn't raise his hands, though. Instead, he grabbed a wooden spoon and jabbed it into the water in an attempt to dislodge whatever had stuck in the drain. Derek rushed forward and slid on the tile, which had become an indoor Slip 'N Slide. Momentum carried him forward until he slid into Vaughn's back and slammed the guy hard against the sink.

Having no doubt Derek could wrangle the suspect into submission, I took off down the hall, looking for the other man. He'd locked himself in the bathroom, but there was no need for Derek to bust down this door. The apartment building was old and cheaply built. I could take down the flimsy interior door myself. Rather than risk a shoulder injury, which could impede my ability to unwrap my Christmas presents, I went straight for a kick, turning sideways and putting the full force of my thigh into it. *BAM!* The hollow door splintered on my first try. *Those squats are really paying off.* I reached through the hole I'd made, unlocked the door, and shoved it open. Vaughn's cohort stood over the toilet, plunger in hand, going at the clogged commode like a pioneer in a butter-churning contest.

I brandished my baton. "Drop the plunger and put your hands up!" Brigit backed me up with a *BOW-WOW* that echoed in the tiny space and said *Do what my partner says or I'll bite you in the ass!*

In seconds, the guy was cuffed and kneeling on the

threadbare carpet in the hall, Brigit standing guard over him. I turned back to look into the bathroom. *Holy heck!* The room had fared no better than the kitchen. The bathtub, toilet, and sink were all clogged with the marijuana, soggy baked goods, and plastic wrap. The moron hadn't had the sense to take the plastic wrap off before trying to flush the baked goods away.

I returned to the living room, dragging my charge along with me. After instructing him to sit against the wall, I addressed Vaughn, who was also on the floor. "You're going to jail, obviously. Is there someone who can take care of the dog for you?"

"My mother," Vaughn said resignedly.

"What's her number?" As he rattled it off, I dialed it on my cell phone and activated the speaker since his hands were cuffed behind him.

A woman's froggy voice came over the line. "Hello?"

"Hi, Mom," Vaughn said. "It's me."

"It's the middle of the night, son! What's wrong?"

"I need you to come to my apartment and get Sasquatch. You'll have to take care of him for a while."

"Why?" she asked.

Vaughn cut angry eyes up at me. "I've been arrested."

"Again?" She muttered a curse. "What did you do this time?"

"Nothing!" he snapped.

"Does it have something to do with all those trips you've made to Colorado?"

"Shut up, Mom! The cops can hear you!"

Derek and I exchanged glances and chuckled, a rare bonding moment for the two of us. Looked like Vaughn had given up on international smuggling and was now smuggling cannabis products into Texas from colorful Colorado. *But is he still dabbling in the animal trade?*

I decided to ask him point-blank. "You still smuggling animals?"

"No," he spat. "I haven't done that since I went to prison."

"So you don't have anything to do with the monkey that's missing from the zoo?"

His befuddled look appeared genuine. "There's a monkey missing from the zoo?"

One of our fellow officers showed up with Vaughn's taco-toting friend in tow. "X-Ray" turned out to be Xavier Reyes, who, according to a quick search online, already had a prior arrest for marijuana possession, though in a small amount. He was currently on probation. Given his association with Vaughn Waggoner and the drugs we'd found here tonight, he could expect his probation to be revoked.

A thorough search of Vaughn's apartment and the men's vehicles yielded nothing that pointed to his involvement in Sarki's kidnapping. Vaughn's computer and phone would still need to be searched, but I sensed that his animal smuggling days were, in fact, behind him.

After Derek took the men to the station for booking, I retrieved Sasquatch from my car and brought him into the apartment to wait for Vaughn's mother to come get him. I pulled a couple of liver treats from my pockets and fed them to Brigit. She'd never let me hear the end of it if I'd done otherwise. After all, she'd performed services here and deserved to be paid for them. I fed another to the chow to reward him for his cooperation.

Half an hour later, after handing his leash over to Vaughn's mother, I gave Sasquatch a nice scratch behind the ears. "Be a good boy for grandma."

"No worries there," she said. "He's always an angel."

She frowned. "Wish I could say the same for my son. I have half a mind to return his Christmas gifts to the store."

My subsequent visits to the area's pet stores and small, mom-and-pop petting zoos had led to me inadvertently stepping in a pile of pig poo, but had yielded no clues as to the whereabouts of Sarki, Fabiana, or Fernando. The only good news was that most of the people I'd spoken with had expressed genuine concern about their welfare and promised to contact me if they heard anything. I'd searched extensively online, too, looking for anyone offering a colobus monkey or hyacinth macaw for sale, or someone who had recently acquired one of the animals. Nothing had turned up.

My original searches only returned sites in English. However, it was possible the animals could have been smuggled out of the United States and sold. Even if there was a site that mentioned the animals, if the content was written in another language it would not have come up. Realizing this, and that Spanish was spoken in virtually every country to the south, I found the Spanish words for colobus monkey and hyacinth macaw and searched for those. A few links popped up with recent references to a *mono colobo* or a *guacamayo jacinto*. I forwarded those to Detective Bustamente, who spoke Spanish fluently. Unfortunately, he'd found nothing helpful in the links. Though Canada was much farther away and French was spoken only by a minority of people there, I nonetheless searched for *singe colobus* and *ara jacinthe*. I got *rien du tout,* nothing at all.

The lab issued their report. The only fingerprints the crime scene tech had lifted from the employee areas of the colobus monkey enclosure belonged to Dr. Greer, Camilla

Bellafiore, and two other zookeepers responsible for caring for the primates. All four had voluntarily offered their prints for comparison. Of course they all had to know that their prints would be expected to be found at the site and would not incriminate them. The current custodial staff had also offered their prints, but none were found at the habitat, probably because they wore gloves when cleaning. I'd driven by Dr. Greer's and Camilla Bellafiore's homes both while I was on the clock and a couple times on my own when I was off duty. Though I spotted Dr. Greer's car in Camilla's driveway one evening, confirming my suspicion that the two might be personally involved, I saw no evidence of a monkey at either of their homes.

By Christmas Eve, I had crossed all of the area pet shops and unaccredited zoos off my list but one. I drove with Brigit out to a property thirty miles west of the city, just past the town of Weatherford. Though the place called itself a sanctuary and had obtained nonprofit status from the IRS, it was immediately clear the facility's owners ran the place to make money and that the animals' welfare was secondary to the bottom line. Before going to the property, I stopped on a small rise nearby and used my binoculars to take a sneak peek at the place. A pair of tigers were kept in a chain-link enclosure no bigger than my backyard at home, their shelter cobbled together from spare plywood. A single, lonely kangaroo stared forlornly out at the horizon from a flimsy fence of lightweight mesh better suited for a chicken coop. One well-placed kick and the marsupial could be on the loose. A trio of ostriches strutted around on a dusty patch, pecking at the hard ground in search of food.

Though plenty of dung sullied the enclosures, no one was working to clean it up. In fact, the only staff who appeared to be on the site was a corpulent man sporting an unkempt beard, scuffed boots, and dusty overalls. He sat in an open garden shed that served as the ticket booth. I stowed the binoculars in the cruiser's glove compartment, drove down to the place, and parked under a big sign that read WILD 'N WOOLY ANIMAL SANCTUARY. I left Brigit in the car. The tigers were already pacing in their inadequate enclosure and eyeing a toddler standing nearby. The big cats might think my partner looked like a yummy snack, too.

As he collected their entry fees from his makeshift booth near the road, the big, grizzly man who seemed to be singlehandedly running the place informed a teenaged couple who came through the gate that they could get their picture taken with a tiger cub for twenty extra bucks. *The practice ought to be outlawed.* People had been killed taking a photo with what they wrongfully assumed was a wholly tamed beast. In reality, a creature's wild nature could never be fully conquered by man. Luckily, the couple declined, probably unable to afford the photo fee. They did, however, buy a bag of sunflower seeds to feed the ostriches.

As they headed into the place, I stepped up to the shed and feigned friendliness as I addressed the man sitting inside. "Hello, there. How's your day going?"

He jabbed a button on the laptop sitting on the TV tray next to him, pausing the movie he'd been watching. "Jus' fine. What can I do you for?"

Though his wording and tone were relaxed, his eyes were wary. With good reason. The research I'd performed before coming out here told me the guy had been fined twice for the shoddy way he operated. The government should've put him out of business.

"Just wondering if anyone has contacted you about a colobus monkey that's up for sale."

He sat up straight, the steely wariness in his eyes replaced by an excited gleam. "There's a monkey for sale? Hell, I'd love to buy a monkey. How much they askin'?"

Sheesh. "The monkey was stolen. From the Fort Worth Zoo."

Like the ostriches, this guy must've hidden his head in the sand. Sarki's face had been all over the news since he'd disappeared. People had been calling the FWPD headquarters, wanting to know whether the monkey had been found. A small group had even held a candlelight vigil for him in the zoo's parking lot. Frankie and I had joined them, sending up a prayer for Sarki's safe return. Frankie knew how worried I'd been, and we figured appealing to a higher power couldn't hurt. The organizers of the vigil passed out safety pins twined with black and white ribbons, the color of the colobus monkey. One had been pinned to my lapel since.

Given the man's response, it was clear he hadn't been approached about buying the monkey. I handed him my business card. "If you hear anything about a colobus monkey or a hyacinth macaw being on the market, please let me know."

"Is there a reward?"

Again, *sheesh.* Wasn't doing the right thing and feeling good about it reward enough? "You'd probably get your picture in the paper, maybe be interviewed on the news."

He grunted, but took my card and tucked it into a pocket on the chest of his overalls. He turned his attention back to the movie streaming on the laptop in front of him. Looked like I could cross this place off my list, too.

Having finished the parts of the investigation that Bustamente had delegated to me, I drove to the station for an update on his progress.

When I rapped on his door frame, he looked up from

his cluttered desk. "Take a seat," he said, gesturing to a chair facing his desk. As I flopped down in the chair, he read my body language. "No luck?"

"None. Nobody in the area seems to have heard anything. I've repeatedly searched online, too. I've seen nothing about a colobus monkey or hyacinth macaw for sale, or being added to a collection or exhibit."

The detective released a long, frustrated breath. "I checked with Sharon Easley again today. She's hasn't heard from anyone in her zoo circles. None of the other zoo employees shed light on the case, either. Nobody who knows Camilla Bellafiore or Greg Greer thinks they are remotely capable of such a heinous crime."

"What about the fur we found in Landis's car and house?" I asked. "What did the lab say about it?"

"They compared it to a sample of the colobus monkey fur and the fur from Landis's cat. It's all feline."

Unless new evidence surfaced, Danny Landis seemed to be a dead end, too.

Bustamente leaned his head back against the headrest and stared up at the ceiling. "The chief isn't going to be happy to hear we've hit a wall. He's getting heat from the public and the press."

I rested my face in my hands. "Where could that monkey be?"

"Who knows," Bustamente replied. "He could be on display in a dentist office in Shanghai by now."

Ugh. The thought made me feel cold and empty. I could only hope that, wherever Sarki was, he didn't feel the same way.

TWENTY-ONE
SILENT NIGHT

Brigit

Brigit wasn't sure why, but her partner had seemed intent on introducing her to every captive animal in the Fort Worth area. Over the last few days, Megan had taken her to all sorts of pet stores and petting zoos. Not that Brigit was complaining. She liked other animals. She'd enjoyed carousing with the puppies at that one shop even though a couple of them had nipped her playfully with their sharp teeth. Still, having once been a prisoner at the city's animal pound, she felt sorry for the animals who didn't have a comfortable home with a loving person like Megan to feed them, and cuddle them, and do their bidding.

At the final store they'd visited, Megan bought Brigit a box of peanut butter dog biscuits. *Yummy!* After wolfing one down herself, Brigit nudged the box, insisting Megan offer one to each of the three dogs up for adoption at the front. They crunched away at the biscuits and, when they finished, thanked Brigit with a wag of their tails.

Megan was quiet on their ride home from the station tonight. At home, she said nothing as she washed up, changed into her pajamas, and slid into bed. Brigit knew

Megan's silence was not a good sign. Her partner was upset about something. Brigit wished she knew what it was. All she could do was curl up next to Megan in bed and give her a wet kiss on the cheek to let her know she cared. *Slup!*

TWENTY-TWO
FA LA LAWBREAKER

The Poacher

The kids woke at the butt crack of dawn on Christmas morning, squealing and shouting as they discovered the gifts Santa had left in their stockings.

Vicki moaned from her place in the bed beside him, not unlike how she'd moaned last night when he'd "stuffed her stocking." After the kids had gone to bed, he'd surprised her with an early present of her favorite perfume. She'd slipped her clothes off, slapped a bow on her bare butt, and summoned him to her bed with a crooked finger.

Knowing he was still on thin ice with her, he sat up. "I'll start the coffee."

"Wake me when it's ready." With that, she rolled over to go back to sleep.

Torn wrapping paper, colorful bows, and ribbon covered the living room floor, the kids happily playing with their new toys. Well, all but the biggest toy.

The Poacher gestured to the rocking horse in the corner. "Harper, aren't you going to ride the horsey Santa brought you?"

She made a face. "I'm too old for a rocking horse, Daddy."

His heart splintered. Harper had been thrilled when Santa had given her a rocking horse three years ago, then later devastated when the police seized it as evidence he had stolen from the Toys "R" Us store he'd worked at. He wondered if she remembered, hoped to God she didn't. Regardless, he'd sworn to himself back then that he'd make it up to her. *Maybe some things can't ever be fixed.*

He padded into the kitchen, got the coffeepot going, and rounded up a rusty frying pan. "Who wants pancakes?"

His older son hollered, "I do! I do! I do!"

The younger one looked up to his brother and attempted to say the same thing but it came out, "Ah-doo. Ah-doo."

Harper raised hopeful brows. "Can you make the smiley-face kind? Pleeeeeease?"

She's still my little girl. "Anything for you, squirt."

After breakfast, the whole family cuddled on the couch to watch the same holiday movies they had already seen a hundred times. It was like the warden and his John Travolta movies all over again. Harper had squeezed in between him and Vicki. When the third show ended, Harper's patience ran out.

She looked up at him. "Can we open our presents now?"

He gestured to all of the new toys lying around. "What about the things Santa brought you? Tired of them already?"

"We'll play with them more later," Harper said. "Please?"

Vicki glanced at the clock on the cable box. "It's not even noon yet."

"I don't care!" Harper said. She looked up at the Poacher and, seeming to sense he was on her side, began pumping her fists. "Pres-ents! Pres-ents! Pres-ents!"

Her brothers joined in, the youngest shouting gibberish. "Pez-iss! Pez-iss!"

"All right." Vicki waved a hand toward the wrapped presents under the tree. "Harper, you pass them out."

Harper was more than happy to provide present-delivery services, picking up each gift, reading the name on the tag, and stacking them before their intended recipient. When her little brother started pulling on the paper, she wagged a finger in front of his face. "Not yet. You have to wait until they're all passed out."

His lip began to quiver and he was on the verge of blubbering when Harper leaned down and gave him a hug. "It's okay."

His expression was confused now, but at least he wasn't going to cry.

When all of the gifts had been distributed, Harper took her place on the rug. "On your mark!" she cried. "Get set! Go!"

The air filled with the sounds of paper tearing and children screaming.

Vicki reached into his gift bag and pulled out the lace teddy he'd bought her. When she realized what it was, she shoved it back into the bag before the kids could see. She sent a coy look his way. "Is this for me or for *you*?"

"Both of us," he replied with a wink.

Harper opened the small box he'd wrapped for her and held up the gift inside, her eyes wide and mouth gaping. "My own cell phone!"

His little girl was thrilled. His heart warmed. Finally, he was showing her he could be the kind of father she deserved, a good father who provided well for his family. *Looks like things can be fixed after all.*

Vicki was less delighted. She turned a frown on him. "What does a seven-year-old need with a cell phone?"

"Aw, c'mon," he said. "Lots of kids her age have them. Besides, she's always asking me questions I don't have the answers to. If she has her own phone, she can look them up herself." Maybe he could've answered more of his daughter's questions if he'd spent less of his time in prison working out and more of it reading.

Vicki frowned again, but it was a smaller frown this time and her tone had softened a little. "I still say it's ridiculous."

He returned his attention to Harper, basking in her delight until she suddenly froze. Her smile faded and she turned to him, her eyes lit with worry, and said something that hurt worse than the time he'd been shanked in the prison shower. "Do we get to keep our presents this time, Daddy?"

TWENTY-THREE
ABLAZE IN A MANGER

Megan

I woke on Christmas morning hoping Santa would have filled my stocking with clear and convincing evidence as to who had taken the macaws and Sarki. Unfortunately, he hadn't. In fact, he hadn't put anything in it at all. Frankie had, though. She'd filled it with a bottle of jasmine-scented bubble bath, a bag of fancy dark roast coffee, and a pair of gel inserts for my tactical shoes.

"That's what you get for complaining about your feet hurting after traffic duty," she teased.

I gave her a hug. The gifts were perfect and thoughtful. "You're the best roommate ever!"

In Brigit's stocking she'd put a fuzzy hedgehog squeaky toy, signing the attached tag from her cat Zoe. Brigit expressed her appreciation by taking the toy in her teeth and shaking it back and forth at warp speed, the hedgehog emitting a squeal with each shake. *Squee-squee-squee!*

Frankie reached into her stocking and pulled out the pair of rainbow-striped skating socks I'd bought for her. I'd also bought her a new derby helmet, a shiny white one spanned by a glittery rainbow to match the socks. She'd cracked her previous helmet when taking a particularly precarious tumble in a recent bout. I'd worried the damaged helmet would fail and she'd end up with a concussion.

She slid her feet into the socks and donned the helmet, turning to and fro in the living room to model them. "I'm so cute! But you know wearing a girlie helmet like this means everyone on the other teams will come after me, don't you?"

"Yep," I said, "and you'll love every second of it."

"Ah, you know me well." She performed a graceful pirouette and curtsy, before throwing out her bent elbows left and right in a derby improvisation. Like my K-9 partner, my roommate could be both sweet and scary.

Brigit had gotten Zoe a new fish-pole-style toy with a fuzzy, wiggly caterpillar dangling from the end. My stingy partner decided she wanted to keep it for herself and took the stick in her mouth. As Brigit trotted around the room with it, Zoe chased after the caterpillar dragging on the floor.

Our gifts exchanged, Frankie and I shared a simple breakfast of cold cereal and hot coffee, enjoying my new dark roast.

Brigit came over to the table and put a paw on my leg, politely offering to clean my bowl for me. I left a little bit of cereal in the bottom and set the bowl on the floor. "Here you go, girl."

After breakfast, Frankie headed off to the fire station and I headed over to my parents' house so I could spend the early part of Christmas Day with my family. Seth was already on a twenty-four-hour shift at the station, so we planned to celebrate the following day.

After forcing down as much as I could of the overcooked and overseasoned holiday meal my mother had prepared, we gathered in the family room to open our gifts. My mother loved the new backpack I'd bought for her, and the polka-dot sweater was a big hit with Gabby, who declared it "Adorbs!" I supposed I had the shoplifter in the pink coat to thank for helping me find the gift. Dad appreciated the case of his favorite imported beer that he rarely splurged on for himself. My three brothers were easy, too. They'd all received gift cards for shopping online. They'd use them for some tech gadget or another, maybe a video game.

By that point, it was almost time for my shift to begin. After changing into my uniform in the bedroom I used to share with my sister Gabby, I headed out, giving each of my family members one last hug and a "Merry Christmas!" My mother's three tabby cats received one head pat apiece, offering hisses in return. They'd never forgiven me for introducing the big hairy beast known as Brigit into the family.

Shortly thereafter, Brigit and I were in our cruiser, winding our way at a leisurely pace up and down the streets of our beat. I'd spent the last several days driving out of the city to shady places calling themselves zoos, wildlife refuges, or animal parks. My search for Sarki and the birds had been fruitless, as had my pleas to the operators of these sites to contact me if they heard of anyone looking to sell a hyacinth macaw or colobus monkey. I'd interrogated a couple of men who'd been convicted of dog fighting in the past. Given their lack of respect for animal life, I thought it possible they could be involved in the zoo thefts. Neither offered me any useful information, though both offered me plenty of attitude.

"What's the big deal?" one of them said. "They're just animals."

I'd been tempted to sic Brigit on the bastard and, after she chewed on him a bit, ask him, *What's the big deal? Humans are "just animals," too, you know.*

But while I'd spent the last few days chasing down the potential leads, I'd exhausted them now. There was nothing more I could do but return to my usual duties.

Brigit and I were only fifteen minutes into our shift when we fielded our first domestic call. Apparently Dad had the nerve to bring his "trampy new girlfriend" to his adult daughter's home for the holiday, and his ex-wife and the woman had ended up in a catfight during which said tramp's hair extensions were pulled from her head and the ex's cheek was scratched by the tramp's clawlike fingernails. Rather than complicate the women's lives with an assault charge, I deescalated the situation by separating the warring parties, mediating a truce, and suggesting the daughter host separate celebrations for each parent next year.

"Don't worry," she told me with a roll of her eyes. "I'm spending next Christmas with friends in Cancún."

Over the next few hours, Brigit and I dealt with three more domestic issues. Two brothers had ventured down memory lane, resurrected a decades-old dispute over a referee's call in a football game, and ended up tackling each other in their living room. A woman and her mother ended up tossing wine in each other's faces and engaging in a screaming match so loud it led to the next-door neighbors calling 911. *Sheesh. Just send each other a card next year and call it a day.* In the final call, a drunk phoned for assistance because his aunt had stolen his car keys and wouldn't return them.

"She did you a favor," I told him as he stared at me with bloodshot eyes. "You get behind the wheel in your current condition and I'll drag you down to the station for DUI. Now do as your aunt says and sleep it off in the guest room."

I was heading back to my cruiser when the radio on my

shoulder again squawked to life, dispatch summoning officers to provide traffic control at a nearby church where a fire was under way. I pushed the button to activate my mic. "Officer Luz and Brigit responding."

In minutes, we pulled up to the church. The living Nativity scene was up in flames, burning as bright as the North Star in the dark evening. As firefighters doused the fire with a hose, a crowd of people formed a semicircle around the smoldering remains of the manger. Frankie circled the collapsed display, using a tool that looked like an oversized hoe to tamp out the embers and prevent further flare-ups.

A few yards away stood a man in a long brown robe, presumably the congregant who'd been playing Joseph. He held on to ropes tied around the necks of a sheep, a goat, and a small, anxious donkey tramping the ground like a tap dancer marking his steps. The donkey's ears were laid back, his eyes wild. But who could blame the poor beast? The fire would have been upsetting enough, but the sounds of the sirens and the water spraying and the wafting smoke were a lot to handle, even for a human being who understood what was happening.

A fire truck and ambulance sat at the curb. Alex stood at the back of the open ambulance. On the tailgate sat a woman in a blue hooded robe, evidently the Virgin Mary. Alex knelt down to inspect the back of Mary's legs. The singed hem of Mary's robe told me the garment had caught fire. Looked like her legs might have been burned, too. *Ouch.* Too bad she only had a plastic doll serving as her supernatural son. If the real Jesus were here, he could heal her wounds lickety-split and she wouldn't have to worry about medical bills. He performed his miracles gratis.

I parked the cruiser in the church's lot. Before exiting the car, I grabbed my neon-yellow gloves with the reflective glow-in-the-dark strips, as well as the orange traffic-wand attachment for my flashlight. I left Brigit inside the car. Traffic duty was extremely dangerous. No way would I risk my partner's safety by taking her into the street with me. Besides, this wasn't a task for a K-9.

The donkey wasn't the only jackass here. Derek Mackey had beat me to the church. While he diverted traffic approaching from the west, I stepped up behind the fire truck and used my orange light to redirect oncoming eastern traffic, motioning for drivers to turn down a side street so they wouldn't get in the way of the firefighters.

It wasn't long before Mary's minor burns had been treated and the embers had been fully extinguished. The firemen packed up to go. Joseph stepped forward with his assortment of farm animals, probably to thank the firefighters who'd responded to his son's birthday bash gone wrong. Unfortunately, the donkey wasn't having it. He yanked back on his rope, pulled it out of the man's hand, and took off running for the street.

Joseph cried out, "Come back!", but naturally the donkey ignored him.

Seth had just removed his gloves. He dropped them to the ground, and he and I both took off running toward the donkey, hoping to head it off before it could run into the traffic that was flowing again.

Seth got to the donkey first, grabbing the rope at the animal's shoulder and pulling him to a stop. Terrified, the donkey brayed, turned, and bit into Seth's hand. By that time, I'd reached them. So had Joseph.

"You all right?" I asked.

Seth muttered some curses under his breath while cupping his injured hand in the other. Red tooth marks formed an arc across his palm like a macabre dot-to-dot puzzle. "I'll be fine."

He handed the donkey off to Joseph, who issued profuse apologies for the animal's behavior. "He pulled out of my grip. I am so sorry!"

"Don't worry about it," Seth replied graciously. "He was scared. I don't blame him." He turned to me, angling his head to indicate the ambulance. "I better get this looked at."

"I'll go with you."

As we approached the ambulance, Alex looked out from the bay where she crouched, returning supplies to a drawer. As she saw Seth approaching with blood running down his hand, her eyes went wide and she gasped, her hands reflexively covering her mouth. She scuttled to the tailgate. "Oh, my gosh! Are you okay?"

He perched on the edge of the bay. "It's only a little bite."

I stood back as Alex bent over to examine his hand. When she did, her uniform shirt gaped at the neck, providing a glimpse of the pink lace bra she wore underneath. *Rookie.* Didn't she know that female first responders should always wear a sports bra? With as much running as our jobs could require, she'd sprain a boob in that flimsy lingerie.

Alex gingerly turned Seth's hand from one side to the other to get a good look at the wound. After flushing it out with a syringe, she applied hydrogen peroxide, cradling his hand in hers as she gently dabbed at the bite marks. "I'm not hurting you, am I?"

Oh, please. Seth had defused bombs in Afghanistan, been bombarded with shrapnel, and bore the scars on his body to prove it. A little nip from a farm animal was nothing to him. Besides, he didn't like to be babied.

"Don't worry. I'm man enough to handle a little antiseptic." He gave Alex a small smile. *Hmm.* Maybe he liked being babied a little bit.

As Alex continued to hold his hand, my mind harkened back to the singers at the mall, the crooner who'd gone down on one knee and taken the shopper's hand. I'd thought the gesture was cute then. Now, not so much.

Having noticed the commotion, Frankie slipped up beside me.

I turned to her, tilted my head slightly to indicate Seth and Alex, and spoke softly. "Should I be concerned *now*?"

She glanced at the two before turning back to me. "Nah. Like I said before, you've got nothing to worry about. Seth's crazy about you."

She was probably right. *But she could be wrong.* I wasn't normally a jealous, insecure person, but the domestic calls had left me realizing that relationships could be tenuous.

Alex wrapped gauze around Seth's hand, tying the ends in a bow as if he were a Christmas present. "There you go. All done."

He looked down at the bow and chuckled. "Thanks."

She went to stand, putting a hand on Seth's strong shoulder for leverage rather than using the frame of the gurney. It was an obvious ploy, an opportunity to touch him.

Seth, however, seemed oblivious to it. He stood, walked over to me, and showed me the bow on his wrapped hand. Leaning in, he whispered, "I can't wait for you to unwrap me."

I wagged a finger at him. "Nuh-uh-uh. You don't want to be the first name on Santa's naughty list for next year."

He slid me a sly grin. "It would be worth it."

The day after Christmas, Seth and I had lunch at an Italian restaurant before returning to my house for our own small, private celebration. We took seats on the couch, side by side, our dogs tussling on the rug.

"You first." He used his bandaged hand to slide a large, flat box in shiny silver wrap my way.

Very few things came in boxes this size and shape. "Let me guess," I said. "TV for my bedroom?"

"Not even close."

What could it be? I ran a finger under the seam and pulled off the wrap. The cardboard box bore no label to give me a clue as to its contents. I pulled the heavy-duty tape from the end, opened the flap, and peered inside. All I could see was the edge of dark wooden frame. Had Seth bought me a piece of art? Maybe a print from the Kimbell Art Museum? Only one way to find out.

I stood, gently turned the box on its side, and eased the frame out. When I realized what I was looking at, I gasped. "Oh, Seth! I love it!"

Before me was a painted portrait of Brigit. The artist had captured the intelligence in her eyes, the proud way she held her head, the playful tilt of her tail, the nuances of color and texture in her thick, shiny coat.

Seth smiled softly, clearly pleased by my reaction. "Remember the sketch artist from the abandoned-baby case?"

Of course I did. Not long ago, an unknown man had come to the fire station and surrendered a newborn baby to Seth under the state's safe drop law. When I'd later noticed a cry for help stitched into the baby's blanket, we realized we needed to find the man. The detective leading the investigation hired a sketch artist who'd questioned Seth and come up with a remarkably accurate sketch of the suspect.

"The sketch artist painted this? Wow. He's as talented with oils as he is with a charcoal pencil."

I leaned toward Seth, wrapped my arms around his shoulders, and gave him a tight hug. I loved the painting, but what had also warmed my heart was the fact that Seth had put so much thought into this gift, had come up with something so uniquely suited for me. Serving with a furry, four-footed partner himself, Seth knew how much my Brigit meant to me. Now, she'd be forever immortalized in this work of art.

I stood and glanced around the room, searching for the perfect spot to hang the portrait. My beautiful Brigit should be the focal point of the room. "Let's hang it over the bookcase."

After I rounded up a hammer and nail from the garage, Seth and I hung the portrait. We engaged in a debate over whether the frame had a slight tilt to the left or right, and confirmed with a level that it had neither.

My art properly installed, it was Seth's turn to open my gift. He donned the goggles and the swimsuit, performing a series of knee bends and circling his arms in the center of my living room as he improvised his best stroke, the butterfly. "These fit great. I bet I can cut my time in these."

He was clearly eager to find out. I suggested we head over to the Y.

A half hour later, I stood at the end of a swim lane, a timer in my hand. Seth raced toward me in the pool, his back arching in and out of the water, his legs sending up a splash with each kick. When his fingers grabbed the edge of the concrete, I pressed the button to stop the timer. "Two minutes, sixteen seconds."

"I broke two-twenty?" It might not be an Olympic-caliber performance, but it was still incredibly fast and a personal best for him. He hooted and hollered and pumped his wet fists in the air. "*Woot-woot!*"

After he climbed out, I draped a beach towel over his broad shoulders. While watching Seth swim shirtless had been a nice distraction from my work-related woes, the army eagle tattoo that spanned his shoulders reminded me of the missing birds from the zoo. *Will we ever find the macaws and the monkey?* I could only hope the new year would bring new evidence with it.

TWENTY-FOUR
TOY TO THE WORLD

Brigit

The dog had no idea why Megan had given her so many special treats and toys yesterday, and why Megan had wrapped them in paper or hidden them in bags. She only knew it had been one of her best days ever!

Today was turning out to be another one. Seth had come over and brought Blast with him. Their human partners were gone now, leaving the dogs to their mischief. Brigit and Blast were currently engaged in a game of tug-of-war with a thick, knotted rope she'd discovered in one of the bags. She was going easy on Blast for the moment, toying with him, letting the Labrador think he had a chance. She issued a soft, playful growl. He did the same in return.

Nobody gets the better of me. She gave him an inch, then another, then another, teasing him along until . . . *yank*! She jerked the rope right out of his mouth. Head held high, she ran a victory lap around the living room. *Ha!*

TWENTY-FIVE
GIG ECONOMY

The Poacher

It was halfway between the Christmas and New Year's Eve holidays when he sat in a coffee shop full of twenty-year-olds, feeling washed out at only a decade older. He used the cheap laptop he'd bought at a holiday sale and the shop's Wi-Fi to look for jobs online. He wasn't having much luck. He'd already applied for all of the skilled trade positions in his line of work, plus any others he was remotely qualified for. Retail sales. Fast-food service. Warehouse work. With everyone on vacation for the holidays, human resource departments hadn't updated their listings. *What am I going to do?*

His burner phone buzzed in his left pocket. He cursed and closed his eyes, willing it to be a wrong number. He should've gotten rid of the stupid phone so he wouldn't be tempted to answer. When Harper had heard that a monkey was missing from the zoo, she'd burst into tears. "Do you think he's okay, Daddy? Do you think whoever took him is being nice to him?"

The Poacher had tried to be as nice to the monkey as possible after he'd offered him the sedative-laced fruit. He'd slid the sleepy creature into the outward-facing baby carrier he'd found in the boys' closet. It would prevent the monkey from escaping and make it easier for him to sneak it out of the zoo. He'd worn black nylon running pants and a long-sleeved black T-shirt. For camouflage, he'd cut holes for his head and arms out of a black garbage bag and worn it like a poncho. *Genius.* It wasn't his idea, of course. He'd heard in prison that an inmate had once escaped when he'd disguised himself as trash.

When the Poacher had seen the beam of the zoo security guard's flashlight coming up the path, he'd curled up behind a garbage can. The guy had walked right past him, none the wiser. The Poacher had scaled the outer wall, dropped to the dry grass at the edge of the road, and rolled until he reached the row of bushes that led to the adjoining neighborhood.

The phone buzzed again. *I should let it go.*

But he didn't. He couldn't. He was nearly out of money again. *Who knew it cost so much to raise a family?* Still, unless the offer was upped, he wouldn't do it. It was too risky. He didn't want to end up back in prison.

He accepted the call, listened to the man on the other end, and asked, "How much?" When he heard how much, he knew he couldn't say no. He also knew he'd need help this time. Help and a trailer.

TWENTY-SIX
MIDNIGHTMARE

Megan

It was near closing time on New Year's Eve and the Shoppes at Chisholm Trail looked like a ghost town. Unwanted or ill-fitting Christmas gifts had already been returned, and shoppers looking for after-Christmas markdowns had already snatched up all the clearance merchandise they wanted. The carolers were gone, too, of course. *Shame.* They'd been a big hit with the customers.

The nail salon had been offering a New Year's special, glittery gold polish with a teeny glass of champagne painted on your thumb. *Cute.* But it was too late now. The nail technician with the strawberry-blond hair turned off the lights in the salon, stepped outside, and headed off down the walkway.

Brigit and I weren't far behind. Given that tonight marked citywide partying and general debauchery, we'd better get back out on the streets. It was sure to be a rough night. The only good news was that Mother Nature had apparently been given orders by Father Time to take it easy on us this New Year's Eve. The outdoor temperature was mild, the winds light, the skies clear.

Over the next three hours, I issued two speeding tickets, arrested one drunk driver, and issued a teenager a citation for illegal fireworks. He'd been shooting off a Roman candle in his driveway, his friends gathered around to watch. The sound and the repeated explosions in the sky over his house had made him easy to find. I'd caught him red-handed. Literally. The last Roman candle he'd shot off had burned his fingers. *That's why the warning label says not to hold the thing, you nitwit.*

The kid was just as burned about the ticket I issued to him. "I didn't know fireworks were illegal! How can they sell them if they're against the law?"

Here we go again. I explained the difference between the county and city regulations and jurisdiction, providing an impromptu civics lesson. Seeing my flashing lights at the curb, his parents came outside and tried to convince me to let the matter slide.

"They're only having a little fun," the boy's mother said, her words slurred, her breath as flammable as the fireworks.

The dad piled on, giving me an unwelcome nudge and wink. "Surely you can just give a warning for a little violation like this."

Not gonna happen. Not with me dating a firefighter who'd be putting his life on the line to extinguish any conflagrations caused by the illegal firecrackers. My roommate, too. Why should they pay the price for someone else's careless and flagrant disregard of the law and warning labels? Besides, this guy had only offered me a weak attempt at charm. At least Vaughn and his cohort had had the decency to offer me hundreds of dollars to turn a blind eye to their criminal activity. Not that I'd take it from either of them, but at least there was some semblance of a quid pro quo.

"Sorry, folks," I told them as I picked up the used

fireworks and dropped them into an evidence bag. "This is a serious offense."

Having not gotten his way, the boy's father eyed the name badge on my chest and issued what he thought was a threat. "I'll be contacting your superiors, Officer Luz."

"Feel free," I replied with a smile. "They'll be happy to hear I'm doing my job."

First the donkey bites Seth, then this jerk chews me out. *Two jackasses in one week.* What were the odds?

With that I returned to my cruiser and set back out on patrol. I cruised by the zoo every twenty minutes or so, slowly circumnavigating the parking lot with my flashing lights on. If I couldn't figure out who'd taken Fabiana, Fernando, and Sarki, maybe I could at least deter them from attempting to steal another animal.

Random bursts of colored lights continued through the evening, accompanied by *ka-bangs*, *pop-pop-pops,* and the elongated *wheeeeee* of those whistling fireworks as they fell to earth. While patrolling the Ryan Place neighborhood, I came upon a small grass fire at the edge of a yard. Several people were gathered about, each of them with a bottle or cup in their hand. The homeowner had a garden hose aimed at the fire. When he noticed my cruiser approaching, he turned the stream of water on the conical firework that had started the mess and washed it down the storm drain, getting rid of the evidence.

He tossed the hose aside as I pulled to the curb and unrolled my window. I wagged a finger at him. "Don't think I didn't see what you did there. I'll be keeping an eye on you."

The group laughed and yukked it up as I drove away. *This is such a thankless job sometimes.*

As the night wore on the temperature plummeted and

a light fog drifted in, the mist dressing the streetlights in halos and making the roads slick. The fog decreased visibility on the roads, too, on what was already a dangerous night. Mother Nature was toying with us.

At twenty to midnight, my cell phone chirped from the cup holder. The readout told me it was Frankie calling. Like me, she and Seth were both on duty tonight while the rest of the city was having fun.

I pulled to a stop down a side street and tapped the icon on the screen to take the call. "Hey, Frankenstein." What were roommates for if not to bum hair spray from and razz a little?

Her tone was tense. "Any chance you can come to the station?"

"Something wrong?"

"It's Seth. He was catching some sleep in the bunkroom and woke up screaming. I think he had a flashback. He acted like he'd shrugged it off, but he's been sitting alone outside for half an hour now."

"I'll be right there." I ended the call without saying good-bye, dropped my phone back in the cup holder, and hooked a U-turn to head to the station. I turned on my flashing lights. When someone I loved was hurting, it was an emergency.

As I pulled into the parking lot, I spotted Seth's silhouette sitting atop the picnic table on the side of the station. Blast sat next to him, the dog's eyes reflecting my headlights as he cast a look our way. I parked, rounded up Brigit, and walked down the side of the building.

Seth turned to look over his shoulder and sighed. "Frankie called you, didn't she?"

"Yes. She was worried about you."

He grunted. "They're making a big deal over nothing."

I circled around in front of him and looked him in the eye. "If it's nothing, why are you out here alone in the dark?"

He sat up straighter and looked around, almost as if he hadn't realized where he was. Another *pop-pop-pop* sounded in the distance, and Seth's jaw flexed. "Those things should be outlawed."

I wholeheartedly agreed. There were plenty of other ways to celebrate holidays without risking fire or the loss of life and limb. One could whack a parrot-shaped piñata, for instance.

I eyed him intently. "You had a bad dream, right?" No doubt the fireworks had activated his subconscious to cough up the nightmare. "You want to talk about it?"

He eyed me back for a long moment before saying, "No. People say talking about these things is supposed to make it better, but that doesn't work for me."

Though I hadn't faced the horrors of war, my job provided me a thorough and repeated immersion into the seedy underworld of life, the depths of human depravity. I didn't like to talk about the things I'd seen on my job, either.

"What *would* help?" I asked.

He reached out to pull me toward him. "Maybe a little of this . . ." He nuzzled my neck. "Or a little of this . . ." He nibbled at my ear. "Or a big bunch of this." He put his lips to mine.

I was so lost in the kiss I didn't hear footsteps approaching on the grass. Evidently Seth didn't, either. Suddenly, a voice broke the darkness.

"Oh!" It was Alex, standing a few feet away. She bit her bottom lip. "Officer Megan. Hi. I didn't mean to . . ."

Catch me and Seth kissing? She didn't say it, didn't seem to want to acknowledge what she had seen.

She raised her shoulders to her ears and offered a coy cringe. "I only came to see if Seth was okay. I'll go now." She swept her hand in an arc, waving awkwardly before turning around and scooting off.

I turned to Seth. "You know she's got a crush on you, right?"

"Alex?" He snorted softly. "I don't think so. She's just a sweet kid."

Frankie and the rest of the firefighters and paramedics streamed into the parking lot in front of the station, twirling noisemakers and blowing fringed horns. Someone carried a boom box tuned to a local radio station playing party music. Alex was among them, seemingly swept up in their current.

Frankie stepped to the edge of the lot and waved me and Seth over. "Come on, y'all! It's almost time for the countdown!"

Seth slid down from the table. We gathered our dogs and hurried over to join the others. I scurried over to my cruiser and turned on my flashing lights. They might not be actual party lights, but we'd pretend they were for the moment.

We danced in the parking lot until the countdown on the local radio began. "Ten! Nine! Eight!"

All of us counted along with them. Next to me, Brigit wagged her tail.

"Seven! Six! Five! Four!"

Brigit woofed, as if counting down, too. *Woof-woof-woof!* Not to be left out, Blast raised his snout and sent up a howl. *Aroooo!*

"Three! Two! One!"

The sky erupted in light and color and *bang-pop-wheees*! Unlike the sounds that had invaded his sleep, Seth was prepared for these noises and even smiled softly as he looked up at the sky.

I tossed my partner a liver treat and cried, "Happy New Year!", before turning to Seth for the traditional midnight kiss.

When we finally pulled away from each other, we looked down to see Blast and Brigit licking each other's mouths. They were welcoming the new year with a kiss, too.

TWENTY-SEVEN
THINGS THAT GO BANG IN THE NIGHT

Brigit

Brigit had spent a lot of time on firing ranges, and was trained to remain calm during gunfire. Still, the sounds tonight were different. The bangs and pops she didn't mind so much. But what was that weird *weeeee*? It sounded like something was falling from the sky.

Blast, who'd been trained in explosives, was familiar with the high-pitched squeal. He licked at Brigit's mouth, letting her know everything was all right. She licked him back to thank him for being there for her. Brigit put on the tough alpha dog act most of the time. But, whether they liked to admit it or not, everyone needed someone else sometimes.

TWENTY-EIGHT
SPRUNG

The Poacher

He'd tried to track down some of the other guys he'd known from prison. Unfortunately, not many of them had land-lines in their names and few of them spent much time on social media. He'd finally touched base with one of the guys from his job-training class in prison. He'd sent the guy a message through Facebook and asked for his phone number. When the Poacher had called on his burner phone and asked if the guy might be up for helping him on a job that might not exactly be legit, the guy had been a total dick.

"I don't know what you've got in mind," he said, "but don't you be trying to drag me down with you. I'm getting my shit together. Got a good job, making some money. I don't need to go looking for trouble. If you know what's good for you, you won't go looking for it, either." With that, the guy had hung up on him.

But the Poacher had other options. Since his release, he'd been taking classes with fellow ex-cons in the eve-nings, trying to broaden his skills. Some of them went out for beers afterward. He knew where one of the guys worked, at a fast-food chicken place, working the fryer.

He'd swung by and spoken to the guy when he'd got off his shift. That conversation had gone much better. Hell, he'd even lowballed the guy, offering him only a couple hundred dollars for his help, expecting to haggle before settling on a price. But the guy had agreed right off the bat.

Now, the two of them were busy doing the job. Ironically, the additional security lights that had been installed at the zoo only served to better hide the Poacher's activity, and the *pops* and *bangs* of the fireworks should mask any noise they might make.

He was nearly into the enclosure when his phone silently vibrated, sending his heart into his throat. The text on his dimmed screen read only *G*, the agreed-upon shorthand to indicate a guard was coming. He turned off his tool and slipped behind an evergreen bush. He held his breath as the security officer approached. His pulse pounded in his ears as the beam of the man's flashlight played around the edges of the walkway and over the surrounding fences, walls, and foliage. *Should I run for it?*

Before he could make up his mind, the guard was on him, no more than four or five feet away. The man stopped and ran his light over the bush, bisecting the Poacher's belly. If it had been a light saber, it would have cut him in two. *Does he see me hiding back here?*

His question was answered when the guard moved on. No, the guard hadn't spotted him.

The ghillie suits had been a good idea. He'd thought it up when he'd been playing hide-and-seek with his boys. The youngest had quickly found his brother lying curled up under the Christmas tree. But when the Poacher had pulled the garland off the mantel and wrapped himself in it, the boys hadn't been able to find him behind the tree only a few minutes later. Military snipers wore the ghillie suits to disguise themselves when hunting a target. The fake foliage on the suit made them blend right in with their surroundings. The Poacher had blended right in, too.

The guard walked a few more feet before abruptly stopping and sniffing the air. He turned his head toward the fence where the Poacher had been working.

NO! The Poacher nearly wet himself. He should run like hell, try to get out of there as fast as he could. But while his mind knew what he should do, his body refused to cooperate. He was frozen to the spot. Turned out to be a good thing his flight instinct hadn't been activated. After another second or two, the guard continued on.

The Poacher inhaled so deep he became light-headed for a moment. A minute later, he received a text of *C* for "Clear." He eased himself out of the bush and returned to his work.

In mere minutes, they were in and out. Once the animal had been loaded into the trailer, he turned to the other guy and held out two hundred dollars in twenties. "There you go."

The guy took the money, counted it, and folded it in half, sliding it into his back pocket. He held out his closed hand for a fist bump. "Nice doing business with you."

TWENTY-NINE
OFF TO A BAD START

Megan

Working New Year's Eve had been no fun, but at least I was free on New Year's Day. My mother, Gabby, and I decided to have a girls' day and, naturally, a girls' day involved shopping at the mall. Gabby had babysitting money burning a hole in her pocket.

We arrived shortly after noon. The mall had wasted no time pulling down the Christmas and New Year's decorations, and replacing them with hearts and cupids for Valentine's Day next month. We meandered through clothing stores, but nothing caught our eye. The bookstore was another matter. I bought a couple of mysteries, while Gabby picked up a young adult novel. The young couple depicted on the cover stood back-to-back with their arms crossed over their chests, their body language a sure signal the book would serve up plenty of teen angst. Mom perused the Valentines-themed romance selections that had been placed on a special table up front, choosing one set in Victorian England. Her choice didn't surprise me. When she'd returned to college recently, she'd discovered a latent interest in history.

As we passed the nail salon, Gabby grabbed my arm and tugged me toward the door. "Let's get our nails done!"

Mom agreed. "I'm game."

Before I knew what was happening, I was sitting at a table in front of the platinum-blond nail tech. Mom sat at the next table, her nails being tended to by the strawberry blonde. Atop each of the three tables was a tiered display of polish in all colors of the rainbow, as well as a velvet-covered hand-shaped ring stand. I recalled the woman at the country club mentioning that her manicurist had a ring stand like these. I also recalled her saying there was no chance she'd left her rings at her nail salon because her technician had explicitly reminded her not to forget them.

I watched as the tech carefully painted my fingernails red and embellished them with pink hearts. The end result might not make me look like a tough cop, but it was fun as heck. The tech finished by applying a sizable dollop of shea butter lotion to the back of each of my hands and massaging it into my skin.

I lifted the back of my hand to my nose. "*Mmm.* This stuff smells really good." It worked well, too. My hands hadn't felt so soft in ages.

Gabby succeeded me in the seat, while a middle-aged woman in a blue turtleneck, jeans, and ankle boots took my mother's place in front of the strawberry blonde. Though the woman was casually dressed, her perfect coif and designer tote bag said she'd likely come from one of the upper-crust neighborhoods nearby. The overflowing tote told me she'd already done quite a bit of shopping. She set her tote on the ground and lifted a paper coffee cup to her mouth to down the last sip. As she raised the cup, the overhead lights gleamed off a cocktail ring on her right index finger. The ring featured a large blue topaz atop a white gold split-shank setting. *Gorgeous.* She dropped her cup into the trash can under the table and removed her ring, having to twist it back and forth to force it past her knuckle. Once it was off, she gently slid it onto the velvet finger on the holder.

Preliminaries dispensed with, the tech asked, "What color would you like?"

As the woman perused the display of polish, the tech pulled her cell phone out of a drawer on the back of the table and typed on the screen, apparently sending a text. The customer selected a subtle pink and placed the bottle on the table between them. "Let's go with this one."

A few minutes later, the strawberry-blond tech finished with the polish. While her client's fingertips set under the small, heated air dryer, the tech pulled her cell phone out and sent another quick text. A minute or so later, the woman's nails were ready. The tech applied the shea butter lotion to the woman's hands, too, gently rubbing it in. "All done." The tech eased the velvet hand forward. "Don't forget your ring."

"Wouldn't want to do that," the woman agreed, plucking her ring from the holder. She had no trouble at all sliding it onto her finger now.

Gabby's nails were ready, too. She squealed, holding them up for the world to see. "I love it!"

I pulled out my wallet. "My treat," I told my mother and Gabby. They thanked me with hugs. I stepped into line at the register behind the woman in the blue turtleneck. Her topaz caught the light again as she inserted her debit card into the chip reader. When she was done, I handed cash across the counter to cover the cost of our manicures, as well as a generous tip. Maybe it would bring me good karma.

As we ventured out of the nail salon, we found ourselves face-to-face with the barbershop quartet. The same four men who'd been dressed in Dickens costumes and singing Christmas carols just days ago were back, only now they were singing a love song and dressed in typical barbershop-quartet attire. All four sported white pants and white shirts, with red and white striped vests and straw hats with wide red bands. Their bow ties, which were red with white hearts, gave a nod to the upcoming romantic holiday.

Though the four men approached the woman in the turtleneck, she dodged them, turning right and heading down the walkway at a fast clip, probably aiming for the parking lot. My mother, Gabby, and I stopped to listen.

They strolled among the shoppers who'd gathered, singing the Beatles' classic "I Want to Hold Your Hand," vocalizing and harmonizing and clapping their hands, to the delight of the crowd, who clapped along, too, at just the right points in the song. Just as he'd done when singing "Sleigh Ride," the shortest one went down on one knee in front of Gabby, taking her hand when they launched into the chorus. My sister threw her head back and laughed. The man gave her a grin before standing and resuming his stroll. When the four men finished their song, the shoppers erupted in applause. Launching into "All My Loving," they strolled off down the walkway to entertain shoppers at the stores farther down.

My mother watched their retreating backs and declared their act, "Cute."

Gabby groaned and countered with, "Corny."

The family peacekeeper, I diplomatically brought everyone together with, "It's both. Cute and corny."

No longer distracted by the singers, we picked up on the smells from the nearby food court wafting our way. Onions. Garlic. Tomato sauce.

"I'm starving!" Gabby grabbed her stomach with both hands as if it might implode. "Let's get some pizza."

A few minutes later, we were gathered around a table in the food court. My mother and Gabby were sharing a cheese pizza, while I'd opted for a southwestern salad. Given the amount of time I spent sitting on my rear end in my cruiser, I had to watch my diet.

Gabby went to pick up her drink, and the cup slid right through her hands. "That lotion is slippery."

I'd noticed it, too. I'd had a hard time keeping hold of my plastic fork. I pulled three napkins from the dispenser on the table and handed one to Gabby, another to my mother, and kept one for myself, using it to pat some of the excess lotion from my hands.

I was crunching my way through a mouthful of raw veggies when my cell phone jiggled in my back pocket. I pulled it out and checked the screen. Detective Bustamente was calling. "It's work," I told my mom and sister as I jabbed the button to take the call. I put the phone to one ear and a finger to the other to block out the buzz of conversations taking place around us. "Hello, Detective. Happy New Year."

"It's not starting so happy," he said. "Another animal was taken from the zoo last night."

"No!" Diners at nearby tables looked my way. I turned my back and hunched over in an attempt to create some privacy. "What was taken?"

"A springbok. From what I understand it's a medium-sized antelope ..."

"Native to Africa."

"You're familiar with them?"

"Brigit and I walk the zoo sometimes." Probably more often than we should, but no sense telling him that.

When I pressed him for details, he said, "You know what I know. I'm on my way to the zoo now to find out more and take a look around. Chief's coming, too. He's called a press conference for later this afternoon. Can you meet us there?"

"Of course. I'll be there ASAP."

Today was supposed to be my day off, but I wasn't about to miss out on another chance to help in this investigation. While assisting a detective could give my career a boost, my reasons in this particular matter were primarily personal. It broke my heart to think of the confusion and fear these poor animals must be suffering after being removed from the homes and animal families they were accustomed to. This crime was cruel. I'd do whatever I could to help bring them home and put the perpetrator behind bars.

"Sorry," I told my mother and Gabby. "I have to cut our girls' day short. Detective Bustamente needs me at the zoo. A springbok was taken last night. It's an antelope from—"

"Africa," Mom said. "We heard."

Gabby's face tensed with worry. "I hope you catch whoever's doing this."

"She will," Mom said with a confident lift of her chin. "Megan and Brigit haven't had a case yet that they couldn't solve."

While I appreciated my mother's support, I feared she might be wrong. We'd been unable to determine how the thief or thieves had removed Sarki from the monkey habitat, and we'd had no luck trying to identify who might have kidnapped the beautiful birds. None of the angles we'd worked had brought us any closer to solving the crime. But maybe whoever had taken the springbok had left a clue this time, some piece of evidence that would lead us to their door.

I gave each of them a quick hug and rushed to my car. I sped home, changed into my uniform, and rounded up Brigit. We climbed into the cruiser and off we went.

My partner and I found Detective Bustamente and Chief Garelik at the African Savanna exhibit. The chief was a hulk of a man, with silver-bullet hair, gunmetal-gray eyes, and a double-barreled demeanor.

"Hello, Chief." I extended my hand.

"Officer Luz." He took my hand and gave it a solid shake that threatened to buckle my knees.

Brigit raised her paw to shake, too, but the chief ignored her. She returned her paw to the ground and issued a soft snort as if to reprimand him for his poor manners.

Gathered with the detective and the chief were Sharon Easley, the CSO, and a stocky black man wearing the zoo's standard mock-safari attire.

Easley introduced me to the man. "He's our hoof-stock keeper. He was feeding the springboks an hour ago and noticed one of them is gone. A male. His name is Dinari. There's no sign of the animal on the zoo grounds."

Knowing springboks lived up to their names and could jump quite high, I asked, "Did they seem upset by the fireworks last night?" Fear could be a powerful motivator. Maybe Dinari had put extra effort into his leaps and made it over the wall.

The keeper said, "They weren't crazy about the noise. None of the animals were. They were huddled together the last time I checked on them before I went home last night, but they weren't pronking like I'd expect if they were especially spooked."

The CSO backed him up, looking from me, to the detective, to the chief. "My team patrolled regularly last night and kept a close eye on the animals, looking for signs of extreme stress. We didn't notice any. Some of the animals seemed restless and some went into their private areas, but none of them exhibited any behaviors that caused us alarm."

"Did your team report anything else?" Bustamente asked the CSO. "Anything unusual in any way?"

"One guy came back saying he'd caught a strong whiff of garlic behind the African Savanna exhibit." He offered a shrug and an apologetic smile that the useless tidbit was all he had to offer. The smell had likely been carried on the wind from one of the restaurants on University Drive. Many of them had extended their hours for the New Year's holiday. Or maybe it had been a residual aroma from the zoo's café.

"All right then," the detective said, moving things along. "Let's check out the enclosure."

The chief begged off then, his appearance here a goodwill gesture. As the head of the Fort Worth Police Department, his law enforcement duties were mostly administrative. "I've got to get back to HQ." He bade the zoo employees good-bye before turning to the detective. "Come brief me when you're done here."

Just as Camilla Bellafiore had shown me and the detective around the colobus-monkey digs, the hoof-stock keeper led us around the ten-acre habitat, which the springboks shared with other nonpredator species native to Africa. Giraffes. Zebras. Ostriches. Again, I left Brigit safely secured in a locked staff-only area so she wouldn't frighten the animals.

This enclosure was similar in design to the monkey exhibit. An entry comprising a roofed outdoor corridor with brick walls on each side and heavy metal gates at either end secured by key-card devices. A large center area landscaped with grasses and trees to simulate the springboks' natural habitat. A deep, moatlike perimeter and high walls to prevent escape.

I turned to the others. "I've assumed Sarki was probably taken by someone using a ladder to get into the enclosure to snatch him. He'd have been easy enough to carry. But how could a person climb up a ladder carrying one of these animals?" I gestured to the remaining springboks, which were grazing fifty or so yards away. While the springboks stood about three feet tall at the shoulder, their heads and horns added another couple feet at least. Plus, they were over five feet long from nose to tail, and weighed around seventy-five pounds on average.

The detective thought out loud. "If the animal were unconscious, I suppose they could have strapped it to their back."

It was possible, maybe, but it seemed unlikely. The horns would have poked the thief. Even so, the only other possibilities my mind came up with involved some type of airlift by helicopter or crane. Surely the security guards would have noticed a chopper or crane hovering over the zoo. We discussed these scenarios and agreed all of them were unlikely.

Still musing aloud, I said, "So if the animal wasn't brought *up* out of the exhibit, could it have been taken out *under* the exhibit?"

"A tunnel, you mean?" the detective asked.

"Exactly."

We split into two groups and circumnavigated the entire exhibit, looking for places where the ground had been disturbed, the concrete cracked. We found some scat, but no evidence of a tunnel. It had been a long shot anyway. Tunneling into the zoo from outside would have involved extensive digging with high-powered equipment, as well as detailed maps and surveys to avoid hitting buried gas lines or plumbing. We reconvened at the exit gate, all of us at a loss.

The detective recapped. "So we've pretty much ruled out the idea that someone came down into the closure, or dug up into it. That means they had to come *through* it."

We examined the perimeter walls. Again we found no evidence of damage. Again we met at the gate.

I eyed the metal bars. "What if they came through the gate somehow?"

The CSO shook his head. "I've looked at the card-reader records. The only one in and out in the last twenty-four hours was him." He angled his head to indicate the zookeeper.

Bustamente grunted. "There's got to be an explanation. It's not like someone came here and waved a magic wand and *poof,* the animals disappeared."

Not yet ready to give up on the thought that someone had come through the gate, I stepped closer and turned sideways to give it a more thorough inspection. Only two or three inches separated the bars. Someone would have to be as flat as a paper doll to fit through the gate sideways. *How else could someone have come through this gate?*

I stepped even closer, my face only inches from the metal. Starting in the upper left corner, I ran my gaze back and forth over the gate, my focus traversing the top cross bar, then the middle one, stopping at the bottom cross bar. I squatted down for a better look. In the corner where the horizontal bar met the outermost vertical bar, the metal was rough, gloppy looking. It was the same at each spot where a horizontal bar met the outermost vertical bar. In other words, it could mean a center panel had been cut out of the gate, then welded back together.

I looked up at Bustamente. "Look at these joints. The welding looks sloppy, like it was done quickly."

He put his hands on his knees and bent down to take a look. "You're right. Do they all look like that?"

After the zoo director, the CSO, and the keeper each took a look for themselves, we moved en masse to the outer gate. Spotting us through the slats, Brigit wagged her tail from the courtyard where she waited. Sure enough, this gate appeared to have been hastily welded, too. Even so, the metal held together, just as sloppy stitching could hold fabric together. It didn't have to look nice and smooth to function properly.

I cut a glance at the detective. "Does it mean anything?"

He pointed to the locked gate that secured the courtyard. "Let's take a look at that one."

We stepped into the courtyard and looked the gate over both inside and out. We saw no evidence of substandard welding on that gate. *Hmm.*

Bustamente pointed out the open gate. "Let's go look at the gates on the monkey habitat and compare them to the gates on other enclosures."

We returned to the colobus monkey enclosure. Yep, the gates to that enclosure had been sloppily welded, too. The gates at the nearby gorilla enclosure were welded by someone who had either taken more time or had more skill. The places where the metal was joined were smooth. *But what does that tell us?*

A gorilla watched us from across the habitat as Bustamente turned to Easley. "Were all of the gates installed at the same time? The ones at the monkey enclosure and this one?"

"Originally, yes," she said. "But some of them have been damaged and replaced. I'd have to go through our records to be able to tell you for certain when each of them was installed."

Before she spent precious time looking up information that might not be necessary, I suggested we return to the springbok enclosure. "If we think someone took the springbok out the gate, he'd have had to get out of the courtyard somehow. Maybe Brigit can show us where."

We traced our steps back to the courtyard outside the springbok habitat. I led her to the gate and issued the order for her to track a disturbance, hoping that the group of us traipsing all around the place wouldn't confuse her.

I needn't have worried. Brigit sniffed around the gate, glanced over at us, and put her nose back to the concrete, proceeding to lead me to the back of the courtyard. She snuffled around the fence a bit and sat, issuing her passive alert.

Bustamente and I stepped forward and looked at the metal bars supporting the wooden privacy fence that surrounded the courtyard.

"There." I pointed to a spot on the upper cross bar where the metal had clearly been melted.

"And here," Bustamente said, pointing to a similar spot along the bar to the left.

Two poorly welded cuts appeared on the bottom cross beam also.

I said aloud what the two of us were thinking. "Whoever stole Dinari cut a panel out of this fence and the gates. That way, the animal could be removed without activating the alarm connected to the outer bars of the gate."

Brigit, too, said aloud what she was thinking. *Woof!* Translation: *Liver treat!*

I tossed her two treats and scratched her ears. "Good girl!" I placed another liver treat on top of the panel of fencing to mark the spot and waved for the others to follow us. "Let's take Brigit around to the other side of this fence and see if she can show us where the thieves exited the zoo."

We exited the courtyard and circled around the outside of the savanna habitat. As we approached the fence, a bird swept down and plucked the liver treat from the top of it. *Probably should've marked the spot with something inedible.*

I led Brigit to the panel of fencing and again issued her the order to trail. She put her nose to the ground and snuffled around before sniffing her way up the fence. Dropping her snout back to the ground, she set off, we mere humans in her wake. Though she lost the trail a few times at places where one pathway intersected with another and led us in a few inadvertent circles and figure eights, she eventually picked the trail back up each time. *My partner's nose is the best in the biz.*

In the end, she led us past all of the exhibits, past the garbage and storage areas at the rear of the zoo property, until she stopped at the back fence where the zoo gave way onto an older upscale neighborhood. Once again, welding marks were visible on the fence supports. Brigit earned two more liver treats and a two-handed scratch at that special spot at the base of her tail. She wolfed down the treats and closed her eyes in pure doggie bliss as I dug my nails into her fur.

Bustamente turned to the CSO. "You got cameras on this area?"

"We do."

He led us a dozen yards away to a metal pole that stood around ten feet tall. A camera was mounted on the end of it. The lens was coated with what appeared to be snow, but the temperature was in the upper forties and we'd had no flurries.

"Dammit!" spat the CSO. "What is that stuff covering the camera?"

As the men squinted upward, trying to figure it out, I realized what the substance was. "It's flocking. You know, the artificial snow that's sprayed on store windows and

Christmas trees?" Heck, they'd used gallons of the stuff to decorate the store windows at the mall.

The detective sighed. "So much for the camera footage."

Even if we couldn't obtain actual video of the thieves, at least we had determined the methods they'd used to access the springbok and move it off the zoo property. Still, while we'd figured out *how* the thieves had committed this crime, the biggest question remained.

Who?

THIRTY
INS AND OUTS

Brigit

When Megan had first asked her to trail from that gate, Brigit had picked up the disturbance caused by Megan, Detective Bustamente, and those other people from the zoo. But Brigit was smart enough to know that Megan didn't want her to follow that trail and lead them right back to themselves. They already knew where they were. So she led Megan on the much lighter trail, the one she could barely detect, the one that was even more difficult to follow once they were out in the main part of the zoo where so many people had walked back and forth, interfering with the scent. It had taken all of her concentration, but Brigit had managed to pick it up again each time she lost it.

From the scent trails left where the thieves had come in and out of the zoo, she could tell that two men had come into the zoo alone, and that they'd left with one of those animals with the horns. Brigit thought it might be nice to have a pair of pointy horns like that hooved creature. If she had horns, she'd be able to scratch that sweet spot at the base of her tail herself.

THIRTY-ONE
FAIR SHARE

The Poacher

They hooked up at a gas station in the town of Temple, making it about a two-hour drive for each of them. But while he didn't mind going halfway when it came to driving, he'd decided on the drive down that going halfsies on the cash wasn't fair. The Poacher had done all the work, taken all the risks. He'd bought the equipment, paid the assistant, too. Delivered the antelope to that rancher out in Glen Rose. All his prison buddy had done was make a few phone calls. *He should get half the take for that?*

He handed the envelope over.

His buddy opened it, counted the money inside, and looked up at him, slack-jawed. "What are you trying to pull, man? There should be two grand in here. Where's the other half of my money?"

"Twenty-five percent is more than fair!" the Poacher snapped. "I had to do all the real work, and I nearly got caught by a security guard last night." Okay, so he was exaggerating. The guy had sniffed the air and moved on. Still, he *could* have gotten caught and, even though the guard had eventually walked away, the Poacher had spent a few seconds in utter terror. "All you've done is dial some numbers and talk to people."

The guy's eyes narrowed and his nostrils flared. "If I didn't talk to those people, there'd be no deal. You'd have nothing! Thanks to me, you've got thousands of dollars in your pocket."

The Poacher snorted. "I got less than two grand in my pocket. I dropped eight hundred on the trailer." It was the cheapest one he could find and pocked with hail damage, but it got the job done. "I had to buy supplies and pay a lookout, too. You're coming out pretty good, bro."

That seemed to shut his buddy up. The guy tucked the envelope into his back pocket and raised his hands. "All right, man. We're cool."

The Poacher returned to his truck. A *ding* came from his pocket, along with a jiggle. He pulled out his cell phone to find a text from Harper—or, as he'd listed her in his contacts, Squirt.

I love you Daddy! I love my phone too!

He felt his mouth spread in an involuntary smile. Stealing those animals had been illegal. But if he'd done it to make his daughter happy, he wasn't a bad man.

Was he?

THIRTY-TWO
PRESS CONFERENCES AND PRESSURE COOKERS

Megan

We left the zoo, and soon my butt was back in the same fake-leather wing chair in the chief's office where I had sat as he'd chewed me out for Tasering Derek. This time, the detective sat in a matching chair next to me. The oversized chief sat on the other side of his oversized desk in an oversized chair. A veritable zoo of animal heads stared over his shoulder with their unseeing glass eyes. *Creepy and ironic.* I averted my gaze from the chief's collection of carnage.

"Good God a'mighty," he muttered. "What's that on your hands, Officer Luz?"

I cringed. "It's a Valentine's manicure, sir. I wasn't supposed to be working today."

"You expect to fight crime looking like a fairy princess?" Before I could respond, he barked. "What's going on over at that zoo? And what's with the people of this city? They're as worked up over that monkey as they are when a child goes missing. And now we've got some kind of deer gone. Thank heavens Christmas is over or we'd be accused of letting one of Santa's reindeer be kidnapped."

Despite his hyperbole, and his incorrectly referring to the springbok as a deer rather than an antelope, he had a point. People had accused the department of not doing enough to find Sarki. As I'd been writing a woman a speeding ticket a few days ago, she'd hissed, "You're out here giving innocent people a hard time when you should be looking for that monkey!" *Innocent, my ass.* Though I had to admit I would've much rather been looking for Sarki than working traffic duty. Another person had pulled to the curb at Forest Park as I'd let Brigit out to relieve herself. "When are y'all gonna find that poor monkey?" he'd demanded. *As soon as my dog finishes taking her dump,* I'd wanted to say. Instead, I'd said, "Soon, we hope."

The public's concern was the reason behind the press conference, which would begin as soon as we concluded our briefing. The chief needed to assure the public and the press that the department was doing all it could to bring the cuddly creatures back home.

The chief's rant over, he looked to the detective. "Give me the poop, Hector."

Detective Bustamente summarized our efforts and the evidence efficiently and effectively. "When the hyancinth macaws went missing, there wasn't enough evidence to prove they'd been stolen. The zoo chalked it up to human error on the part of a custodian and didn't file a report. When the monkey turned up gone, Officer Luz and I performed an inspection of the enclosure along with zoo staff. We found no obvious signs of a break-in. The most likely scenario seemed to be an inside job, with the monkey being sold to a private collection, circus, roadside zoo, or somewhere out of the country. Officer Luz spent a lot of time trying to track the animals down online, and personally contacted all of the wildlife parks and pet stores in the area but had no luck. I interviewed zoo staff extensively, and both Officer Luz and I paid a visit to the custodian, but we came up with nothing. Today, Officer Luz noticed that the secured gates had been cut with a welding torch. Brigit trailed the thieves to an outer fence that had also been cut and welded back together."

The chief took it all in, his head bobbing as he thought. "So whoever did this knows something about welding?"

"Looks that way," Bustamente said. "Of course we told the zoo staff not to mention that fact to anyone. We don't want word getting out that we know how the job was done. The thieves might skip town if they know we're on to them."

"Got it," the chief said. "But the welding, that's your only lead at this point?"

"Yes," Bustamente admitted.

The chief grunted. "We're in the middle of the oil patch here, not to mention all those planes being built over at Lockheed and the cars at the GM plant. We're up to our balls in welders. Is there some other angle you can explore?"

I looked up in thought and there, looking back at me, was a hairy javelina with tusklike bottom teeth. A bobcat not much bigger than Zoe. A pronghorn antelope that looked remarkably similar to the stolen springbok.

"Oh, no!" I sat bolt upright in my seat. We'd assumed that whoever stole Fabiana, Fernando, and Sarki intended to sell them to a collector or zoo, but what if the thief intended to sell the springbok for sport? Rather than living out a life of leisure with its herd at the zoo, it could be pursued and killed by hunters it wouldn't know to be wary of. After all, as a zoo animal, Dinari was accustomed to humans, trusted them. "Maybe the thieves are planning to sell the springbok for hunting!"

The chief steepled his fingers and frowned. "You could be on to something. Trophy hunters pay upward of thirty grand to shoot an African bongo. About half that for a wildebeest. A little under ten thousand for an Arabian oryx."

The hunters didn't have to travel to Africa or Arabia to do it, either. Thanks to the proliferation of canned hunting ranches throughout the state, they could kill these rare species in their own backyard.

The chief pulled a pen and a legal pad from his desk, plunked the pad down on the desktop, and held his pen aloft. "Give me some talking points for the press conference."

We gave him a quick list of bullet points he could cover. The crime had taken place overnight. Given the type of animal that was taken this time, we suspected more than one person was involved and that a large vehicle, a truck, or trailer would have been needed for transporting the springbok. Crime scene techs were currently on-site looking for fingerprints the thieves might have left behind.

He looked up at me. "What's that monkey's name again? Snarky?"

"Sarki," I said. "No *n*."

He jotted it down. "Got it." He turned his eyes on me. "Whatever you do, make sure your fingernails don't show on camera."

I flinched. "Yes, sir."

With that, we headed down to the first floor briefing room where press conferences were held. Two dozen reporters from local newspapers, radio, and television stations filled the chairs. Several more who'd been unable to snag a seat stood along the back wall beside a number of camera operators with equipment perched on their shoulders. A tech from the department's PR office sat behind a projector that displayed a rotating series of photos on the screen at the front of the room. Hyacinth macaws, a colobus monkey, a springbok.

Derek stood in the front corner of the room, ostensibly to keep order. But I knew why he was really here. Because he was the chief's hunting buddy and golden boy, and because having both a female K-9 team and an alpha male cop on the case would make good optics. The chief hadn't risen through the ranks on his law enforcement skills alone. He had public relations acumen, too.

The chief took his place at the podium, while Derek, Detective Bustamente, Brigit, and I lined up behind him as a show of force. I kept both of my hands tightly curled around Brigit's leash to hide my manicure. My stomach fluttered as if filled with tiny parakeets from the zoo's Parrot Paradise exhibit. Press conferences could go either way, helping us or hurting us. Sometimes the press was the police department's best partner in fighting crime and maintaining accountability when officers went astray. Other times they were a thorn in our side, making us look inept or worse. We had a love/hate relationship.

The chief launched into a short monologue, informing the press that yes, despite our increased patrols around the zoo, another animal had been snatched from under our noses. "I've assigned a team of my best people to relentlessly pursue those who'd dared to take Sarki and the other beloved creatures from their homes at the zoo."

Best people? Aw, shucks. I somehow managed to blush and beam at the same time.

Trish LeGrande, a cheesecake reporter from Dallas with a breathy voice, pumpkin-spice hair, and a Texas-sized bosom, shot her hand into the air and stood, teetering on her stilettos. "Do you have any clues as to who might have committed these crimes?"

The chief's response was intentionally vague. "We're working some angles."

"What angles exactly?" Trish demanded.

"I can't give you more details at this time," the chief said. "But I feel confident we'll close in on the thieves soon."

He hadn't seemed so confident a few minutes ago in his office, but I knew he had to put on a brave face out here, to give the people hope.

The grilling began, reporters badgering the chief with essentially the same question slightly rephrased, as if he'd somehow be tricked into giving away his secrets. Eventually, the reporters gave up, and turned their attention to my partner.

Trish pointed a pink-tipped finger at Brigit. "Is that the K-9 who was shot recently?"

The chief confirmed. "Yes, it is."

Trish tilted her head in a coy manner. "I can see that the fur on her chest hasn't fully grown back yet. Isn't it soon for her to be back on the job?"

The insinuation that I'd force Brigit back to work before she was ready cut to my core. I loved this precocious pooch with all my heart.

The chief responded with, "The dog's handler can best answer those questions."

Uh-oh. Is he expecting me to address a room of reporters? On live TV? I could face violent creeps on the job and barely bat an eye but, thanks to my unpredictable stutter, public speaking scared the heck out of me.

Chief Garelik glanced back at me and held out a hand to invite me to the podium. "Officer Luz?"

There was nothing I could do. My heart pounded and I willed my stutter to stay at bay as I stepped forward. The chief eased aside as I led Brigit to the podium. When the dog realized she couldn't see anything from behind the large lectern, she stood on her back legs, put her front paws up on the top, and, as if to respond to the question herself, *woofed* into the microphone.

I raised a hand to indicate my partner. "You have your answer."

The reporters chuckled. No doubt my partner's impromptu performance would become the day's sound bite.

I leaned into the microphone, speaking slowly. "Brigit is not only my partner and packmate, but she's my best friend. If I'd had any concerns whatsoever about her b-being ready to return to work, I would not have allowed her back on duty. She's very smart and very driven to do her job, and she let me know she was ready to resume patrol." It was true. She'd quickly become bored being cooped up at home. All there was to do at the house was guard the backyard against squirrels. Squirrel patrol was the petty duty of mere house dogs.

Trish was relentless. "The bullet struck her chest. It was a serious injury. Surely it's slowed her down some."

"Not a bit," I replied. "She's b-better than ever." *Yay!* I'd gotten through my interview with only two little stutters.

I retreated and the chief resumed his place at the podium, responding to several more questions.

The final question, asked by a reporter from the local NPR radio station, was less forceful and more supportive. "What can the public do to help?"

"Several things," the chief replied. "We ask anyone with security cameras who lives or runs a business in the vicinity of the zoo to share their footage from last night with us. They can also keep an eye out for these animals." The chief pointed at the screen on which the springbok currently appeared. "Somebody out there has seen something, knows something. We ask that anyone with information call the number on the screen or 911. Thanks, folks."

With that, he raised a hand in good-bye and left the podium. He passed us as he aimed for the door, commanding us under his breath, "Find those animals!"

As if we haven't been putting enough pressure on ourselves. Now I felt like a pot roast in a pressure cooker. Lots of tension and lots of heat.

As Derek went to follow the chief, the detective grabbed his arm and pulled him to a stop. "You're not just for show, Officer Mackey. Pay a visit to the businesses along University Drive near the zoo. Get their security tapes. Ditto for the houses on Winton Terrace. The thieves brought the springbok out of the back of the zoo where it borders the street. They must have parked there."

As much as I despised Derek, adding a third person to the case would help us move the investigation along faster. For the sake of Fabiana, Fernando, Dinari, and sweet little Sarki, I'd suck it up and work with the jerk.

Detective Bustamente and I returned to his office at the station and holed up for a powwow. While we waited for Derek to round up the security camera footage, we needed to move ahead on the other two angles—the wildlife trafficking angle and the welding angle.

I'd already spent quite a bit of time working the wildlife trafficking angle to no success, but because Sarki and the birds would only be valuable alive, I had not contacted any of the trophy-hunting outfits. The missing sprinkbok was another matter. Dinari could be worth more dead than alive, especially to a wealthy trophy hunter looking to add to his collection. Trophy hunters liked tamer prey for a couple of reasons. One, they were easier to shoot because they were habituated to humans and didn't fear hunters nearly as much as their wild-born counterparts. And two, because they'd been raised in artificial environments, they made more attractive trophies, not bearing the scars and shabby fur of truly wild animals.

Bustamente wagged his fingers at me. "Get on your laptop and find all of the trophy-hunting ranches in the area. We've got to move quick before that springbok's head ends up hanging on someone's wall." He tossed me a pad of sticky notes. "Write the names and phone numbers on those notes and hand them to me as you go."

I set my laptop up on the corner of his desk, logged in to the Internet, and ran a search. I started with ranches in Tarrant and surrounding counties, jotting down the names and phone numbers, and making a row of sticky notes in front of Bustamente. Meanwhile, he was on his phone, calling each of them.

"If anyone tells you they've got a single springbok for sale," he said to the person on the other end of the line, "get their contact information and pass it along to me right away." He gave the person both his office and cell numbers. "Any time, day or night."

I continued my search, eventually cyber-venturing into the next counties and secretly wishing the station would hire an intern. While I was glad to be part of such an important case, my skills were being squandered simply searching for information online. A college kid could compile this list. But I supposed not all detective work was particularly challenging or exciting. Again, if I wanted to be a detective, I'd have to take the bad with the good.

When the list seemed to keep growing and growing, I ran a search to find out how many trophy-hunting ranches there were in Texas. Google told me that there were over five hundred. *Sheesh.* I, in turn, told Bustamente, "There's more than five hundred in Texas alone. Thousands across the U.S." This task could be never-ending.

He looked down at his desk, which was covered with sticky notes three deep. "I'll call the local TV stations, see if they can prod those up the chain to get this story on the national news. Meanwhile, find out something about welding. Everything I know about it could fit in this cup." He raised his coffee mug, sloshing stale coffee over the rim and onto a couple of the sticky notes.

"Same for me," I said. "The only thing I know about welding is that they teach it in prison."

"Did Danny Landis learn welding while he was in the joint?"

"No. He took the custodial program."

While the detective phoned the local television offices, I schooled myself in basic welding. Evidently there were many different types of welding and welding torches. Stick. MIG. TIG. Arc. Oxy-fuel. Fixed-position. Gas metal arc. Solid core. Flux core. The latter sounded like something from *Back to the Future.*

One article noted that an acetylene torch gives off a smell similar to garlic. *Aha!* When the detective was between calls, I mentioned this intriguing fact to him.

"What do you know," he said. "The CSO's 'useless tidbit' about his team member smelling garlic wasn't so useless after all."

On the contrary, it told us what type of tool the thieves had used to cut through the metal. Now, we just needed to get our hands on that particular tool, seize it as evidence. Armed with general information about welding, my next step would be to figure out where in the area a welder might be found.

While he waited on hold for a station manager, Bustamente gave me a suggestion. "Search job listings for welders. That'll tell us who hires them."

"Good idea."

I searched several job-hunting Web sites. Indeed. Monster. Career Builder. Several large companies in the area had listings for welders, including the ones the chief had mentioned earlier. Lockheed Martin, the aerospace company in west Fort Worth. The General Motors plant in nearby Arlington, where my father worked. Oil and gas companies. Outfits that installed pipes, tanks, and sprinkler systems. Sheet-metal businesses. Of course there were smaller companies that did fence work. Collision-repair shops employed welders, too.

While searching online, I discovered the local community college offered a two-year welding program that would result in a Level 1 certification upon completion. Welding instruction was offered as part of the art curriculum at several area universities and art schools, allowing students to explore metal sculpture. Welding was even offered at some local high schools, including Trimble Technical High School, which sat within my beat. The Texas Workforce Commission also offered welding instruction through community learning centers.

To make sure I'd covered all the bases, I ran a search of recent arrests to see if anyone had been caught stealing animals or using welding equipment to access a building in a burglary. After I typed in key terms, an arrest report popped up. The report had been filed recently by one of the officers who worked in the westernmost division. He'd arrested a supervisor at an oil and gas company after hidden surveillance video showed the man stealing welding tools and equipment from a job site. The list of items stolen included three acetylene torches.

I connected to the detective's wireless printer, circled my finger on my computer mouse pad, and clicked. His printer sprang to life, spitting out a copy of the report.

Bustamente completed his calls and hung up the phone. "School me."

I gave him a quick rundown of the information I'd found. There were many businesses in the area that employed large numbers of welders, but there were small outfits and freelancers, too. Many different types of educational facilities offered welding instruction in the city. "I also found something interesting. Take a look at this." I retrieved the printout from the tray and handed it to him.

He read it over and looked back up at me. "Is this guy still in custody?"

"I haven't checked, but I doubt it."

The chances were slim. Bail for most people who committed property crimes was generally set low enough that they could bond out.

Bustamente tapped some keys on his keyboard, maneuvered his mouse, and performed a few clicks before leaning in to look more closely at the screen. "He was released the next day. No attorney of record."

The guy had represented himself. Not a smart move. If he were poor enough, an attorney would have been appointed to represent him. Presumably, he didn't qualify for free representation. Of course some people who didn't qualify nevertheless had a difficult time scraping together the money for a retainer. That could be the case here. There were also people who were too arrogant to hire legal counsel, who thought they could fight the system on their own. Those people were stupid. The procedures were complicated and the prosecutors were clever.

"Where should we start?" I asked.

"With the man who was arrested."

"And then?"

After some discussion, we both agreed that a welder who was gainfully employed by a large company seemed least likely to need the money from the sale of stolen zoo animals. A starving student or freelance welder without a stable income seemed a better bet. Of course there was also the possibility that someone had bought an acetylene torch, a welding mask, and the other necessary gear and learned basic metal cutting and welding from a video on YouTube. After all, we couldn't be certain the job was sloppy only because the thieves had been in a hurry. Maybe it was due to a lack of training.

I shared my concerns with the detective. "The thief might not be a professional welder. He could be self-taught."

He grunted. "A few online tutorials and everyone thinks they're an expert."

I'd used online tutorials myself. But despite watching three makeup lessons, I'd yet to master the smoky eye.

Given all the time in the world and no other duties, we could visit every welder in the county. But with limited staff and all of us with other work responsibilities, we had to prioritize. I'd visit several of the schools where welding instruction was offered, and Detective Bustamente would visit the others. Maybe one of the teachers could tell us if anyone in their class was a viable suspect. I'd also visit some of the smaller freelance welding businesses, and anyone who appeared to be working solo.

The detective pushed back from his desk and stood. "Let's go pay the thief a visit."

Rising from my seat, I speculated. "I wonder if Danny Landis owns an acetylene torch. He could have learned basic welding from a buddy in prison, right?" After all, he'd expressed an interest in learning the trade.

"Let's pay him another visit, too," Bustamente said. "But we need to be careful. We don't want to get tunnel vision."

The detective made a valid point. Wrong conclusions could be reached when an investigator focused too much on one potential suspect rather than keeping an open mind. Still, we hadn't been able to definitively rule Landis out. He could be behind the animal thefts, after all.

The detective grabbed his coat, I rousted my dozing partner, and off we went.

We parked at the curb in front of the large suburban brick home belonging to the former supervisor at the oil and gas company. In the drive sat a four-wheel-drive Chevy Silverado High Country crew cab pickup in a deep blue color. This model came with heated and cooled seats, and lots of sparkly chrome accents, you know, for tough guys. I peeked in the window as we made our way to the door. Yep, leather interior, too. With its Blu-ray entertainment and Bose sound systems, the truck would've set the guy back around sixty grand. The guy had certainly splurged. But pickups were a status symbol among men in the state of Texas. Heck, among women, too.

We made our way up to the porch and knocked. When the man answered, he said nothing, waiting for us to take the lead. He crossed his arms tightly over his chest and tucked his hands into his armpits, a smug grin on his face as the scent of his $130-a-bottle Acqua di Giò cologne wafted up my nose.

I looked past the man into the house. On a hook inside the door hung a stylish men's leather jacket. Beyond that, in the living room, sat a leather couch and a big-screen television nearly as wide as I was tall. It was tuned to a movie on a premium cable channel. My observations told me that, in addition to being arrogant and stupid, this man had expensive tastes and was prone to indulge himself. My guess was that his salary as the welding foreman didn't provide sufficient funds to keep him in the luxurious manner to which he aspired, hence he'd stolen the equipment for resale.

Bustamente introduced us, not bothering to offer the man a hand. It was just as well. I wouldn't want to get any of his underarm sweat on me. "We're aware you were arrested on suspicion of stealing welding equipment."

"I know my rights," the man spat. "I don't have to talk. The First Amendment says so."

His smug grin grew even smuger. My presumption had been right. This man was both arrogant and stupid. The First Amendment addressed free speech. It was the Fifth Amendment that protected individuals from being forced to incriminate themselves. But no point in giving him a civics lesson.

Undeterred, the detective asked, "We're wondering if you also took the springbok."

The man's face clouded in confusion. "Spring box?" he said, apparently forgetting he didn't have to talk to us. "What's that? Some kind of tool?"

"Springbok." The detective enunciated more clearly this time. "It's a type of antelope. It was taken from the zoo last night."

"An antelope?" The man scoffed and raised both his hands and his voice. "What in the world would I want with an antelope?"

"Do you hunt?" I asked.

"Hell, no," the man said. "I'm not getting up before dawn to cover myself in doe piss and sit in a freezing-cold stand in the woods."

Another glance over his shoulder told me he was more

likely to find his entertainment on the enormous TV in his living room.

Bustamente cut me a look that said, *It's not him.*

I cut him one back that said, *I don't think so, either.*

"Thanks for your time," the detective said, to which the man responded by slamming his door in our faces.

"That was fun," Bustamente said.

"Oodles," I agreed.

We headed back to my cruiser and, twenty minutes later, pulled up to Danny Landis's home once again. He was outside, wrangling a long extension ladder from the luggage rack atop his SUV. His wife stood on the lawn nearby, their son on her hip. Danny's face clouded when he saw my squad car stop at the curb. So did his wife's. Their son seemed happier to see us. He raised his small hand and waved. The detective and I waved back, offering the little boy smiles as well. *His dad might be an ex-con, but that tiny tyke sure is a cutie.*

Bustamente levered himself out of the car and addressed Landis. "Let me give you a hand with that ladder."

While I retrieved Brigit from the back, the detective helped Landis ease the ladder off the vehicle and lean it against the rusty shed out back.

I stepped up next to his wife and gestured at the ladder. "Your husband found work?"

"Guess you could say that." She shifted the boy to her other hip. "Danny put up flyers and got paid to hang peoples' Christmas lights. Now that the holidays are over, he's getting paid to take them down. I don't much like it. All those rich wives hiring my husband to get up on that tall ladder. They don't want their own husbands doing it, but it's okay for my husband to climb up there and maybe break his neck."

I felt for her. "I wouldn't like that, either. My boyfriend's a firefighter and I worry about him all the time."

She issued a *hm* that said she felt for me, too. *Surprising what people can have in common, huh?*

The ladder dispensed with, the men returned to the front yard where Landis turned to us. Unlike the last guy we'd interrogated, he was neither arrogant nor stupid. He was simply uneducated, unskilled, and overburdened.

"What do you want?" he demanded.

Bustamente filled him in. "There's another animal missing from the zoo. A male springbok."

No point in trying to keep the animal's identity a secret this time. The information had already been provided to news outlets and presumably reported on the radio and TV.

"Why are you back here?" Landis demanded. "You looked around last time and didn't find nothin'."

Bustamente didn't beat around the bush. "We'd like to look again."

Landis stiffened. "You got a search warrant?"

"No," the detective admitted. He cut me a discreet look. There might not be enough evidence to support a search warrant, especially given that we'd found nothing to incriminate Landis on our earlier visit.

Landis frowned. "Maybe you should go get one. I'm tired of being wrongfully accused, everybody pushing me around all the time."

"I don't blame you," Bustamente said. "But put yourself in our shoes. You were there when the birds went missing and you know your way around the zoo. That makes it seem like you could be the one who took the animals. To be honest, we don't think there's much chance you did it, but we've got to check out all possible leads. Otherwise, it makes us look bad, like we didn't do our jobs. I need to work. Like you, I've got a family to take care of."

Landis's frown loosened a bit, but didn't entirely disappear. When he spoke, though, he sounded far less convicted. "I still think maybe I should get a lawyer and fight back."

Rather than threaten Landis, the detective seemed to realize, as had I, that the man only wanted a sense of control ovcr things, somc sign of rcspcct. "You could hirc a lawyer," Bustamente acknowledged. "But I'm hoping you'll work with us on this. We're hoping to eliminate you as a suspect. Then we can move on to finding whoever actually took Dinari."

Landis's frown melted away entirely, and he gazed wistfully off into the distance, as if picturing Dinari in his mind. "Those animals are pretty. Funny, too. Sometimes they'd get to bouncing around like the broncs at the rodeo." He turned back to us and cocked his head. "All right. Have at it." He circled his hand in the air to indicate the house and yard.

Again, we searched his SUV, the house, the attic, and the shed. Again, we found nothing, no welding torch, mask, or other clue pointing to his guilt. And again, we harbored a tiny residual doubt that, nonetheless, Danny Landis could be our guy.

THIRTY-THREE
THIS K-9 DON'T CARE

Brigit

The cat had run and hidden under the bed again, as if it thought Brigit might try to chase it. *Sheesh.* Felines were such narcissistic creatures. Brigit had much better things to do with her time than pursue a house cat. Didn't that silly feline realize Brigit was on duty? Probably not. Brigit had seen plenty of dogs with jobs. Guard dogs. Cadaver dogs. Explosive detection dogs like Blast. Other police K-9s, of course. But she'd never once seen an employed cat. *What a bunch of mewing moochers.*

THIRTY-FOUR
YOU'RE NOT THE BOSS OF ME

The Poacher

Christmas was over and the new year had begun, but Vicki had yet to begin her search for work. When he'd asked about it she'd snapped at him. She said she'd liked being a stay-home mom the past few weeks and wasn't ready to go back to waiting tables. "Besides," she'd said, "you're making enough money for us to get by."

The weight on his shoulders threatened to crush him.

He still hadn't been able to bring himself to tell Vicki he'd been fired from his welding job at the oil and gas company. Even if he could bring himself to tell her, she'd want to know why and when, and then she'd ask how he got the money he'd handed over to her and how he'd paid for all those nice Christmas presents he'd bought. If he got a new job, he could tell her he'd left the other job voluntarily for a better opportunity. But he hadn't heard back from any of the jobs he'd applied for, and the cold calls had led nowhere.

Each weekday, he continued to pretend to go to a job he didn't have. He'd even had to pretend to be working out of town on the nights he'd pulled the zoo heists. She'd been especially disappointed that he'd purportedly been called to handle an out-of-town emergency on New Year's Eve. She'd bought a bottle of cheap champagne so the two of them could celebrate. Luckily, she seemed appeased when they'd celebrated last night. He might have been a day late, but for once he wasn't a dollar short. That antelope had brought him enough cash to last a few weeks.

Maybe the new year will bring me a new job, he thought as he rolled slowly down Industrial Avenue, an appropriately named street in a warehouse district southwest of the I-30/I-35 mix-master. He planned to make more cold calls today, see if maybe he'd stumble upon something. If he couldn't land a welding job, maybe somebody would need some help in their warehouse.

By mid-afternoon, his hope was gone. Nobody was hiring full-time. Nobody needed help on a part-time or temporary basis, either. *They'd keep him in mind in case something came up.* But if something didn't come up soon, he'd find himself out on the streets. What's worse, he might cause Vicki and the kids to end up out on the streets, too.

His only option seemed to be self-employment. Here in Texas, people had a lot of state pride. They went gaga over anything in the shape of the state or a star, which not only stood for the Lone Star State but also represented the Dallas Cowboys. Heck, in prison they'd learned to weld by making star- and Texas-shaped metal wall art. If you added the words "God Bless Texas," even better. The prisons sold the inmates' work in their gift shops. He could buy some scrap sheet metal for next to nothing and try to make a go of it, maybe sell the stuff at the flea market or a craft show. Of course he'd need a place to ply his trade.

As he headed out of the area, a freestanding garage with

a FOR RENT sign posted on it caught his eye. The metal pull-down door was dented in several places and the cinder-block walls were covered in graffiti, but that didn't much matter. If he rented this small garage, he could do work here and store the trailer in it, too. He'd originally planned to resell the trailer after using it to transport the antelope, but he'd changed his mind and decided to hang on to it. It could come in handy for transporting tools and supplies and such. He hadn't yet registered the trailer in his name. The tax and registration fees would set him back another hundred bucks he couldn't spare right now. He'd incur a small penalty when he finally filed the paperwork, but keeping the trailer out of his name could also reduce the risk of it being traced to him if someone reported seeing it near the zoo. Of course, Vicki didn't know about the trailer. He hadn't told her. She'd only ask what he needed it for, why he'd spent good money on it. He'd rented a unit at one of those public storage places for stowing the thing, but he couldn't use that space to work in. It was against the rules. But if he could move the trailer to this garage, he could kill two birds with one stone. *Two birds. Ugh.* He thought of the macaws and felt a twinge of guilt in his gut.

He turned into the asphalt drive, cut his engine, and pulled out his phone. He dialed the number on the sign. When a man answered, he asked. "How much you askin' for the garage on south Jones Street?"

"Four fifty a month, plus three hundred damage deposit. Cash only."

The $750 would take a big bite out of his remaining cash, but what choice did he have?

"Will you do month to month?" The Poacher didn't want to be stuck with a long-term lease if things didn't work out and he ended up not needing a workspace.

"Long as you pay in advance," the guy said. "If I don't have the next month's rent by the twenty-fifth of the month, you're out and I get someone new in there."

They arranged to meet at the bay first thing the next morning to exchange cash for keys. Maybe the year was off to a promising start, after all.

THIRTY-FIVE
THE INVESTIGATION GOES SOUTH

Megan

Knowing I was likely to get more information and clues from visiting the welders in person than I would by simply giving them a phone call, I'd made a list of small shops and solo welders to visit, grouping them by location. Fortunately, they tended to be concentrated in a few primary pockets. The oldest industrial section of the city lay just to the south and west of the intersection of Interstates 30 and 35. It was the closest to the zoo and sat within my usual beat. Farther to the south, where I-35 met I-20, was Carter Industrial Park. A third, much newer industrial area called "AllianceTexas" spanned the property around Alliance Airport directly north of the city. The rents at the first two parks were much lower than those at AllianceTexas, so it seemed to make sense to focus on those locales first.

I'd planned to start off the morning by visiting the places inside my beat and work my way south. But before we could head out, Detective Bustamente summoned me into the station by knocking on the inside of his window and waving his arms to get my attention as Brigit and I headed to our cruiser in the parking lot. I rushed inside, jogging down the hall, Brigit's nails clicking on the tile as she ran along with me. In the detective's office I found Derek and the detective hunkered over a map of the city spread out on the desk.

"Did we get a break?" I stepped closer so I could look at the map, too.

Bustamente said, "You know that flocking stuff that was sprayed on the security camera at the zoo?"

"Yeah?"

"Officer Mackey discovered it was also sprayed on a bunch of security cameras along Winton Terrace and other neighborhood streets in the area. The thieves thought it would prevent them from being picked up on cameras, which it did, but it also gave us a rough map of the escape route they used." He pointed to streets he'd marked with yellow highlighter. "See this? Looks like they drove through neighborhoods all the way south to Interstate 20. I've requested footage from businesses along the frontage road down that way." He capped the pen and used it to point out the area where he'd requested video. "Maybe they picked something up."

I looked up, my gaze going between Derek and the detective. "What about the footage from the cameras as they were sprayed?" Surely they'd captured the thieves when they'd come to disable the devices.

"Typical MO," Derek said. "Guys dressed all in black and wearing ski masks."

"Judging from their builds and the way they moved," Bustamente added, "there appears to be at least two of them."

The news was both disappointing and hopeful at the same time. Disappointing in that we still had nothing concrete, hadn't yet identified the lawbreakers, but hopeful in that maybe we soon would.

"What about fingerprints?" I asked. "Any word yet?"

"Crime scene lifted some," the detective said, "but most belonged to zoo staff. There were no hits on the others."

In other words, if the other prints belonged to the thieves, the thieves had never been arrested so their prints weren't in the database. It was also possible the other prints were made by zoo visitors trying to peek over the fences and see what was going on behind the scenes, or other zoo employees whose prints we hadn't obtained.

Bustamente promised to call both me and Derek once he reviewed the camera footage from businesses along I-20.

As Derek, Brigit, and I headed out of the station, I tossed Derek a "Good job, Mackey." Honestly, all he'd done was follow a trail of proverbial bread crumbs in the form of fake snow spray. It didn't take a flocking genius to figure it out. A rookie could have done the same. But I might as well play nice.

My reward for congratulating the Big Dick was a snide, "Wish I could say the same for you, *Luz-er.* Everyone knows you'd be nothing without that dog."

His words made me falter as I walked. *It's not true, is it? That I owe all of my success to Brigit?*

As if she knew she'd been used as a pawn, Brigit yapped and lunged at Derek. He jerked out of her reach and cackled.

I loaded Brigit into our patrol car and climbed into the driver's seat. *Derek is wrong,* I told myself. *Don't let him psych you out.* Brigit did an outstanding job as a K-9 cop, no doubt about it. But she hadn't done it alone. My intellect and guidance had been integral to our success, too.

As I threw the car into reverse, I mentally shifted gears, too. Given that it appeared the thieves had headed south, it made sense for me to start my investigation down that way. Carter Industrial Park was not far from the Tarrant County College campus where the welding classes were offered, so I decided to start with the school and head on to the industrial park from there.

Brigit and I traced the thieves' presumed route, looking for clues along the way but seeing none. When I reached I-20, I turned east, exiting on Campus Drive and turning into the parking lot of the college. With students out on winter break until mid-January, the lot was mostly empty, only a few cars parked in the staff spots. A skeleton crew manned the administration offices.

I stepped up to the woman at the counter. "I'm hoping to speak with your welding instructors. Can you help me out?"

"I'm not sure anyone's in over there, but I'll check." She picked up the phone on her desk and dialed a four-digit number. A few seconds later she raised her brows and lifted her chin to let me know someone had answered. "It's the front desk. There's a police officer here wants to talk to you." She paused a moment. "Uh-huh. All right." She hung up the phone and turned back to me. "You can head over. It's in the building marked 'STEC'." She pointed to a map on the wall beside us for reference.

I thanked the woman and headed to the building. I found a surprisingly slight man dressed head to toe in welding gear. Heavy-duty boots housed his small feet. A thick welding jacket protected his torso. A raised welding mask topped his head, making it look as if an openmouthed monster was about to chomp down on him from behind. The stubble on the man's face couldn't be called a five o'clock shadow because one, it was only nine in the morning, and two, the white-blond hairs didn't darken his cheeks. If anything, they made him appear ghostlike. Same for his flame-blue eyes.

I introduced myself and Brigit. "You may have heard about the missing animals from the zoo," I said.

"Saw it on the news," he replied. "It's got to be an inside job, right? I mean, how do you get an antelope out of the zoo without someone noticing?"

"That's exactly what we're trying to figure out," I said. "And it's why I'm here. Can you tell me whether you've got any current or former students who might have been involved in something like this?"

The guy wasn't an idiot. "The thieves cut into the animal cages?"

"It's a theory we're working on," I said. "We need you to keep that theory to yourself, okay?"

"Sure." He stood a little straighter, as if proud to be on the inside of a high-profile investigation.

"So?" I said. "Any students that come to mind? Any of them ask any odd questions that could indicate their involvement? Seem to have suddenly come into a chunk of money?"

He looked up in thought, which basically meant he was looking up at his mask. Unfortunately, his mask gave him no answers. He returned his gaze to my face. "No. I can't think of anyone in particular. I mean, we get some people in the classes who have criminal records, but it's usually for DUI or drugs. Some type of petty theft, maybe. Nothing related to stealing animals that I know of. Of course they don't all mention the fact that they've got a record."

"All right." I handed him my business card. "If anything changes or you think of someone, give me a call."

Shortly after leaving the community college campus, Brigit and I rolled up to a warehouse just south of Altamesa

Boulevard. Despite the cool outdoor temperatures, both bay doors were open. Men in coveralls, knit caps, and heavy canvas work gloves milled about inside, carrying pieces of sheet metal and loading them into the back of a commercial truck.

I raised a hand in greeting. "'Morning, guys. Got a second?"

They exchanged glances, probably wondering why a police officer was wandering into their warehouse.

Once they'd gathered, I looked around. "Is this everyone?"

They murmured in agreement.

I pulled out a flyer the police department's public relations division had prepared and held it up. "As you might have heard, these animals were taken from the zoo." The men eyed the flyer, which included the same photos of the macaws, the colobus monkey, and the springbok that had been used in the slide show at yesterday's press conference. "I'm just out asking around, trying to find out if anyone has seen anything or knows anything about the animals, where they might be. We'd love to get them back."

A man at the front cocked his head, his eyes wary. "Some reason why you're coming to my shop?"

Better not to disclose the secret that a welding torch had been used to circumvent the zoo's security system and gain access to the animals. But common sense said the springbok must have been taken away in some type of truck or trailer.

"A truck or trailer would have been needed to transport the springbok," I said. "There's lots of trucks and trailers in industrial areas like this." I offered a casual shrug. "That's all." The man's features relaxed as I held out the flyer. "Would you mind posting this?" I asked. "We're trying to spread the word. We really need the public's help on this one. If we don't find those animals soon, there's no telling what could happen to them."

"All right." He took the paper from me.

"Thanks." I raised a hand again to the group, this time in good-bye. "Please let us know if you hear or see anything."

They gave me another murmur of agreement.

I repeated virtually the same routine at three other places. I paid special attention to the welders who worked for the fencing company. After all, the canned hunting ranches required extra-tall perimeter fences to keep some of the exotic wildlife trapped inside. It was possible someone installing a fence at a hunting ranch had been approached about stealing an animal from the zoo, or perhaps had come up with the idea after seeing the wild animals on-site. Then again, maybe I was looking for connections where there were none.

Brigit and I spent the rest of the morning in the area, visiting machine shops and pipe companies, leaving flyers and business cards. A couple of the freelance welder shops were locked up and dark, the welder either out on a job or taking an extra day of vacation. Who could blame them? If I were my own boss, I'd give myself an extra day off, too, plus an employee-of-the-year award.

Our final stop was at an auto body shop. Bandera music blared from a radio inside, where we found two Latino guys in oil stained gray coveralls working on a shiny red car sitting up on a lift. A classic Plymouth Road Runner. I'd learned a lot about cars, could identify many of the makes and models, both from writing traffic tickets as a cop and from dating Seth, who had an affinity for muscle cars.

Unfortunately, the grease monkeys knew nothing about the stolen monkey. Nothing about the other animals, either.

They shook their heads. The one with the mustache added, "Sorry."

"Here's my card." I handed out what felt like the millionth business card of the day. "If you hear anything, please call me."

As I walked out, the back wheels of the Plymouth began to spin. I knew how the car felt. It seemed I was spinning my wheels, too.

THIRTY-SIX
EGGROLL OVER

Brigit

Seth came over and brought Blast with him. *Yay!* One sniff and she knew he'd also brought egg rolls, fried rice, and lo mein noodles. *I gotta get me some of that.*

A few minutes later, Seth and Megan sat on the couch, eating their dinner. Megan had filled Brigit's bowl with wet dog food in an attempt to keep her from begging, but Brigit wasn't fooled. Human food was always better than dog food. Still, she knew if she was too insistent Megan wouldn't share. She had to play this right if she was going to score an egg roll and some noodles.

She sat patiently across the coffee table from them, blocking their view of the television. They couldn't ignore her when she was in their way. She batted her eyes and whined softly to say *Please?* She drooled some, too, but not on purpose. The drool just came naturally.

Megan groaned. "Move, you mangy mongrel." She tossed a bit of egg roll off to the side so Brigit would move out of the way of the TV. *Such an obvious tactic.*

Brigit scurried over and gobbled down the yummy tidbit before returning to her spot between Megan and the screen. It was a delicate dance the two had performed many a time.

Megan tossed a noodle this time, using the chopsticks to fling it all the way into the kitchen. "Go get it, girl!"

Oh, she'd get it all right. Brigit dashed to the kitchen, narrowly beating Blast, and slurped the noodle up off the floor, wolfing it down. Even if she had seen *Lady and the Tramp,* Brigit wouldn't have shared her noodles. They were her favorite. She'd let Blast have the broccoli, though. She wasn't a fan.

The noodle dispensed with, she returned to her spot in front of the TV. Megan groaned again. Their dance continued until the food was gone and all that remained were the fortune cookies. Megan tossed Brigit a piece of cookie and Brigit caught it midair. Blast did the same.

Her mission accomplished and her tummy full, Brigit flopped down flat on the rug so Megan and Seth could see the TV. *Enjoy the show.*

THIRTY-SEVEN
NOT TOO SHABBY

The Poacher

It was a few minutes after eight in the morning when he held out his first month's rent and damage deposit to a man who didn't believe in written leases, issuing receipts, or, from the smell of him, deodorant. *Phew.* The Poacher accepted a single key in return. It was on a key chain that said "World's Best Grandmother." *Should I be concerned about that?* For all he knew, the guy had killed some elderly woman and was now renting out her properties. He hadn't offered his name.

The Poacher gestured to the graffiti. "How would you feel about painting the place?"

"I would feel that the lease is as is," the man said. "You want the building painted, you can do it yourself." With that, the man returned to his car, leaving a stench in his wake. He gunned his engine and drove away.

Cheap son of a bitch. The Poacher climbed into his truck. As he looked over his shoulder to back up, he spotted Harper's pink cell phone tucked into the map pocket on the inside of the passenger door. Maybe Vicki was right. Maybe Harper was too young for a cell phone.

He leaned over and retrieved the phone. The movement

caused the screen to come to life. Any irritation he'd felt at his landlord for being so tightfisted or at Harper for forgetting her cell phone was immediately forgotten when he saw she'd chosen a photo of the two of them at the zoo for her screen saver. *Damn, I love that little squirt.* He slid the phone into the glove box for safekeeping. He'd have a talk with her later, let her know she needed to do a better job of keeping up with it or he'd have to take it away.

He headed off down Vickery. After paying additional deposits at the electric and water companies to have service turned on at the building, he made a stop at a hardware store for supplies. He returned to the garage with three gallons of their cheapest white paint, painter's tape, and a set of rollers and brushes. After sweeping up the trash around the building, he set to work, painting over the graffiti. It took two coats and most of the day to repaint the outside of the building.

He'd nearly soiled himself when a police cruiser rolled slowly by, a dark-haired female cop at the wheel and a huge furry dog in the back. She'd glanced his way but had only raised a hand off the wheel in greeting. He'd returned the gesture, momentarily forgetting he had the roller in his hand and inadvertently splattering himself with white paint.

He spent the rest of the day doing the best he could to smooth out the dents in the bay door and the hail damage on the trailer. He didn't need one of his torches for that task. A simple butane lighter provided enough heat to enable him to work the metal, force it back into place. The hail damage was a surprisingly easy fix. A little heat and the metal practically popped itself back into place.

Now that he'd done what he could outside, he turned his attention to the inside of the garage. He hosed down the floor and walls, dusted off the bare fluorescent bulbs overhead, and wiped the grime off the small panel of glass in the heavy steel door on the side of the building. Burglar bars were affixed over the window, the afternoon sun shining through them and casting a hashtag-shaped shadow on the stained concrete floor. If Harper were here, she'd whip out her sidewalk chalk and challenge him to a game of tic-tac-toe.

By then it was dark and time to get home for dinner. He hadn't stopped for lunch and his stomach was growling like a lion. Stowing the leftover paint and supplies inside, he locked up and took a final look at the place. It was still a basic cinder-block building, nothing fancy. But it looked less shabby than it had this morning. Tomorrow, he'd pick up some sheet metal and put himself to work.

When he arrived home, Harper met him at the door. "Hi, Daddy!"

"Hey, squirt." He bent down and gave her a hug, whispering in her ear. "Did somebody forget something in my truck?" He pulled her cell phone from his pocket and held it up.

Her eyes went wide and bright with the fear that he'd take her phone away. "I'm sorry, Daddy!"

He held it out to her, but yanked it back as she went to take it from him. "You promise to be a good girl from now on and remember your phone?"

She nodded her head so hard it was a wonder it didn't pop off her neck. "I won't forget it again. I promise!"

He reached out and ruffled her copper hair, handing her the phone at the same time. "All right, squirt. Let's get some dinner."

He walked into the kitchen, where Vicki stood at the stove stirring a pot of spaghetti. She still wore her pajamas. She hadn't even bothered to dress today. No point in asking her whether she'd gone out to apply for any waitressing jobs. Meanwhile, he'd been busting his ass trying to find work, to think of some way to bring in some money. But he knew better than to bring it up. She'd tell him she deserved some time off after taking care of everything on her own while he was in jail, that it was his turn to work and pay the bills. She'd be right about that, too. Still, it chapped his ass.

She turned and gave him a smile and his ass felt a little less chapped. "Where's my kiss?"

He stepped over and planted a peck on her cheek.

She leaned into it before pulling her head back. "Why is there paint in your hair? And on your clothes?"

Uh-oh. He thought up a quick lie. "The boss asked me to help paint some signs at a drilling site."

She seemed to accept his response and asked nothing further. Unfortunately, she dropped a financial bombshell on him. "Refrigerator went out today. An appliance repair guy came out and looked it over, said it's shot." She held up the spoon she'd been using to stir the spaghetti to point at the cooler on the floor. "I put all the food in the ice chest so we wouldn't lose it. I thought I'd go pick out a new fridge tomorrow, maybe get one of them shiny stainless steel ones with the automatic ice thing in the door. That'll make our lives easier."

Like hell it would. A new fridge could cost a thousand dollars or more. He'd already spent a big chunk of money today on rent and deposits. "Maybe we should look at used refrigerators."

She scoffed and cut him a look, her lip quirked in disgust. "You'll buy your daughter an expensive new phone, but someone else's icky old fridge is good enough for me?"

"I didn't say that." He let out a loud breath. "We spent

a lot on Christmas and need to watch our money right now. The fridge is coming at a bad time is all."

She cocked her head. "We could finance it. That way we'd only have to pay a little each month rather than a bunch up front."

He supposed he couldn't argue with her logic. Well, he could, but he knew it would probably land him back on the floor in the boys' bedroom. He forced a smile. "Sounds like a plan."

She perked up as she turned back to thc stove. "Maybe I'll replace this old oven, too, while I'm at it."

His gut clenched. Ironically, all this talk about refrigerators and ovens had killed his appetite.

THIRTY-EIGHT
P TRAPPED

Megan

On January 4th, Detective Bustamente and I made visits to several businesses on the I-20 frontage road just west of I-35. They'd rounded up their camera footage for us to take a look at. Based on the route indicated by the trail of flock-covered home security cameras, we surmised the poachers had driven down this way to access the interstate.

Our first stop was at a hair salon. We were met at the door by the manager, a woman in her mid-thirties with dark hair slicked back in a shiny, perfectly coiffed updo. She led us through a fog of hair spray and dye fumes to a small room in the back that served as a storage area, break room, and office. Brigit lay on the floor next to the desk as the woman rounded up chairs and showed us how to work the program that played the footage.

"Take all the time you need." She returned to work, leaving us to watch the recording on her laptop.

While the business had an outdoor camera, it was positioned over the door and angled to primarily take in the sidewalk and parking lot. The angle was typical. Owners and managers installed the cameras to catch criminals trying to break into their places of business. They weren't concerned with the traffic going by on the street.

We leaned in, as if that would somehow give us a better vantage point, but all we could see was tires going by. Some tires were big and some were small. But none of them gave us any clues about the thieves we'd begun to call the Poachers.

As we headed out, we thanked the woman for her time.

"No problem." She turned back to the client in the chair in front of her, readied her shears, and gave the ends of the client's long brown locks a definitive *snip*.

We made our way next door to a thrift store. This time, we got tires plus about six inches of each vehicle that went by. We continued on, to no avail, until we watched the footage from a large gas station with a convenience store and diesel pumps specifically designed for eighteen-wheelers. The place was open twenty-four hours, which meant it was more prone to crime. For this reason, its security cameras covered a greater area. Still, while the cameras captured license plates of vehicles at the station, they lacked the resolution to get the license plates of vehicles driving past on the frontage road. We could identify some makes and models, however.

We made note of several vehicles that went by. A dark green Chevy Suburban. A red Toyota pickup truck hauling a horse trailer. An unmarked white delivery van. All were large enough to transport the springbok. The clock at the bottom of the screen ticked away the hours and minutes. Midnight. One A.M. Two A.M. The number of cars going by increased shortly after everyone rang in the new year, but decreased as the night turned to very early morning.

At 3:17 A.M., a semi pulled slowly out of the gas station.

At first, it was visible on only the first of the three outer cameras. As it continued, it filled the screens of both the first and second cameras. A couple seconds later and the truck's length took up the lenses of all three perimeter cameras, blocking our view of any traffic in the farther lane of the two-lane frontage road. Just as the back end of the eighteen-wheeler cleared the first camera, I caught a quick glimpse of the tail end of an enclosed white trailer. It looked to be a five-by-ten-foot size, or maybe a six-by-twelve, the type commonly used by building contractors or others for hauling tools and equipment to job sites.

I jabbed the button to pause the footage. "Did you see that?"

Bustamente's head bobbed. "I did. Looked like the back of a commercial trailer."

I dragged the feed back a few seconds and we watched again. Yep, definitely a smaller trailer behind the semi. "Do you think the poachers purposely timed it so they'd be hidden by the eighteen-wheeler when they drove past the cameras?"

"It's possible."

Unfortunately, the freeway entrance ramp sat only a few yards beyond the gas station, meaning that the vehicle pulling the trailer likely pulled onto the highway. That section of the interstate sat below the land that flanked it, and was bordered by tall noise-abatement walls. In other words, no cameras on the frontage road would be able to capture images of the cars driving down in what was essentially a topless tunnel. *But the traffic cameras might.*

I turned to the detective. "We need to see what the traffic cameras on I-20 picked up."

Bustamente concurred. "I'll put in a request. Meanwhile, you get back out and talk to some welders."

I spent the rest of the day paying a visit to the welding

instructor at Trimble Tech High School and meandering around the industrial area bordered roughly by Vickery on the north, I-35 on the east, Rosedale on the south, and Henderson on the west. I talked to a number of people, nearly all of them men, but with a couple of Rosie the Riveter-type women in the mix. While I saw several white trailers at the places I visited, there was no way for me to tell if any of them was the same one we'd caught a glimpse of in the video, hiding behind the eighteen-wheeler.

By late afternoon, I had made my rounds and was feeling flustered and frustrated. While I tried to maintain some hope the traffic cameras might yield a clue, I was afraid to hang too much hope on their footage. We didn't know exactly what time the springbok had been taken. It could have been in a number of the larger vehicles we'd noted, or the trailer could have had nothing to do with the theft of the beautiful antelope.

We had twenty minutes left in our shift. Making a pass through the Chisolm Trail mall would kill the time.

I parked in a reserved spot and let Brigit out of the back of the cruiser. As always, she popped a quick squat on the grassy patch nearby before we headed down the walkway. With it being January and nearing the dinner hour, things were slow, only an occasional shopper strolling about. Up ahead, I saw the barbershop quartet enter the glass-enclosed area of the mall. They strolled along in a single-file line, snapping their fingers as they sang Billy Joel's jaunty love ballad "For the Longest Time," the strains just loud enough for me to hear from this distance.

I raised a hand in greeting to some of the store personnel along the way. Several of them stood at their doors, with so little to do, looking bored. A glance into the nail salon told me that it was slow, too. Only one nail technician was on duty, the strawberry blond who'd handled my mother's manicure. The chairs both in front and in back of the other tables were pushed in, telling me no other techs were on duty. The strawberry blond had no client at the moment, and was using her downtime to scroll through her cell phone. I was tempted to take Brigit over, see if the woman would give her a pretty paw-dicure. But using human manicure implements on a dog would probably violate the health code.

When we reached the center hub, I pulled the glass door open and we stepped inside. Brigit's salivary glands went into instant overdrive, drool dripping from her lips. *Might as well get her some dinner.* She'd been cooped up in the cruiser more than usual today, and had been very patient about it. I'd get her some people food as a reward.

We aimed straight for the kebob stand, where I placed my order with the teenaged boy behind the counter. When it was ready, I slid the meat off the stick and tore it into pieces for my partner. She inhaled it, hardly chewing, smacking her lips after each bite. When she finished, I ruffled her ears. "You need to work on your table manners, Brigit."

We were on our way out when a fortyish brown-skinned woman in a snappy tangerine-colored peacoat called out to me from the other side of the space. "Officer! I need your help!"

As she hurried my way, I did the same, taking long strides.

"What's going on?" I asked as we met by the carousel.

She held up her left hand. Other than a pretty orange polish, her hand was bare. "It's my rings!" She used her right hand to point behind her. "I think they went down the sink in the ladies' room!"

"Show me."

We hurried into the ladies' room, where she pointed at

the nearest sink. "That's the one I used. I was drying my hands at the machine when I realized my rings were gone."

"You're sure you had them on when you came in?"

"I'm sure about it," she said. "I just got a manicure. I took them off while the girl was working on my nails, but I know I put them back on before I left. She reminded me not to forget them."

She must be talking about the strawberry blond. She was the only nail tech on duty. The reminder seemed to be part of the tech's routine. She'd done the same thing for the woman who'd had her nails done after my mother. It was thoughtful of her to make sure her clients didn't forget their jewelry.

"Did you take them off before you washed your hands?" I asked.

She shook her head. "No. The only time I take them off is for manicures and to clean them at home. I never take them off in public like this."

"Stay right here," I told the woman. "Don't let anyone use that sink. I'll get the mall manager and see what they can do."

"Thanks. I'm praying they're caught in the trap!"

I scurried over to the mall's administrative wing behind the carousel at the back of the center court. I found one of the assistant managers there, and told him what was going on.

"It's odd," he said. "This is the third woman who's reported losing rings in the mall since Thanksgiving."

Hmm. From reviewing the department's crime statistics, I knew certain crimes, like drunk driving, burglaries, and domestic violence, followed predictable patterns. They increased around the holidays and during the summer months when people were on vacation or grumpy from the unbearable heat. But other times, crimes occurred in random spurts, with certain statistics increasing for no apparent reason. I supposed it could be the same for situations like this, more people inadvertently and randomly misplacing their property around the same time.

"I'll have one of our maintenance crew meet us there," the manager said, picking up his phone. He dialed a number and spoke with someone on the other end. "Bring your toolbox to the ladies' room. A customer's rings went down the drain."

He joined me and Brigit, and we made our way to the restroom. The manager stood at the door while the maintenance worker came in carrying a large metal toolbox and a plastic bucket.

"I hope you find them!" cried the woman in the peacoat as she stepped back out of the way.

The man placed his toolbox on the tile floor, flipped open the latches, and removed an adjustable wrench. He pushed the bucket into place under the P trap and set to work, twisting the coupling until it was loose. Residual water ran into the bucket as he carefully removed the pipe. He turned the pipe and poured the contents into the bucket. A distinct *plop* could be heard as something heavy fell into the water.

He pulled the bucket out and we all looked down into it. Well, we humans looked down into it. Brigit, on the other hand, stuck her face into the bucket and took a drink. *Slup-slup.*

"No, girl!" I pulled her back.

Soap clouded the water a little, but not so much that we couldn't see something shiny at the bottom of the bucket. The maintenance man pushed back his shirtsleeve, reached into the bucket, and pulled the item out, holding it up. Rather than a wedding set, it was a birthstone ring, silver with an oval-shaped opal.

The woman gasped. "That's not it!" She hunched over the bucket. "Is there anything else in there?"

The man shook his head. "That was all that came out." After handing the ring to the mall manager, he picked up the P-shaped pipe, retrieved a soft-bristled cleaning brush with a bendable handle, and inserted it into the drain to dislodge anything that might be stuck inside. The brush emerged from the other end having moved nothing along. The pipe was empty.

"No!" the woman cried, putting her hands to her face as her eyes filled with tears. "Where could they be?"

She glanced frantically around, her gaze moving over the countertop and then underneath it as she crouched. She checked the stall she'd used. The maintenance worker and I helped her search to no avail.

"How did the rings fit?" I asked. "Were they loose?"

"I've lost a few pounds recently," she said. "My husband got me a treadmill for Christmas. They weren't as tight as they used to be, but they weren't loose enough to just fall off my hand."

I remembered the lotion the techs had put on our hands when my mother, sister, and I got manicures on New Year's Day, how slippery it had made our hands. "Did the tech put lotion on your hands?"

"Yes," she said. "She was very generous with it."

Seemed the rings could have slipped off afterward while the woman was rifling through a clothing rack, or sorting through smaller items in a bin. "Is it possible they slid off somewhere in the mall while you were shopping?"

She bit her lip at the thought.

"Let's retrace your steps," I suggested. "Start with where you were most recently and we'll work our way back to the nail salon."

We followed the woman's path from the bathroom back

to the bookstore, and from the bookstore to the shoe section of a department store. We found nothing. No engagement or wedding ring. We ended up back at the nail salon. While I scoured the walkway with my flashlight, the woman went back into the salon and spoke to the technician. Tears streamed down her face as she came back out. Unable to speak, she merely shook her head.

I put a supportive hand on her back. "I'm so sorry," I told her. "But maybe they'll turn up. Let's give the mall management your contact information and a description of the rings. The store managers, too. Maybe someone will find them."

I made the rounds with her a second time as she provided her name and phone number.

We headed out to the parking lot together. When Brigit and I reached our cruiser, she thanked me for helping her.

"I'll keep my fingers crossed," I told her.

She issued a mirthless chuckle. "Maybe if I'd crossed my fingers, the rings wouldn't have come off." She headed into the parking lot, swiping at a tear as she went.

THIRTY-NINE
LAPS IN JUDGMENT

Brigit

Brigit wasn't sure why Megan scolded her for lapping water out of the bucket. When humans put a bowl of water on the ground, wasn't it usually for a dog to drink from? She hadn't much liked the soapy taste, though. *Yuck.*

The scolding and soap aside, Brigit hadn't minded the mall bathroom too much. All it had were sinks and toilets, no tubs. Brigit hated bathtubs. Every time Megan tried to call her into the bathroom at home, she knew it was for a bath. She'd run and hide under the bed. If Megan was going to force her to take a bath, Brigit wasn't going to make it easy on her. And Megan seemed to always want to give Brigit a bath just when she was smelling her most interesting, right after she'd rolled on a dead squirrel or in some wonderfully foul muck. Maybe if Megan would try rolling on a rodent corpse, she'd realize how good she could smell, too.

FORTY
ENTREPRENEUR

The Poacher

He'd decided to try a new strategy, one he'd heard about from some of the other guys at those classes he'd been taking at night. They'd said anyone could go to the county clerk's office and sign up to run a business under a made-up name. That way, a person could work under the name of a company rather than his own. You didn't even have to officially incorporate. The guys said that nobody ever checked up on them when they worked under a business name. The people who hired them assumed that whoever owned the company would have done a background check and that they were vouched for. The secret was not to let people know you owned the business. Of course it was all there in the public records for anyone to check, but nobody ever did.

The thought of hiding behind another identity not only gave him hope, but also gave him a secret little thrill. It would be like being Batman or Superman or, perhaps more appropriately in his case, Iron Man. Nobody knew who they really were, either.

It was just past eight thirty in the morning when he walked into the county clerk's office and headed straight up to the gray-haired woman at the counter. "I want to register a business."

She reached under her counter, pulled out a form, and plunked it down in front of him. "Fill this out." She pointed to a table along the side of the room. "There's pens over there."

He stepped over, grabbed a pen, and looked down at the form. It was called an "Assumed Name Certificate." The first blank asked him to fill in the name under which the business would be conducted. *Huh. What name should I use?*

He chewed on the end of the pen as he thought. He called out to the woman. "Can I be Iron Man?"

"Don't think so," she said. "That name's probably trademarked."

Darn. He chewed some more on the pen. Maybe he should try "Skywalker Welding." When he worked with his torch, he felt like Luke Skywalker wielding a light saber. But that name was probably trademarked, too.

"Torch for Hire?" No, that sounded like he was offering to burn places down for money. The last thing he needed was to be suspected of arson.

"AAA Welding"? He'd once heard that it was good to go with a name that started with *a* so you'd be first in the phone book. Then again, nobody used a phone book anymore. The Internet didn't display listings alphabetically, so there was no point in going with such a boring name. Besides, the name had probably already been taken by a business formed back in the day when people still used the Yellow Pages.

What about "King Midas Metalworks"? Yeah. That's the one. Everything King Midas touched turned into gold. Anything the Poacher touched seemed to turn into shit. Maybe the name would turn things around for him. He put the pen to paper and wrote KING MIDAS METALWORKS in the space.

The next blank asked for the business address. He wrote down the address for the garage he'd rented. He wasn't sure how long he'd stay there, though. The place was cold and drafty, the pipes squealed every time he used the bathroom, and the ventilation in the bay sucked. But he'd already plunked down rent for the month, plus the deposit, and he'd sunk a little money and a day's worth of time into sprucing the place up. He'd stick it out until he could afford something better.

When he finished filling out the form, he handed it to the clerk along with a twenty-dollar bill to cover the filing fee. After, he drove to one of those storefront business centers and ordered a box of basic business cards. He grabbed a burger at the place next door while the cards were printing.

He wasn't sure it was worth the cost to set up a Web site, but he could make a Facebook page for King Midas Metalworks for free. He drove to the closest public library branch and spent some time setting the page up. He found a free image of a king online and posted the picture to the page. He made up some reviews, too.

"You can count on King Midas Metalworks!"

"Their workers do a good job at a fair price."

"Best in the business!"

That last one was definitely a stretch. He'd only learned to weld a few months ago, in prison. Other than a few days at the oil company, cutting some air holes in the top of that secondhand trailer he'd bought, and the quick and messy jobs he'd done on those gates at the zoo, he had little actual experience. But he'd take his time and make sure he did a good job for anyone who hired him.

He set up an e-mail account for the business, and sent messages to local drilling companies, fabrication businesses, and auto body shops to let them know King Midas Metalworks had welders available on short notice for temporary assignments. Of course he'd already contacted the same places, but they hadn't given him the time of day as an individual. Maybe they'd take him more seriously now that he had a business name. He included his cell phone number in the e-mail. He even took a chance and called one of his former coworkers at the oil company to ask whether he had any contacts who might need a welder on a short-term basis. "I'm with this new company," the Poacher said. "King Midas Metalworks."

"Never heard of it."

Of course he hadn't. It had only been in business for five hours. "The owner would be impressed if I could bring in some work for us."

"Don't know nobody who's looking to hire," the guy said. "If things change, I'll be in touch. But you won't believe this. The boss man? He got fired for stealing equipment."

The Poacher's blood froze. He'd been terminated after equipment turned up missing, equipment he hadn't taken. His supervisor had blamed him, made him the scapegoat. Because the Poacher had been fired, he'd been forced to go to work at that Christmas tree lot, to steal those animals from the zoo, to break his little girl's heart and see her cry. And now it turned out it was the boss himself who'd taken the tools? *Motherfu—*

"You still there?" the other guy asked.

"Yeah, I'm still here," the Poacher replied, gritting his teeth so hard it was a wonder they didn't crumble.

"Police came and hauled him away in handcuffs." The man hooted with laughter. "You shoulda seen it!"

"Wish I had." He wished that prick who'd framed him would do some time behind bars, too.

When they ended the call, the Poacher called the human resources department at the oil and gas company to see about getting his job back. "I shouldn't have been fired," he told the woman. "My supervisor stole the equipment, not me."

"Sorry," she said. "We've already filled your position. But we'll keep you in mind if we have another opening."

A lot of good that would do him. He needed a job *now.*

Disgusted, the Poacher went about his business, or went about trying to drum up some business, anyway. He also bought a few pieces of sheet metal and other supplies. Until something turned up, looked like he'd be cutting out stars. While he was at it, he might as well make a sign for his place, too.

FORTY-ONE
DEAD ENDS

Megan

By the end of the week, we realized we were once again at a dead end. The traffic cameras had been little help. While the cameras at the gas station were protected by the cover over the pumps, the light fog that had seeped into the area on New Year's Eve had left condensation on the unprotected lenses of the traffic cameras. Between the water droplets and the cloudy air, all the highway cameras picked up were blurry images of vehicles. The white trailer appeared to be attached to a large, dark vehicle, most likely an SUV judging from the rectangular shape. But we couldn't be sure. Heck, we still didn't even know if the vehicle had anything to do with the disappearance of the springbok. It felt as if we'd become so desperate for a break in the case that we were grasping at straws.

Two more weeks passed, and we reached late January with no forward movement. Despite having wallpapered the city with flyers about the missing animals, no one had called in with a fruitful tip. There'd been plenty of fruitless tips, however. A purported sighting of Sarki in Forest Park that turned out to be a skunk. A report of Dinari in a pasture north of the city. I'd raced up there only to find a white-tailed deer with unusually straight antlers. Someone had reported a possible sighting of a hyacinth macaw, too, but it turned out to be a blue-and-gold macaw that had escaped its home when the owner's child neglected to fully close their patio door. At least we'd been able to return the bird to its home before a cat went after it or it starved to death.

The most frustrating thing about serial crimes is that when the crimes ceased for any significant length of time, law enforcement had no way of knowing if the criminal had decided to stop his behavior or was merely lying in wait, biding his time until everyone lowered their guard before striking again. Sometimes, the perpetrator moved on to commit crimes elsewhere. Other times, the lawbreaker disappeared into thin air. Jack the Ripper had never been caught. Neither had the Zodiac Killer. Of course we weren't dealing with a murderer here, but the animal thefts were nonetheless a serious crime.

It was a blustery Wednesday afternoon and a motorist was in the middle of a misogynistic rant, cursing me out for writing him a speeding ticket, when Detective Bustamente called my cell. *Too bad I can't write this guy a ticket for being an ass.*

A vein pulsed in the man's forehead as his hands strangled his steering wheel. "You think you've got something to prove 'cause you're a woman and I'm a man, don't you? You've got penis envy! You—"

I raised a finger to silence the driver. "Hold that thought. I need to take this." *And, by the way, I'm very happy with my lady parts, thank you very much.*

Keeping a close eye on the jerk, I accepted the call. "Hello, Det—"

It was my turn to be interrupted. "Get to the station

pronto. We got a new tip. It sounds legit. We may have located the springbok."

Finally! A break! Sometimes you have to go looking for clues. Other times clues come looking for you. "I'll be right there."

I scribbled the rest of the citation as quickly as possible and handed it to the man. "Drive safely, sir." *And kiss my lady butt, too.*

I hopped back in my cruiser, gunned my engine, and swerved around the idiot's car just as he went to pull out. He jammed on his horn. *HOOOONK!* I flipped the switch on my dash and gave him a *WOO-WOO* right back.

At the station, I leaped from my car, retrieved Brigit, and sprinted inside, dashing to the detective's office. "This is great news! Where's the springbok? Are Sarki and the birds with it?"

His face was somber. *Uh-oh.* He gestured to a chair. "Take a seat, Officer Luz," he said softly, his voice resigned.

I hesitated, as if continuing to stand could somehow make the bad news he was about to deliver go away. But eventually I lowered myself into a chair. Brigit lowered herself to a sit at my feet.

"There's no easy way to tell you this," he said, "but the springbok is dead. It was shot by a hunter and taken to a taxidermist for mounting."

"No!" My hands gripped the armrests so tightly it was a wonder I didn't break a nail. This scenario is exactly what we'd feared. *God help those Poachers when I find them.* I'd show them as much mercy as they showed Dinari.

"The taxidermist is in Glen Rose." Bustamente rose from his chair. "Let's go."

We hopped into my cruiser and set out.

Glen Rose was a small town in Somervell County, with a population of less than three thousand. The town was mostly known for its Dinosaur Valley State Park, a natural area along the Paluxy River. Way back, dinosaurs had left footprints in the mud around an ancient ocean. The ocean had long since receded, but a river and the dinosaur tracks remained. Also in Glen Rose sat the Creation Evidence Museum, complete with a replica Noah's Ark and a hyperbaric biosphere intended to simulate atmospheric conditions that existed on earth prior to the time God flooded it. Notably, and perhaps ironically, the museum was established and directed by Carl Baugh, a researcher who'd led the excavation of numerous dinosaurs, including the *Acrocanthosaurus* in Texas and *Diplodocus* in Colorado. Baugh and his team uncovered a number of dinosaur tracks in the area. He'd proposed a number of possible creation models, taking science into account. Of course his exhibits and findings were not without controversy. Some questioned the authenticity of the "Burdick Track," a purportedly human footprint found among the dinosaur tracks in a tributary of the Paluxy. The unusual length of the foot would be commensurate with a human around seven feet tall. The museum also featured what was allegedly a fossilized finger, though some decried it as a fake. The ages-old debate on creation versus evolution was alive and well in these parts.

The taxidermist operated out of a prefab metal building along a county road directly west of downtown Glen Rose. As we pulled up to the place, we were greeted by the bared fangs of a mountain lion that appeared ready to spring from its log base and rip us to shreds, if only it were still alive.

We exited the car onto the gravel drive, our feet and Brigit's paw sending up small poofs of dust as they hit the surface. Brigit took one look at the puma and launched into a growl, her fur bristling along her back.

"Don't worry, girl," I told her. "That cat's harmless."

She approached it cautiously, her ears back, before seeming to realize it was immobilized and lifeless. She gave it a thorough sniff before we proceeded inside. The bells on the door jingled as it swung closed behind us.

We found ourselves in a foyer of horror. Skins spanned the wall, the heads of their bearers still attached, some with mouths open as if crying for help. A huge moose mounted on a board sat on the floor, leaning back against the wall, looking up at us with his one glass eye. With the other eye missing, he appeared to be winking. An owl mounted on a tree limb stared our way, looking perennially perplexed as to how he'd ended up in this situation.

A tall, skinny man with wild salt-and-pepper hair and an unkempt beard came through an open door at the back of the foyer. He wore an untucked flannel shirt, faded jeans, and scuffed boots. He took one look at my uniform and said, "You must be the folks from Fort Worth."

Bustamente nodded and held out his hand, introducing himself. I did the same. Brigit followed suit. He bent down to address her. "Aren't you a pretty girl?"

Brigit wagged her tail to let the man know she wholeheartedly agreed with his assessment.

"I suppose you want to take a look," the man said.

If, in fact, he had Dinari, we wouldn't only be taking a look, we'd be seizing the animal as evidence. But no need to address that point until we'd confirmed the animal's identity.

He motioned for us to follow him into his work area, and led us over to a large table covered with a bloodstained canvas tarp. As he grabbed an edge of the tarp, my insides squirmed, but I fought the feeling. I'd never survive as a detective if I couldn't face things head-on. Still, I took a deep breath to steel myself.

He pulled the cloth back to reveal the head and shoulders of the animal. If the ringed horns, cinnamon-brown and white fur, and distinct black stripes on its cheeks and side weren't enough to tell us the creature lying on the table was Dinari, the series of numbers and letters tattooed inside his lower lip identified him with one hundred percent certainty. Our nightmare had become a reality. The springbok we'd hoped to save was dead, shot for his trophy head.

Brigit raised her snout and sniffed Dinari's face, but quickly backed away, emitting a soft whimper. She, too, seemed to realize the tragedy of the situation.

Though we were certain of the animal's identity, it never hurt to cover your ass. Bustamente snapped a pic of the animal's face with the tattoo exposed and sent it via text to Sharon Easley for confirmation. A minute or so later, we received our reply. *The numbers match. That's Dinari.*

"It's him," Bustamente told the taxidermist.

"Damn," the man muttered as he looked down at the springbok. "Guess I was hoping you'd tell me I was wrong. Once I saw that tattoo I knew there was a problem." He looked back up at us. "I didn't let on that I had suspicions. Figured if I did, the guy might take the animal elsewhere."

Bustamente gave the man a pat on the back. "You've done everything right. We can't thank you enough for giving us a call. Of course, we'll have to take the animal as evidence. But we'll break that news to your customer so you don't have to."

"I'd appreciate it," the man said. "He ain't gonna be happy about it, I'd say."

The taxidermist assured us the animal could survive the one-hour drive to Fort Worth without risking decomposition, but advised us to get the animal into a freezer ASAP.

While Bustamente called for a crime scene team to bring a van out here to pick the animal up, the taxidermist rounded up the hunter's name and phone number for us, jotting it down on the back of a piece of junk mail and handing it to me.

I glanced down at the name he'd written. Philip Broadwell. *Uh-oh.* My insides squirmed. "Detective?" I said when Bustamente ended his call. "We've got a problem."

Philip Broadwell was an old-money Fort Worth native who'd retired a few years ago after working for decades in the railroad industry. He now served on the city council—or at least he would until this news got out. If it became known a city official killed the zoo animal, the public would likely demand his resignation.

I pointed to the name on the envelope and Bustamente responded with a decisive grunt. "This case just keeps getting hairier, doesn't it?"

The case had already been a public relations nightmare for the police department. It would be nothing short of a disaster once the press got wind of this. We'd have to handle the matter delicately, make sure we didn't do anything without notifying the top brass.

The taxidermist looked from one of us to the other. "Something wrong?"

Bustamente gave him a small shake of his head. "Nothing we can't handle. By the way, have you mentioned anything about this to anyone? Told anyone about the springbok or the man who brought it in?"

"No. The guy just brought it to me this morning. I work alone. Haven't talked to anybody since, other than whoever answered the phone at the police department and you folks."

The detective cocked his head and aimed a pointed look

at the man, speaking slowly and with authority. "You'll need to keep everything about this under wraps. Not a word to anyone about the animal, who brought it to you, the fact that we've been out here. Understand?"

The man dipped his head in acknowledgment. "I most certainly do."

We shook hands again and thanked him before heading back out to the cruiser. As I drove the three of us back to Fort Worth, Bustamente phoned the chief and gave him the terrible news. *Dinari dead, killed by a council member.* He pulled the phone back from his ear when the chief, predictably, exploded in a string of expletives.

When our boss quieted down, Bustamente put the phone back to his ear and listened. "Yes, sir," he said. After a short pause he added, "We'll meet you there." He returned the phone to his pocket and turned to me. "Head for the city hall. We're assembling at the mayor's office."

An hour later, the detective, Brigit, and I checked in with the mayor's assistant and were escorted into her office. She sat in a paisley tapestry wing chair, her face pinched. The chief sat on a love seat, man-spreading and taking up the entire seating space.

Bustamente nodded to Chief Garelik and turned to the mayor, dipping his head as a sign of respect. "Madam Mayor, I'm Detective Bustamente." He raised a hand to indicate me and my partner. "Officer Megan Luz and her partner Sergeant Brigit."

After raising a hand to indicate there was no need for her to get up, Bustamente and I reached over the coffee table to shake the mayor's hand and sat down on the sofa. Brigit sat on the rug between us. Our bums had just met the fabric when the mayor's assistant escorted Philip Broadwell into the room. He wore tan chinos and a thick sweater with a short zipper at the collar, distinctly

L.L.Bean. His wire-framed glasses rested on his narrow nose, and his gray hair was slicked back on his head. He was old enough to look distinguished, but far from doddering.

After quick introductions, he tentatively lowered himself into a chair. "What's this about?"

The rest of us waited for the chief to take the lead. "That animal you bagged this morning? It's the missing springbok from the zoo."

His face seemed to contract momentarily in confusion before everything went wide. His eyes. His mouth. Even his nostrils. "Oh, Lord," he said on an exhale. "This is bad." He seemed to know the public would demand justice. An eye for an eye. A tooth for a tooth. His head for Dinari's.

The chief eyed him. "You know what you were killing?"

"I knew it was a springbok, sure," Broadwell replied. "It's not illegal to hunt them in Texas. But did I know it was the one missing from the zoo? Of course not!"

The mayor seized the bull by the horns, so to speak. "We've got to get out ahead of this. Let's call a joint press conference and put the news out ourselves, so we can control it, before some nosy reporter gets wind of it."

Broadwell balked. "I don't have to be part of that, do I?"

"Hell, no," the chief said. "You stand up there and confess, you're likely to get shot yourself. We'll have to identify you, of course, but we'll do our best to point out that hunting springbok is permitted in the state. Nobody can expect a hunter to tell the difference between a zoo animal and another springbok, especially from a distance."

The chief would paint the incident as yet another tragic chapter in this ongoing saga, and place all blame squarely at the feet of the kidnappers.

"Even so," the mayor said, addressing Broadwell, "we'll have to prepare a statement, too. The press will want something straight from the horse's mouth."

I cringed at the animal reference. It hit too close to home.

The mayor turned to the chief. "Until this settles down, we'll need officers here at city hall, at least one unit at Philip's home, too. We don't want this to get out of control."

While the chief and mayor were concerned about PR and backlash, the detective was concerned with nailing those responsible. "Where'd you shoot the animal?"

"Squaw Vista Ranch," he said. "It's on the west side of Squaw Creek Lake, a little north of Glen Rose. It's a smaller hunting ranch, a few hundred acres at most."

"Who'd you deal with out there?" Bustamente asked.

"A guide named Colt," Broadwell said. "Young buck, but he knows his stuff. He manages the game, too. He's told me several times before that if there was ever anything in particular I wanted to shoot that they didn't have on-site, he could bring one in for me."

I chimed in now. "Did you see a black-and-white monkey there? Maybe a couple of bright blue parrots?"

Broadwell shook his head. "No. Just exotic and game animals. Some hunting dogs." He went on to tell us he'd paid the six grand trophy fee in cash. "Their usual fee for a springbok is sixty-five hundred, but Colt said they were offering a cash discount. It sounded reasonable. I know credit card companies charge ridiculous fees, and businesses don't like to risk a chargeback." He exhaled sharply. "Colt was really pressuring me to use their on-site taxidermist. Now I know why. But I went with my usual guy. He doesn't charge as much."

After a few more questions, our powwow was complete. The mayor and the chief summoned folks from their public relations departments, while the detective, Broadwell, Brigit, and I went to obtain a search warrant for the Squaw Vista Ranch. With Broadwell providing sworn testimony about his morning's hunt and Detective Bustamente providing photos of the dead animal and its telltale tattoo, the judge had no reservations granting us the warrant.

Minutes later, the detective, Brigit, and I were backtracking our way west in two separate cars. The detective brought a squad car along to transport Colt back to Fort Worth after we arrested him. *I've sure put a lot of miles on my cruiser today.* At least they'd been productive miles. By the time we arrived at the hunting ranch, it was dusk. We made our way into the log-cabin-style lodge to find a bunch of men in camo gear drinking beers and telling tall tales about the one that got away.

A waitress in tight jeans and an even tighter knit top spotted us and came over. "Y'all need help with something?"

"We're looking for Colt," the detective said.

"That's him." She pointed to a thirtyish, sandy-haired man shooting whiskey with a group of other guys at a table near the back. Nobody at the table had spotted us yet.

We weaved our way through the tables, a few of the men looking down at Brigit and ogling her. While German shepherds weren't hunting dogs, they were nevertheless working dogs, something these men could appreciate.

"That's one fine bitch," one of them said.

Another gave a whistle. "Ain't she something."

I had to agree.

We stepped up to the table. Colt froze when he saw us, a shot glass poised at his lips, a sure sign of guilt if ever I saw one. He expressed no curiosity as to why two members of law enforcement were staring him down and another was sniffing his boots. Yet another sign of guilt. Most innocent people expressed an interest in finding out why a police officer singled them out.

Bustamente jerked his head to indicate the front doors. Colt set his shot glass down and addressed his tablemates. "I'll be right back."

The detective and I flanked Colt as we stepped outside.

"How'd you get Dinari?" Bustamente asked. No beating around the bush or pulling punches.

"Dinari?" Colt said.

"The springbok," the detective said.

Colt scratched at his chin, the facial touch a common sign of a person who was lying. "We buy our springboks from a breeder down near Kerrville."

"Cut the crap," the detective said. "I'm talking about the one from the zoo and you know it." When Colt said nothing else, Bustamente cut his eyes to me, his look saying *Get your handcuffs ready.* He returned his gaze to Colt. "You're under arrest. You have the right to—"

As I took his right arm and slipped a cuff on it, Colt panicked and tried to turn out of my grip. Dumb move. A few quick maneuvers and I had the guy facedown on the hard-packed dirt, my knee in his back. My partner barked encouragement to me. *Arf! Arf-arf!*

Colt turned his head and spit out dirt. "Stop! I'll talk!"

Undeterred, the detective continued to recite the Miranda warning that everyone in law enforcement had memorized and could repeat in their sleep. Even if Colt was willing to talk voluntarily, it was best to read him his rights first so there'd be no question about the admissibility of his statements in court.

Bustamente finished with, "Do you understand the rights I have just read to you?"

"Yeah," Colt snapped. "I'm not a moron."

That's debatable.

"With these rights in mind," the detective wrapped up, "do you wish to speak to us?"

"Maybe."

I pulled Colt up to a sitting position on the ground. He turned his head and used his shoulder to wipe dirt from his cheek.

Bustamente crouched down to Colt's level. "Did you take the springbok from the zoo, or did you buy it from someone who did?"

"I want immunity before I talk," Colt said.

Ugh. Conditions. If he wanted immunity, it likely meant he wasn't the one who'd actually taken Dinari from the zoo. We'd have to get a prosecutor involved and he'd have to get a defense attorney. We'd lose precious time, but at least we'd finally have a real lead.

We hauled Colt to his feet and began to lead him to the detective's cruiser.

He dug his heels in. "Wait! Why are y'all taking me to the car? Can't we work things out here?"

"That's not how it's done," Bustamente said. "For you to get immunity, we've got to book you first. You'll wait in jail while we round up an assistant DA. You can get a lawyer then if you want. Of course it's late now. You'll spend the night in a cell."

"I'll have an arrest on my record?" Clearly he didn't like the idea. He should've thought about that before he involved himself in illegal animal trafficking.

"Yes. The arrest will be on your record."

"What if I talk to you here?" Colt asked.

"We'd appreciate it," the detective said. "It would allow us to move forward on our investigation right away and it might encourage the prosecutor to go easy on you. But there's no guarantees."

"Would I still be arrested?"

"Yes."

"Damn!" His shoulders slumped. "Guess I better wait to talk to a lawyer then."

As I opened the back of Bustamente's cruiser to load Colt inside, a series of pops sounded from off in the distance. My first thought was fireworks, but a moment later I remembered where we were. With night-vision scopes, hunters weren't limited to daytime hours. More pops sounded, followed by a sick squeal and whoops.

Colt glanced in the direction the noise came from. "Someone just bagged themselves a pig."

"They weren't the only ones," I snapped as I shoved him into the car.

FORTY-TWO
HAVE YOU HERD

Brigit

Brigit heard the popping sound off in the distance. She recognized that sound. It came from guns. She'd heard it many times before. But when she heard the squeal, she knew what had happened. The same thing had happened to her not long ago. A loud *pop* and then a hot, burning feeling in her chest. Then everything had gone dark . . .

She knew things had gone dark for the springbok they'd seen earlier, too. She'd recognized the animal's scent, knew it came from the zoo. Things had gone dark for that big cat at this ranch, too. Same for that big thing with antlers, and all those creatures whose skins were stretched out inside. Only for them, things would never go light again.

Brigit had been lucky. Her light had come back.

FORTY-THREE
TURNING TO GOLD

The Poacher

He walked in the front door feeling defeated. He'd eked out a few bucks selling the metal stars and Texas-shaped wall decorations to local nurseries and a gift shop up in the stockyards district. But he hadn't earned nearly as much as he'd hoped and definitely not enough to keep them afloat much longer. Vicki still hadn't applied for jobs. In fact, she'd been talking lately about maybe taking some classes at the community college. Computers and stuff.

"I'm tired of being on my feet all day," she said. "I want to work in an office. I'll have to work on my typing speed, though. Nobody's going to hire me if I can only type twenty words a minute."

At least Harper took his mind off his woes for a bit. "Daddy-daddy-daddy!" she'd cried, running to him as he came in the door. "Look what I made you in art class today!"

Valentine's Day was still three weeks off, but she'd used pink construction paper to make a big heart. She'd written "I love you Daddy!" with glue in the middle of the heart and covered it with silver glitter. As always, she'd written her name in big letters at the bottom of the heart, putting a cute little tail on the *p*.

He took it from her. "I love it, squirt. I'm going to hang it up at work so I can look at it all day."

Vicki glanced over from where she stood at the stove, browning ground beef. "Where would you hang it up? You don't have an office. Aren't you out in the field most of the day?"

Uh-oh. He'd screwed up. "We have lockers in the work trailer," he lied. "That's what I meant. I'll hang it on my locker." He turned to Harper. "All of the other daddies will be so jealous." He reached out to tickle her and she giggled before his fingers even touched her.

The following morning, he made a loop with some of the remaining painter's tape, stuck it to the back of the heart, and hung it on the wall inside his garage. After, he put the final touches on the sign he'd been building for his shop, KING MIDAS METALWORKS spelled out in corrugated sheet metal. Sturdy, but lightweight. He spray-painted the letters in a shiny copper color, the same shade as Vicki's and Harper's hair. A little of the paint had ended up on the floor, but his landlord could hardly complain. The concrete floor was already covered in oil stains and cracked in a number of places.

Once the paint had dried, he rolled up the wide bay door and carried the sign outside. Metal brackets left over from a former tenant remained affixed to the outside wall over the door. He found a ladder and carried up the sign, planning to fasten it to the brackets. Before he could get to it, he felt his cell phone jiggle in his pocket and heard his ringtone. He wrangled his phone out of the back pocket of his coveralls. He didn't recognize the number, but it had an 817 prefix, meaning it was local. *Is someone finally calling to hire me?*

He jumped down from the ladder, nearly busting his ankle in the process. He scrambled to accept the call. "Hello?"

"Is this King Midas Metalworks?"

Dammit! He needed to remember to answer with his business name. "Yes, this is King Midas. How can we help you?"

The caller was the owner of an auto body shop. They had some jobs they needed welders for.

"I got three cars needing work," the man said. "How many guys can you send me?"

"We've had high demand lately," the Poacher lied. "But I've got one guy I can spare." *Me.* "Good guy. You'll like him."

"When can he start?"

"Right away," the Poacher replied.

"Send him on, then." He proceeded to provide the address of the shop.

The call completed, the Poacher pumped his fist. The job would be temporary, but it was better than nothing. It had taken longer than he'd liked, but it looked like the new year was bringing him a fresh start, after all. Just in time. The money was running low again.

He carried the sign back into the garage. He'd hang it later, after he finished at the body shop. He locked the place up and drove off.

The collision-repair business was in a low-rent area on the east side of town, where Fort Worth bordered Arlington. The body shop was housed in a brick building painted black with the name of the shop in big yellow letters on the side.

The Poacher wandered into the small office area to the side of the three bays and addressed the man who sat at the counter, ordering parts on a computer. "I'm from King Midas Metalworks."

The man turned out to be not only the owner, but also the manager and chief mechanic, all in one. He led the Poacher into the bay, where a rock station played through speakers mounted overhead. Thank goodness it wasn't country music. His supervisor at the gas company had always played country and the Poacher couldn't hear it now without thinking about how the man framed him and wanting to punch something.

The boss introduced the Poacher to the other two guys on his crew and directed him to a crumpled Nissan 350Z parked in the last bay.

"Whoa," the Poacher said. "Someone did a number on this car." The front end was smashed in a foot or more, and the back end was crushed twice that much.

"Eighteen-wheeler in front," the boss said. "Postal truck at the rear. He got sandwiched between them. Lucky to be alive." The man gestured to a row of mangled cars sitting behind the garage. "Those need work, too."

Good. These banged-up cars will keep me busy a while.

The Poacher retrieved his tools from the covered bed of his truck and set to work. It felt good to be putting his skills to use, to be earning honest money. For the first time in a long time, he felt a tiny tingle of pride.

FORTY-FOUR
PLEA DEALING

Megan

After loading Colt into his cruiser last night, Detective Bustamente and I had spent an hour collecting evidence. While we'd found nothing in the lodge or on the ranch grounds, Colt's cell phone and wallet had given us some damning proof that he'd engaged in felonious behavior.

The cell records showed an incoming phone call from Broadwell. It also showed two incoming calls prior to New Year's Eve from a phone number with a 210 area code, which indicated the calls had come from the San Antonio area. The calls were made two days apart. Our guess was that the first call was a cold call by the poacher to assess potential interest in the springbok. The second was likely to arrange the terms of payment and delivery. The second call took place on December 31, New Year's Eve. Dinari had disappeared from the zoo that night.

When considering ex-cons as suspects earlier, I'd dismissed Bruno Molina. He'd been convicted of illegally trafficking in reptiles smuggled into the country from Brazil. Stealing animals from zoos didn't seem to be his modus operandi. The fact that he was a four-hour drive down the road in San Antonio had also led me to believe he was not likely involved. Given the San Antonio phone number on Colt's phone, however, the detective and I were rethinking Molina as a suspect. Unfortunately, the 210 phone number was linked to a prepaid, untraceable phone. We'd attempted to ping the phone last night, to no avail. Whoever had used the phone had either destroyed it or removed the battery so cell towers couldn't locate it.

We'd contacted the San Antonio Police Department and they'd sent a detective out to speak with Molina, but the guy claimed he had nothing to do with the zoo heist. His live-in girlfriend vouched for his whereabouts on New Year's Eve, when Dinari had been stolen from the zoo. Their bar tab and pics on her phone proved Molina had spent the entire evening with her at a nightclub on San Antonio's River Walk, remaining until well after the midnight countdown, providing him an irrefutable alibi.

Colt's wallet, on the other hand, contained two bank slips that were highly incriminating. One was dated New Year's Eve with a time stamp only an hour after the second phone call from the untraceable phone. The slip documented a cash withdrawal of $4,000 from Colt's bank account. The second bank slip showed that he'd made a cash deposit of $6,000 yesterday.

When Colt failed to return for his whiskey, the waitress had summoned the owner of the hunting ranch. The man had been none too happy to find out his game manager and top hunting guide was doing off-the-books, under-the-table deals with clients and pocketing the profits.

It was Thursday morning now, and the detective and I were at the district attorney's office, holed up in a small conference room with a senior prosecutor, Colt, and his criminal defense attorney, our notepads and pens at the ready. We performed a delicate dance. Colt and his attorney didn't want to admit too much and cause him to incriminate himself in case the deal fell through. But before the prosecutor agreed to anything, we had to know he actually had valuable information to offer.

The prosecutor pointed out to Colt and his attorney that we had plenty of evidence to nail him, including the testimony of Philip Broadwell and the owner of the ranch. We also had a zoo animal whose death needed to be avenged, both for the animal's sake and to satisfy the public. "Full immunity is off the table," he said, "but we'd be willing to waive jail time and impose a reasonable fine if you'll name the person who sold you the springbok and agree to testify against that person in court."

Frankly, if it were up to me, I'd insist the guy spend some time behind bars. One night in the police station's lockup was too little for a creep like him. But this was legal warfare, not my battle to fight. Besides, I was so filled with anticipation I could hardly sit still. Every nerve ending in my body buzzed with excitement at the thought of finally finding out who'd been behind the animal thefts, of arresting the bastards and parading them past the press and taking their mug shots, of watching them be convicted and sent to prison.

Colt and his attorney exchanged glances before the lawyer turned back to address his counterpart. "My client can't provide a name or a detailed physical description. Only a vehicle make and model."

Wait. *What?* "Not even a license plate?" I asked.

Colt looked sheepish. "There weren't any. They'd been taken off."

The buzz in my nerves intensified, but not in a good way. It felt as if I were on the verge of being electrocuted by frustration.

After a bit more haggling, they agreed Colt would pay

a fine of two grand in addition to forfeiting the six grand he'd been paid by Broadwell.

The price agreed upon, my impatience got the best of me. I fluttered my hands in front of me, as if they could draw unspoken words out of Colt. "Tell us! Tell us everything!"

Bustamente and the prosecutor both cut me a look, but said nothing.

Colt finally spilled what few beans he had, confirming our conclusions about the phone calls. "A guy came by before sunup on New Year's Day. He didn't come onto the ranch property but just pulled onto the grass next to the road outside the gate. I met him out there and handed him the cash. He was wearing a ski mask, so I can't tell you what he looked like other than that the little bit of skin I could see around the eyes was white. His voice wasn't the same as the guy I had spoken to on the phone."

I wondered why only one man delivered the animal, but I realized it could be any number of reasons. The guy on the phone might want to lie low, keep his potential exposure to a minimum. Or maybe he had a date on New Year's Eve. Maybe he was down in San Antonio arranging the deals and had someone up here in north Texas taking care of the dirty work, stealing the animals and delivering them. *Maybe Molina is in this, after all.*

Bustamente continued his interrogation. "What did the man say to you?"

Colt raised his shoulders. "He asked if I was Colt and if I had the money. That was it."

Bustamente asked, "Anything distinctive about his voice? An accent maybe?"

Colt shook his head. "Just a normal voice."

"Okay. Go on." The detective cocked his head, ready for Colt to continue.

Colt sat up a little taller in his seat and rested his elbows on the conference table. "The guy had the springbok in a white trailer."

"An animal trailer?" Bustamente asked.

"No," Colt said. "An enclosed one, like the kind used to haul equipment."

"How big was it?"

"A ten- or twelve-footer maybe?" Colt surmised. "Anyway, it had dents all over it, major hail damage."

The detective and I exchanged glances. The dents could be a helpful clue. After all, white trailers were fairly common. But one with extensive hail damage would be less so.

"Anything on the trailer?" Bustamente asked. "A logo or a company name?"

"No. Just a plain trailer. He opened the back and I climbed inside and brought the springbok out. It was spooked and tried to jump, but I know how to handle these animals and was able to get him inside our high fence without too much trouble."

I felt my eyes narrow as I reflexively glared at the man. *Gee, jackass, I'm glad you didn't have too much trouble leading a stolen zoo animal to his death!*

He wrapped things up. "The guy drove off and that was it."

"What kind of vehicle was he driving?" Bustamente asked.

"Dodge Ram pickup. Solid black. I'm not sure of the year, but it looked like a base model. No fancy chrome or anything on it."

Bustamente jotted a note on his pad, as did I, before asking, "Anything distinguishing about the truck? Wheels? Bumper stickers? Parking decals? Maybe some hail damage, too?"

"No," Colt said. "The truck didn't have any hail damage, and I didn't notice any stickers, but it had a camper top on the bed."

Another glance was exchanged between me and my mentor. While there were likely dozens of black Dodge Ram pickups in the area, maybe even hundreds, there probably weren't many with a camper top on them. Of course I was assuming that whoever had stolen and delivered the animals lived in north Texas. That may not be the case. He could live down in San Antonio, too. The guy on the phone could be the second guy we'd seen on the security camera footage from the houses by the zoo. Maybe the two of them intentionally targeted a zoo far from their home to throw off suspicion. Regardless, the camper top was a significant clue.

When we'd obtained all the information we could, the detective, Brigit, and I left, telling Colt and his attorney we'd be in touch if we had any follow-up questions. The detective and I paused by our cruisers in the parking lot to discuss the information Colt had provided and debate how to proceed on what we'd learned.

"First thing we do," Bustamente said, "is share the vehicle description with the media outlets. The press and the public can help us track down that truck and trailer. I'll contact our public relations department so they can get moving on it. I'll also put the word out across law enforcement networks. It wouldn't surprise me if we heard something very soon."

Bustamente wasn't generally the type to count chickens before they hatched, so I took his prediction seriously. My spirits soared. *This case could be solved quickly!* As soon as we arrested the Poachers, we could set about bringing Sarki, Fabiana, and Fernando home.

Although we anticipated someone calling in with a tip that would lead us to the vehicle and thieves, it couldn't hurt to remain proactive. "I'll search the DMV records for black Dodge pickups in the area." The DMV records wouldn't note whether the truck had a camper top, but I knew I was looking for a pickup potentially owned by a welder. After finding the names on the DMV site, I could run the names through my browser, see if any of them were identified online as a welder, maybe on a social media or job-related profile. "I'll try to determine if anyone who owns a black Dodge pickup is also a welder."

"It's a plan," Bustamente said.

We climbed into our respective cruisers. A glance at the clock on the dash told me it was nearly lunchtime. I figured I'd run by the fire station, give Seth the big news about the break in the case and see if he could take a lunch break with me. The two of us had hardly spent any time together lately. Our work schedules seemed to be in constant conflict, and I'd been running extra patrols by the zoo on my own time, too.

We pulled into the fire station a few minutes later. It was a chilly day, so the bay doors remained closed. I led Brigit in the front door and we made our way down the hall, glancing into the various rooms looking for Seth. When we reached the rec room, I peeked through the doorway. There he was, sitting on the end of a couch, staring at the station's big-screen television, Blast lying next to him. Although there were two other couches in the room, both of them empty, Alex was seated on the same sofa as Seth. She sat on the other side of Blast, who had his head draped over her thigh. She ran her hand down the dog's side and cooed sweet nothings to him.

My hand reflexively went to my baton. *This doesn't look good.* If I didn't know better, I'd think Alex and Seth were a couple.

I forced myself to remove my hand from my nightstick.

Seth and Alex were coworkers, and Blast was an irresistibly sweet dog. There was nothing here to worry about. Was there?

Brigit's tags jingled as we stepped into the room and both Seth and Alex looked up. But while Alex's face reddened with what I assumed was guilt, Seth's brightened.

"It's my girls!" he said, rising from the couch and coming over to give me a kiss on the cheek.

Blast remained on the couch, going only so far as to lift his head and send a look Brigit's way. That didn't sit well with her. She issued a soft growl and an accusatory *yap!*

I gave her leash a discreet tug. *Don't demean yourself, girl. If he's going to toss you aside for a belly rub, he doesn't deserve you.*

"We got a break in the zoo investigation," I told Seth.

"You did?" This came from Alex, who'd evidently been eavesdropping from the couch. She sat bolt upright. "Did you find the animals?"

Might as well include them both in the conversation. She seemed genuinely concerned.

"We found the springbok," I said, looking from one of them to the other.

"That's great!" she said.

"Not really," I replied. "He's dead. Shot by a hunter at one of those canned hunting outfits."

Her free hand went to her mouth in horror. "That's awful!"

"Damn," Seth muttered. "That's all kinds of wrong." He reached out and gave my hand a squeeze, seeming to realize how frustrated and upset I must feel.

"The good news is that the guy at the ranch who bought the springbok gave us some valuable information. The man who delivered the antelope was driving a black Dodge Ram pickup with a camper top. He had Dinari in a commercial utility trailer that was covered in hail dents. The chief is going to put the word out. In fact, there it goes right now."

I pointed to the television screen, where a red banner with the words BREAKING NEWS scrolled across the bottom of the screen. Photos of Fabiana, Fernando, Sarki, and Denari appeared over the anchorwoman's shoulder. As we all watched and listened, she reported essentially the same information I'd just given them, except she added the fact that a local government official had unknowingly killed the animal at a trophy hunting ranch. She didn't name the official, promising more details to come on the five o'clock news.

"Had lunch yet?" I asked Seth.

"I was just thinking about it." He gestured to the door. "Let's go. Your choice."

Ten minutes later, we were seated in a booth at Spiral Diner, an eatery that mixed classic 1950s style diner décor with a menu of up-to-the-minute vegan cuisine. After seeing all the dead animals at the trophy hunting ranch, I was in the mood for a plant-based meal. Brigit sat next to me on the booth seat, while Seth and Blast sat across from us.

After we placed orders for both ourselves and our partners, Seth eyed me intently across the tabletop. "You were right about Alex."

"Of course I was," I replied. "I'm always right about everything."

"I wouldn't go that far," he teased.

I took a sip of my drink. "So you realized she's got a crush on you." A queasy feeling churned in my stomach. "What finally clued you in?"

"She did."

"Outright? She told you she was interested?"

"Not in so many words. But she asked me about you, about our relationship. How we'd met. How long we've been dating. Whether it was serious."

He left the obvious question unanswered. *And what did you tell her?* I wanted to scream. But I wasn't about to play the role of jealous, insecure girlfriend. It would be beneath me. In fact, I decided to take a totally different tack. I shrugged. "Could be innocent questions. Maybe she was only trying to make conversation."

Seth recoiled slightly, as if hurt by my words. *I'd been petty, hadn't I?*

I sent him a smile across the table. "Of course if I'd just joined your station, I'd have set my sights on you, too. You're the hottest guy there."

A grin played about his mouth. "Stop objectifying me."

He was eating it up and we both knew it.

"Then stop having such gorgeous green eyes," I said. "And those shoulders?" I moaned. "So broad and strong. Not to mention those firm pecs and muscular arms. Six-pack abs, too."

When I stopped talking, he cocked his head and gave me a roguish grin. "Feel free to keep working your way down."

The server arrived with our food and set our plates in front of us.

I pointed to my meal. "I'm going to work on this instead."

FORTY-FIVE
CHEATERS NEVER PROSPER

Brigit

Blast eyed her vegan meatballs over the table, but Brigit ignored him. She wasn't about to share her meal with him after the way he'd treated her, barely giving her the time of day when she'd showed up to surprise him at the station earlier. If he wanted some of her lunch, then he should've climbed off the couch and come over to sniff her butt. Well, two could play that game. His butt would remain unsniffed for a while, too.

FORTY-SIX
AN UNHAPPY CAMPER

The Poacher

He was crouched on the backside of the 350Z, finishing up, when the radio station playing on the speaker overhead wrapped up a song and turned to breaking news.

"This just in," said the disc jockey. "The Fort Worth Police Department has issued a press release stating that they have recovered one of the missing zoo animals. Unfortunately, the springbok was shot dead at a trophy hunting ranch in Somervell County. Springbok are legal game in the state of Texas and the hunter, who is an official with the city of Fort Worth, was unaware the springbok was Dinari, the animal that had been taken from the city zoo. Police believe the animal thieves could be driving a black Dodge pickup truck with a camper shell."

Holy shit! He wobbled, having to put a gloved hand to the concrete floor to steady himself. His breaths came fast inside his mask, the air ricocheting off the glass, as the deejay continued his report.

"The thieves also used a white trailer with obvious signs of hail damage. The mayor and police chief are asking for the public's help in tracking down these vehicles, and ask that anyone with information please call the Fort Worth Police Department."

The Poacher extinguished his torch but remained hunkered down behind the car, glad that his welding mask hid his face so that the mechanics couldn't see the panic on it. His black Dodge pickup sat right outside the bay, the camper shell virtually screaming, *It's us! The deejay was talking about us!* At least the trailer wouldn't point to him. He'd managed to get rid of all but the most stubborn dents near the bottom.

As soon as he left here today, he'd head straight for his garage and take the camper shell off. He'd take a key to the truck, too, scratch it up, maybe write some bad words on it, give himself an excuse to have it repainted. If Vicki asked, he'd say the truck had been vandalized while he'd been out in the field. He'd removed his license plates when he'd delivered the springbok, and the police obviously didn't have a plate number or they'd have mentioned it. Without the shell, his truck would look just like hundreds of others in Fort Worth. Seemed everybody here had a pickup in their driveway. *I just need to get to my garage without getting caught.*

When the boss circled around the back of the Nissan, the Poacher nearly shit himself. He looked up, but didn't raise his mask. *It's over for me, isn't it? I'm going back to prison.*

The boss gestured to the car. "How's it coming? The guy who owns the car is on the phone, wanting to know when he can come pick it up."

"Nearly done," the Poacher said. "Ten minutes or so."

The man nodded and circled back around the vehicle out of sight.

The Poacher breathed a sigh of relief. *Looks like it's not over for me, after all.*

FORTY-SEVEN
TIPPED OFF

Megan

The department's phones lit up for days after the initial report about the Dodge pickup had been released to the public. Detective Bustamente and I followed up on all of the most promising tips first, and when none of those panned out we moved on to explore the more dubious ones.

Every hunter in the state who drove a black Dodge pickup seemed to have been reported by his neighbors as a possible suspect, regardless of whether his truck had ever borne a camper shell. The hunters didn't much appreciate being questioned about the zoo animals and implicitly accused of breaking the law, either.

It had taken me a number of hours, but I'd used the DMV records and a Google search to identify a couple of welders in the north Texas area who drove black Dodge pickups. Unfortunately, a visit to each of them told me that neither had a camper shell on their truck. Both also had solid alibis for New Year's Eve, and a number of witnesses who were willing to put them at parties, one of the men later falling drunk into bed according to his wife. "He couldn't have found his way to the bedroom door, let alone the zoo."

When two more weeks went by and we'd been unable to identify a potential suspect, Bustamente and I put our minds together again over coffee in his office.

"Maybe the thief didn't own the truck," I suggested. "Maybe it was a rental. Or maybe he'd borrowed it from somebody and they had no idea what he'd used it for."

"He could be from out of state," the detective added. "It's also possible the truck wasn't black, but just looked black in the dark of night. Maybe it was green or blue."

I groaned. "So what do we do now?"

Bustamente heaved a sigh and slumped back in his chair. "I think we've done what we can, Officer Luz." He gestured to a pile of file folders on his desk. "I've got fifteen other investigations demanding my attention, and the captain needs you out on patrol. Neither of us can keep putting the time into this that we have been, especially now that we'd be chasing down information that isn't likely to get us anywhere."

"We're going to give up?" I didn't like that idea. I'd never been a quitter.

"Part of being a good detective is resource management," Bustamente said. "You've got to know when to cut your losses and move on. Where this zoo case is concerned, it's time."

"The bad guys win this one, then, huh?" Another idea I didn't like.

"If it's any consolation, they seem to have given up on taking any more animals from the zoo. The three thefts all took place in the span of a month. It's been more than a month since Dinari was taken on New Year's Eve. We might not have solved the crimes, but we seem to have deterred them from committing another. It might not be a complete victory, but I'd still call that a win."

It didn't feel like a win to me, but what could I say? I

stood to go. "Thanks again for including me in the investigation, Detective."

He offered a small smile. "I'd have been a fool not to. You've got a good head on your shoulders, good eyes, too. When you make detective, you'll show the rest of us up." He pointed to the door. "Now get back out on those streets."

I gave him a salute, rounded up my partner, and headed out the door.

Brigit and I had been patrolling for over three hours and I was bored to death. Traffic tickets, petty thievery, and noise complaints paled in comparison to working a wildlife trafficking investigation. But when I'd had to U-turn on Vickery to catch up to a speeder and found myself once again in the industrial area flanked by I-30 and I-35, I figured it couldn't hurt to make yet another cruise through the area.

I hooked a right on south Jones Street, casting casual glances left and right. Some of the warehouses and garages were open and bustling. Others were closed and rusting. *Wait. What's that?*

A shiny copper sign on a small garage caught my eye. It read KING MIDAS METALWORKS. Given the name, it must be a welding business, right? The name rang no bells, though. It hadn't come up when I'd run my search for welding businesses after Dinari had been taken. It must be new.

I turned into the asphalt drive and parked my cruiser in front of the bay door, which was closed. I logged on to my laptop and ran a quick search. According to public records, the business had been formed in early January by a man named Trevor Fleming. The business had several reviews online already. *"You can count on King Midas Metalworks!" "Their workers do a good job at a fair price." "Best in the business!"*

Fleming had been slow to put his sign up. Surely I would've spotted the sign if it had been up long.

I rounded up Brigit from the back and took her to a small strip of dirt next to the road so she could relieve herself. A little ground beetle meandered along the curb. Brigit gave it a sniff and appeared poised to eat it until I gave her leash a tug and said, "Nuh-uh. Not a snack."

As the beetle waddled off, my subconscious mind coughed up the Beatles' song "I Want to Hold Your Hand" that the barbershop quartet had been covering at the mall. I found myself humming the tune as I led Brigit back to the building and circled around to the regular door on the side. I tried the handle but the door was locked. The small window in the door was covered with burglar bars that prevented me from putting my face right up to the glass, but I cupped my hands around my eyes and did my best to see inside.

The place was dark, lit only by the meager sunlight streaming through the dusty window at which I stood. My eyes made out a large rectangular shape inside. *Is that a trailer?*

I pulled my flashlight from my belt and shined it through the glass. While I investigated with my eyes, Brigit investigated with her nose, snuffling around the edge of the door. *Snuffle-snuffle.*

The beam of my flashlight landed on a flat piece of white metal. Angling the beam slightly, I could make out a tire at the bottom and a metal tongue sticking out in front. *Yep. It's a trailer, all right.* The trailer was in decent shape, certainly not extensively hail damaged like the one used to deliver the springbok to the hunting ranch. There were a few dings along the bottom that could have been hail damage, but given their placement it was more likely the dents had been made by gravel pinging against the metal.

What's more, the trailer bore a logo, a copper-colored crown under which KING MIDAS METALWORKS had been spelled out in black stick-on lettering.

Snuffle-snuffle.

I shined my flashlight about, spotting nothing else of interest, only a pink heart cut from construction paper with a sweet sentiment scrawled across it. *I love you Daddy!* The artist had signed her name, Harper, giving the *p* a curled-up tail in an act of alphabetic rebellion.

Brigit was still sniffing along the door frame when I finished my inspection. "C'mon, girl. Back to the car."

The two of us returned to my cruiser. After loading Brigit into the back, I ran Fleming's name through the motor vehicle records. I knew Detective Bustamente had said not to devote more time to the zoo case, but it wouldn't take more than a few seconds to run a search and see what might come up. The results showed no trailer or vehicle, black Dodge pickup or otherwise, in his name. *Who owns the trailer? And how'd he transport the trailer here? He must drive something, right?*

It wasn't uncommon for married couples to share vehicles. Many times when I pulled a driver over, the car registration they offered me was in the name of their spouse. To determine if Fleming had a spouse, I looked up his driver's license, then ran the address through the system again to see if another Fleming had a driver's license at the same address, which was an apartment. *Nope.* It was possible if he had a wife, that she hadn't taken his name. I ran a search of the marriage licenses. *Nope, again.* The guy had never been married, at least not in the state of Texas. *Hmm.* I supposed he could be driving a car owned by a friend or family member. Younger drivers often borrowed cars, as did people with bad credit who couldn't get financing on their own.

I made a mental note to make a run by this shop on another day, see if Fleming might be here. More than likely it would lead nowhere, but it couldn't hurt and nobody could complain. The garage sat within my beat.

Beat. Beatles. There went my brain again, making connections and forming thoughts behind the scenes while my focus was on something else. Again, the lyrics to "I Want to Hold Your Hand" ran through my mind.

I put Brigit in the back and opened the driver's door. As my butt hit the seat, an epiphany jarred loose in my brain. I started the car, gunned the engine, and, tires squealing, aimed for the mall.

FORTY-EIGHT
WHIFFS AND SNIFFS

Brigit

Brigit stared back at the garage as Megan drove away. Brigit had been about to issue an alert, to signal Megan that she'd caught a whiff of a springbok at the garage. It wasn't any old springbok, either. Brigit's advanced nose could tell it was the very springbok who used to live at the zoo, the one who they'd found dead a while back.

Whoa!

Brigit crouched to stabilize herself as the cruiser's engine roared and the car took off. Wherever they were going, they were going there fast. Brigit wagged her tail. *Maybe I'll get to play chase!*

FORTY-NINE
ONE LAST HURRAH

The Poacher

He'd had only a couple days' downtime between the gig at the auto body shop and this one, installing aluminum carport covers at a new condominium development on the southwest side of town. The woman who'd hired him had asked if he ran background checks on his employees. He'd lied and said yes. Then again, since he knew his own background and he was his only worker, maybe it wasn't actually a lie. Besides, she'd only asked if he ran a check, not whether his supposed employees had passed muster. If she wanted to know if anyone working under the name of King Midas Metalworks had a criminal record, then she should have asked outright.

His burner phone buzzed in his pocket. He had no qualms answering the call this time because he could trust himself to say no. Money was tight for sure, but things were starting to take off for his welding business and the heat he'd felt after the police said they were looking for a black Dodge pickup with a camper shell had begun to subside. He'd dodged a bullet there. Vicki was too busy with the kids to watch much TV and, when she did, it was something she'd recorded earlier. She'd forward through the commercials and news teasers. She never watched the actual news reports, said they were too much gloom and doom. Even if she had heard the police were looking for a black Dodge pickup with a camper top, would she have suspected him? The Poacher wasn't sure. She hadn't had much faith in him when he'd first been released from prison, but that seemed to have changed. The color of his truck had changed, too. He'd driven it all the way out to Abilene and paid $600 to have it repainted a basic white. With the f-word scrawled all over it, the guys at the shop hadn't asked why he'd brought it to them. When they'd asked if he'd wanted to go with black paint again, he'd said, "No. Too hot in the summer. Let's go with white."

He glanced down at the screen. It was another 210 phone number, different from last time. Molina ditched burner phones as often as he ditched girlfriends. The guy was a player. Or at least he'd claimed to be when the inmates swapped stories in prison of their sexual exploits. The Poacher had said nothing about Vicki. It didn't seem right. She was much more than a piece of ass to him.

The Poacher accepted the call. "Hey, Mo."

"Hey. Got another proposal for you."

"I only answered to tell you I'm not interested," the Poacher said. "My business is picking up and—"

"There's fifty grand in it for you."

Fifty thousand dollars? Hell, it would take the Poacher longer than his prison sentence to earn that kind of money. "You must be high."

Molina snorted a laugh. "I got a customer who's willing to pay big bucks for the big kahuna."

"Kahuna?" the Poacher repeated. "Is that the thing with the white nose and the long tail that looks like an anteater?"

Molina snorted again. "Trevor, has anyone ever told you that you're dumb as a box of rocks?"

A lot of people had told him that. More than once, too. Maybe they were right. He had done some stupid things in his life. But sometimes he wondered what he might have done if they'd expected more. "Just tell me what the hell you're talking about."

"The black rhino, man."

Molina was suggesting he steal a huge, horned animal that probably weighed upward of a ton? "Are you screwing with me?"

"No, man. Their horns are worth a shitload of money. In Asia they use it to make some kind of magic dick powder. Gives you a boner that lasts for days."

The Poacher wasn't sure why anyone would want a boner that lasted for days, but that wasn't the point. The point was that fifty thousand dollars would mean he wouldn't have to stare at his cell phone, willing someone to call with a welding job. He could pay off that new high-tech refrigerator Vicki had bought. His pickup, too. He could finally put the truck in his own name, feel like a real man. Maybe he could even start a college fund for Harper. It would be ten years before she'd be heading off to a university but, while time in prison had passed slow, his time back on the outside seemed to be flying by.

Even so, while the money had him considering the offer, he had to think about the risk, too. He could get caught this time. A pair of birds and a tiny monkey had been easy to sneak out of the zoo. The antelope had taken more planning, but was still small enough to manage. A huge animal like a rhino was a different matter. *Could it even be done?*

He'd taken Harper and the boys to the zoo several times both before and after he'd stolen the animals. While Harper had been busy reading the posted signs that gave information about the animals, the Poacher had been scoping things out. He'd noticed the zoo had installed more security cameras around the outside, and that there seemed to be more security staff on duty. But he also noticed there weren't many cameras at the far end of the zoo, where it backed up to McCart Street. They probably figured someone would have to be crazy to try to sneak an animal out that way where they'd have to exit onto a public street and could be spotted. But that section of McCart was an oddity, an angled shortcut from Forest Park Boulevard to Park Hill Drive that ran behind the businesses sitting on a small, triangular parcel of land. None of the businesses on that stretch faced McCart. *If I put up cones at either end of the cutoff, people would think it was closed and go another way . . .*

Molina's patience ran out. "I need an answer, bro. You ain't interested, I got other people who can get me one from somewhere else."

He thought he could do it without getting caught, and he definitely wanted the money, but there was one other thing to deal with before he'd agree to do the job. "Whoever you sell the rhino to, are they gonna kill it?"

Harper had bawled when she found out the springbok had been shot. She'd seen the antelopes at the zoo, spent fifteen minutes just watching them graze. *Aren't they pretty, Daddy?* Even though she'd squealed in disgust when she'd seen a rhino sniffing the poop pile in their enclosure, she knew it was just what rhinos do and she'd be just as upset if it were killed.

"Nah, man," Molina said. "They're not going to kill it. They'll just saw its horn off. It doesn't even hurt them."

The Poacher wavered, but when a text from Vicki came in on his other cell phone—*dentist says I need root canal and crown*—he knew what his answer would be. "All right. I'll do it."

FIFTY
FINGERED AND NAILED

Megan

As I hustled Brigit down the walkway at the mall, I was careful to steer clear of the door of the nail salon. I didn't want the technicians to know my partner and I were on-site. Ditto for the barbershop quartet. When I heard them singing the Temptations' classic "My Girl" up ahead, I scurried into Victoria's Secret to hide behind a rack. Not easy when the garments contained so little fabric.

Once they'd passed by the door and continued down the walk, I slunk out, keeping Brigit on a short leash by my side. We entered the mall's center atrium and strode quickly to the manager's office. The same manager who'd been on duty when the maintenance man had checked the P trap was on duty again.

I took a seat in his office. "I need contact information for all of the women who reported their rings missing."

"Okay." He arched an inquisitive brow. "Something going on?"

"Following a hunch."

He frowned slightly at my vague response, but I wasn't ready to say more until I knew whether I was right. He turned to his computer, tapped some keys, and ran his finger over his mouse pad. I pulled a pen and my small notebook from the pocket of my uniform and jotted down the names and numbers as he read them aloud. When he finished, I stood. "I'm going to give these women a call. If things check out, I'll be in touch."

I stepped back out into the atrium, finding a quiet spot along the back wall to make the calls. I dialed the number of the woman who'd thought her rings had gone down the sink. "It's Officer Megan Luz, from the mall. I have a few quick questions for you. First, did you happen to see the barbershop quartet after you had your nails done?"

"Yes," the woman said. "They weren't far from the nail salon. Pretty talented group."

In more ways than one, I suspected. "Did any of the men touch you in any way?"

"The shortest one went down on a knee and took my hand. It went along with the lyrics of the song."

"Do you know the name of the nail technician who did your manicure?"

"No," she replied. "But she had reddish-blond hair, like Nicole Kidman. What's all this about?"

"Just gathering information," I said. "If it leads somewhere, I'll let you know. In the meantime, don't mention to anyone that I've contacted you and asked you these questions, okay?"

"Okay."

I phoned the other two women. They, too, had received manicures from the Kidman lookalike, as well as a handholding from the short singer from the barbershop quartet. Nan Ishii was my next call.

After I told her who was calling, she said, "Did you find my rings?"

"No," I said, "but I'm pulling some information together. I noticed your nails looked very nice when I came to your house the day your rings went missing. Had you gotten a manicure recently?"

"Hmm," she said. "Probably. I get them all the time."

"Where?" I asked.

"No particular place," she said. "Wherever I happen to be when I need one. There's nail salons everywhere."

"Have you ever used the one at the Shoppes at Chisholm Trail?"

"Yes, several times."

"Do you pay by debit card or cash?"

"I use my debit card for almost everything."

"Check your bank records," I said. "See if you have a debit at the mall's nail salon just prior to the day you realized your rings had disappeared."

She was silent for several seconds as she checked her records. "There was a debit the day before."

"Do you remember who did your manicure?"

"No. Sorry."

"Do you recall whether you saw any singers when you left the salon?"

"I did." Her voice was sure this time. "They came right up to me. I thought maybe they were collecting for a charity or something, but they were just caroling for the holidays."

"Did any of the men touch you? Take your hand?"

"I think so," she said. "They kind of all circled around and I'd had a glass of wine beforehand, so I can't say for certain."

I thanked her for the information and told her I'd be in touch if anything panned out. From there, I phoned Colonial Country Club. It took a few minutes for the receptionist to track down the assistant manager, but when they did she gave me the name and number of the member who'd been playing tennis at the club and accused the landscape staff of stealing her rings. I phoned the woman and confirmed that she'd had a manicure the morning she'd lost her rings, and that the strawberry blond "who looked like Emma Stone" had done it. She also confirmed that the short man from the barbershop quartet had come over and taken her hand right after she'd left the salon.

I had not only suspicion now, but a theory. The tech had scouted out clients with expensive rings, applied copious amounts of greasy lotion to their hands so their rings would slide off easily, and texted the short man in the quartet to let him know both when a target had sat down in her chair and when the target was leaving the salon. To cover her own ass, she made sure to remind the women not to forget their rings.

Even though I felt certain my theory was correct, I had no proof. The security cameras at the mall wouldn't be able to pick up on whether the singer had slid the women's rings off their fingers. The footage would be too grainy and far away. I'd have to run a sting, catch the singer in the act. Literally.

I placed a quick call to Summer, one of my fellow female officers. She was off duty today, but always up for a good bust. I gave her the scoop.

"If we snag these two," I said, "there'll be a margarita in it for you. Nachos, too."

"You had me at tequila."

She agreed to meet me at the mall. But first, she'd run by the station and get the fanciest ring she could find out of the lost-and-found box. People turned in all kinds of things they'd found on the streets. Jewelry. Wallets. Someone had once turned in what they thought was a valuable gold coin. Turned out to be a subway token from Budapest.

After giving the mall manager a heads-up, I slunk into the bookstore that sat across the walkway from the nail salon and kept an eye on the place through the front window, having to work hard not to be distracted by the display of new releases nearby. Brigit sat by my side. A few shoppers cast glances our way as they entered or exited the store. One even asked for recommendations of good crime novels.

He raised his palms. "You'd know, right?"

I pointed to a procedural by one of my favorite authors on the new-release rack. "Try that one. You won't be disappointed."

He grabbed a copy and held it up. "Thanks!"

Maybe I should ask the store for a commission.

A few minutes later, a text came in from Summer. She'd *arrived,* evidently with *a big honking diamond* on her finger. I kept her at bay at the store next door until the seat opened at the table manned by the strawberry blond. I texted Summer back. *Now!*

She darted across the walkway, her golden curls bouncing. She slowed to a reasonable pace as she approached the door of the salon. She'd worn a cute pair of rhinestone-studded ankle boots along with jeans and a colorful Versace cardigan I also recognized from the lost-and-found box. Out of curiosity, we'd looked up the garment online after it had been turned in. It retailed for over seven hundred dollars. I couldn't imagine having that kind of money to spend on a sweater, and then not keeping up with it. But it was the perfect disguise to make Summer look like a spoiled sorority girl from nearby TCU rather than a street-smart cop.

Summer entered the salon and slid into the seat at the strawberry blond's table. The tech pushed the velvet hand forward. Summer made a show of removing the ring and daintily slipping it onto the holder. The tech discreetly pulled her phone from the drawer and sent a text, probably giving the short guy from the quartet a heads-up that a mark was now sitting in her chair.

I watched as the tech painted Summer's nails, applied the greasy lotion, and pushed the velvet hand forward again. Her lips moved. Though I couldn't hear what she said, I knew she was reminding Summer not to forget her ring. As Summer put it on, the tech pulled out her phone and sent another text.

Summer and the tech moved to the counter. I saw the barbershop quartet strolling up the walkway, the short one setting the pace. I wondered if the other men were involved in the jewelry theft, or if the short guy and the nail tech were the only ones in cahoots.

Summer paid for her services and walked out of the salon. Five steps later, she hit a wall of men in red and white, singing about how they wanted to hold her hand. The short one went down on his knee and took Summer's hand, while the taller three removed their hats and shook them like tambourines over their heads. Were the shaking hats intended to distract her? Could be. Magicians used tricks like that all the time. Drawing your attention to one hand while the other was doing something sneaky.

The short man released Summer's hand and surreptitiously dipped his fingers into the pocket of his vest. As he began to rise, Summer raised her arm to signal me that he'd slipped her ring off her finger. Brigit and I were on the move. In seconds, Summer, my partner, and I had turned the tables on the men, blocking their way now. While the taller three men merely appeared perplexed, the short guy took one look at my uniform, turned, and took off running.

It's go time.

Summer and I took off after him. Given that she wore ankle boots, she soon lagged behind. Although I was giving it my all, the guy was nimble, weaving in and out of shoppers with great agility. *This is a job for Brigit.* I reached down and released my partner's leash on the go, giving her the signal to take the crooning crook down. "Get 'im, girl!"

Her nails scrabbled on the cement before she shot off like a rocket. A young mother who didn't see Brigit coming wheeled a baby stroller into Brigit's path, but rather than waste time circling around them, my partner hurdled the stroller with ease, the baby's head turning as he watched a dog sail over him and land on the other side.

Brigit gained on the man and made a graceful leap onto his back, snatching his hat in her teeth as she did so. *Whump!* The man was down on the pavement and screaming, Brigit pinning him to the ground. I finally caught up to them. I ordered Brigit off the man's back, replacing her weight with my own, my knee in his back. Before he could gather his wits, I gathered his hands, pulling them up behind him and slapping on the cuffs. *Click-click.*

Summer caught up to us, panting from exertion. While Brigit lay to the side, happily chewing the brim of the guy's straw hat, I rolled him over onto his back and patted his vest pocket. Sure enough, I felt something hard inside. I stuck my fingers into the pocket, retrieved the ring, and held it up.

"Busted," I said. "You'll be trading your red stripes for black ones."

As if realizing his only hope was to pass the blame onto the nail tech, he cried, "Kylie made me do it! It was all her idea! She said if I didn't she'd post revenge porn online!"

What kind of porn would feature a member of a barbershop quarter? My mind coughed up a visual of this guy wearing only his vest, shaking his hat, and singing "She'll Be Coming 'Round the Mountain." I cringed. *Ew.*

Summer and I hauled the guy to his feet and began to lead him to the nail salon so we could arrest his cohort. As we did, the other three members of his quartet tentatively came up.

"What's going on?" asked the tallest one.

It seemed clear to me the short guy and the nail tech had worked alone, without the knowledge of the other three men. Even so, my first priority was to get the tech rounded up.

"Hold that thought," I said.

We proceeded en masse to the salon, shoppers stopping on the sidewalk to gawk and activate their cell phone cameras. As we approached the salon, a *ding* sounded in the other pocket of the suspect's vest. I pulled out his phone to find a text from Kylie. *Did you get it?*

I held the phone out in front of us to take a selfie. "Smile!" I sent the pic of me and the guy to Kylie, along with a text message that said, *No, I got arrested instead.*

We'd just reached the door of the salon when Kylie came barreling out of it. Brigit lunged at the end of her leash, ready for another chase. To her it was a game, and she loved to play it. I unclipped the lead once more, gave her order and off she went, the hat still in her teeth.

Hearing Brigit thundering up behind her and seeming to realize she'd never outrun a police K-9, Kylie circled a lamppost and ran back into the salon. She darted behind her rolling table, stepped on the lever to release the brake, and shoved it. The table rolled toward Brigit, who evaded it with a sideways roll of her own.

The girl moved behind the adjacent table, snatched up a handful of polish, and hurled the bottles one by one at Brigit like some warped kind of knife thrower. I dashed into the store, slipped in a puddle of Mango Mania polish, and went down on my butt. Kylie continued to hurl bottles of polish at me and Brigit. I put up a hand to protect my eyes, and a bottle bounced off my forehead. *Ow!* I levered myself to my knees and dove at the table in front of Kylie, grabbing the lip and turning it over on her. She fell backward and found herself buried under cotton balls and nail files.

In seconds, she was in handcuffs, too, leaning up against the back wall next to her former lover. Summer and I glanced around the salon.

While I thought the place was a disaster, Summer, living up to her bright and hopeful name, had a different assessment. "It looks like a Jackson Pollock painting."

Brigit's fur was smeared and smudged with two dozen colors ranging from peacock blue to flamingo pink. My uniform had fared no better. I looked down at myself. "Think the cleaners can do anything about this?"

Summer was less positive. "Doubtful. You might have to throw it out."

Darn. A new uniform would set my budget back. "Which manicure did you get?"

She held up her nails. They were pink with white polka dots and mini cupid decals on her thumbs.

"That's perfect for Valentine's Day," I said.

"Yeah," she said wistfully. "Now I just need someone to spend it with."

We turned to what was now a barbershop trio and explained that their tenor had been swiping rings off the hands of slicked-up shoppers who'd had their nails done by Kylie. The three, in turn, turned on the former fourth member of their chorus.

"You're out of the band," the tallest one said.

The next shortest one turned to me and Summer. "He

insisted on developing our choreography. Now we know why."

The third guy leaned in to whisper something to the other two and, with a "One, two, three, four," they launched into an entertaining rendition of "In the Jailhouse Now."

FIFTY-ONE
HATS OFF TO YOU

Brigit

Baths were bad enough, but tonight Megan had poured some foul-smelling liquid all over her first. It was awful! Brigit sneezed and sneezed to clear the awful stench from her nose. After Megan had rinsed the yucky stuff off, she'd given Brigit a bath with the usual peach shampoo, digging in extra hard with her fingers to get through the thick fur, all the way down to Brigit's skin. That part wasn't so bad. Brigit always liked a good scratch.

Afterward, Megan wiped her down with a towel, first in one direction and then the other. Of course that wasn't going to stop Brigit from doing a full-body follow-up shake to get rid of the water left behind. Megan shrieked and held up the towel to protect herself from the deluge. The obligatory shake dispensed with, Brigit felt a case of the zoomies coming on.

Weeeee!

Off Brigit went, fueled partly by a primal need to rid herself of the horrible fruit scent and partly by an unbridled joy that the torture of the bath was over. She leaped up onto the couch, rubbed herself along the pillows at the back, and leaped back down. She put her right shoulder down to the rug, running with her back feet, performing a cockeyed canine version of a wheelbarrow. When her right side was done, she turned around and did the same thing on her left side.

Megan came into the living room and barked orders at Brigit, insisting she stop. But they were off duty now, equals as far as Brigit was concerned. *Not gonna happen, sister.*

Flopping over on her back, the dog wriggled and writhed, curling one way then the other in a furry frenzy.

Almost done. Just one more step.

Brigit rolled to her feet and bolted past Megan into the bedroom. She sprang from the floor and sailed through the air, landing on their bed. She stretched her front paws out and scooped the soft covers toward her until they formed a big, comfy pile. When it was just right, she flopped down on it. *Aaaaah.*

FIFTY-TWO
THE ART OF THE STEAL

The Poacher, aka Trevor Fleming

They'd done it. Stolen the rhino.

Who's dumb as a box of rocks now?

Trevor could hardly believe they'd gotten away with it. But his plan had worked.

Like last time, he'd sprayed leftover flocking spray on the security cameras on the homes and businesses nearby so they wouldn't record him. The cops thought the thief drove a black Dodge pickup, but he was in a white truck now, the kind you saw a dozen of any time you went anywhere in Fort Worth. Hell, local companies had fleets of them. The cops wouldn't be on the lookout for a white truck, so he shouldn't have any trouble on the road.

He'd placed orange cones at both ends of the McCart cutoff, along with signs he'd snatched from a construction site that read ROAD CLOSED. He'd parked his pickup and trailer at the curb in the restricted area. He'd had to peel off the stickers that spelled out the name of his business on the side of the trailer, and use paint stripper to get rid of the crown logo, but he could reapply them later. He and his partner had worn the ghillie suits again to camouflage themselves as they'd made their way through the zoo.

Beforehand, the Poacher had watched some videos online and seen that circus trainers used bull hooks to train and control elephants. The comments showed that many people thought it was a cruel practice. The bull hooks reminded him of the batons the prison guards used to keep the inmates in line. He wouldn't know where to get a bull hook, but he figured a long piece of PVC pipe would work, so he'd picked up a couple lengths at the hardware store. He thought they might have trouble with the rhino, but the animal came right along with only a little prodding. They'd gotten in and out in no time.

It was four in the morning when the two men stood on either side of the rhino at the back of the open trailer. According to his Internet search, a black rhino could weigh up to three thousand pounds or more. Trevor had bought a wide, heavy-duty ramp for this job. Gently tapping the rhino's armor-plated bottom with the pipe, they eased the animal forward. The rhino balked at the top of the ramp, refusing to move another inch. Trevor's gut clenched so hard it hurt, nearly as bad as the time his cellmate had sucker-punched him. They needed to get the hell out of there as quickly as possible or someone might catch them!

"Come on, big guy," Trevor whispered. "Get in there!"

"What's wrong with him?" asked his partner.

"I don't know. Maybe he doesn't like that it's dark in the trailer." His boys slept with a night-light on. Harper did, too. You'd think something this big wouldn't be afraid of a little darkness, but who knows.

The other guy turned on his flashlight and carried it into the trailer, securing it to the front wall with a roll of duct tape and a pocketknife he'd pulled from the pocket of his cargo pants. *Smart.*

Trevor gestured to the tape. "How'd you know to bring that along?"

The guy shrugged. "I always carry duct tape and a Swiss army knife. Can't tell you how many times it's saved my ass."

Trevor realized he probably didn't want to know what all the guy had done with a blade and duct tape.

They returned to the rhino's side and the two of them prodded the big beast again. This time, the animal walked right into the lighted trailer. Trevor pumped a fist. *Yes!*

When he went to shut the back door of the trailer, he realized he might have celebrated too soon. The rhino's butt was too big. The doors couldn't close all the way. They'd never be able to get the lock on it if it wouldn't shut!

"Dammit!" Trevor spat.

They poked the PVC pipes through the three-inch gap, tapping the beast's enormous buttocks, but the rhino was in as far as he could go.

Trevor felt panic welling up in him, squeezing his lungs. "What the hell are we going to do?" he wheezed.

The other guy grunted. "Ain't no *we* anymore. My job was to help you get the rhino out of the zoo and into the trailer. From here out it's on you. Time for you to pay up."

"Come on, man!" Trevor said. "You can't leave me hanging like this!"

The other guy glanced around nervously. "It's no good being out here this long." He fingered the pipe, gave it a meaningful swing, and tapped it hard against the palm of his hand. *Thwack*. "I want my money. *Now.*"

Unless he wanted to be beaten with the pipe and left for dead, Trevor had no choice. He went to the cab of the truck and got the cash. All one thousand dollars of it. The other guy might be smart in some ways, but he'd underpriced his services. Of course, Trevor had lied and said he was only getting three grand in the deal.

He handed the cash over. The man counted it quickly,

tucked the envelope into the neck of his ghillie suit, and dropped the pipe into the bed of the truck, where it landed with a *clang*. As he backed away, he said, "Heads up." He tossed the duct tape to Trevor.

Trevor caught it. "What am I supposed to do with this?"

"Put your suit over his ass," the guy said, turning away. He spoke over his shoulder as he retreated. "Cover the gap with tape. Use your belt to hold the doors closed."

Wow. The guy was amazingly resourceful. It was a wonder he didn't have a better legit job.

Trevor did as his partner had suggested. When he finished, he realized he'd been here far too long. *I gotta get moving.* He left the cones and the ROAD CLOSED signs. He'd worn gloves when he'd snatched them, so there'd be no prints to tie the crime to him. He started his truck and pulled out, running over three cones as he drove off, leaving them crushed on the street behind him.

He was heading slowly down a residential street when he spotted a roofing company's sign in a yard. Looked like the homeowners were having new shingles installed. Also looked like they'd hired a sloppy crew. The street was littered with nails. But Trevor couldn't swerve around them or he'd risk tipping the trailer. His heavy, horned cargo could lay that thing on its side in a heartbeat. If that happened, he'd be royally screwed.

He grimaced as he rolled over the nails and hoped for the best. He'd made it three more blocks and thought he was home free when he felt the drag kick in. He looked in the rearview mirror and saw the trailer tipping to the left. He unrolled his window and stuck his head out. One look back and he could see the trailer's tire going flat.

A string of colorful expletives exploded from his mouth like Roman candles. He had no spare tire for the trailer. Hadn't thought to get one. Duct tape was good for a lot of things, but it couldn't patch a tire. There was no way he could haul a three-thousand-pound animal for sixty miles on a flat. He was already taking a chance the thing would fall out the back when he got on the freeway.

His only choice was to take the rhino to his garage. Once the stores opened in the morning, he could buy a new tire for the trailer and weld some metal strips across the back to make sure the rhino was secure and hide its enormous armored ass from view.

He gingerly pressed the gas pedal and set off slowly down the street. The tire had gone totally flat by then, and the back corner of the trailer dragged on the street, sending up a shower of sparks like a beacon in the night. He spewed more curses. *I might as well have a spotlight shining on me!*

At least he could get from the zoo to his garage by smaller neighborhood streets, where he was less likely to be spotted. A camera might pick him up, but with any luck law enforcement would dismiss the white truck as unimportant if they happened to watch the footage later.

He weaved in and out of the streets, the trailer continuing to send up sparks, along with a *krrrrrrr* sound of metal dragging on asphalt. Luckily, no one was on the road at this time of night. All he saw was a couple of frisky cats chasing each other across the street.

He was heading north through the Fairmount neighborhood when headlights came at him from the other direction. He slowed, hoping to minimize any sparks. The last thing he needed was to draw attention to himself.

As the car approached, his eyes made out something on top of it. *Could it be pizza delivery? This time of night?* As it drew closer, he gasped. *It's a cop car!*

He knew he should jump out of the truck and run, but he couldn't seem to get his arms and legs to cooperate. *I'm done for. It's over. Vicki will find another guy to stick bows on her butt for. Harper will know her daddy is not a good man.*

As the squad car came upon him, the driver's window went down and a hand reached out, palm raised in the universal gesture that meant STOP. He had no choice but to comply. The cruiser pulled up next to his truck and the bulky, rusty-haired officer at the wheel made a circling motion with his hand, telling him to roll down his window.

Weighed down with dread, Trevor felt heavier than the rhino behind him. He pushed the button to lower the window and waited for the man to tell him to put his hands up. But he didn't.

Instead, the cop said, "Saw those sparks all the way down the block. Looks like you've got yourself a bum tire."

The officer had pointed out the obvious. *I wonder if anyone ever told this cop he was dumb as a box of rocks?*

"Dragging a trailer like this," the cop said, "it'll tear up the roads."

"It just happened," Trevor lied. "Luckily, I don't have far to go."

He hoped the cop would leave it at that, but the guy climbed out of his cruiser, walked over to the trailer, and bent down to take a look. *No!* Trevor briefly toyed with the idea of grabbing the PVC pipe from the truck bed and whacking the cop over the head with it. He could knock the guy out and take off. But he'd gotten this far without committing violence. It was hard enough getting work with a nonviolent offense on his record. He'd be totally doomed if he was convicted of assaulting a cop.

The officer reached out to the tire, tugged a nail out of the rubber, and held it up as proud as King Arthur when he'd freed the sword Excalibur from the stone. "Here's your problem."

No, YOU are my problem! Trevor wanted to yell. But he offered the guy a grateful nod. "Thanks. I'll get that flat fixed first thing in the morning."

The cop stepped to the back of the trailer and glanced over at the door. "What you got in here, anyway?"

Terror choked Trevor. But before the cop could realize that Trevor hadn't responded, he offered his own answer. "Looks like some bushes."

His partner had saved Trevor's ass by suggesting he lay his ghillie suit over the rhino's rear end.

"Yeah," Trevor squeaked out. "It's bushes. I'm a gardener."

The cop came back around the trailer and headed up the side of the bed. He'd said nothing about the fact that the truck and trailer were missing license plates. He must not have noticed.

The cop reached down into the bed and picked up the length of PVC pipe Trevor's partner in crime had dropped into it. "What's this for?"

Uh-oh.

Again, the cop gave Trevor an easy out. "You install lawn sprinklers, too?"

Thank you! "Sure do."

Still holding the pipe, the cop eyed him, his eyes going squinty. "What're you doing out here this time of night?"

"It'll be sunup soon," Trevor said. "Just getting an early start on the day." The sun wouldn't be up for over two hours, but the lame excuse was all Trevor could think of. *Had the cop bought it?*

The cop laid the pipe back down and walked up to Trevor's door. As he did, a female voice came over the radio on his shoulder, informing officers there'd been a collision on Henderson, not far from where they were. The officer pushed the button on the radio and turned his head to the side to speak into the mic. "Officer Mackey responding."

Hallelujah! If the cop was going to respond to the car wreck, that meant he was done here, right?

The cop released the button and turned back to Trevor. "Since you don't have far to go, I'll let you carry on. But you get that flat fixed before you get back out on the road. Hear me?"

Trevor nodded. "Loud and clear, sir."

The cop rapped his knuckles on the side of the truck door, climbed back into his patrol car, and drove off.

Box. Of. Rocks.

FIFTY-THREE
MASSIVE MIGRATION

Megan

A search of the nail technician's apartment had led to a treasure trove of rings. While she'd had some of them resized and redesigned, the rings that had been snatched more recently had yet to be modified. Once they were no longer needed as evidence, we'd be able to return the rings to their rightful owners. I'd called the victims to let them know what had gone down, and they'd been thrilled to hear the news. Both the tech and her boyfriend would face charges. Brigit and I could add another successful bust to our ever-expanding list of successes.

The morning after Brigit and I arrested the nail technician and her barbershop boyfriend, we were on duty again. Realizing I hadn't finished my research into Trevor Fleming, the owner of King Midas Metalworks, I ran his name through the criminal database. I got a hit. Not entirely surprising given that welding was one of the trades taught in the state's correctional institutions and, thus, a higher than average number of welders had records. But still, I felt a little tingle nonetheless.

The records told me that Fleming had been convicted of felony theft after stealing thousands of dollars in merchandise from the toy store where he worked on the receiving dock. He'd had an earlier misdemeanor conviction for stealing from a grocery store where he'd also worked, but for that crime he'd received only a fine and community service. For the felony conviction, he'd spent eighteen months in the Darrington Unit, the same unit where convicted wildlife trafficker Bruno Molina had done time.

The dates of Fleming's incarceration overlapped with Molina's for three months, at the beginning of Fleming's term and the end of Molina's. *Hmm.* Still, there were over fifteen hundred men in the Darrington Unit at any given time. The two might have never even met. Fleming had been released late last year, shortly before the disappearance of Fernando and Fabiana, the hyacinth macaws, the first of the animals to go missing from the zoo.

It could all be coincidence. But it also couldn't hurt to stop by and pay him a visit.

I headed to King Midas Metalworks. I went to the side door, Brigit coming along with me. I tried the handle. Not only was the door locked, but a piece of sheet metal had been leaned up against the window, blocking any view inside. I put an ear to the door but heard nothing. I led Brigit around to the garage door and put an ear to the edge. Still no noise. But even though my nose wasn't as skilled as Brigit's, it didn't take a canine's superior olfactory senses to smell the hint of garlic in the air.

I rapped on the bay door. "Hello? Anybody there?"

There was no answer.

I circled around to the side door again and knocked there. "Hello? Anyone inside?" Still no response from within. I supposed the garlic smell could be residual. Maybe he'd performed some welding work in the bay last night or early this morning. Or it could be coming from the food truck idling half a block away, serving up breakfast burritos and home-fried potatoes to the blue-collar folks who worked in the buildings nearby.

Brigit and I returned to our cruiser.

A half hour later, I was rolling west on Berry Street when my cell phone chimed with an incoming call from Detective Bustamente. I pulled into the parking lot of a sandwich shop that was not yet open for business and tapped the icon to accept the call. "Good mor—"

"They got a black rhino."

What?!?

As if he'd heard my thought, he said, "One of the black rhinos is missing. A male named Mubanga. Sharon Easley says the name means 'strong.' The thieves must have taken him last night."

My first thought was, *How in the world could they steal such an enormous animal?* My second thought was, *If we don't find that rhino right away, it will be killed for its horn!*

The horn is what made the rhino so valuable to poachers. Some thought, wrongfully of course, that the horn had magical medicinal or aphrodisiac qualities. Frankly, if a guy needed rhino horn in order to perform well sexually, maybe he should just remain celibate. I had a hard time believing men ingested the powdered horn with the hope of being more pleasing to their partner, anyway. It was all about the men and making their own little "horn" happy.

Brigit and I had to get to the zoo. *Now.* "We're on our way!"

I flipped on my lights and siren, and we hightailed it to the zoo. As we entered, my eyes sought out Janelle in the ticket booth. She shook her head sorrowfully. We hurried inside and found Detective Bustamente, Director Easley, the zoo's chief security officer, and a keeper at the enclosure, along with Derek Mackey and the chief.

Every vein and capillary in the chief's face seemed to

be throbbing. As Brigit and I rushed up he turned on me and barked, "I thought I told you to put a stop to this!"

While Derek was the chief's golden boy, I was his whipping girl. It was utterly unfair, sexist, and wrong. But it was also a matter to address at another time. Right now, priority one was finding the rhino.

I turned to Bustamente. "Same MO this time?"

He nodded. "They cut through the secured staff gates to get the rhino out. But we don't know where they exited the zoo."

It was no wonder. The perimeter of the zoo comprised miles of fencing. It would take humans a significant amount of time to inspect the entire outer fence and find the welding marks. But my partner could take us right to the thieves' exit point.

"This way, girl." I led Brigit to the secured entrance of the rhino habitat and ordered her to trail the disturbance.

The bright look in her eyes said, *Sure, boss.* She put her furry head down, snuffled, and picked up a trail right away. Off we went, the others trotting along behind us, leading our own little entourage. Fortunately, since the rhino's disappearance had been discovered before the zoo opened for the day, the trail remained undisturbed by zoo visitors. Brigit led us on a direct route to a relatively short stretch of fencing.

The detective and I inspected the metal fence supports. Sure enough, they bore the telltale signs of having been cut and welded back together.

Derek put a foot up on the bottom rung and his hands on the top of the fence, raising himself up to look over it. "The street's blocked off here. There's signs and a bunch of orange cones. Some are knocked over."

I looked up at him. "I'm not aware of any construction on McCart Street. Are you?"

"No," he said. "I don't see any trucks or a road crew, either."

We hurried to the zoo exit and jogged our way along the fence. The chief and Derek were out front, running side by side, the CSO not far behind. Brigit and I were on their tail, my partner's pace limited by my capabilities. Detective Bustamente, who probably hadn't exercised in decades, lagged behind, as did the zoo director, though a glance back told me she may have been maintaining the detective's slow pace so as not to embarrass him.

The chief and Derek reached the road first, and started scouring the dried grass and street for clues. When I arrived, my heart pumping double time and my lungs panting, I issued the order for Brigit to continue to follow the trail from the outer side of the fence. While I caught my breath, she snuffled along the fence until she caught the trail again, and followed it a few feet into the street. She sniffed around in circles, telling me the thieves had walked around in the area, probably loading the rhino into a truck or large trailer. When she realized the trail stopped there, she sat and stared ahead, issuing her passive alert.

I ruffled her ears and fed her three liver treats. "Good girl!"

FIFTY-FOUR
I KNOW A RHINO WHEN I SMELL ONE

Brigit

Yummy treats! Brigit wolfed them down and nuzzled Megan's pocket to see if she might get another. She did. Megan was such a pushover.

While the humans put up police cordon tape and looked around for clues, Brigit basked in a sunny spot on the dried grass. She might appear to the others to be lazily staring off into the distance, but her nose and mind were actually processing quite a bit of data. Brigit smelled the rhino here. Two men, too. She'd also caught a strong smell of the rhino and one of the men at that garage Megan had taken her to earlier. The animal and the man had been inside, but he hadn't come to the door when Megan knocked. Brigit had noticed that sometimes people were quiet and still when Megan knocked on their doors. But Brigit knew they were there on the other side.

There's no hiding from me and my nose.

FIFTY-FIVE
KNOCK-KNOCK. WHO'S THERE?

Trevor Fleming

He wasn't sure who had knocked on the door of his shop this morning. From the voice, he could tell it was a woman. There'd been a jingling sound, too. *Keys, maybe?* She was probably a solicitor. He was constantly finding flyers with coupons stuck in the door frame of his shop, advertising some lunch place or another in the area. Knowing people came by and might peek inside, he'd leaned a piece of scrap sheet metal against the door so nobody would be able to see in through the glass.

With both his truck and trailer inside the garage, there wasn't much extra space. He also doubted whether he'd be able to load the rhino back into the trailer himself. He'd left the animal inside while he'd welded metal bars across the back of the trailer. The torch was virtually silent, so it didn't seem to bother the animal. The fumes were another matter. It wasn't a good idea to weld in an enclosed space, but he didn't have much choice. When it became too much, he raised the garage door a few inches to allow a minimum of ventilation.

He finished with the bars, opened the bay door, and backed his truck out. He drove to a trailer dealership and bought a hydraulic jack and two new tires. He'd learned his lesson about not carrying a spare. He returned to his garage to install the tires. But even though he'd be done preparing the trailer in just another hour or two, he wouldn't dare venture out with the rhino until dusk. Going out in broad daylight was too risky.

When he raised the bay door to put his truck back inside, he was met with fresh, funky fumes that had nothing to do with welding.

"Holy cow!" He waved his hand in front of his face and looked down to find a heaping pile of rhino dung behind the trailer. More lay inside the trailer, between the rhino's feet. *This is what my life has come to. A steaming pile of shit.*

He grabbed a dust pan and a garbage bag and set to work.

FIFTY-SIX
GETTING THE POOP

Megan

While the chief left the zoo early on to call an urgent press conference, a crime scene team arrived to collect evidence and search for clues the rest of us might have overlooked.

As the evidence team looked around, I told the detective about Trevor Fleming. "He's got a welding business, and he did time in the Darrington Unit at the same time Bruno Molina was serving his sentence there. Fleming was released only a short time before the animals started to disappear."

"What was he in for?"

"Theft," I said. "He stole merchandise from stores where he worked."

Bustamente's lips pursed in one direction, then the other as he thought things over. "I'd say it's a long shot. Criminals tend to stick with what they know, repeat the same type of crimes. But there's always the occasional exception. When we finish up here, we'll swing by."

The crime scene team left an hour later, having found next to nothing. They'd taken the cones and signs with them in hopes of lifting prints that might identify the poachers, but we'd have to wait for the results.

The security cameras on the rear of the businesses that backed up to McCart Street had also been coated with flocking. As before, the thieves had donned ski masks and sprayed fake snow on the lenses of residential security cameras in the area, too, though in a different pattern than last time. This pattern seemed to imply that, rather than driving south, the poachers had headed north with the rhino, probably aiming for I-30. Once they hit the interstate, it was unclear which way they'd intended to go. The rhino could be halfway across the country by now, or south of the border in Mexico.

After the crime scene team left, Detective Bustamente and I swung by King Midas Metalworks. We listened at the doors and knocked, but once again it appeared nobody was on-site.

We spent the rest of the day visiting businesses on the presumed escape route to watch their security camera footage. Unfortunately, nothing on the video streams jumped out at us.

It was growing dark when we reluctantly called it a day. The lab had called. Though they found a number of prints on the cones and road signs, none could be identified. If any of the prints belonged to the rhino thieves, they had never been arrested and their prints did not appear in law-enforcement databases. We had no clues to explore, no leads to follow up on. Though someone had called in a possible sighting of the rhino on a livestock transport truck near the Texas-New Mexico border, the El Paso County sheriff's department followed up and confirmed that the truck carried only large hogs headed for a slaughterhouse.

As we parted in the station's parking lot, Bustamente gave me a pat on the shoulder. "Go home and relax, Officer Luz. You've been going the extra mile for weeks. You've earned it."

I was heading home, planning to follow the detective's advice and relax in a warm bath with a glass of wine, when I thought, *What the heck. I'll swing by King Midas one more time, see if anyone might be there.* I wanted to feel like I'd made some progress, even if it was just checking Trevor Fleming off my list.

For the third time that day, I found myself knocking on the door and getting no response. Ditto for the bay. It was dark enough outside now that I'd be able to tell if there were lights on inside the place. But no telltale illumination shined around the edges of the sheet metal that blocked the window. An ear to the doors yielded no sounds coming from inside.

Brigit put her nose to the ground and began to snuffle. When she'd edged far enough away that her leash tugged my hand, I said, "Let's go, girl," and turned to head back to the car. But she didn't follow me. Instead, she pulled on her leash and woofed, insisting I go with her. *Hmm.*

I looked in the direction she was trying to pull me. All I saw was an uncovered metal dumpster at the back of the lot. She'd probably smelled a rat or a piece of trash with a food remnant stuck to it, but it couldn't hurt to indulge her. "Okay, girl. Show me what's got you interested."

She led me over to the garbage bin. *Whoa.* I waved a hand in front of my face. I'd expected a stench, but this odor was particularly rank.

Brigit reared back, put her front paws on the edge of the dumpster, and sniffed along the edge. When she reached a certain garbage bag, she grabbed it with her teeth and tried to pull it out. It was sunk down among other bags and too heavy for her to lift. She turned pleading brown eyes on me and whined.

"If you think I'm going to pull out a bag of garbage for you, Brigit, you are sorely mistaken." There were a lot of things I'd do for this dog, but dumpster diving was not one of them. "Let's go."

She refused to budge, nipping at the bag and tugging with her teeth again until it tore open. When it did, she sat down next to the dumpster, issuing a passive alert. *Are there drugs in the bag? Is that what she's trying to tell me?*

I pulled out my flashlight and shined it into the hole she'd just torn. *Holy crap!* The bag was filled with enormous turds. Quite possibly rhino-sized turds.

"Good girl!" I tossed Brigit a liver treat and ran her back to the car. She complied now that I'd discovered the clue she'd led me to. I put her in the cruiser, rounded up an evidence bag, and ran back to the dumpster. I turned the bag inside out and improvised a glove with it, reaching in and plucking a poop from the pile, much like I gathered Brigit's droppings. I turned the bag right side out again, and ran back to my car.

I grabbed my cell phone and called Detective Bustamente. "I've got the poop on Fleming!"

"Excuse me?"

"I found droppings in his dumpster. Huge ones! I'm pretty sure they're from a rhino."

"You were supposed to be relaxing," he said, though I knew he didn't expect me to apologize for my overzealous work ethic. "Could the droppings be from a horse?" he asked. "Or a cow?"

What a party pooper. "I suppose they could be." My hopes faded. Fort Worth's nickname was Cowtown, and the city hosted a never-ending lineup of stock shows. It was possible someone had mucked a stall and thrown the refuse out here. But still, this garage bin was off the beaten path. It seemed an odd place for someone to get rid of a bag of animal excrement. I pointed this out to the detective. "The rhino could be in his garage right now!"

"We'll need to have someone identify the scat before we can get a search warrant. I'll contact Sharon Easley, see if she can put us in touch with a keeper."

"All right. I'll head to the zoo." It was after dark now, and the zoo was closed to the public for the day. Would a keeper still be around? I crossed my fingers.

We ended the call. He phoned me back a minute later. "She's got a keeper coming, but it'll be half an hour before he can get there."

The rhino's life could be at stake. We didn't have time to waste!

The words of Danny Landis echoed in my mind. "I've learned more about animal dung on this job than I ever wanted to know."

"I've got a better idea," I said. "Let's ask Danny Landis. He used to clean up this stuff. He'll be able to tell if it's from a rhino."

"It can't hurt," Bustamente agreed. "We can stop by his place and still be at the zoo in half an hour if he can't tell us. I'll meet you at his house."

I turned on my flashing lights, hooked a left turn, and punched the gas. In minutes, Detective Bustamente and I stood in front of Danny Landis.

He scoffed and raised credulous brows. "First you accuse me of stealing those animals, and now you want my help trying to save them?"

Bustamente ducked a contrite head. "That's pretty much the long and short of it."

Landis cut a scathing look at the detective before turning it on me.

"Sorry." *Really, what else could I say?* I held out the bag. "Here's the poop. Can you please tell us if it belongs to a zoo animal?"

He took the bag, unzipped it, and jerked his head back

as the stench hit him. "*Hoo-ee,* that smell takes me back." He peered down into the bag. "Yep, that crap belongs to a zoo animal. A rhino, to be exact. You can tell by the type of grass and leaves in it."

Bustamente extended a hand to Landis and I did the same, giving it a firm and grateful shake. "Thanks so much!"

Landis offered a nod. "Nail those sons of bitches."

One whiff of the poop and the judge issued a search warrant posthaste. Bustamente, Brigit, and I returned to the garage and knocked on the doors for the fourth time. There was still no answer. But this time we didn't have to take no answer for an answer. We were legally authorized to break into the place and search for evidence.

While the burglar bars at the glass were too tightly placed to stick a hand through, my nightstick should fit.

"Stand back," I told the detective as I pulled my baton from my belt. I flicked my wrist and extended it with a *snap!* I slid the stick through one of the small squares in the bars and jabbed at the pane. *Bam! Bam! Bam!* Eventually, the glass splintered. One more solid jab and it shattered, tinkling to the concrete inside. With the bars so closely placed, I couldn't reach through to unlock the door. But if the sheet metal wasn't held in place by something heavy, I could use my nightstick to move it from blocking our view. I gave the sheet metal a jab to see if it would budge. The sheet fell backward and crashed to the floor with a tinny clang. Bustamente and I shined our flashlights into the space, banging heads as we both went to look inside. I pulled back, deferring to my superior.

"Is Mubanga there?" I cried. *Please say yes!*

Bustamente backed away, shaking his head. My heart sank.

I peeked inside. There was no rhino. No trailer. No truck. There was nothing other than the cheap piece of scrap sheet metal, an overlooked plop of rhino poo, and the pink construction-paper heart on the wall. *When did Fleming leave with the rhino? And where has he gone?*

The detective turned to me. "You got a cell phone number for this guy?"

"I might be able to get one." I whipped out my phone and ran a quick Internet search for King Midas Metalworks. When a phone number popped up, I dialed it. There was no telltale ring from inside the shop, meaning the number didn't belong to a landline here. I hung up, not waiting for an answer. No sense letting Fleming know we were on to him. He might disable his phone.

I gave Bustamente the number and he made a call, asking for the department's technical division to ping Fleming's phone. If we could find his cell phone, we'd find him, too.

"In the meantime," the detective said, "let's swing by Fleming's residence, see if he's there."

We slid into our cruisers and raced to the address listed for Fleming in his driver's license record. We arrived at the rundown complex in mere minutes. My eyes scanned the lot, but I saw no black Dodge pickup at all, with or without a camper shell. No trailer, either. *Has he hidden them somewhere? Has he delivered the rhino to the buyer already?*

Brigit and I darted up the steps to the second floor of the apartment complex, Bustamente coming up after us.

A light was on in the window. *Someone's home.* I banged my fist on the door. *Bang-bang-bang!* "Fort Worth police! Open up now!"

A few seconds later, a click and a sliding sound told me someone was releasing the dead bolt. The door swung open to reveal a young couple in their early twenties, both wearing bewildered expressions.

"Where's Trevor Fleming?" I demanded as the detective stepped up next to me, huffing slightly from the climb.

"Who?" the young man asked.

The woman turned to him. "That's the name of the guy who lived here before us." She turned back to me. "We get his mail sometimes. It's all past-due notices."

"When did you move in?" I asked.

"About a year and a half ago," she said.

There was no on-site management, but it was questionable whether they'd be of help anyway. From what I could glean, Fleming had left the apartment to serve his time in prison. His forwarding address was likely the Darrington Unit, if he'd bothered to provide one at all. The tenants gave me the property manager's phone number. I thanked them and dialed the number as Bustamente and I headed back down the stairs to our cruisers. All I got was a voice mail. The property manager didn't seem too concerned about potential emergencies.

"Dang it!" I spat.

Bustamente's cell rang. He put the phone to his ear. "Oh, yeah?" He turned to me and quirked his brows, offering a thumbs-up that told me the tech team had tracked Fleming through his cell phone. "Where?" He paused for a second. "All right. Stay with me." Bustamente turned the bottom half of his phone away from his ear. "He's in town. Just a few blocks from here."

I raised victorious fists in the air. "Woo-hoo!"

The detective gestured to my car. "Get in. You drive. I'll navigate."

I slid behind the wheel and cranked the engine. *Stay strong, Mubanga! Brigit and I are coming to your rescue!*

FIFTY-SEVEN
SMELLS LIKE ACTION

Brigit

The cruiser smelled like rhino poop, but it also smelled of human adrenaline. When Megan smelled like this, it often meant they were in for some fun. Of course other times Megan smelled like adrenaline and nothing happened. Police work was a crap shoot.

Megan drove like a bat out of hell, increasing the odds of a takedown. Brigit wagged her tail in anticipation, wondering what lay in store for her and her partner tonight. Whatever it was, she hoped it would earn her a whole box of liver treats.

FIFTY-EIGHT
ROADBLOCKS

Trevor Fleming

It took everything in him not to lay on his horn as yet another asshole cut him off. Now he knew how long-haul truckers felt when people constantly cut in front of them.

He'd been on the road for over half an hour and had gotten nowhere. He hadn't even made it to the interstate. He'd stupidly left his garage during the height of rush hour. Now, something had happened up ahead, a wreck of some sort. He could see the flashing lights on a fire truck and a couple of cop cars. *Just what I need. Police.* But what could he do? He was boxed in.

Another siren sounded behind him as an ambulance rolled up, slowing down to get through the traffic. Only the far right lane was getting through. The cars continued to merge to the right, continued to cut him off when he attempted to take his turn. Everyone was so damn impatient! He raised his middle finger at a woman in an SUV who refused to let him over. She raised hers right back. *Bitch. Really, how did this state ever get a reputation for being so friendly?*

He inched forward for ten full minutes before finally reaching the accident site. Traffic came to a total standstill as a cop blew a whistle and held up a hand. Someone was pulled from one of the banged-up cars, placed on a gurney, and wheeled over to an ambulance by a young paramedic with caramel-colored hair and nice curves. If he didn't already have Vicki, he might be tempted to make a stop at the fire station later, get a closer look at this girl.

A *clang* sounded behind him and the truck lurched as the tongue of the trailer bounced. The rhino seemed to have had enough of the trailer and wanted out. He only hoped it wouldn't use its horn to tear through the aluminum siding.

When his patience ran out and he feared someone might notice his trailer rocking, he gave up on merging right. Instead, he eased into the center lane and turned left down a side street. It had him heading in the wrong direction, but once he circled south around this mess he could turn north again.

A block down, his dashboard flashed as a warning light came on. He was running low on gas. *Dammit!* If he'd had half a brain, he'd have filled up the truck last night before stealing the rhino.

Box. Of. Rocks.

FIFTY-NINE
PING, BANG, BOOM

Megan

Thank goodness for technology! While hi-tech gadgets made it easier for criminals to get away with crimes, it also gave law enforcement new ways to intercept evidence and locate suspects. The triangulation system the department's tech gurus were using now could access data from cell phone towers, measure the relative strength of the signals, and pinpoint the location of a cell phone within a very small range.

With Bustamente telling me where to go, we made our way through east Fort Worth, heading west, our lights flashing. Even so, we weren't making great time. It was the tail end of rush hour, and a major wreck on Vickery had traffic backed up. Even when drivers tried to get out of our way, they had a hard time pulling over with so many cars on the road.

His phone still at his ear, the detective cut a glance my way. "They're saying the signals haven't changed for a few minutes now. Either he's stopped somewhere, or he's ditched the phone."

I prayed it was the former. *Please, God! Help us save this rhino!*

He pointed down a side street up ahead. "Turn left there. It'll get us out of this mess."

I made the left turn.

When we reached the next block, Bustamente repeated what he was being told on the phone. "He's on the move again."

The information was both good news and bad news. It was always easier to nail a nonmoving target. But at least with the signal in motion again, we knew he hadn't ditched his phone.

Bustamente pointed through the windshield. "He should be right up there somewhere."

I squinted and leaned over my steering wheel for a better view as we sped along. *Not seeing a trailer or a black Dodge pickup with a camper shell. No . . . No . . . Wait!* "That must be him!"

A few cars ahead, we could see the back end of a white trailer. The back doors were open a few inches, but secured with some type of crossbars.

As we drew closer, we could see foliage through the narrow opening.

Bustamente grunted. "You sure that's him? It looks like that trailer's full of trees."

"Maybe it's the rhino's food."

"Can a rhino even fit in a trailer that size?"

I was wondering the same thing. I unrolled my window and stuck my head out to see up ahead. To my dismay, I couldn't tell from this distance and angle what type of vehicle was pulling the trailer.

"Is it a black Dodge pickup?" Bustamente asked.

"I can't get eyes on it." The cars between our cruiser and the trailer were taking their sweet time pulling out of the way. Never mind that the law required them to pull right, they didn't want to give up the two-second advantage they might have over a driver coming up behind them.

The detective pointed to a Penske rental truck in the adjacent lane. "Think Fleming's in that truck instead?"

"Could be." *Ugh!* The uncertainty was frustrating. *We had to follow the right vehicle or he could get away!*

But which vehicle was the right one?

SIXTY
HOWL

Brigit

When Megan had unrolled her window, Brigit had caught a strong scent of rhino. She'd also caught the faint sound of a freight train heading their way. She wondered if it would sing its song. Regardless, she'd sing hers.

She raised her snout and began her deep, throaty wail, the prechorus, if you will. *Rrrroooo!*

SIXTY-ONE
DISAPPEARING ACT

Trevor Fleming

AAARGH!

He banged his hand on his steering wheel, tempted to bang his head on it, too. That cop and her dog were following him in their cruiser.

What the hell do I do now?

The engine of his pickup strained and revved with all the weight it was pulling. The truck was supposed to be capable of pulling three times the rhino's weight, but it was an older model and the engine wasn't what it used to be. *RrrrRRRR!* With his luck, the motor would blow and he'd be caught red-handed. He'd be sent back to prison, for who knows how long this time. Everyone had their shorts in a wad about the ugly, stinky beast in his trailer. By the time he was released, Harper would probably be out of high school. If only he could somehow ditch the trailer, maybe drive over a deep pothole and cause it to unhitch. But no. He'd made sure it was securely attached to the tow bar, even added a heavy-gauge safety chain. It had seemed like the smart thing to do at the time.

RrrRRRrrRRRRR! The engine continued its protest.

I'm screwed! Royally and thoroughly screwed! He wasn't King Midas. He was King Dumbass.

He debated making a run for it, but he knew the cop would sic her dog on him. He couldn't outrun a shepherd that size. He also debated a surrender, thinking maybe he could put the blame on Molina and work out a plea deal, when another sound met his ears, another engine rumble, this one deeper and more powerful and followed by an elongated *WOOO-WOOO.* A freight train approached from the north, its headlights visible off to the left.

Wait. Maybe this train is my way out!

He continued on, putting the pedal to the metal but managing a mere thirty-eight miles per hour with all the weight he was pulling. The cop's lights continued to flash in his side mirror, joined now by the headlights of the train as it gained on them from the left.

"Come on!" he yelled in encouragement to his truck. The engine responded with another roar and a shudder. *Is it going to die?*

The cop gave him another block or two to pull over and, when he didn't, she activated her siren. *Woo-woo-woo!* A competing blare from the train drowned it out. *WOOO-WOO!*

Up ahead, just south of the Page Avenue intersection, warning lights flashed, alerting oncoming traffic of the approaching train. Most of the major roads had overpasses or underpasses so that vehicle traffic didn't have to stop for the trains, but this spot happened to be one of the few in the city with an actual crossing. He usually cursed the trains, but not tonight.

Still, he'd never make it through if the minivan in front of him didn't get out of his way. He jammed the ball of his hand against his steering wheel and added his own horn to the mix. *HOOOONK!*

A hand came out of the minivan's driver's window, another middle finger raised. Texans wouldn't give up their guns, and they were just as stubborn when it came to lane positions. Hell, they weren't even yielding to the police cruiser.

He pulled up close to the van's bumper and the driver brake-checked him, the red lights on the back of the vehicle flashing. But he had nothing to lose at this point. He didn't punch his brakes in return. He kept going, tapping the minivan's back bumper with the front bumper of his pickup. His truck was called a Ram, after all. *Bam!*

The minivan driver swerved in surprise, punched the gas to avoid another ramming from behind, and eased over onto the shoulder. If she'd expected him to pull over and exchange insurance information, she had another think coming. Her mouth gaped as he rolled right on by.

The white arms of the railroad crossing began to descend up ahead. "Come on!" He slapped his dashboard as if spurring on a horse. "Go! Go! Go!"

The arms continued their descent. To his left, the train continued its approach, the horn blaring a solid note as the engineer must have realized the pickup and trailer on the street alongside the tracks was racing the locomotive toward the intersection. *WOOOOOOOO!*

The arm bounced as it reached the bottom of its arc. An instant later it bounced again, this time over his hood as he drove through the railroad crossing. He felt another jerk and jolt as the trailer's wheels hit the tracks.

WOOOOOOOOOOO!

He wasn't sure what would happen if the trailer didn't

clear the tracks before the train. The rhino would be roadkill. That was certain. The train might even derail. But would the impact break the safety chain and cause the trailer to detach from his truck? Or would he and his truck become roadkill, too?

His heart twisted. Harper would forever hate him for causing the death of another animal. *I'd deserve it if I died here.*

He closed his eyes and held his breath. A second later, he felt the trailer bounce over the other side of the tracks. A split second afterward he felt the *whoosh* of air as the train rushed past the back of the trailer, missing it by only an inch or two.

He opened his eyes. *We made it!*

SIXTY-TWO
THE TELLTALE TAIL

Megan

Boxed in at the intersection, I banged my hand on the steering wheel and let out a wail of frustration that was completely drowned out by the blare of the train horn. *The rhino is in that trailer!* We knew it now. Why else would the guy have risked his life racing a train?

But while we knew the rhino was in the trailer, both were now on the other side of the Union Pacific train, which seemed to be crawling at a snail's pace and have no end of graffiti-covered cars. Of course it was actually fortunate the trailer was on the other side of the train, rather than mangled under it. That meant Mubanga was still alive, still had a chance to be recovered.

As the train rattled over the tracks in front of us, I grabbed my radio to contact dispatch. "We need backup. Immediately!"

The dispatcher said, "What? I can't hear you over the noise."

I tried again, imploring the dispatcher to get backup en route before the truck and trailer could get away. Still, she couldn't hear me. *Argh!*

Bustamente had the same problem with his cell phone.

He couldn't hear the techies on the other end, and they couldn't hear him.

Our only hope was to put some distance between my cruiser and the train. One glance to my right told me there was no hope of squeezing in front of the line of cars filling the lane. Checking my rearview mirror, I discovered that the driver behind me had left only a few inches between us. I'd only be able to turn left if the car behind me backed up and gave me some room to maneuver. Of course that car could only back up if the car behind it backed up, too, and so on. Texas roads were full of tailgaters.

I threw my gearshift into reverse and motioned with my arm for the driver to back up. But between Brigit blocking his view of me and the fact that he was looking down, his gaze locked on his cell phone, he didn't notice that I was trying to reverse. I pressed my horn to no avail. Ditto for the public address system on my car. Though I demanded he "Back up! Now!", he never even looked up from his phone. The train noise was too darn loud. All the detective and I could do was sit there, fuming in frustration, as the train cars rattled by, one by one by one.

Finally, six long minutes later, the red caboose sailed by and the splintered crossing arm lifted.

The driver of a minivan walked up the shoulder, waving her arms to get my attention. "Hey! Officer! Some guy in a truck rear-ended me!"

I had bigger things to worry about than a fender bender. The life of a critically endangered black rhino was at stake. Her mouth gaped as I gunned my engine and flew over the tracks, my head whipping side to side as I looked for the trailer and tried dispatch again. "Can you hear me now?"

"Loud and clear."

Thank goodness! I told her we needed backup in our area. *Pronto.*

Though it was possible the rhino rustler intended to hide the animal somewhere else within the city limits, he could be planning to make a break for one of the interstates. Heck, he could have reached any of the three major freeways while we were stuck behind the train. But the techies would be able to tell us where he was.

Or so I'd thought.

"You're kidding me, right?" Bustamente said into his phone before turning to speak to me. "They lost the signal. He must've ditched his phone."

I grabbed the mic from the dash once again to contact dispatch. "We need units on Interstates thirty-five, twenty, and thirty," I demanded. "Air support, too. Be on the lookout for a black Dodge pickup pulling a white trailer. We have reason to believe the stolen rhino is in the trailer."

A dozen voices came back, my fellow officers responding to my plea. Unfortunately, given how much time had passed since Trevor Fleming had barreled through the crossing, he could be miles away by now. Time was of the essence when trying to catch a fugitive and, as each minute ticked by, the chances of catching Trevor Fleming and rescuing the rhino diminished.

A call came in about a fight at a bar near the university. Another came in about a suspected drunk driver. Another came in about a robbery at a gas station. But nobody contacted dispatch to report seeing Fleming or his truck and trailer.

The detective and I debated our options. We could continue to patrol the area, hoping to find Fleming, but with other units keeping an eye out it seemed redundant. We figured the best thing we could do was keep an eye on his shop. He might try to go back to it. Of course he might decide to ditch his truck and trailer and make a run for it, too. If he did, he'd need help. He could call Uber or Lyft, or even a good old-fashioned cab. Or he could abscond on foot.

"Or he could go to his home," the detective said, "wherever that might be."

If only he'd updated his driver's license record when he'd been released, or registered his trailer at his home address.

As we pulled into Fleming's old apartment complex to retrieve the cruiser Bustamente had left there earlier, I had an epiphany. I turned to the detective. "I already checked the DMV records to see if Fleming owns a trailer or a black Dodge pickup. No trailer or vehicles are registered in his name. I thought they might be registered in his wife's name, but he's not married."

"And?"

"What about his kid? Remember that heart on the wall of his shop? It said *I Love You Daddy* and had a girl's name on it." I remembered the curly tail on the letter *p*. "Harper. That was her name. Maybe she can lead us to him."

I logged in to my laptop and ran a search of the birth records. Sure enough, there was a Harper Fleming who'd been born seven years ago and fathered by a Trevor Fleming. Her mother was listed as a Victoria Skarsgard. The residence listed for both the father and mother was the address where we now sat. In other words, useless.

"Run the mother's name through the DMV files," Bustamente said. "See if she's updated her address."

I ran Victoria's name through the system. *Bingo!* We hit a mother lode of information.

Two vehicles were registered in her name. One was a 2012 Dodge Caravan minivan. The other was a 2006 Dodge Ram pickup—black. The address shown on the registrations was the same, and was on a street in nearby Polytechnic Heights. Victoria's driver's license showed the same address. It had been issued a little over a year ago, apparently after she'd moved out of this apartment and into her new residence. We now had a license plate number for the truck and a possible home address for Fleming.

The detective opened his door. "Let's go say howdy."

While Bustamente moved to his cruiser, I contacted dispatch and provided the tag number for the truck. Meanwhile, the detective and I rolled out, heading for what we suspected was Fleming's current residence to see if he might be there or what anyone there might know.

Minutes later, Bustamente and I pulled up to the house in our separate cruisers. I retrieved Brigit, and the three of us stepped up to the door of the small house. Bustamente raised a hand and knocked on the door. *Rap-rap-rap.* When no one answered, he knocked again, louder. *RAP-RAP-RAP.* His efforts elicited a wail from a toddler inside the house, followed by a woman's voice hushing the child.

"Who is it?" she demanded from the other side of the door.

"Fort Worth Police," Bustamente called.

She opened the door a few inches, revealing her scowling face and a blubbering toddler clinging to her side. He glanced our way with pink, puffy eyes before rubbing his wet face on the shoulder of her sweater.

She tilted her coppery head to indicate the little boy affixed to her. "You woke my baby. I'd just got him down, too."

"Our apologies, ma'am," Bustamente replied. "We're looking for Trevor Fleming. Is he here?"

She hesitated a moment and her eyes narrowed, wary and weary. "What do you want with him?"

The detective was purposely vague. "We think he has some information that could aid us in an investigation. Do you know where he is?"

"He's putting in overtime at work."

"At his shop?"

Her brows formed a puzzled V. "No. At the drilling site in Weatherford. He's a welder for Cloud Point Energy. What shop are you talking about?"

Bustamente and I exchanged glances. Evidently Trevor Fleming had failed to inform his girlfriend about his termination from the drilling company. Just as evidently, he was not out working in Weatherford.

Bustamente was vague once again and, in fact, feigned ignorance. "Maybe I'm confusing him with someone else. I thought he had a bay somewhere in town, did some freelance welding work now and then? Maybe under the name King Midas?"

She shook her head. "No. He just works for Cloud Point."

She looked from one of us to the other, and the wariness in her eyes was forced out by another emotion. *Shame.* As she processed things, her expression made her thoughts easily readable. She'd let her ex back into her life, and he'd led the police right to her door. *Fool me once . . .*

She hesitated a moment before wincing as if in pain. "Is he . . . Is he in trouble again?" Her voice was tight and soft, a dolphinlike squeak.

"Honestly?" the detective said. "He's in some pretty big trouble. But if we don't find him right away, things will be even worse for him."

She issued a soft choking sound before turning her head and pressing her lips to her baby's temple and closing her eyes. She turned her face downward. "Once a screwup, always a screwup," she whispered.

SIXTY-THREE
DING-A-LING

Brigit

The cat at this house wasn't scared of Brigit like that other one had been. He'd been batting a ball around the place, the toy giving off a *ding-a-ling* as it bounced off the walls and playpen. But when he saw Brigit at the door, he abandoned the ball, sauntered over, and raised his head to sniff Brigit's chin.

She looked down at him. *Hello, inferior species.*

Undeterred, he raised a paw and tapped her cheek. *You're it!* He ran off down the hall, the only participant in his game of tag. Couldn't the silly cat tell she was on duty right now?

SIXTY-FOUR
UP, UP, AND AWAY!

Trevor Fleming

Now that he was driving a constant speed, and had added some gas to his tank, his engine seemed to be doing better. His heart had nearly burst in his chest when he'd passed a couple of police cars, but none of the officers seemed to take an interest in him. He heard the *whup-whup-whup* of a police helicopter drawing near as he headed west on Interstate 20, but it had only circled overhead and angled off. It hadn't hovered or followed him like it would have if they were looking for him. Maybe he'd panicked for no reason. Maybe that cop that had been behind him at the railroad tracks hadn't been after him, after all. Maybe there'd been no reason for him to take the battery out of his cell phone and ditch it. He'd thought they might have been using it to track him, but it must have all been a crazy coincidence. *Right?*

SIXTY-FIVE
DADDY'S GIRL

Megan

Detective Bustamente and I were seated in Vicki's small living room, explaining why we were there and why we suspected her boyfriend had been involved in the zoo thefts, when a sweet, soft voice sounded from off to the side.

"Daddy stole Sarki? A rhino, too?"

We turned to see a young girl standing in the hallway. She had her mother's coppery hair, but while her mother's blue eyes were full of regret, the girl's hazel eyes were full of tears.

Her lip trembled. "Daddy told me he was going to be good now."

Vicki waved her over and pulled her close, one arm wrapped protectively around the girl's back and the other cupping her head. She bent her head down and spoke quietly into her daughter's ear. "I'm sorry, Harper. Daddy messed up again."

While we realized the girl needed comforting, it would have to come later. There'd been no reported sightings of the truck and trailer. We needed to find Fleming *now.*

Bustamente asked, "Do you have any idea where he might be, ma'am? Where he might be taking the rhino?"

Still encircled in her mother's arms, Harper turned to face us.

Vicki shook her head and answered the question. "I got no idea at all."

Bustamente exhaled a loud breath. "But he's in your pickup, right? The black Dodge with the camper shell?"

"I suppose he is," she said. "Only it's not black anymore. Someone took a key to it a while back and he had it repainted white. They damaged the camper top, too, so he took it off."

I threw up my hands. "That's why nobody's spotted him!" Law enforcement had been looking for a black truck with a camper shell, not a white truck without one. I was fairly certain the person who'd scratched up the truck was none other than Fleming himself, but there was nothing to be gained by pointing out to Vicki what a deceitful man she'd been living with. She seemed to be getting that point all on her own.

I pressed the button on my shoulder mic and contacted dispatch yet another time. "That black truck with the camper shell everyone's looking for? Turns out it's a white truck with no top on it."

Dispatch quickly issued an update.

Bustamente and I exchanged glances. We both realized the blunder over the truck's color had cost us quite a bit of time and given Fleming an advantage. He could be thirty or more miles from Fort Worth now, in any direction, increasing the search area exponentially. There were untold numbers of places to hide a rhino in that square mileage.

Harper stared intently at me as I told Vicki how we'd tracked Fleming before coming to her house. "We pinged his phone and found him at Page Road, but we got separated when a train came through. After that, we lost the signal on his phone. He must've taken the battery out. We have no way of knowing where he and the rhino are now."

Harper spoke now. "You can tell where somebody's phone is at?"

"Yes," I told her. "Cell phones give off a signal that can be traced."

She tilted her cute, coppery head. "So if my phone was in Daddy's truck, you could find it?"

Bustamente and I exchanged glances again. Hopeful ones, this time.

I addressed Harper, keeping my voice upbeat and calm. "Is your phone in your daddy's truck, honey?"

She turned her head and looked up at her mother, her eyes bright with worry.

Vicki ran a hand over her daughter's hair. "It's okay if you left it there. I won't be mad this time."

Relieved, the little girl turned back to me and nodded.

Bustamente was already on his cell, calling the tech team back. "What's your phone number, sweetie?"

Harper stood up straight and proud. "I got it memorized." As she called out the number, the detective repeated it to the techies.

The detective drummed his fingers impatiently on his knee as he waited for them to give it a try. I was equally anxious, my knee bouncing like a railroad piston.

A minute later, Bustamente said, "They've got it. He's on the 820 loop at Camp Bowie Boulevard."

I updated dispatch with the information.

"Roger that!" called the helicopter pilot over the airwaves.

The loop ran through the neighboring suburbs of White Settlement and Lake Worth. I asked dispatch to give their departments a shout, too. We needed as many eyes as we could get looking out for Fleming and his endangered cargo.

"Will do," she said.

We waited in virtual silence for word to come in that someone had Fleming in their sights. *Come on!* I willed my fellow officers. *Get that bastard!*

Derek's voice came over the radio a few seconds later, his siren audible in the background. "I'm on the loop near Chapin Road. I should be on him soon."

A flash of white-hot fury threatened to incinerate my insides. I'd busted my ass on this case, and Derek would get the glory? The same guy who'd summoned me to the Fiesta Mart claiming he'd spotted Fabiana and Fernando when all he'd seen were some parrot piñatas? I could handle another officer nabbing Fleming. But Derek? *Grrrr!*

I took a deep breath, extended my baton, and twirled it to calm myself. *Swish-swish-swish.* I added my mantra. *Peace be with me. Peace be with me.* It didn't help. I still wanted to take my baton to Derek like he was one of those piñatas.

Bustamente, who was still on the phone with the techs, banged a fist on his knee. "Not again!" He turned to me. "They've lost this signal, too."

Harper looked from the detective, to me, to her mother. "What does that mean?"

Vicki answered for all of us. "It means they don't know where Daddy is anymore."

Harper turned to me. "Maybe he's going out to that place with the horses."

The detective and I looked to Vicki for details. She shrugged. "I don't know a place with horses." She looked down at her daughter. "What are you talking about?"

The girl toyed with a length of her hair. "Daddy took us out there last weekend," she told her mother, "after we went to the zoo."

Bustamente asked, "Do you know why he went to the horse place? Did he talk to anyone?"

Harper continued to run her little hands down her hair, a soothing mechanism just like my baton twirling. "I don't know why. He didn't talk to anybody. He just drove real slow and looked around."

Had he been scouting out a hiding place for Mubanga? Or maybe making a dry run to the delivery point? It seemed possible, even probable.

"Where is the horse place?" Bustamente asked the girl.

"It's in the country. You go on that road between the airports."

The road between the airports . . . Was she referring to Highway 199? Also known as Jacksboro Highway, the road ran between the airfield at the military's joint reserve base on the west side of Fort Worth and Meacham Field, a smaller airport northwest of downtown. The airports were miles apart, but the flashing beacons and the planes flying in and out of them would be visible from a car traveling Highway 199. The road intersected Loop 820 not too far north of where Fleming was last pinged. But from there it wasn't far to county roads and open land with big barns where it would be easy to conceal a large animal.

"Harper," I said, "if we got in the car, could you show us where your daddy took you?"

"I think so," she said. "I always look out the window and see things." In other words, she might spot some landmarks that would help us find her father and rescue the rhino.

I stood. "Harper, do you want to help save Mubanga?"

Her worried eyes brightened. "Yes!"

I swung my finger to indicate the door. "Then let's go!"

SIXTY-SIX

IT

Brigit

Megan rousted Brigit from where she'd been lying on the floor. Looked like they were heading out. But before she left, she had one small matter to attend to.

She sidled along until she came up to the cat, who'd been sitting under the coffee table pouting because Brigit had refused to play tag with him. Brigit put out her paw and gave him a poke. *Not it!*

SIXTY-SEVEN
EYE IN THE SKY

Trevor

He'd nearly jumped out of his skin when Harper's phone had chimed with a reminder to clean out her kitty's litter box. But thank goodness it had! He hadn't realized the phone had slid under the seat of his truck. *How many times have I told her she needs to keep up with that phone?*

Her phone explained why the helicopter that had circled him earlier and flown off was now shining its spotlight on the loop only a mile or so behind him. He'd hurled Harper's phone out the window, where it had promptly been pulverized under the wheels of a semi truck. *Ping that, suckers!*

He took the exit for Jacksboro Highway, circled around the ramp, and headed northwest on the road. Only a few more miles and he'd reach the ranch, hand over the rhino, and collect his big bucks. He'd have to go into hiding after that, at least until he figured things out. But he could survive quite a while on fifty grand in cash.

He'd made it a good way down the road when he heard the *whup-whup-whup* growing louder again. He arched his neck to look out his window. The police helicopter was back and seemed to be following the same highway he was on, running its searchlight over the fields and pastures along the sides of the road. He gripped the wheel so tight his knuckles threatened to pop clean out of his skin.

What do I do now?

SIXTY-EIGHT
LANDMARKS THE SPOT

Megan

We made our way in Bustamente's cruiser, the detective at the wheel and yours truly riding shotgun, with Brigit and Harper in the backseat. Harper was an incredibly observant little girl. She'd not only directed us to Highway 199, but continued to let us know we were on the right track.

She pushed back the hood on her panda-themed coat and pointed up at the Lake Worth water tower. "I remember that water tower with the blue stripe around it." A few miles later, she recognized another water tower in the city of Azle. "I remember 'cause it has three Ss on it."

The S shapes were intended to resemble the waves on Eagle Mountain Lake, which sat to the east of town.

As we went along, the helicopter trailed us, scanning left and right with its searchlight, making sure we in the cruiser hadn't missed anything. After all, we were confined to the pavement and had limited visibility in any direction, but those in the helicopter had much greater range and could see all over, into places not visible from the roads.

Harper sat up taller in the back, her little hand curved around the top of my seat. "Can you go slower?" she asked the detective. "I need to look for the donkey. That's where we turn."

Uh-oh. Any donkey she might have seen in the daylight last Saturday was unlikely to be standing in the same place tonight. We might not even spot him in the dark.

I turned to address her. "What if the donkey moved? Is there another way you could know where to turn?"

She shook her head.

I fought the urge to scream. I needed to relieve some tension. Too bad I couldn't twirl my baton in the cruiser. There wasn't room.

Harper's hand shot forward, her little finger pointing. "There's the donkey!"

I needn't have worried about the donkey moving. This donkey was a ceramic yard decoration that someone had set atop a stump. He wore a broad smile and a cowboy hat, and had a piece of straw clenched in his buckteeth.

Detective Bustamente negotiated the turn and there, way off in the distance, appeared two tiny red lights. But were they the lights on the back of some farmer's car? Or were they the rear lights on Fleming's trailer?

SIXTY-NINE
THE SCENT OF SUCCESS

Brigit

Even without the windows down, Brigit's nose picked up the scent of rhino on the air. The thing had pooped in the trailer again, releasing that unmistakable odor.

Brigit was excited about the thought of getting to see the big animal up close and personal. At the zoo, she could only watch from afar. Maybe they'd even become friends.

SEVENTY
A NICE NIGHT FOR A SWIM

Trevor

The helicopter was closing in. His mind whirled like the blades of the chopper. *What do I do? What do I do?* He couldn't think straight. But if he had any hope of getting out of this, he had to ditch the rhino.

He pulled over under a live oak tree, the lower branches scratching along the top of his truck and the trailer with a *screeeeeee.*

He leaped from his truck, grabbed his mask, gloves, and tool from his truck bed and circled around the back of the trailer. *Ugh!* The rhino had unloaded again. The feces littered the floor and the stench filled his sinuses.

He turned on the welder and, as quick as he could, cut through the metal bars that had held the rhino in place. A small herd of longhorn cattle who'd been grazing in the pasture wandered over to watch, chewing their cuds with idle curiosity.

Once the bars were cut, he swung the doors open, yanked the ghillie suit off the rhino's butt, and tossed it on top of the trailer, spreading it flat for additional camouflage. Maybe the chopper wouldn't be able to spot his truck and trailer hiding under this huge tree.

He scurried over to the fence. The bovine audience squinted against the harsh glow as he quickly cut through the barbed wire. When he finished, he tossed his mask and welder aside and ran to the truck. He grabbed the ramp from the bed and situated it behind the trailer.

"Come on out!" he called to the animal.

But the rhino didn't budge.

He reached out and used his hands to pull back on the rhino's armored buttock, but the beast took only one tentative step backward. *He's got to move faster!*

He pushed the rhino's butt to the side and squeezed past his hip into the trailer. The rhino turned his head as far as he could to the left to look back at Fleming. Fleming put both hands on the rhino's shoulder and pushed. "Come on, now! Back it up, big butt!"

Finally, the rhino began to move. He took four steps back before shifting his weight in another attempt to see behind himself. As the animal shifted, he pinned Fleming to the inside wall of the trailer. *Oh, Lord! I can't breathe!* Fleming flailed his arms to no avail. He was hopelessly trapped and pretty sure that cracking sound he'd just heard was a rib giving way.

The animal moved again of its own accord, backing the rest of the way down the ramp. On solid ground now, he stopped and stared into the trailer as Fleming melted to the floor in such agony his mind attempted to shut down. But after a few breaths, he managed to get the pain under control enough that he could pull himself to the end of the trailer and slide down the ramp. A few more breaths, and he levered his crushed body to a stand.

He scuttled as best he could to the bed of his pickup and retrieved the PVC pipe. Using it as a prod, he guided the rhino into the pasture. The cattle greeted the rhino with snorts and *moos* that seemed to ask, *Who and what are you?* A short, grunting *mo* translated as *Cool nose horn, buddy.*

Having ditched the animal, he headed back to his truck, grimacing against the pain. He was almost to the door when a set of headlights shined down the road. He ambled to the tree and hid behind it, hoping whoever was in the car would pass on by.

No such luck.

The car slowed as it approached and stopped twenty yards away. He peeked out from behind the tree. With the bright beams blinding him, Fleming couldn't make out what kind of car it was, but when the flashing lights illuminated on top he knew it was a law enforcement vehicle.

A voice came over the public address system. "Daddy? It's Harper."

They'd brought his little girl out here? *Is that how they'd found me?*

He fell to his knees, the pain in his ribs nothing compared to the raw ache in his heart. *Betrayed, by his own precious daughter.* He supposed he'd betrayed her, too, by stealing the animals she loved to watch at the zoo.

"Be good, Daddy," Harper said. "Raise your hands like we do in school."

He slowly raised his hands and came out from behind the tree, walking slowly in the direction of the cruiser. But when he reached the hole he'd cut in the fence, he sidestepped out of the headlights and made a run for it.

SEVENTY-ONE
STAMPEDE

Megan

The rhino and cows simply stared as Fleming darted past them. While they seemed mildly curious about what was going on, they didn't seem the least bit upset. It appeared safe to deploy Brigit. Out here in the dark on this scrubby land, I'd never be able to track Fleming as quickly and effectively as she could.

I let her out of the car and unclipped her leash, issuing the order for her to take Fleming down. Brigit was off in an instant, running between the rhino and the cows, their heads turning in unison to watch her race off into the pitch-black field.

Whup-whup-whup. The chopper drew in close and descended lower, hovering over the field. *WHUP-WHUP-WHUP.*

The cattle, who'd been calm and content only a moment before, started to shuffle and moo.

Uh-oh. I turned to face the helicopter and motioned with both arms for it to retreat. "Move back! Move back!"

WHUP-WHUP-WHUP!

The chopper rose, but it was too late. The rhino swung his head around and took off at a gallop in the same direction Fleming and Brigit had gone. I watched in horror as the cattle followed suit, forming a stampede, their thundering hooves releasing the scent of fresh dirt and vibrating the ground beneath my feet. *Brigit and Fleming are in their path.* My blood turned to shards of ice. They could be trampled to death, like Mufasa in *The Lion King.* No doubt Brigit had already taken the man down and was holding him in place, waiting for me to come cuff him. She was a well-trained dog and might remain in place as ordered, despite her instincts telling her to ditch the ex-con and run for her life.

I yanked my flashlight from my belt, turned it on, and ran through the hole in the fence, taking off after Mubanga and the cattle. My instinct was to call out to Brigit, but I knew doing so might only confuse her, draw her back through the stampeding animals. The animals ran straight ahead for what seemed an eternity before they vectored off to the left. I swung my flashlight left and right as I rushed after them, scanning the ground desperately for any sign of Brigit.

Please! I begged any deity that might be listening. *Please protect Brigit!*

SEVENTY-TWO
IN STINKS

Brigit

She was holding the man down, waiting for Megan to arrive and take over, when the ground under them began to shake. She smelled the dirt and dung kicked up by the cows running at them, smelled the cattle's scent growing stronger. The rhino was coming, too.

Her training told her to stay here, to keep watch over the man until Megan showed up. But her instincts told her *you might want to rethink that.*

She also smelled water ahead. She didn't like baths. *Maybe these animals don't, either.*

SEVENTY-THREE
POND SCUM

Trevor

The dog dragged him across the pasture and into the pond, out of the path of the stampede, continuing on until the water was so deep she had to swim.

She saved my life.

He'd been awful to take the zoo animals from their homes, yet a dog had shown him mercy. He didn't deserve it. But maybe the dog was trying to tell him something, that it was never too late to be good, that he might still be redeemable. It was just too much.

He burst into sobs.

SEVENTY-FOUR
THE RETURN OF THE RHINO

Megan

Woof! Woof-woof!

A cry of joy burst from me. *She's alive! Brigit's alive!*

"Brigit!" I called. "Where are you?"

Woof-woof!

I ran toward her bark and found her at the edge of a pond. Fleming knelt on the ground next to her, his hands raised in the air. Both of them were wet—Brigit with water from the stock tank and Fleming with both pond water and tears.

After I cuffed Fleming, he looked up at me. "Your dog saved my life."

I bent down and wrapped my arms around my soggy, smelly partner, giving her a tight squeeze and a kiss on the snout. "She's a good girl. Just like your daughter."

He gulped back a sob. "She is, isn't she?"

Fleming's clothes bore remnants of the cow patties in which Brigit had taken him down, so we were more than happy to allow Derek to transport the man back to the station in his cruiser.

The detective and I drove Harper back home. She was quiet on the ride, staring out the window. We didn't want to push her to talk. The night must've been confusing and difficult for her, and she was probably trying to make sense of it all.

Back at her house, I bent down to look her in the eye. "Thank you for your help, Harper. We couldn't have found Mubanga without you."

She merely nodded, but when we turned to leave, she called out after me. "Is it fun to work with a dog?"

I looked down at my partner, ruffled her ear, and turned back to Harper. "Best job in the world."

She gave me a timid smile. "Maybe I'll be a police like you when I grow up."

I gave her a big smile in return. "I hope you will. You'd be good at it."

Fleming told us everything, cooperating completely, evidently deciding it was never too late to be good. Bruno Molina was in custody in San Antonio within the hour, as was the man who'd helped Fleming steal the animals. The creep who'd been waiting on the rhino to be delivered to his ranch was also rounded up. He wouldn't talk, but we surmised he planned to remove Mubanga's horn and sell it. He was well connected in safari circuits, and had a trophy room in his house full of animal heads and pelts from all over the world.

It took some investigative work to determine who Molina had sold the macaws and the monkey to, but the animals were eventually tracked down to a petting zoo in Florida. Fabiana, Fernando, and Sarki were all returned to the zoo. Mubanga was, too, though the keeper who'd been dispatched to round him up from the pasture said he seemed reluctant to leave a heifer who'd seemed impressed by his double horn. Maybe the darn thing was an aphrodisiac, after all.

The chief called a final press conference on the matter. He awarded me and Brigit a special commendation for our work in the zoo theft investigation. I beamed as he pinned the award on my dress uniform. Brigit wagged her tail as he pinned hers on her collar.

He shook my hand and Brigit's paw afterward. "Good work, Officers."

Our photo made the front page of the paper again, and Trish LeGrande interviewed us for a special news segment called "Ladies in the Law." Yep, Brigit and I had made quite a name for ourselves.

On Valentine's Day, Seth took me out to dinner at Joe T. Garcia's, a Mexican restaurant where we'd had our first date. Brigit and Blast tagged along, having a date of their own. While I sipped a frozen margarita, Seth gazed at me intently. "I realized something recently."

"What is it?" I asked.

"That I'm completely and irrevocably whipped."

"Oh, yeah?" I unsuccessfully fought a smile. "What brought you to that conclusion?"

"Let's just say it was an utter lack of temptation."

In other words, Alex. He was telling me that despite her being sweet and gorgeous and great in the kitchen, he had no interest in her. And if he couldn't be tempted by someone like her, he'd found the woman for him. *Me.*

His profession of undying devotion complete, he slid a smile and a small black velvet box topped with a red bow across the table. "I hope you like it."

My pulse racing, I gently took the box in both hands

and eased the top open. Inside was an exquisite and unique ring in rose gold with brown gemstones. Not an engagement ring, but a treasure nonetheless. "It's beautiful, Seth!"

"The stones are andalusites. They're the same color as your eyes. That's why I couldn't resist them."

Awwww. I reflexively put my hand to my heart. "I love it!" I removed it from the box and slid it onto the ring finger of my right hand. "It fits perfectly."

I bent down and picked up the bag containing the gift I'd bought for him. "I got you something shiny, too." It was a new chrome exhaust pipe for his Nova. The old one had given way to rust and was unbefitting a classic muscle car.

"It'll look great," he said. "The other cars will be jealous."

After a delicious dinner and sopaipillas for dessert, the four of us climbed back into Seth's Nova.

On the way to my house, he made an unexpected turn.

"Where are you going?" I asked.

He cast me a roguish grin. "You'll see."

He pulled into the Fort Worth Police Department headquarters, parked, and led me inside. We rode up the elevator, but he refused to answer any questions I asked him on the way. We stepped out on the floor where the chief's office was located. The floor was dark, lit only by dim after-hours lights.

Brigit and Blast followed along as Seth led me over to a bank of chairs that faced the door of the chief's office. He sat me down in one of them, backed up and eyed me, then stepped back over and moved me to the next one over. He backed up again. "That's where you were sitting the first time I laid eyes on you."

"I remember." It was the first time I'd laid eyes on him, too. I'd been sitting here waiting to meet with the chief, to find out if he was going to fire me for zapping Derek with my Taser. Seth and some other guys from the bomb squad had been meeting with the chief and walked out of his office. Seth had caught my eye, been a wonderful, if quick, distraction from my then-pending woes.

Seth gave me a soft smile. "I took one look at you and thought, 'I didn't know they made women like that.'"

His words made me feel warm and tingly all over. As he slowly made his way forward and dropped down to one knee, my heart pounded in my chest. *Oh, my gosh! Is he proposing?* Brigit and Blast came over to see what Seth was doing on the floor, taking seats next to him. He pulled another velvet box from his pocket. "The other ring was a gift for you, but if you accept this one, it'll be a gift for me."

Happy tears welled up in my eyes. He opened the box and removed the ring, holding it out. It was brushed gold with a round diamond, absolutely gorgeous. "What do you say, Megan? Shall we form a pack?"